A STRONGER IMPULSE

A Pride & Prejudice Variation

JULIE COOPER

Quills & Quartos
PUBLISHING

Edited by Grace Oliver and Regina McCaughey-Silvia

Cover by Holly Perret

ISBN 978-1-956613-33-9 (ebook) and 978-1-956613-34-6 (paperback)

To Lisa, my dear friend in every season

"...and in his behaviour with me, there were stronger impulses even than pride."

— GEORGE WICKHAM, *PRIDE & PREJUDICE*

PROLOGUE

June 29, 1811

Fitzwilliam Darcy fought the temptation to close his eyes. This stretch of road was a rough one, and if he allowed himself to doze, he would surely find himself in an undignified sprawl on the vehicle's floor, however well-sprung his carriage. He ought to have ridden; not only would it have been faster, but guiding his temperamental, unsuitably named stallion, Gallant, would have required his attention. He would not have had this endless time to *think*—an enforced time of contemplation bringing him no peace whatsoever.

This journey was an attempt at escape. He would not lie to himself, even if his visit to Ramsgate was well justified. Their comfortable house, Sea Cliff Lodge, beckoned, invigorating seaside breezes would refresh, and his sister would appreciate amends for his recent neglect. But these were excuses, not reasons.

The truth behind his flight had little to do with his sister, and much more to do with a certain green-eyed beauty of regrettable family and little fortune. Why had he ever chosen to spend the summer at a leased home in dull, insipid Hertfordshire? A stupid choice.

But what further insanity had led him to propose *marriage* to one of its inconsequential, inappropriate inhabitants?

He ought not have insulted her at their first meeting. He knew that. He ought to have simply danced with her instead of allowing his general exhaustion to rule him, instead of uttering a slur upon her hair colour—taken in at a glance and thoughtlessly spoken. It was not well done, and he had been instantly sorry. But how was he to have known how soon she would captivate him—heart, body, and soul?

Elizabeth was not a typical light-eyed redhead, with spotty porcelain skin—though there were a few sun-kissed freckles on her perfectly shaped nose. Miss Bingley called her skin 'brown' and 'coarse' when it was actually golden—a bit exotic, even. Her eyes were large, expressive—twinkling with enjoyment or condemning with reproach—leaving one in no doubt of her feelings. He had the strangest impression that he had seen her before, that she was somehow known to him, but she was so unique, so utterly unforgettable, it was impossible. Take her hair, for instance; that it was red was an unquestioned truth. But to call it *only* 'red' was a serious misstatement. It was every imaginable hue of the shade, from chestnut to deepest ruby, thick and luscious, and it was all he could do not to imagine it spread upon his pillow.

He *knew* better than to pursue insolent, ineligible beauties. The stupid proposal must be yet another symptom of this dratted muzzy-headedness, a bone-deep fatigue infecting what he knew was a blessed and privileged existence. The lassitude had already robbed him of closeness with those he held dear. His correspondence had become terse and impersonal. His attendance at his club had become a trial. In the drawing rooms of his friends, he felt only hunted and pursued by the dynastic concerns of the *ton*. When Fitzwilliam's dandified elder brother, Viscount Mallory, had approached him—*again*—for a 'loan' until his next allowance, he had simply written out the draft, rather than ensuring it went to payment of the man's debts or the needs of his young family.

It was all he could do to maintain his current business interests—new opportunities were victim to a wall of indifference he was too drained to scale. He had never enjoyed ballrooms, but even once-heartening pursuits, ranging from hunting and fishing to scientific societies, lost their appeal in the depths of his exhaustion. Thus, his foolish decision to summer in Hertfordshire, the site of the country house he had helped Bingley lease, hoping for relief and respite.

But Bingley could seldom interest him in their favourite entertainments, so why he had agreed to attend the party in the Meryton assembly rooms in the first place was puzzling. Why his attempted apology took the form of requesting a dance—she of unfashionable gown and untameable hair that not even a linen cap could contain—was bewildering. And why he had fallen so swiftly in love with her, someone so much the opposite of demand, duty, and decorum, was a baffling, unsupportable mystery.

His declaration of love to Elizabeth Bennet was insanity itself.

She had no fortune, his aunt's ridiculous parson as the heir to her father's estate, and a family which, for the most part, was a mortification. For any *one* of these reasons, he ought never to think of her again. And yet, these difficulties might be overlooked—after all, he had wealth sufficient for ten penniless wives, her birth was good enough, and *surely* she would not maintain close connexions with such kith and kin if she were raised up to a higher sphere.

Neither was she precisely unsuitable; however, she was *different*. Different from the fragile blooms sprouting amongst the *ton*, different from the stiff and starchy females who were regularly thrown—or throwing themselves—at him, and her unique hair colouring was the least of it. Miss Bingley was quick to call her 'unwomanly', but in this opinion, he could not agree.

Elizabeth—as he called her in his mind—preferred tramping about the weeds and thistles of the countryside—alone—more than the cultured paths of formal gardens. He had observed her at every event she had attended as she'd easily shared friendly witticisms and anecdotes with her neighbours. Never anything cutting or mean, only the humorous or intriguing. She laughed much, talking effortlessly, drawing out the shyest with the skills of a master conversationalist; Miss Bingley styled it 'boldness' and 'flirtation', but it was not. She was simply…interested.

And when her sister, Miss Jane Bennet, had been struck by fever whilst dining at Netherfield—the result, doubtless, of Miss Bingley's stuffy, airless dining parlour during an excessively sultry June evening—Elizabeth had walked miles in the hot sun searching for some type of herb or weed with which she had brewed a tea. She'd appeared before them all damp with sweat, her hems laced with dirt and grass stains, declaring Mr Jones's remedies to be inadequate and insisting upon her own.

He ought to have been disgusted, like Miss Bingley and Mrs Hurst, instead of attracted to dewy, glistening skin, unkempt ruby curls, and clinging muslin. He ought to have joined their critique of her instead of mentioning that his own mother had enjoyed working in her stillroom and that her Culpepper's *The English Physitian* held pride of place in Pemberley's extensive library.

Assuring himself that the admiration would fade in time, he had pretended he'd only amused himself during an otherwise dull period, that despite his desire for rest, his sleepless imaginings of holding her, kissing her, were a temporary addiction. He might have ignored the disruption to his peace of mind and remained at Netherfield until Christmas had he only kept his mouth shut.

The morning had begun with the arrival of a missive from Lady Catherine, imploring him to present himself without delay at Rosings and address himself to her intimate concerns regarding his unmarried state and her preferences for changing it. How many times had he informed her that such a union was impossible? A spike of misery had clawed him at the very thought of presenting his refusals once again. At that very moment of despondency, Miss Bingley had intruded upon him in the library, weeping into her handkerchief and laying the problem of her brother's romance at *his* feet.

"You must prevent Charles from making an error of monumental proportion," she had cried. "Offering for such a girl, from such a family! It is not to be borne!"

"He has offered for someone?" Darcy asked, incredulous. "Who?"

"No! As yet, he has not. But the entire countryside is speaking of his intentions towards Miss Jane Bennet! Penniless, inappropriate girl. Surely you can stop him!"

"You know your brother—he falls in and out of love with every change of season."

"His preference for the sly thing is beyond what I have ever before perceived in him. I do not exaggerate the danger!" She dabbed at her eyes, looking up at him pleadingly.

He *ought* to have done as he had in times past—observe Bingley with Miss Bennet, determine whether the girl was truly attached or whether it was yet another idle, meaningless flirtation—then distract him away from it before his attentions attracted notice or expectation. The notion made him unutterably weary.

Why could not the people in his life manage themselves? Why must he repeat to his aunt, again and again, a rejection so distasteful to her? Why could not Bingley heed the countless warnings already given him? Why should Miss Bingley look to *him* as her brother's caretaker?

In very real dismay, he had mounted Gallant and galloped over fields and pastures, only to come upon the temptation herself: his Elizabeth, unruly curls hidden by a cap, an apron covering her light and pleasing figure, a basket full of weeds upon her arm. She looked like a peasant girl, simple and wild, and yet those marvellous eyes of hers caught and held his gaze as an equal. Heady, piercing desire shook him. His heart leapt, then beat too fast as he halted the steed beside her and impulsively blurted his love from atop it in mortifying, passionate awkwardness.

"Miss Elizabeth, it is all in vain. My sentiments cannot be repressed. You must allow me to tell you how ardently I admire and love you."

He would never forget her humiliating response: laughter. She believed he was joking, teasing her. Her look and manners were open, cheerful, and engaging as ever, but without any symptom of peculiar regard, or any participation of like sentiment. Obviously, she did not believe him truthful, or want any part of his love.

It was a fortunate reprieve. Allowing the 'joke' to stand, he had galloped away from her, leaving her staring after him. He had ordered his man to pack his trunks, written brief apologies to both Lady Catherine and Bingley for being unable to delay a journey to the coast to visit his sister, and fled Netherfield so quickly, it was barely polite.

<hr />

The road smoothed and widened as his carriage drew closer to the seaside village of Ramsgate, but Darcy's head still pounded as though he were being dragged down a rutted lane. He heard the sounds of gulls and breathed deeply of the salty air, hoping his brain would clear. He anticipated Georgiana's response at seeing him unexpectedly on her doorstep, and smiled. The action felt unfamiliar, even odd; he wondered if he should practise it before arriving, resisting the urge to dig out a mirror from his kit for fear it, instead, resembled a grimace.

As he drove past the various medical establishments on Chapel Place, he wondered if he should perhaps make an appointment for a sea cure. He immediately shuddered at the thought of trying to explain himself, of giving voice to complaints of discomfort in a life he knew to be uniformly desirable. He could only imagine what his father would have thought of such a display of weakness. No, the best possible cure had been removing himself from Elizabeth's taxing presence, exchanging sleepless nights for peace of mind. *Press on, Darcy*, he commanded himself in familiar refrain.

At long last, his carriage turned onto his own drive, and he rested his tired eyes upon Sea Cliff Lodge.

Entering the large, well-lit hall, Darcy was surprised by the quiet of the place. No servants greeted him; he directed his own man and Frost, his coachman, to deal with his trunks. The music room was empty, so he proceeded up the stairs to his sister's favourite parlour. He almost called out when he reached it—as he heard low murmurings from within—but head throbbing, he could not bring himself to make the effort.

He strode into the pale blue room, expecting to see his sister—perhaps bent over her writing desk or her sewing, conversing with her companion, Mrs Younge. Instead, he halted in shock.

Georgiana was wrapped in what could only be described as a passionate embrace; her arms were locked around the neck of a man, her fingers clutching his hair. The man's hands were...were...

Darcy made a sound—not words, some exclamation that could not begin to express his horror. He did not know what he meant to say; he was already choosing his second, planning the scoundrel's death. Perhaps he would not wait for a field of honour—a gutter was too grand a place for this ne'er-do-well to die.

Georgiana heard him...he saw her startle...saw the moment she recognised just *who* was witness to this gross impropriety. She shrieked, dropping her hands and shoving at her lover; the man stumbled back awkwardly, whirling to see the source of the interruption, his face reflecting annoyance, not shame.

"Wickham!"

"Fitzwilliam! It is not what you think..." Georgiana's plea faded at his obvious fury, but she caught her courage and tried to continue. "We are to be married—"

But Darcy could not look at her, only at the villainous source of her potential ruin. "*Marry?* You think to marry my *sister?*" His tone was incredulous, his anger spiralling beyond his control. "That so vile a blackguard as you should even *speak* with her is an outrage, much less..." His words choked off, cut into shreds by rage. He could hardly draw breath to fill his lungs.

George Wickham laughed. "This is rich," he said between guffaws. "If you could only see your red face, Darcy! I suppose your puritanical tyranny would not allow for men and women to behave as mere mortals. Your bride shall anticipate a buss on the cheek for her wedding night bliss, with only your money to keep her warm, eh?"

Darcy stood frozen, chest heaving. He watched, as though from a distance, Wickham's continued hilarity. Darcy reached out to his sister, intending to order her from the room so he could throw the first punch. His mouth worked around the words but failed to form them. He tried to stretch his arm to her—but it was unresponsive to his brain's demands. His vision clouded, black and red dots obscuring his view. His limbs grew heavy, unyielding. He thought perhaps he was seeing through a red haze of his own making, his fury tunnelling through his senses and paralysing him. He attempted to reassert control of his body—failed, and collapsed where he stood, his consciousness fading to the sound of Georgiana's screams.

1

SCARCELY ESCAPING DISCREDIT AND MISERY

If one wished to assign blame for the impossible situation, Lizzy felt the onus ought to rest at Mr Collins's too-large feet. Of course, it was her mother who had enacted the actual expulsion, but Lizzy understood her—as much as one could ever understand Mama. Mrs Bennet had been overly encouraged by Jane's triumphant match with Bingley into believing that she could be as easily rid of her least favourite daughter.

I was too slow to recognise the signs of Mama's intentions—so obvious, in retrospect.

"How *could* I have guessed, though?" Lizzy argued with herself. "Whomever Mr Collins marries will eventually become *mistress* of Longbourn. It is impossible to conceive of receiving *either* of my parents' approbation for my assumption of *that* position!"

Of course, Cousin Collins was repellent to her, but even had he not been, she had been taught to believe, from a very young age, that she would *never* marry. Her mother's small portion was to be split between her other sisters; none was to come to her. Mrs Bennet had told her so often enough—and who would marry one so impoverished?

While her father...her father said nothing to her at all. Ever.

Even without her shock, distaste and dismay at the ridiculous proposal, she must refuse Collins's offer. That refusal would be *expected* of her. A niggling idea escaped her control. What would her parents have done, she wondered, had Mr Darcy's interest been a serious one? But she stopped this line of thought immediately; he had never, by word or deed, indicated any feelings other than contempt and half-hearted apology. The one dance they had shared over the course of his one-month visit was not any sort of courtship, and a couple of sentences muttered from atop a horse were hardly a proposal. Had not they all agreed that his departure shortly thereafter only hastened Jane's happiness? Absent his gloomy, disapproving friend, Bingley and Jane had been engaged within a fortnight. She had vowed to never think of it again.

And for a few days after her mother's threat of expulsion, Lizzy had truly expected her mother to change her mind. Mama had never been known for her constancy. In fact, it was an unwritten rule of the household—Mama's temper flared, and an hour later, whatever punishments and discipline administered were forgotten and never enforced.

Father certainly neither supported nor encouraged obedience to his wife. And while he never spoke to Lizzy, neither did he engage much with *any* of them. His life was spent in his book-room, unaffected by the moods and tempers of the ladies of Longbourn. An appeal to him, of course, would be useless.

Nevertheless, Mama *knew* the work Lizzy performed to make life at Longbourn more comfortable! Lizzy had taught herself to brew teas for easing Mama's megrims and Kitty and Lydia's monthlies, as well as a poultice excellent for relieving the pain of Mr Bennet's gout. Amongst her sisters, she was the peacemaker, able to divert the most stubborn argument, and so clever at wordplay and skilled at pantomime that she had often been able to turn a row into giggling fits. Mama had been sending her into the village on little errands since she was six. She had been sewing her own dresses, and many of her sisters', since the age of nine or ten. Many were the evenings where she read aloud to them all—and she had noted her father doing as poor a job at pretending not to listen as Mary.

Sir William had once complimented her abilities after she had recited a scene from *Hamlet*, saying she had made his blood run cold. "As good as a play, listening to you, Lizzy-girl!" he'd enthused.

Still, after three days had passed in which her mother would not look her way even once, she'd had a new thought: *Perhaps I ought to tell Mr Collins I have changed my mind.* But even as she had steeled herself to approach him, Charlotte had come to Longbourn with news of her engagement.

And after that conversation, Lizzy had seen the resentment—and disgust, even—in Mrs Bennet's eyes, and known Mama would never change *her* mind before Friday—the day Lizzy was to be sent away.

⊰❦⊱

"We will visit Mr Bingley's relations in Scarborough, and after, he has taken a cottage in Brighton for our wedding trip. It will be lovely to be near the seaside, and it is said to have the most glorious gardens!"

"Now you are simply boasting. Lizzy, Jane is crowing about going to Brighton—"

"I was not, Lydia. I was simply telling—"

"I have to leave," Lizzy interrupted the argument in progress.

Her sisters had congregated in the green parlour, the coolest one in the house on this unusually sultry early-July afternoon. It was presided over by a large portrait of Percival Earnest Bennet, a sharp-eyed ancestor who stared imperiously down his nose at all who dared gather in his illustrious presence. Mrs Bennet hated it, of course, but her husband would never agree to its removal.

Her sisters peered up at her blankly. Well, all except for Mary, who avoided addressing Lizzy whenever possible and used the opportunity to turn the page of her book, as if no one had spoken. This did not trouble Lizzy, as those to whom Mary *did* speak were often subjected to Fordyce's constructive criticisms.

"Are you going to the village?" Kitty asked.

"No," Lizzy replied. "I mean, I have to leave Longbourn. On Friday, I am to be taken to London with Mrs Long, who visits her sister's family there. Mama has instructed her to drop me at her brother's, who, apparently, lives and works there." She held up a small, faded trade-card. "She has ordered him to find me a position, she says."

Jane's brows rose. "No, surely not, Lizzy. You must be mistaken."

Lizzy's stomach clenched a little. Most all of her prospects rested with Jane, but she could not predict Jane's response with any certainty.

Jane was very sweet, very kind. Lizzy cherished the hope that, once married—an event occurring in less than a month—Jane would invite Lizzy to live with her at Netherfield. Netherfield was twice the size of Longbourn, and she knew she could easily keep out of Miss Bingley's way. Her plan had been to ease into the situation— and especially once Jane was with child, there would be a hundred ways she could make herself useful. She knew that Jane was genuinely troubled by the treatment Lizzy often received at Longbourn and, had she been permitted, would have taken her part on any number of occasions.

But that was the trouble, was it not? She had not *been* permitted, and there was not a rebellious or confrontational bone in her sister's body. Jane could never think ill of anyone, living to please her difficult, fractious parents and soon—it was to be presumed— Mr Bingley. Neither did Jane think for herself when she could help it, and the idea of her presenting defiance to *anyone* was ridiculous. But surely a desperate circumstance would inspire a room amongst so many at Netherfield?

"Mama has been angry at you before," Lydia offered, not sounding particularly concerned. "Stay over with Charlotte a few days, and it will all blow over. I cannot believe anyone would blame you for refusing that nincompoop Collins. He is utterly ridiculous. She is in a temper, is all."

Lizzy bit her lower lip. "She said none of us are to go near the Lucases ever again, now that Charlotte is engaged to Collins. That we must avoid speaking to them. She is telling her friends I am to visit her brother in town, and she told *me* she will eventually report that I have married from there. I am never to return. She...she is not reasonable."

"Does she even *have* a brother in London?" Kitty asked. "I have never heard of one."

Lizzy shrugged, fingering the faded parchment card proclaiming 'Edward Gardiner, Solicitor', and remembering the letter with its address in Cheapside. "She must. She gave me his card and a letter for him. And she has not the imagination to invent one."

The Bennet sisters all nodded, except for Mary, who had not turned a page in some time and hastily did so to prove she was not listening.

"But a position? Surely not," Jane protested, her expression troubled.

"Perhaps you might convince Mrs Long to take you with her instead," Kitty suggested.

They all looked at her incredulously. Mrs Long was the last person to whom one would admit the truth of Lizzy's status at Long-bourn, or from whom to expect a rescue.

"Perhaps I could become a companion," Lizzy suggested, hoping Jane might take the hint.

"But you *have* no experience, no references! Who would employ you?" Lydia asked.

"Lydia, it is not the *who*. *Any* position would be a degradation!" Jane declared.

"Perhaps...perhaps, Jane, you might be able to do so?" Lizzy dared suggest, when it became clear that Jane would never think of it herself. "Not now, of course, but after your marriage? Not for payment, obviously. Only as a help and comfort to you?"

An awkward silence ensued. *Please, please, please,* Lizzy thought, holding herself very still.

Jane opened her mouth, shut it again; it was several moments before she spoke. "Naturally, you must not go into service. It is only...Miss Bingley is barely reconciled to our marriage as it is. I would not like to disturb Mr Bingley's peace, with Mama so likely to change her mind."

Lizzy felt the colour rush to her cheeks and glanced at the portrait of Great-Great-Grandfather Bennet. Did not his lip curl ever so slightly at Lizzy's predicament? Unsurprisingly, Jane refused to believe that Lizzy's position in the household had grown so tenuous.

"I am certain by the time your wedding is past, she will be more accepting," Lizzy assured, trying to keep the desperation from her voice. "If it were discovered that I had entered service, it would be humiliating for her too. Only if word were to get out, of course. It might not."

She did not threaten her sisters with publicising such an outcome. Firstly, the very idea of anyone knowing was terrible. Secondly, she did love them, faults and all. Lizzy would never intentionally harm their reputations.

"I-I suppose I could mention the idea to Mr Bingley. After the wedding, that is," Jane said carefully, obviously terrified at the thought.

"To be sure," Lydia interpolated. "We would not want to cast the line before the bait is well hooked."

Jane gave her a hurt look, which Lydia contrived not to notice.

But it was Kitty who voiced aloud Lizzy's worst fears. "What if this uncle is wicked? What if he-he places you with a cruel mistress?"

Lydia chimed in. "What if he sells you to a brothel?" She sounded both horrified and intrigued.

"What novels you read, Lydia! I shall not go to this uncle, of course! I will send a note to Mrs Long early Friday, saying plans have changed and that I will ride with you, Lydia, when you depart with Harriet to Ramsgate the same day. And then, I will hide."

"Hide? But where? How?" Jane, Kitty, and Lydia asked nearly in unison. Even Mary could not continue her pretence of reading, gawking at Lizzy in astonishment.

"The woods between Longbourn and Netherfield's boundaries are seldom visited by anyone," Lizzy explained, trying to sound rational and calm, instead of desperate and terrified. "The old woodsman's cottage is vacant, since our father built the bigger one. The weather is good, and I have warm clothing for nights. Mama did not say I must leave my belongings."

"That is because most of your clothing belongs in the rag bag," Lydia scoffed.

This was not at all true, Lizzy knew, because neither of her parents wanted the neighbourhood to remark upon *any* difference between Lizzy and her sisters. Her dresses were simply duller and darker, without decoration or trimmings—long ago, she had learnt the wisdom of calling no attention to herself and asking for nothing. Still, her wardrobe was sturdy and well made, if disagreeable in other ways, and for assemblies, Kitty, Lydia, and Jane had all shared their ribbons and lace to help her look more presentable.

"How would you eat? What of wolves, or other forest creatures?" asked Kitty fearfully.

"You would grow dirty and wild," Jane added, horrified.

Lydia rolled her eyes. "You are always so dramatic, both of you. I never heard of wolves in Longbourn's woods, and Lizzy, no one is going to sneak out there to feed you with contraband from Mama's kitchen. Instead, we will make your lies into truth: you *will* leave with Harriet and her aunt on a visit to the shore in my place."

At this proclamation, all the girls turned to Lydia—Mary, Kitty, and Jane with astonishment, and Lizzy with some suspicion.

Mary spoke first, unable to help herself. "Lydia Bennet, after the detestable fits of temper you threw in order to gain permission to miss Jane's wedding, were I your parents, I would not *permit* you to beg off now!"

"You have certainly been looking forward to spending the rest of the summer on the coast," Lizzy hurriedly put in, before Lydia and Mary began bickering. "You have talked of nothing else this age." It was inconceivable that Lydia would relinquish her longed-for, begged-for holiday simply as a good deed.

"That was before," Lydia replied complacently.

"Before what?" Kitty asked.

Lydia's expression turned sly. "Before I learnt that an entire regiment will soon be stationed near to Meryton, and for the rest of the year! I overheard Mr Goulding discussing it with Papa, and I have been wondering how to avoid going away ever since. This will do nicely. Harriet hasn't the will to overrule me—she always does whatever I say, though she *is* three years my senior. I will tell her that you are peaked and require the sea air, and I cannot, in good conscience, leave you behind when it is within my power to see you restored. She must be a good Christian, and take you instead of me."

Mary harrumphed at this, turning back to her book with a sniff.

"Will not her aunt object to a change in guests?" Lizzy asked.

Lydia snorted inelegantly. "Why should Mrs Morris care which friend Harriet brings along? Frankly, I do not think she would notice. Her head is always in a book, and half of the time, she calls me 'Lilian'. The perfect chaperon. We would have been able to do as we pleased."

Jane's eyes widened at this, and she and Lizzy exchanged a glance. *Lydia ought never to be allowed to accompany Harriet anywhere at all,* their look agreed.

"Let Mama believe you have gone to London," Lydia continued. "How would she know otherwise? I daresay she will be so thrilled I intend to stay at home, she will pay little attention to the doings of Harriet and her aunt. It *would* have been such a lark, and I *am* a little sorry to miss it. Still, what is the use of such freedom in a poky little town like Ramsgate? Especially when an entire regiment of lovely redcoats will be quartered *here*. Harriet will be so jealous when she learns of it."

"I pray you do not inform her," beseeched Lizzy.

"Oh, I shall not, to be sure. It will be such a good joke. But one of the Harringtons is sure to write her. I would have had to feign illness myself to avoid leaving, and this is much more convenient. I shall have to have a new dress for the wedding and will need to shop."

Mary chided her for encouraging falsehoods, and Jane chided them both for bickering.

"I am very sorry to miss your wedding, Jane," Lizzy said softly to her, swallowing a sudden lump. She did love Jane best; it was not her fault she had no pluck. For that matter, she would miss all her sisters. Perhaps even Mary.

"Do not think another thing about it, Lizzy," Jane replied, sighing heavily. "It cannot be helped." She gathered up her embroidery. "And no one had better inform Mama of Lizzy's true destination," Jane added, with a warning glance at Mary. "Else we shall all be taking turns leaving food in the woods for her, and likely be eaten by bears."

The Thursday evening before her departure, Lizzy could not sleep. She had never before suffered from an insomnious complaint, but then, she had never before ventured into the unknown with such little security. What if Jane would not eventually permit her to live at Netherfield? Should she, perhaps, attempt to write to her unknown uncle? But why should a man who had never made any effort to be a part of her life pay to receive a letter from her? Might Mama change her mind after all?

The entire day had been a difficult one. She had, briefly, hoped Mama's feelings had softened, for all of Lizzy's favourite breakfast dishes had been laid out—Bath buns and French breads and the little white sugar biscuits Lizzy called 'fairy cakes'. But then Mrs Hill had tucked three new handkerchiefs in her reticule, reminding Lizzy, in her fastidious way, not to lose them, whilst Cook had written out her receipt for pigeon pie—the spices therein were a great secret. Mama had *not* been responsible for the treats.

Jane had given her a guinea, Kitty two hair ribbons, and Lydia her cameo bracelet, saying she did not wear it any longer, even though Lizzy had seen it on her only the day before. Even Mary had handed her a pamphlet containing excerpts from the Book of Revelation, urging her to care for her soul. Their gifts touched Lizzy, for her sisters had each been wordlessly taught that she was of smaller importance to their family circle, and they could have treated her however they wished without fear of retaliation.

But the most wrenching encounter of the day had come from, of all people, her father. When she'd been much younger, she had persistently tried to gain his attention, speak to him, try for *some* kind of response—had even misbehaved at times, feeling that a switching would be better than the vast nothingness of his disinterest. It had not worked; to him, she did not exist.

It had been the great trial of her early years, and eventually, she had ignored him as well, hating him with a sort of childish animosity. But she had not been formed for unhappiness; when she had finally discovered the reasons for his bitterness, she had buried her hatred and done her best to simply accept his indifference. And on those rare occasions she knew she had earned his attention—always against his will, by some wit or cleverness on her part—she had only smiled to herself and betrayed no sign of her victories.

As she had begun the climb to her bed chamber this evening, however, he had halted her with a hand on her arm. When she turned to him in some amazement, he held out a book, which she accepted with a small curtsey. He turned away without a word.

For long moments, she watched his back as he disappeared down the corridor towards his book-room, feeling a renewed surge of bitterness, hatred, and longing. Then she gazed down at the worn leather covers, the faded gilt lettering of *The Pilgrim's Progress*, even reading the inscription inside, marking it as the property of Lady Sarah Ashley, one of Mr Bennet's patriarchal grandmothers who had been a lady-in-waiting or some such to the queen during the reign of Charles II. A valuable volume, really.

But she knew with a crushing finality that whatever plans she might or might not be able to form with Jane, whatever forgiveness she might eventually earn from Mama, she could never, ever again call Longbourn her home. Mr Bennet had finished with her.

2

NAMING NO NAMES

The hundred-mile journey to Ramsgate was accomplished in near-silence. Lizzy felt too sad to attempt much conversation. Mrs Morris usually had her nose in a book, while Harriet plainly believed Lizzy to have been stricken as an invalid since the last party they'd attended together. And the first time she and Harriet—accompanied only by Harriet's maid, for Mrs Morris could not be bothered—journeyed to the town proper, Lizzy was astonished by the sight of what must have been a thousand soldiers, probably more, meandering about the streets of the village. Lydia could have had a different redcoat beside her every day of the week.

"Oh my," Harriet murmured, looking around delightedly. "How sorry Lydia will be when she hears of this."

"Why, Lydia will be so..." Lizzy trailed off, imagining her sister's fury and, even, an insistence upon joining them directly, whether or not it meant Lizzy was thrown out on her ear.

Harriet laughed, but then tossed her curls. "Hmpf. I shall write nothing to her yet. Lydia is a great deal of fun, but she *does* like to claim the best admirers for herself. I do hope you will not be so boring." What she meant, of course, was her expectation of the exact opposite. Where Lydia would have shined, Harriet now wished her companion to fade into the background.

The following week proved Lizzy correct. By turns aimable and temperamental, giddy and officer-mad, the pretty and popular Harriet Thorpe was happiest when Lizzy faded into the background. The aunt was completely inept at chaperonage—she called Lizzy 'Lilian' if she called her anything at all—and paid little attention to her charges. However, Mrs Morris had been spending her summers in Ramsgate for many years now, and she was well known to its inhabitants. They found no lack of invitations to soirees, concerts, dances, teas, and the like, and Mrs Morris was usually agreeable enough to attend so they could as well. Lizzy was careful to seat herself with the matrons, watching rather than participating. The longer she could stay in Harriet's good graces, the better.

Her natural bonhomie made her situation—living very quietly, avoiding dancing and other activities as if she were an invalid in truth—more difficult, and Lizzy struggled to stay optimistic. She reminded herself that living in Mrs Morris's lovely home, perched atop Ramsgate's East Cliff, was hardly a punishment. It was built in a circular row of other fine houses rimming the cliff, with marvellous views of the ocean on one side and a large park on the other. Its library was quite good, even including a copy of the very interesting *Practices of Physiks*, which Lizzy had long wished to study. Each morning she rose with dawn's first light, long before the rest of the household, walking the shoreline, taking in the crisp cold air and the vastness of the ocean. She told herself that Jane would not see her put into service by some hitherto unknown, uncaring uncle; she was the furthest thing from cold-hearted. It was irrational to believe Jane might.

Still, Lizzy felt very much alone and lonely. Her presence was only tolerated by Harriet, who quickly made other friends whose company she preferred. It was a constant reminder that Ramsgate was but a temporary reprieve.

It was two of Harriet's new friends, Miss Martha Beaton and Miss Diana Cavendish, however, who imparted the first news of real interest.

"Of course, my father is known to Mr Darcy," Martha crowed. "Papa is sure to gain me an introduction if he comes. They say he has ten thousand a year."

Lizzy, who had been paying little attention to their banal conversation, looked up from her book. "Mr Fitzwilliam Darcy?" she asked, struggling for a casual expression. "He is here?"

"Mr Bingley's friend from London!" Harriet cried. "We have met him! Eliza even danced with him once, I recall. She was the only one he danced with not of his party for the whole of his visit."

The other girls turned to her with their first indication of interest, but Lizzy waved dismissively. "It was not what you would think," she explained. "Mr Bingley urged him to dance with me, but he refused. 'The carrot-headed chit?' he asked. 'You must be joking. If no one else will dance with her, why should I?'"

The insult had infuriated and embarrassed her; she had spent so much time trying to tuck every ruby curl out of sight! Even now it invoked a remembered annoyance.

"He did not," Martha breathed.

"Oh, but he did," Lizzy asserted.

"Appalling behaviour in a gentleman," Diana said, but she sounded amused, and Lizzy knew the story would be repeated around dinner tables that evening. But what did she care?

"That is what I told him."

"You did what?" the three girls chorused.

"He knew that I heard him, the hateful creature. I simply turned to him and said, 'You are mistaken, Mr Darcy, if you suppose that I would ever agree to dance with a man who cannot behave in a more gentleman-like manner.' I left him standing there with his mouth gaping like a fish while that wonderful Mr Bingley laughed at him. 'Twas very satisfying."

"But did you not dance with him?" Martha questioned.

"Not by choice. He approached me at Sir William Lucas's party with a condescending apology and asked if I would partner him. I almost refused, but my friend Charlotte Lucas pinched me and said I would accept, so I had to, else make a scene. But it was utter agony to act polite, and the worst dance of my life!"

And the best dance of my life. To be on the arm of the handsomest man she had ever seen, the envy of her friends, to dance with one so skilled, to meet his dark-eyed gaze, to trade banter and to know he had been amused—or perhaps even impressed by her wit...well, it had been a high point. Had he been a different man and she a different girl, she might even have thought him attracted to her for a moment or two of it. But subsequent encounters and his haughty coldness in her presence had cured her of that fancy, all concluding in that mocking, insulting declaration. Determinedly, she forced the memory away.

"He is the one who owns Sea Cliff Lodge," Diana explained, naming the grandest home on the East Cliff. "It is said he took it for his young sister, but perhaps she is an invalid, for we have never once seen her, not even walking out on the Green, although the house is definitely occupied. There was even a rumour he is visiting. Or was. No one seems to know the truth of it, though."

Miss Bingley had frequently spoken of Miss Darcy, had claimed her to be the pinnacle of every female accomplishment. But then, Miss Bingley was usually effusive in the presence of Mr Darcy.

"I have never heard any report of her being an invalid. In fact, she was said to be in perfect health and countenance."

"How odd!" Diana exclaimed.

"Perhaps we should call upon Miss Darcy," Lizzy suggested.

"Why should we?" Martha asked.

"Why should we not? We *are* neighbours," Lizzy replied.

"She is not yet out, I believe," Harriet said with obvious reluctance.

"We do not propose to ask her to a ball, only to leave our cards."

But Martha—who moments before had been boasting of her father's connexion to Mr Darcy—scoffed, "What, and appear to be elbow-rubbers or climbing ivy? As if I would."

Instantly, Harriet agreed, nearly sneering her refusals at Lizzy, turning the conversation back to sleeves and lace trims.

The truth was, Lizzy realised, that the girls were each of good family—but none of them frequented the circles in which the Darcys were accepted. It was unsurprising that Miss Darcy would shun her neighbours; her brother had hardly been gregarious, and if he was visiting, he would be unlikely to set the neighbourhood afire with his presence.

Still, it did incite her curiosity, and every time she passed their property, she wondered. Was *he* there? *Would* she see him again?

⬥

Fitzwilliam Darcy wakened to see that he had been left quite alone. *Ah,* he thought. *An improvement.* He could not know where his keepers were—or if this reprieve meant a visit from one of his relations was imminent. He only knew he must take advantage of every moment of privacy.

Say your name, he told himself. *Say it aloud. Fitzwilliam.*

"Bloody saints!" he said and tensed. *Incorrect. Try it again.*

"Devil take you!" *No. Wrong. Once more. Gain control.*

He caught sight of the leather manacles encasing his wrists, tying him to the bed. A wave of defenceless fury exploded through him at the sight. He forced the rage down. It would not help. *Say your name.*

"Bleeding Fitz-blast-will-bugger it!" *Better.*

It had been like this since he had awakened from the horror at Sea Cliff Lodge—finding himself in a strange room, with no idea of where he was or how much time had passed—no more than a week or two, he thought? No concept of where Wickham or even Mrs Younge might be. And his sister nowhere in sight.

He had regained full consciousness to see his uncle, Lord Matlock, his cousin, Colonel Fitzwilliam, and his aunt, Lady Matlock. He had tried to ask about Georgiana, but all that had escaped his lips was a stream of profanities. He knew it was not right, that he had not said what he'd meant, but could not force the correct words past his cobbled tongue, only virulent expletives; it made him sick to think of it.

I am a gentleman! I am not insane!

For the first few days, they had been patient with him, trying to be soothing. He had tried too. But a week had passed, and still they spoke too fast or too low. They mumbled and stuttered as his mind blinked in and out of awareness—he often could not grasp all of what they told him; he felt weak and sick, unable to prevent what words he could utter from doing as they would. They simply stared, appalled, as he swore at them with the vigour and lucidity of a seasoned sailor. Abruptly, the earl ceased visiting at all. A sinking fear began plaguing Darcy.

He and Fitzwilliam were Georgiana's guardians. But if he were declared *non compos mentis*, who would be *his* guardian? The answer was obvious—the earl. Pemberley, his fortune, his investments—wealth beyond the earl's wildest dreams. His uncle was not a bad man, truly...but his eldest son was an exceedingly expensive wastrel. The allure of believing in his nephew's madness might be stronger than familial duty, even reputation. Colonel Fitzwilliam was Darcy's only real hope—but then *he* also disappeared without warning. As each day passed without word, Darcy's fears grew stronger.

Finally, absolutely frustrated in his need to gain control of his life and discover his whereabouts, his sister, anything at all—he had attempted to simply leave. The doctor who ran the place, Mr Younge, had tried to stop him; Darcy had planted him a facer. However, Younge had called quickly for reinforcements. Hence, the manacles. They loosed him only to use the chamber pot and to feed himself a tasteless gruel, whilst the medicines had become stupefying. Heaven only knew what Younge had said of the incident to the earl—certainly no one had baulked at his restraints.

That was not my wisest moment, he thought drily. In retrospect, he had been too weak, too sick. Had he fully had his wits about him, he would have waited. He could have pretended continued weakness until an opportune moment, then made a real escape—gone to Sea Cliff for his things and his man, and hopefully Georgiana as well. Of course, there was still the matter of his continued inability to communicate. And was he even still in Ramsgate?

Regardless, he improved daily now; he understood what was said to him, especially when the speaker took his time about it. His weakness was diminishing, and he could feel his strength returning. He had grown adept at avoiding swallowing the doctor's cordials, of dumping them into the gruel whenever his keepers failed to watch. Of course, it also meant he could never finish a meal and was losing weight. He was constantly hungry.

Darcy had worked out that the physician who held him, Mr Younge, *must* be some relation of Mrs Younge—Georgiana's companion—and said companion *must* have been complicit in planning Georgiana's ruin with Wickham. He ought to have put it all together sooner—the doctor would probably be able to retire on what he would charge the earl for Darcy's care. If the physician was of the same ilk as Georgiana's companion...his conscience would not stop him from dishonesty.

And since Darcy no longer bothered trying to speak aloud in the presence of others—no need to give anyone more evidence of weakness—he must take advantage of this time alone. He must cease wondering when he would see Fitzwilliam or the earl again. *Do not think of them*, he told himself. *My family. My gaolers. Georgiana.* He would not give in to his weakness; he would cling to the thin veneer of civility he still possessed. He would press on. He forced his mind away from his sister, from his restraints, from his fury, from his fear.

Your name, he thought. *Say it.*

3

SAVED FROM SOMETHING
LIKE REGRET

The day of Jane's wedding dawned cold and clear; Lizzy tried to blunt the sense of loss and homesickness by making her daily tramp longer than usual. Instead of walking down to the ocean and back again, she took a more indirect route along the cliff tops.

She had been this way once before, curious to see where Sea Cliff Lodge's property met the pathway leading down to the beach, noting its small iron gate that was barred from the other side. This morning, however, it was ajar. Could some resident of the place be strolling on the public path? Unlikely, at this hour. Perhaps a gardener had availed himself of it for some reason.

The temptation to enter suddenly struck her—a small adventure, really, perhaps to discover forbidden views of the home and its occupants. Quickly, however, she dismissed the notion as nonsense. It was far too early for the Lodge's residents to be about, and even supposing she *did* catch sight of Mr Darcy, what would she say? 'Hello, I am trespassing at this hour to catch a glimpse of you?'

The very idea of being caught standing here, staring at his gate, filled her with a sense of dismay that had her quickening her steps along the cliff path.

None of her usual solace was found in the crashing waves and majestic ocean views. It was cold and somewhat desolate, the wind screaming loudly in her ears. It matched her mood, however, and she struggled to put her thoughts into some sort of rational order. But the frustration and unfairness of her situation plagued her. Why was she, who had nothing to do with any of her parents' troubles, somehow to blame? Cold droplets began spattering like angry tears. *Return now, Lizzy,* she warned herself. There was no comfort to be found in these thoughts, in this weather. She paused, looking out at the violent waves, suddenly realising that she was not alone on the bluff top.

A girl stood at the cliff's apex, her back to Lizzy, several yards away. Too close, *much* too close to the edge. And as Lizzy watched, horrified, the figure leant forward, teetering upon its brink.

Lizzy did not hesitate, pitching herself towards the girl, grabbing a handful of pelisse to tug her away from the cliff's edge. They both stumbled back.

The girl blinked up at her in surprise. "Oh!" was all she said.

Though she was young, perhaps Lydia's age, the other girl was built upon solid lines, her figure womanly, and something about her face was vaguely familiar.

"Perhaps we should move away from this place," Lizzy suggested.

But the girl looked away. "I do not believe I shall," she said, her cultured accent soft but determined.

"Please!" Lizzy forced her voice to a firmness she did not feel. Yet, a certain candour seemed appropriate. "Whatever your troubles, jumping is no solution."

"You know nothing of my troubles and are no judge of what fate I deserve," the young lady replied softly, bitterly. "I have brought all of them upon myself."

"Of course I do not know specifically," Lizzy agreed. "But Trouble and I are well acquainted—he has followed me everywhere I go, since the day I was born. I am so used to coping with his tricks and tests, perhaps I can be of some use to you?"

But the girl only looked away.

Lizzy took in the expensive clothing, suddenly remembering the unbolted gate from Sea Cliff Lodge; as well, there was that haunting familiarity. It was the eyes, she decided. She was not so handsome as her brother, and her eyes were blue rather than dark, but they had the same shape, a slightly exotic uptilt.

"You are Miss Darcy, I believe?" she enquired. "I am Miss Elizabeth Bennet."

Miss Darcy swivelled her head sharply back to Lizzy, gasping slightly. "How do you know who I am?" There was fear in her gaze.

"Oh, I only guess at your identity. I know your brother, you see—"

But at these words, the girl scrambled away from her, a hopeless sort of fury in her expression.

"Liar! You may stop your extortion right there! I have nothing left! I can give you nothing! You may tell George that she has taken it all and then some!" She raised her hands, then let them fall to her sides. Her head drooped, as if the small defiance had drained her. "Leave me now, if you have an ounce of pity in your soul. Allow me a bit of dignity for this, at least."

Lizzy closed her mouth, which she realised was gaping in astonishment. "I assure you, Miss Darcy, I do not know of any George connected to you, and you have nothing to fear from me. I met Mr Darcy earlier this summer, several times, whilst he resided at Netherfield Park with Mr Bingley."

At the mention of Mr Bingley and Netherfield, Miss Darcy met Lizzy's eyes once more. The fear in them had only marginally receded. What to say? How to say it? She found herself babbling.

"Mr Bingley is to be wed today, as a matter of fact, to my sister Jane. How I wish I could be there for the wedding! I thought of leaving my card for you when I learnt we were neighbours...but then...I did not," she trailed off, feeling somewhat foolish.

To her relief, however, Miss Darcy sat heavily on a nearby boulder —a few feet away from that dangerous edge.

"They would not have given me the card, had you left it," she said bitterly.

Lizzy sat beside her, still wondering how to offer comfort. "And why is that?"

For long moments, Miss Darcy replied nothing, and Lizzy thought she might refuse to speak of her troubles. But then she did. "You may as well know...my brother is a living corpse. His brain, his mind is gone. Or so Lord and Lady Matlock assure me."

"What...Mr Darcy? It cannot be true! This is too awful!" Lizzy could not imagine Mr Darcy in such a state. *Poor, poor Miss Darcy!*

"My opinion precisely. I cannot bear it! I *will* not bear it any longer!" She began to sob with quiet heartbreak.

"Oh, my dear," she soothed, placing an arm about the weeping girl, feeling utterly helpless in the face of such grief.

But something did not quite make sense; Miss Darcy might well not be receiving visitors, but she ought to receive her calling cards, just the same. "Why would they not give you my card, had I left it?"

"I am kept a prisoner there. I cannot speak with anyone. I am only out now because there is no one awake to stop me."

"You are a prisoner of this...Lord Matlock?"

"No, not him. The earl was only here for the first week of Fitzwilliam's illness. Shortly thereafter, Colonel Fitzwilliam departed—Matlock's younger son that is—once the earl left for his country seat. Lady Matlock comes down from London occasionally, but she never stays long, and barely notices me when she does."

"Then who keeps you a prisoner?"

But a certain mulishness crept into Miss Darcy's expression, and she answered nothing.

"Your brother...he is at home, with you?"

Her eyes again filled with tears. "Oh, how I wish! I would nurse him, and gladly, for the rest of my life! If only!" She buried her face in her hands, her shoulders shaking with the force of her grief.

As Lizzy patted Miss Darcy's back, she found a tear in her own eye. Mr Darcy, so handsome, so fit, and once...so alive. "I knew your brother only briefly, but it seems impossible that he should be so ill now. Did the earl take him back to the country?"

"No," Miss Darcy replied, through bitter, choking sobs. "Anywhere else would be better than where he is, at Younge's. It puts him in *her* power." Abruptly she clamped her mouth shut.

What were those wild accusations Miss Darcy had first charged, believing Lizzy was there for a threat of some sort? *'I have nothing left! I can give you nothing! You may tell George that she has taken it all, and then some!'*

This is a great mystery indeed, Lizzy thought.

But as Miss Darcy's sobs faded into bleak despair, it seemed somehow less so. She had no idea who George was, but obviously, someone in Miss Darcy's household, a female, was extorting her, and using her brother to do it. And she apparently felt unable to go to her powerful aunt and uncle with the matter.

"Leaping from this cliff solves nothing," Lizzy said at last. "And it will ruin any opportunity you have in the future to help Mr Darcy. You will not always be as powerless as you feel today."

"My brother suffers *because* of me," she insisted. "It is all my fault. Every awful thing that happens to him is my responsibility. Nothing you can say will change it."

How the girl could possibly be responsible for Mr Darcy's physical ailments was beyond comprehension, but plainly she believed it to be so. "Please explain," Lizzy said softly, "how ripping your brother's heart from his chest—a result which your death would surely cause—would improve his situation."

"You speak as though he would ever know. I tell you, his mind is gone."

"You have seen him? You know this for certain? I have some experience with illness, and I have seen fevers and blows to the head cause temporary incapacity. I saw Mr Darcy less than a month ago; these must be *very* recent developments. It is much too soon to give up hope."

"There is *nothing* I can do to improve *anything!*" she cried.

"Perhaps not," Lizzy said. "But you can certainly make it worse. And you have hit upon the one way to do it."

Miss Darcy again buried her face in her hands. "He would be better off without me."

"I doubt he thinks so," Lizzy replied. "I am certain you are the person he loves best in all the world. But if you reject him and—and *end* yourself, he will hurt—much more deeply than you can understand, and every day for the rest of his life. He would much rather have you alive and flawed, even a veritable thorn in his flesh."

"How can you know?" Miss Darcy asked, as if she despaired of hoping and yet, was desperate to believe.

"Because I, too, have sisters I love."

They sat there together for some time, the angry wind whipping up their skirts with chilling force, the occasional spatter of rain dampening their shoulders, the endless rhythm of crashing surf beating at the base of the cliffs far below.

At last Miss Darcy gave a shuddering sigh. "I did not come here to jump," she said at last. "I just wanted…it all to stop. To be finished."

"Listen to me, dear," Lizzy said earnestly. "You must have felt dreadfully alone to consider such an action. But nothing is ever as hopeless as it seems. I walk hereabouts every morning, and if you were to join me, surely we could come to more productive conclusions as we talk together. Things have a way of working out." She took the girl's cold hand in hers. "Promise me you will meet me again tomorrow, Miss Darcy."

Lizzy practically held her breath waiting for the answer. It came as a slow nod.

"I...yes. It is very kind of you, Miss, um, Bennet, did you say?"

"Not so kind. I have been wishing to make a friend, and here you are. We can help each other—with loneliness, if nothing else. Please call me Elizabeth, or Lizzy, as do all my friends."

"I am Georgiana. My brother called—*calls* me Georgie," she answered shyly.

"Then come now, Georgie. Let us take ourselves in out of the cold, and hope for better weather tomorrow." She stood, pulling the younger girl up with her. "There is a very pretty walk to the beach, and the wind is not so strong down there." She kept her conversation light as they made their way back.

At the gate, Georgiana turned to her. "They will not let me see him, not even for a moment. Do you really believe I have any cause for hope?" she asked. "Could they possibly *all* be wrong about my brother's condition?"

Lizzy took her hands. "I have no way of knowing for sure, but when old Mr Goulding had an apoplexy, he proved *his* doctors wrong. They thought he would never walk again, but he manages with a cane. We must never discount the human spirit. Your brother is a strong man. You must be strong for him."

Georgiana nodded, slipping inside, bolting the gate behind her. Lizzy watched as she trudged slowly up the path, head bowed. It was only when she was out of sight that Lizzy felt her own trembling, so hard that she had to lean against the gatepost to steady herself.

What just happened?

It seemed too fantastic, too terrible. Mr Darcy, his mind ruined? Could it be so? There was so much else the girl had said, and so much she had not. Who was stealing from her? Why could she not confide in any of her family? Why would they not allow her to visit Mr Darcy? What and where was the place that held him—Younge's?

She barely remembered the return walk to the Morris home, her mind was so full of questions. And yet, to whom could she turn to assist her? To assist the Darcys? There was no one.

⬥

Harriet and her friends were to walk to the shops that afternoon; Lizzy joined them, paying particular attention to signs she had all but ignored previously. She had often passed residences of physicians and surgeons, their tastefully lettered signs announcing their various specialties—*Mr Eustace Perry, Surgery, Wounds, Fractures, Luxations, Tumours, and Ulcers*; *Dr James Oliver, Physician, Seller of Famous Nostrums*; and even *Mr Horace Grenville, Bowed Legs Corrected*—but most in this town advertised their medical sea cures. She had not realised just how many there were, and she avidly read each one, unable to keep from searching for the name 'Younge'.

However, it turned out to be rather obvious. Diana and Martha stopped at a flower seller just beyond Gilbert Lawn to select a posy. While waiting for them to make their selections, Lizzy glanced across the narrow street at a row of four-storey terraced houses with elegant ironwork balustrades. She had passed them half a dozen times since arriving in Ramsgate, never before noticing the neatly inscribed placard on the closest building: *Younge's Home for the Convalescence of Invalids*.

It was innocuous in appearance, perfectly respectable, without a flutter of a drapery to indicate its occupants. She had most likely found it. What to do now? Was there anything *to* do?

She had no excuse to even knock on the door, much less to be admitted to its inner sanctums. So intently was she watching the place, however, that she failed to note when the other girls had paid for their purchases and were already headed for the next shop.

"Eliza," Harriet snapped impatiently when she realised Lizzy had not moved. "Quit standing about alone in that stupid manner, and come along with us before you are mistaken for a flower seller yourself."

And that quickly, Lizzy had an idea.

4

FORMING SUCH A PLAN

It was five days before an opportunity to act upon her design presented itself, and Lizzy would likely have talked herself out of the notion as useless, had not Georgiana's situation been so dire. Each early morning, she walked with the younger girl, who was beset by worry and troubles. That morning, she had showed Lizzy a letter she had received the day before from the countess. It was full of exhortations regarding Georgiana's duty to *marry* her cousin and co-guardian, Colonel Fitzwilliam, and to do so before her brother's possible demise meant a delay for mourning. It was the most tactless, insensitive missive Lizzy had ever read.

"I would not answer her at all," Lizzy replied, handing it back. "How far her son might approve of her interference in his affairs, I cannot tell, but she certainly had no right to say any of it to you in his absence. Did he ever speak to you of marriage? He has not written?"

"No, never, and I have not heard from him," Georgiana admitted, plainly in some state of shock. "I wrote him in care of Darcy House, as is usual whenever he's gone to London. But I have no idea whether she—I mean, whether my letters are posted."

Another reference to the mysterious 'she' intervening again—but Lizzy knew by now that pressing Georgiana would yield nothing except tears. The girl was no good at deceit yet obviously was too fearful to reveal any more.

So even though it was perhaps a silly plan, with little chance of useful result, neither did it hold much risk. The scheme was simple enough: purchase a few flowers, present herself at Younge's servant's entrance, and say Lady Matlock had ordered her to bring them to Mr Darcy. If she wore her oldest dress and roughened her accents, she could perhaps pass for a flower seller or maid. At worst, they would refuse to let her bring them to him herself, even if she tried to insist—but why should the house servants care whether she did? It was but one more chore, and they were doubtless busy enough.

All she wished for was a brief visit to judge the strength of his illness for herself, or perhaps even see some sign of improvement that had not been conveyed to Georgiana. If successful, she might try it again in the future. If he was as ill as Georgiana had feared, Lizzy would whisper to him of his sister's love and prayers on his behalf and know that in this, at least, the poor girl had been told the sad truth.

The likeliest outcome was the waste of the coin on the flowers, and although the money was dear, at least she could hope that they might cheer him a bit; she refused to count the cost.

Harriet and Mrs Morris were away visiting an elderly relation, an outing for which Lizzy's presence was discouraged; it gave her the freedom to carry out her private errand. She felt deeply conspicuous when she slipped out of the house alone, without a maid to accompany her. It was one thing to walk out alone at first light, when there was hardly a soul about to notice. But it was a bright, clear day, and the park and walkways were alive with people. Luckily, she saw no one she recognised. Besides, amongst the brightly coloured gowns and feathered millinery, her drab brown wool and linen cap gave her a like appearance of most of the servants scattered amongst the crowds.

After obtaining a cheerful bouquet, Lizzy walked purposefully to the rear entrance of Younge's and knocked, rehearsing in her mind what she would say, hoping to sound both dutiful and determined.

"I have a—" she began, but the harassed-looking woman at the door interrupted her.

"Are ye the help from Mrs Finch? Yer late!"

"I was told to bring these flowers for Mr Darcy," Lizzy said firmly, hoping to carry her point. "I know nothing of any other assignment."

"Flowers! Next the doctor will be wantin' a crown fer his head. Pfft!" The woman glared at Lizzy. "Too many folks in this town, what with troops overrunnin' the place, takin' all the best help. 'Tis a mystery to me why we pay Finch three pounds a year for nothin'. Ye can take those flowers upstairs to him and stay put for a bit. His coun-*tess* be comin' to visit him and with almost no notice, today of all days, when Mrs Tipple be gone to her sister's. *Flowers*." She shook her head in disgust. "I usually do fer him when the fancy folk come, but I have to be at the door. Keep yer mouth shut. Straighten his bedclothes. Fill his water glass. Sit still, an' look sharp. The doctor's given him somethin' so he won't have no fits. Go on upstairs, then. Two flights up, last door on the right. When it's over and done, come down and ask fer Smith. I'll get yer pay." She opened a door leading to a set of stairs, making a shooing motion towards Lizzy.

Well, that was unexpected, Lizzy thought as she walked through the quiet corridor, looking about her as she made her way to the door as directed. For a private retreat at the seaside, it seemed absurdly opposed to fresh air—all the windows were covered in heavy velvet draperies, cloaking the place in shadows. The whole was a hushed atmosphere, heavy rather than peaceful. The doors were tall, substantial, and most of them were open, revealing neat, empty chambers. She saw no other servants, heard no sounds of people talking or going about their business. It was almost as if she were alone in the place. Finally, she reached the last door on the right and paused before it.

She had been given an almost incredible opportunity to see Mr Darcy—but for the first time, she considered that *he* would also be seeing *her*. Of course, she was breaking every rule of propriety, and the very idea of a young, genteel lady entering a gentleman's bedroom, for *any* reason, even a sickroom, was beyond the pale. But he was a patient, a sufferer, not a man—not really. And instead of the disgust and dread a lady ought to feel at such a situation, there came upon her the same emotions she felt the time she had unexpectedly been on hand at the birth of a tenant's son. Inquisitive, yes, and a bit afraid—but also an intense desire to help, to ease.

Could she help? Probably not. But could she try? *Always, always.* She opened the door.

Darcy clamped his mouth shut at the creak of door hinges. The room was kept so dim that he could tell nothing about the arrival except that it was a female and, judging by the mobcap, a servant. She was likely there to tend to the fire or empty the chamber pot. But then she did a strange thing—strange, at least, to his previous experience with the servants here, a silent bunch who barely glanced his way unless compelled. She walked directly to the windows and pulled back the heavy draperies, allowing sunlight to flood into the room. He had to close his eyes to slits to cope with the force of it.

"There! That is much better. When one is feeling poorly, I believe sunshine to be of great benefit."

Her voice was strangely familiar, a pretty, almost lilting sound imbued with good cheer—and the complete opposite of any he had ever heard in this place.

She worked for a few moments at the window latch, but it evidently would not open. "That is too bad," she murmured. "The fresh sea breezes are very restorative, I find." Then she turned to face him.

It was *her*. The face from his most private dreams and memories, the ones he quickly banished whenever they occurred to him. Even with the ugly cap covering her magnificent hair, she was lovely. Although not precisely beautiful, she possessed that certain something, in her air and manner, in her expression, in her uncommon green eyes—some arresting allure. Her long, slender fingers clutched a bouquet of yellow flowers tied with a ribbon, a glorious splash of colour against the dull brown of her gown.

He *must* be dreaming. The doctor's potions did that to him—one could hardly tell what was real. He must not have spit out enough into the gruel during his pretence of eating. His captivity and the medicines had made him foolish. She could *not* be here, staring at him in astonishment, her eyes fixed upon the manacles lashing him to the bed. It was impossible.

But then she spoke with such vast understatement, he had to smile.

"Mr Darcy. Oh, Mr Darcy. This *is* a pickle."

⬥

Lizzy could not quite fathom what to do. She had been prepared for the sight of him, sick, perhaps unconscious, even in some state of maddened insensibility. She had not been prepared for him to look at her with that same penetrating dark gaze, acute intelligence and questioning arrogance in equal measure. She had not been prepared for the sight of his strong throat, the vee of dark hair exposed at his broad chest. She had not been prepared for the sight of him cuffed to the bed, as if he were a dog.

Then he smiled at her, a smile that lightened his countenance, a smile that clutched at her heart.

"Miss Elizabeth, it is all in vain. My sentiments cannot be repressed. You must allow me to tell you how ardently I admire and love you."

She shoved the memory of his mockery from her mind. His face was paler than the white of his nightshirt, and he had lost weight since she'd last seen him. There were deep shadows under his eyes, and his cheekbones were sharply cut into the aristocratic planes of his face. She suddenly realized that she was staring rudely; she must explain her presence.

"I am sorry, Mr Darcy, for your current predicament. I have been talking to Georgie, you see, who is so deeply worried for you, and we—well, *I* determined that if I could talk my way in to see you, perhaps she might be reassured. I did not think I would be so successful, but when I brought the flowers, Smith—she seems to be running the place at the moment—thought I was a maid and ordered me to sit with you whilst the countess visits. I assume your visitor to be Lady Matlock." She realised she was blathering and felt her cheeks redden—something she hated and had striven to conquer ever since John Lucas had told her she looked 'red all over' when she blushed. She took a deep breath, trying to compose herself.

He opened his mouth—to speak, she thought—when suddenly there came voices from the corridor beyond the door she had left open. She thrust the flowers into his water glass—placed out of his reach, she noticed, even if he'd had the use of his hands—and hurried to stand before a little stool placed in the corner near his bedside just as two persons entered.

One of them was Smith, who glanced at the open drapes and gave Lizzy a quick glare before curtseying to the other woman. "Please ring or send the girl if you need anything at all, milady," she said in a low-voiced humility, sounding nothing like her earlier tone. "I shall close these curtains."

But the woman only gestured for her to go. "Leave them," she demanded imperiously, and Smith skittered from the room.

Lizzy curtseyed and opened her mouth to greet her, but the woman did not even seem to notice her, walking directly towards Mr Darcy. *She believes you are a servant, silly girl,* she chided herself, clamping her lips shut and folding herself onto the low stool, doing her best to disappear.

The necessity of keeping her head meekly bowed impaired her view of the countess, but she could peer through the lace edge of her cap and see the lady's profile. She was dressed in the latest style, a long-sleeved, high-necked gown of white French cambric, sporting an antique ruff collar of thin white muslin and a long scarf of light-blue silk tossed artlessly over her shoulders. A white chip hat decorated with white feathers edged in a matching blue perched atop the grey ringlets piled high upon her head. The effect was expensive elegance, designed perfectly for one who was habitually seen and admired.

"Well, Fitzwilliam," she began, her voice the authoritative tones of those who were unaccustomed to contradiction. "I have been investigating brides for you."

Lizzy could not help it, swivelling her head towards Mr Darcy in surprise; she could not see his face, however. Nonetheless, his manacled hands fisted. He said not a word.

"It was a short list of possibilities because you have all but retreated from society in recent months."

Why would she be directing his choice of brides? And she is wrong about his sociability. He attended nearly every event we held. Perhaps he had not been overly convivial, but he was no hermit! Why does he not object?

"Had your insanity burst into fruition a year ago, my choices would be so much the more plentiful."

Insanity? He appears as sane as she is. How can she speak of weddings while he is ill, manacled to a bed? This is in every way ludicrous! Perhaps he would voice opposition now, but though she waited, it did not come.

The woman warmed to her topic. "I considered Miranda Barkley. No living parents—her uncle is her guardian, you might remember —he certainly paraded her before you at every musicale and ball-room last year. Only a baronet's daughter, but she is a biddable girl with no more will than these wall-papers. Easily influenced and ample fortune." She sighed, shaking her perfectly coiffed head in disappointment. "Sadly, she is recently betrothed to Shelby's second eldest."

Mr Darcy answered nothing.

"Did you know that Lord Whitcomb has died? Which of course leaves the very *amiable* Lady Whitcomb available. But I have learnt that Lord Eastham has apparently already satisfied the lady's penchant for virility—they are currently involved in an *affaire d'amour* that has all the *ton* tittering. Truthfully, it is best she is out of the running. While I could manipulate her easily enough into wedlock, it would not be prudent to tie you to such a harlot. One would never be sure whether any heir she provided was truly a Darcy. Any wife *I* furnish will understand the import of providing heirs who *are* heirs. Society might consider you an eccentric and an eremite, but they will *never* think you a cuckold."

Lizzy was blatantly staring at the pair now—not that the countess looked her way once during this fantastic speech. Mr Darcy's hands remained fisted, his knuckles white. Then, finally, Lizzy saw it—Mr Darcy's protest. His head began shaking, a negative motion. The countess took no notice.

"My third candidate is a young woman of delicious dowry, whose brother administers her portion. Again, no living parents, which is to the good. She is also the only one of the three who has managed to garner so much as a dance with you, so I can assume you find her pleasing enough. She is older, which is preferred—at one-and-twenty, she must be feeling the pangs of desperation. A bit headstrong, a great beauty—neither quality is ideal. Still, she would not be foolish enough to offend those of greater consequence. Her father, unfortunately, was in trade, but her brother was raised as a gentleman. It is, actually, a bit of a surprise she was not snatched up quickly on the marriage mart. Of course, had you wanted her, you could have taken her—but *your* wishes are no longer of any import."

She took a deep breath. Lizzy noticed she had not once met Mr Darcy's eyes.

"The earl has threatened to go to the authorities, even the Lord High Chancellor himself, if necessary, to have you declared *non compos mentis*, with Matlock as your guardian, of course. I suppose, were it not for his pride, he might already have begun the process. He has at last agreed with me that honour demands an attempt, at least, to salvage your line. Our hope is that if some small part of your mind has not been breached, you might recognise your duty when I bring you your bride. We are not monsters; we mean to do the thing correctly. We will raise your children, of course, as based upon Mr Younge's observations, you must be permanently incarcerated, for your own safety as well as others'. The earl thinks the dowager house at Pemberley can be converted into a secure private residence for you. Mr Younge has agreed to move with you, when alterations have been completed."

Mr Darcy shook his head in a much more exaggerated manner, a firm 'no'.

The countess looked at him, *really* looked at him, Lizzy thought, for the first time, and her brow furrowed. "I must say, your eyes hold an expression of some intelligence. The doctor warned us, however, that while his medications do occasionally produce the appearance of lucidity, beneath the surface, only an animal resides." Sighing, she shook her head, and whirled on Lizzy, startling her with the sudden acknowledgement. "Girl!"

Lizzy stood, keeping her head low, biting her lip to keep words of protest at bay.

"You are to see that he receives the best of care. I shall go down now and repeat the same to Mr Younge. If anything is lacking, I shall hear about it! Only the best, do you understand?"

Since she did not wait for an answer before turning away, Lizzy gave none. The countess sighed heavily and resumed dictating to Mr Darcy. "It is settled then. I shall begin making arrangements for your marriage. It might take time, for discretion is of the utmost import, and I shall have to approach the situation delicately. Still, I have no doubt of my eventual success."

Again, Mr Darcy shook his head, more firmly now. How could she refuse to see it?

But though the countess still faced him, she did not appear to notice. "Miss Caroline Bingley will be the next Mrs Darcy by Michaelmas. Mark my words."

Mr Darcy frantically began shaking his head in the negative, but he may as well have not even been present. Turning on her heel, the countess quit the room.

5

IN HOPES OF A LETTER

Lizzy felt nearly speechless with dismay. Everything in the lives of *both* Mr and Miss Darcy was terribly wrong. She moved around to where the countess had been standing, and she could see Mr Darcy's face. It was a study in despair.

But as soon as he realised she watched him, his expression smoothed into the implacable Mr Darcy she had once known. He seemed utterly *himself* other than his lack of speech. And he had never had all that much to say.

"Mr Darcy," she began tentatively, "I apologise for my intrusion into your private affairs. I only hoped to—" She broke off, wondering why someone as herself, who had not even the support of her family, could have possibly thought she could be of any help.

She stepped a little closer, determined to reassure him of her respect for his privacy. "Well, it does not matter. I promise, of course, that I shall say nothing of—"

Without warning, his manacled hand grasped her wrist. She had not even realised that he *could* touch her. A small noise escaped her lips, somewhere between a gasp and a shriek. She tugged her arm, but he had a grip like iron and the strength of a madman.

Suddenly, everything she had been told of his insanity screamed through her brain. Her breathing accelerated, even as she jerked harder against the hand clamped fiercely around her wrist. *Stupid girl!*

She panted out her protest. "Oh please, sir...please, release me... oh please, please..."

It grieved Darcy to have frightened her; indeed, he could not bear to, and thus was prepared to humiliate himself completely.

"*Bugger a bit,*" he said, then turned red with embarrassment. He had tried to say, "Miss Elizabeth."

But she abruptly ceased begging him to release her. He looked away from her, and though he did not release her hand, he loosened his grip so she could easily pull away. Amazingly, she did not. He closed his eyes and painstakingly enunciated each word, very slowly and carefully.

"No...*frigging*...fear."

It was not perfect, but after a moment, when she did not move, he dared look at her again. She was breathtakingly lovely to him. What a fool he had been, when he'd had his speech, his health, and his freedom, not to have used it to court her properly. He took in her puzzled, pretty face, regret swamping him. But there was no time for it now.

"*Nugging house slattern,*" he said, then cringed.

"Is this why they say you are...senseless? Because you have...troubles...with your speech?" she asked quietly, pronouncing her words precisely.

Hesitantly, he nodded, mortified but determined to meet her gaze.

"But you can understand everything I am saying?"

He nodded again, listening carefully as she spoke, appreciating her careful enunciation.

"Although of course unusual...it is not an unsolvable problem. If *I* could, in a matter of moments, begin to understand you, anyone could. If I had writing materials, you could simply write out your requests."

Darcy sighed, shaking his head. He had no idea if he could write a sentence, but it did not matter. The greater problem was that the earl was uninterested in seeing him healed and restored to his former place. And his aunt's incredible revelations today showed the plans his relations had formed. Marry him off to a wife the earl would presumably control and thus control the Darcy fortune, while still producing heirs and keeping up appearances—a small nod to honour, and probably the most he could expect. He must not allow it. But first things first.

"*What the devil*...no..." He clenched his teeth, straining for control. "Wh-wh..."

"I will guess your words. Nod once if I am correct. Did you mean to say 'what'...? 'When'...? 'Where'...?"

He finally nodded firmly.

"Where? You do not know where you are? You are at Younge's, 'a private establishment for the convalescence of invalids' according to the sign on the door." She smiled at him, seeming pleased with herself for understanding, as she believed. He felt even more the idiot.

He shook his head in the negative.

"Oh, but you are. I can assure you—"

He squeezed her hand to recall her attention. "Wh-where house?" He closed his eyes in frustration, for that had been incorrect. At least he had not sworn at her.

"Where is the hospital? Why, in Ramsgate. Did they not even tell you in which town you reside?"

He shrugged. There were more important issues. "*Son of a b—*" He stopped himself—that, in itself, an improvement. "Son. No."

"Not son. Father, mother, brother, sister?"

He nodded at the last, wholly impressed with her quick comprehension.

"Sister, then? Georgie? Yes, I have met her; we have even become friends."

He nodded in surprise, wondering how it could be true but grateful that it must be, grateful his sister must not be in Wickham's control. The relief of it was intense. Now, if Georgiana could simply send his man over, Pennywithers would help him depart, would take him to Pemberley, would see things put right. "S-s-s…"

"Sea Cliff?"

No. He shook his head.

"See? Send? Seek?"

He nodded, then shook his head in the negative.

"Oh, I spoke too quickly. Go back. Send? She should send someone? But that is the trouble, you see. She, apparently, is not allowed any say at all. She has written to your cousin, Colonel Fitzwilliam, but something strange is happening at Sea Cliff. Her maid and your man have been let go and not replaced, she says. She will not explain other particulars, but she does not believe her letters are posted. Someone there is interfering in…in some way." She looked perplexed, troubled. "It is why I determined to try to see you for myself. She is…she is very distressed."

Younge. Mrs Younge was, apparently, still very much involved in his sister's care. Lady Matlock had hired her in fact, and thus would trust her implicitly. Obviously, the Younges had seen a new means of taking his money, and even though Elizabeth had mentioned nothing of Wickham, he might yet be a threat in the future.

"I know you cannot wish to marry Miss Bingley, or anyone, really, under such circumstances. I see Georgie daily. We walk out early in the morning together—"

She broke off suddenly, her head swivelling towards the corridor, where the countess had left the door ajar, and suddenly, he could no longer see her, his hand empty—she had held it within hers for the entire conversation.

Abruptly, the door swung open; it took him a moment to remember to close his eyes to slits, but the servant did not look at him—few ever did. She marched abruptly to the window and pulled the drapes shut. And though it made it easier for him to inconspicuously observe the scene before him, he longed for the return of sunlight.

"I told ye to come see me once the countess be gone!" the servant, Smith, scolded, her tone suspicious. "Ye din't have no business here once she left!"

"Sorry, ma'am," Miss Elizabeth said in a docile voice, very unlike her usual tone. "I wasn't sure but if she were gone for good and was afraid to leave for fear she weren't. I figured to give it another few minutes for good measure."

This appeared to mollify the woman, but her dissatisfaction was plain. "Hmph. I heard ye talkin' to the patient. They is not to be assaulted by the coarse expressions of the uncivilised. He don't understand ye anyway. We do not allow them curtains opened. Exposure to raw sunlight be damaging to our patients' nerves."

It was all Darcy could do not to snort. The woman was obviously parroting such foolishness as that reprobate, Younge, babbled.

"Yes, ma'am," Miss Elizabeth replied meekly, instead of giving her a deserved scolding.

"The doctor don't like strangers about, 'specially on this floor. Get ye gone before he sees ye up here. Though how he expected me to do what's needed by meself is anyone's guess." She thrust a coin at Elizabeth.

"Thanks to you, ma'am." Miss Elizabeth took it.

The other woman turned towards the door, and Elizabeth followed, glancing back at him once with a look he could barely see, much less interpret.

Wait! he wanted to call. *Come back! Stay!* But of course, he could not say it. Could not stop her. Could do nothing at all, as she left him lying alone in darkness. He still felt the imprint of her hand in his and fisted it shut, as if he could keep the sensation of it from disappearing with her.

<hr />

Lizzy walked slowly back to the East Cliff, deeply troubled. Mr Darcy's situation was both better and worse than she had feared. He was plainly as sane as herself. She could not know what had become of his speech, but old Mr Goulding's speech had been affected by his apoplexy. He did not spout curses, of course, but he had difficulties with it, which had improved somewhat over the following months. Any physician worth his salt ought to be aware of the possibility after an attack of the brain. The earl and countess ought to have sought another opinion rather than accept one diagnosis and begin searching for brides. Why had Lady Matlock refused to try to *actually* communicate with him? And why, if she thought him mad, would she advocate a marriage to Miss Bingley? And would Miss Bingley agree?

But after a few moments of reflection, Lizzy sorrowfully concluded that Caroline Bingley just might. She was not a woman with depth of character. If the earl and his countess offered wealth enough, if she felt their sponsorship would offer prestige enough, if they locked him out of her sight and allowed her to rule...Pemberley— yes, that was the name of his estate, about which she had once spoken of so enviously—she would likely be tempted. And even if Mr Darcy recovered so completely that he was able to escape the earl's clutches, why, he would still be married to her. Marriages did not simply dissolve because one did not wish them to remain intact. It was in every way terrible.

"Should I write to Jane and beg her to involve Mr Bingley?" she asked. With Jane married, this, at least, was an avenue open to her. She knew, of course, that her father would not pay the postage to receive any letter of hers, and none of her sisters were good correspondents—which was just as well, she had told herself; she needed no help in annoying her hostess with postal costs and had little to repay any. Besides, could Mr Bingley stand against an earl? It seemed unlikely. Further, the Darcys needed help immediately, but she had no idea where in Scarborough to write, although she did know the name of the house in Brighton—*The Breakers*, she remembered. But when would they arrive there? Jane had not known how long they would remain in Scarborough. And would Jane even agree to speak to Mr Bingley about it?

There *must* be something else that could be done...but what?

◆◆◆

"We must get your brother out of that hospital!" Lizzy was walking along the beach with Georgiana, shivering a little in the early-morning air. "Mr Darcy is as sane as I am. I happened to be there while Lady Matlock visited—at least I assume it was she. She took me for a servant and barely noticed me. For that matter, she barely noticed your brother. She just talked *at* him, informing him she was forcing a marriage upon him—and to Miss Bingley of all people."

Georgiana had been enormously relieved and grateful to learn that her brother's mind was intact, but again and again, they returned to the subject of his future. A sharp breeze whipped a cold current of air around them, causing their damp skirts to flatten against their limbs and Lizzy's hair—forever escaping its cap—to momentarily blind her. Impatiently, she brushed it away.

"But you must have more sympathetic relations who could, perhaps, challenge Lady Matlock's care of him?"

Georgiana frowned. "She only answers to the earl, and they act together in this, I am sure. My Darcy relations would *never* defy Lord Matlock."

"Still no word from the colonel?"

"I do not know that the colonel could stop his father, regardless. His elder brother, the viscount, will be no use at all."

"Who *would* the earl listen to? There must be someone!"

Georgiana shook her head. "No one, really. My aunt, Lady Catherine de Bourgh, the earl's elder sister, might annoy him into some sort of delay. Perhaps. But one can never predict what she might do."

Lady Catherine de Bourgh! Mr Collins's adored patroness! "Is she the sort of person who would approve of a forced marriage to Miss Bingley?"

Georgiana laughed, albeit bitterly. "No. She has always wanted him for her own daughter. But I do not believe Anne—her daughter—would wed him without his consent. I do not believe Anne wishes to wed anyone at all."

"Then you must write your aunt, and at once, to inform her of the situation. Tell her that a-a nurse from the hospital told you he is of sound mind and that she must halt any suggestion of a wedding while he heals."

"I doubt any letter I wrote would reach her."

"Write the letter with her direction, and I will have it posted. We *must* try."

"*She* will be curious as to who I am writing. *She* snoops constantly, hovering over me, and if she did not sleep so late and run the house so slackly, I would never even be able to meet you."

It was the most Georgiana had ever said of this mysterious 'she'; such was her distress, that she did not appear to realise what she had spoken. Some near relation installed in the household as a companion, perhaps?

"It is fortunate that she does such a poor job of it," Lizzy replied, not commenting on her suspicions of the woman's identity. "Write two letters, one of the same sort as you have already written to Colonel Fitzwilliam. Let her read it. Allow her to believe you hopeless and helpless and she in control. I have heard of Lady Catherine—my cousin is her vicar, as it happens. He thinks quite well of her. Bring me the letter to Lady Catherine tomorrow morning."

Georgiana looked dubious. "You must understand, Elizabeth—I have never known Lady Catherine to do aught but make situations worse. At least, any situation of import. She is not helpful in any ways that matter."

"Can you think of anyone else? Anyone at all?"

The younger girl's expression fell, and a tear rolled down her cheek. "No. There is no one."

"Then we must try it and see. Georgiana, in all our fears and worries for Mr Darcy, let us remember: the worst did *not* happen. He yet lives, his mind is intact, and he is very much still the brother you have always loved. You must not forget or give up hope. Will you promise me that much?"

Slowly, Georgiana nodded. And Lizzy wondered whether Lady Catherine could possibly be as useful as Mr Collins had always claimed or as incapable as Georgiana feared.

6

HOWEVER UNCERTAIN OF GIVING HAPPINESS

As if the situation was not trying enough, Lizzy gained new difficulties when Harriet acquired a beau. Colonel Biddleston was the younger brother of a baronet—though he was not young. His age bothered Harriet not at all—she had set out to make a respectable match, and the indulgent colonel fit her ideal well enough. Her dowry was ample. She was pretty, and Mrs Morris was shrewd enough to ensure the integrity of any nuptials. It should not have made any difference to anything, but the change in Harriet was immediate.

She had never been overly friendly, and Lizzy understood; Lizzy had not fulfilled the liveliness nor the fun Harriet had expected to have with Lydia. But suddenly, she actively pushed Lizzy away from attending *anything*, encouraging her to stay home and 'care for her health'. The mystery of her new coolness was solved by Martha, who called on her whilst Harriet attended a seaside picnic arranged by a Ramsgate society matron, an event wherein Lizzy's presence was, once again, not welcomed. Martha was in angry spirits because she had not been invited, either, and was in the mood to criticise.

"Harriet says you are too eccentric, but I do not think that at all," Martha explained bluntly, and as if Lizzy had asked for her opinion on Harriet's newly frost-filled manner. "She is jealous."

"Surely you jest," Lizzy vehemently disagreed.

"Oh, not of your looks, of course. It is rather that you are...too interesting."

"That makes little sense." Lizzy shook her head at the other girl's spite. "I am hardly noticed." *I make sure of it.*

"At large parties, yes, you sit with the matrons," Martha agreed. "But in smaller groups, talk can turn to nearly any topic but never one you are unable to converse upon. Old men such as Biddleston like that sort of thing. I watched his attentiveness to your conversation and his smiles at your cleverness, and *I* saw it soon enough. Harriet is well off, pretty, and laughs easily, but at her heart, she is simply dull and stupid. She truly cannot be anywhere beside you without the obvious truth of it shining into her colonel's face."

"Unbelievable!" Lizzy protested, and she tried very hard, thereafter, to be as dull as a moth beside Harriet's butterfly...but all to no effect. Harriet's hints regarding the conclusion of Lizzy's visit increased, even though Lydia's original invitation had been to stay until the summer's end. Lizzy wrote to Mrs Hurst at Netherfield, including a sealed letter for Jane and asking that it be forwarded to Mrs Bingley immediately, boldly begging for a place with them as soon as Jane would allow it.

Although she watched daily, she received no reply.

Lizzy made the early-morning walk to the secluded spot just off the cliff path where she daily met with Georgiana. She could tell by the dejected stance of the girl that Lady Catherine had not, as yet, replied.

"Perhaps there was a delay in receiving your letter," Lizzy suggested.

"Or as is more likely, perhaps she thought it only the foolish imaginations of a foolish girl and paid no attention to it whatsoever."

"Have you had any luck in delivering a note to your brother?" Lizzy asked, trying to distract her from this line of reasoning.

"No," she said more glumly still. "Or rather, I do not believe it. I begged Mrs Younge to give him my letters. She said she would see to it, but there is a smirk in her expression that tells me she only humours me, as one would a stupid child. And why should she think anything else? I have been nothing but her tool."

Mrs Younge! Lizzy thought. It was the first time Georgiana had ever called the mystery woman by name—the very same name as the doctor who held her brother. At last, Georgiana had let down her guard.

"Is Mrs Younge a relation?"

She tried to ask the question casually, but Georgiana immediately paled.

"I should not have mentioned her!" she cried.

"Georgie, dear, you must know you can confide in me. Please say you trust me that far, at least."

Georgiana looked away, and for some time, they walked in silence; Lizzy thought she would say nothing more. But then she said, "Mrs Younge is no relation. She is my hired companion. It is her dead husband's brother who holds Fitzwilliam in his 'hospital'."

Too much power, Lizzy reasoned. All this Mrs Younge need do was threaten Mr Darcy's care in order to get her own way. Several moments passed. "What if you wrote to Lady Matlock? I would happily post it for you. Tell her that Mrs Younge is incompetent and coarse. Tell her that she has threatened to speak of your brother's illness to all of society if you reveal her shortcomings to your family. I cannot believe the countess would stand idly by, and perhaps a new companion would be more sympathetic and helpful. She could hardly be less."

Georgiana bit her lip. "Or perhaps she would confront Mrs Younge, who could tell her the most awful things about me. And...and, Elizabeth, they would be true. I have done wrong, very wrong. I do not know what my family might do if they learnt of it, but it could not help my brother's case. They might even hurry me to the altar without my consent, if not to Colonel Fitzwilliam, to someone else of the earl's choosing. The earl has no incentive to see my brother healed or me happily married. None at all."

Lizzy, of course, had no idea what wrongdoing of Georgiana's could have been so heinous, but that Mrs Younge would exploit it seemed clear. She had always seen the girl's sorrow, her anxiety, her despair, but she had failed to fully comprehend her fear, not until just this moment.

That the earl would push a marriage upon this child was reprehensible, but the situation was beginning to make a kind of sense. She had understood the Darcys to be wealthy, but now she understood just *who* would control those riches if Mr Darcy remained unwell. She must assume that the earl would be a dominant influence in that control, perhaps through the wife he planned to force upon Darcy, and the husband he planned to foist on Georgiana. Undoubtedly, she was her brother's heir; she was neither daring nor confident and would likely always be easily manipulated by her uncle.

No wonder there seems no real attempt at communication or treatment for him! The Darcys were at the mercy of too many unscrupulous people who only cared for themselves.

At breakfast later that morning, however, Lizzy's own troubles increased beyond simply concern for the Darcys.

"It is too, too bad you missed last night's party," Harriet said in dulcet tones.

Lizzy only nodded at the disingenuous remark.

"My engagement was announced," Harriet said, preening. "The colonel and I will be married in a month, and he plans to bring me to his brother's estate, Broadhaven, to introduce me to the baronet. The colonel says it takes thirty servants to run the place, not including the gardeners!"

"My warmest congratulations," Lizzy said, genuinely happy for Harriet. Living with her inattentive aunt could never have been ideal, as she well knew.

Harriet smiled condescendingly. "I suppose you shall be wishing to return to Longbourn soon? I can make arrangements for you. Why, I would send my own maid with you, and you may return her on the post."

Lizzy's belly clenched; here it was, practically an order to leave. "Yes. I will let you know shortly," she promised, then wondered aloud about the baronet's estate, giving Harriet more opportunity to boast—anything to change the subject.

Where could I go? The question beat in her brain as she tried not to panic.

She had her guinea still, and she could survive for a time on it— but what then? If she were to simply appear on the Bingleys' doorstep whilst Jane and Bingley travelled, Miss Bingley might refuse to take her in, besides announcing to the countryside her situation at Longbourn. Would her father allow their rift to be exposed? She feared he very well might, with excuses casting her in no good light.

Between her worries for the Darcys and those of her own, she did not sleep well that night.

Lizzy hurried to her usual early morning meeting, wondering whether Georgiana would even come. A light rain fell from the early-August sky, which was, in and of itself, no great deterrent, but the wind was blowing madly, making the out of doors unpleasant. It was probably foolish to hope so, to rely upon poor, burdened Georgie as her one friend within all the problems of her life.

But there she was, huddled beneath an umbrella that did little to keep the wind-blown damp away.

"Will your wet clothing be noticed?" Lizzy asked worriedly. "Will Younge realise you have been out?"

A gust of wind nearly yanked the umbrella from her grip. "No one notices much of anything any longer. Everyone at the Lodge is in her pocket, but it is a slovenly bunch who only keep up appearances enough to fool Lady Matlock, should she arrive unexpectedly."

Mrs Younge had truly succeeded in isolating both Darcys to the greatest extent possible. "Do you receive pin money? Perhaps you could simply leave if we can find a place for you to go. My visit here will soon end too. I cannot help but believe my new brother Bingley would help you, were he to learn of Mr Darcy's troubles."

"It has not been paid, not on the last quarter day, as was usual. Or else...perhaps it was, and she found a way to take it. If the colonel were here, I could ask him, but..." She shrugged helplessly. "I am sorry to hear you will be leaving. Very sorry indeed. You will go to...Longbourn, is it?"

Lizzy's cheeks were already red from the wind and cold, hiding her mortification. But there was really no reason to hide her situation from Georgiana. "Not there, unfortunately. Longbourn is entailed upon my father's cousin—and he proposed marriage. I refused him. My parents are very...displeased with me, to say the least. A lucky chance gave me the opportunity to come here with Harriet and away from parental wrath. But I am not welcomed home, not at present."

She spoke lightly, but the younger girl immediately apologised. "Oh, Elizabeth...I am so sorry. You have listened to all my troubles again and again, while I have never reciprocated."

"All will be well," Lizzy said, refusing to put more of her own burdens on the girl's shoulders. "I am eager to see Jane again, once she and Bingley are home from their wedding trip. But for now, I have found a new friend in you and feel fortunate to offer you my friendship in return."

"Your friend Harriet is fortunate as well. I would invite you to stay with me, if only I could."

And if only Harriet felt as Georgiana! But Lizzy would not say so; her pride dictated that she admit nothing more. "You are too kind. I would come to you, if it were possible."

For long moments, they said nothing, letting the wind tear at their skirts. Still, despite the miserable weather, it was a companionable silence.

At last Georgiana sighed. "Why does life have to be so difficult, Lizzy?"

Lizzy smiled ruefully. "I do not know. I try to dwell more on all the things that *might* have gone wrong but did not. After all, your brother could be much sicker than he is. A lucky opportunity brought me here instead of to some unknown relation. You and I became friends. It could be worse."

"If you had not come, I shudder to think...I felt so very alone. So hopeless. So...worthless. Nothing has really changed, I know, and yet...what if you had not been up here that morning three weeks ago, Lizzy? What then?"

Lizzy looked down at the pounding surf of the water below; the gusting wind churned it into a chaotic brew, the jutting rocks of the steep cliffside harsh and unforgiving arms clawing downwards to doom's bosom. She took Georgiana's hand and squeezed.

7

ON THE SUBJECT OF HASTY DEPARTURES

Darcy awakened from a light doze to the sound of raised voices. It was enough to startle him, for the place was kept as hushed as a cathedral. How long had it been since Lady Matlock's last visit? A week? Two? Or had he dreamt the whole thing? He could not always avoid the doctor's medicines, not without revealing his determination to escape. His only hope was that they would grow careless and leave him unbound and unattended, thinking him docile, resigned to his fate. Perhaps these noises signified the arrival of Lady Matlock, come with Caroline Bingley and a vicar. His soul was equal parts revulsion and despair.

To his surprise, it was another aunt entirely who stalked into his chamber as if she owned it, followed by the housekeeper and the loathsome Mr Younge.

"It is critical that the patient remain undisturbed," the fellow was bleating. "Any shock to his system, any at all—even foods improperly prepared—could be responsible for the disappearance of the last remaining vestiges of his sanity."

"Darcy. These individuals are under the misapprehension that *I* am subject to my brother's edicts. You shall come home with me, now. Rosings Park is a far superior place for recovery." But though she had addressed him, she did not once glance his way. She only snapped her fingers, and four burly footmen came into his range of vision. One of them wielded a knife, and the doctor and house-keeper leapt back. But ignoring them, the fellow dove beneath the bed; Darcy felt a tug, and one of his leather restraints gave, then the next. The three other footmen hurried forward, and Darcy saw that they carried a litter.

He could walk. Of course he could, but before he could release any words from his cobbled tongue, one of them clutched his ankles and the knife-wielding one took hold of his shoulders. As one, they slung him onto the litter supported by the other two. Then, each grasped a corner and marched for the door as if they had choreo-graphed the manoeuvre.

"My lady, wait. I beg you!" the doctor called, sounding as if he were about to cry.

Darcy could only imagine how displeased the earl would be when he discovered the man had lost his patient and to whom. He felt no sympathy.

Neither was he himself to have any say whatsoever. The litter was carted down the stairs and out the front door, where a large black travelling coach was blocking traffic on the street. The door was thrown open; a little man who looked vaguely familiar poked out his head.

"In here, in here, and hurry up about it," he ordered the footmen.

Two of the footmen grabbed Darcy again, ankles and shoulders; he might have struggled, but by gads, he was in his nightshirt! If he were to run, the entire village would chase after him, likely only to return him to Younge's power. The footmen practically tossed him into the rear-facing coach seat, which had been made up into a kind of cot. One of them climbed in, folding himself onto the floor at Darcy's feet. The little man knocked on the coach roof as another slammed the door shut. Seconds later, they were off.

It appeared as though the man expected some type of resistance from beyond—he continually peered out the curtained window, tapping his foot agitatedly. For several minutes, Darcy waited for someone to say something. The carriage was well-sprung, and lying on his side was a great pleasure, however, so the wait was not unpleasant, even though the cot was far too short for his long limbs. He was not nearly so uncomfortable as the footman crouched near his feet.

Darcy stared, brow furrowed, until the little man's identity came to him—Anne's physician. Davis? Donaldson? No. *Donavan.* Anne had difficulties with her digestive humours, very often feeling ill after eating. She had commented rather sardonically that she did not complain of Donavan's treatments, for his potions did not taste so awful as some and were unlikely to be poisonous. It was hardly a glowing recommendation in a physician.

Finally, after some time, the man's posture eased, and he left off peering out the window, appearing satisfied that there would be no pursuit. If Darcy had expected some sort of acknowledgement from him, however, he was to be disappointed. Donavan withdrew a book and began perusing its pages. Occasionally, he glanced towards the footman, ensuring he hadn't moved. But Darcy may as well have been a bag of bricks on the seat opposite him, for all the attention he was paid.

This illness or affliction had humbled him exceedingly. He had lost, in a few short moments, all of his...rights of self. One might think the physician, with a professional concern, might glance at his patient—even once.

How I wish I could be certain my tongue would obey my brain's commands! He would give the good doctor a setting down he would not soon forget.

But at least there seemed reason to hope. Plainly, someone had communicated with Lady Catherine regarding his circumstances. It *had* to have been Fitzwilliam, for he could not think of anyone else who would, and yet, why? The colonel was just as capable of hiring a doctor and burly footmen and a coach. He might have acted through her in an attempt to avoid his father's censure, but frankly, Darcy himself could barely believe in Lady Catherine's rescue. It seemed unlikely that Fitzwilliam would conceive this plan and then leave it to their aunt, of all people, to execute.

Could *Georgiana* have written to her? Certainly, their Darcy relations were the unlikeliest prospects for her to rely upon for defiance if she wished to present any. Truthfully, he could hardly imagine *anyone* behaving as boldly as Lady Catherine had done today, excepting the colonel. Georgiana had always been terrified of her, so it seemed improbable, and yet...it *was* possible.

The idea that Elizabeth might, somehow, have intervened crossed his mind, but he had already decided that his brain was not to be trusted. It had been a dream. She had *never* come to visit him, *never* appeared at his bedside. It was all in his tangled brain, nothing but a beautiful delusion.

Still, his prospects *must* have, and all of a sudden, changed for the better. They could hardly get worse. Could they?

Lizzy awakened on the morning of her twentieth birthday feeling low of spirits. Not that her birthday was ever celebrated at home, but at least she had not lived with a constant dread of homelessness. It was now necessary to avoid direct conversation with Harriet for as long as possible to delay any discussion of departure. After returning from her early-morning rendezvous, she ate breakfast and returned to her room before Harriet could join her, wondering what she ought to do. Pulling her trunk from the small adjacent dressing room, she began the careful process of folding and rolling, packing all but a few necessities, feeling as though she must be prepared for any eventuality. But she did not have so many possessions that the task took more than a couple of hours. A book passed another, but restlessness soon set in.

Harriet had intended to shop with Martha today, and she had probably left the house by now. But as Lizzy had no maidservant—and was uncertain of her status in the household—she was loath to compel Mrs Morris's servants to accompany her on a walk. She took enough of a risk, she knew, going out alone in the early morning hours. She might, however, walk down the seldom-used clifftop path from the eastern edge of the crescent—still in sight of the Morris row house but in the out of doors, away from the park, with its public paths and public notice. Matching thought to action, she slipped out of the quiet home through the tradesman's entrance.

The wind whipped at her skirts, but at least it had ceased raining. While this neighbourhood traded upon dramatic scenes of the ocean's majesty, her current view took in Sea Cliff Lodge, a mild English country idyll placed improbably within a wild and reckless setting. *Which window is Georgiana's?* she wondered.

Her contemplations were abruptly curtailed by the sudden appearance of a travelling coach-and-four with outriders turning up the long drive approaching the Lodge. When the enormous, lumbering black-lacquered coach—complete with cherubs and gilded Greek gods glistening upon its roofline—passed through the gate, she lost sight of it.

Could this be Georgiana's aunt, answering her letter with a personal visit? Will she take Georgiana with her when she departs? Unexpectedly, her eyes filled with tears, blinding her to any views.

Quickly returning to Mrs Morris's home, she went back to her chamber until she could get herself under better regulation. Georgiana *should* go with her aunt, if that was an option. She needed to be safe within the loving arms of family, family who truly cared, and away from her awful companion and obnoxious Lady Matlock. Perhaps her aunt was here to take charge of *both* Darcys.

And that is good, she reminded herself. Not only would their best interests be looked after, but it relieved her of at least one worry, amongst so many others. It was selfish to grieve at their exodus from her life. She tried opening her book again, but the stupid tears kept blurring the page. A tap at her door startled her from her bleak thoughts. What now?

"Come in," she called.

It was Doris, the upstairs maid. "Excuse me, miss, but you've a message. The lad is waiting a reply."

Puzzled—and a bit alarmed—Lizzy took the note from the maid's outstretched hand and broke the seal.

Dear Elizabeth,

My aunt, Lady Catherine, has arrived and means to take me with her to her estate in Kent—Rosings Park. She says she has already removed my brother from Younge's! Her own doctor will treat him, she says. Oh, Lizzy, I told her an untruth! I told her that I had already invited you to stay with me, and that you would arrive any hour. But she knows you, she said—or knows of you, or at least the Bennets of Longbourn. She says if you arrive soon, you may come with us to Rosings. I hope you will forgive my presumption; I saw my opportunity and took it, and I am hoping you might still wish to come. I also told Lady Catherine that my companion, Mrs Younge, is the sister to the doctor who has been treating my brother, which she did not like at all. She called for Mrs Younge and explained she does not hold with girls my age setting up their own establishments and that I will have no use for a companion at Rosings, for she is more than enough chaperonage, and Mrs Younge may remain here until the earl says otherwise. Of course, Mrs Younge is beside herself, but she dares nothing except casting me warning glares. Oh, please, come if you are able. The stable boy will await your answer.

Georgiana Darcy

"Tell him the answer is yes!" Lizzy replied earnestly. "In fact, perhaps he will help me manage my trunk."

"You's leaving, miss?" Doris asked as Lizzy hastily shoved the last of her belongings into the nearly full trunk.

"Yes," Lizzy said. "I am sorry Mrs Morris and Miss Thorpe are out." She took up pen and ink, hastily scribbling a note of farewell and appreciation for their hospitality and kindness. "I hope you will give them my message of thanks and apologies for my haste— but my arrangements have suddenly come through. Miss Thorpe understood it was expected at any moment." She all but shoved her note at the maid, not feeling the least bit guilty for her rapid departure. Harriet could not care less where next she would go or with whom; she had only wanted her gone.

"Will you help me carry my trunk downstairs?" Lizzy asked, mostly to prevent further questions, shrugging on her warmest pelisse. A few minutes later, Lizzy was following a thankfully strong young man and her trunk down the hill towards Sea Cliff Lodge.

8

Upon Themselves Alone

Lady Catherine was a woman of almost overpowering presence, wearing a carriage dress of *gros de Naples* in a greenish colour not found in nature; the maid who sat beside her nearly disappeared in comparison. There was no such thing as a conversation, only interrogation, and it was a very good thing, Lizzy supposed, that she was accustomed to swallowing her own pride, because the great lady had no difficulty in expressing the most impertinent of opinions.

"You are a relation of Mr Collins," she pronounced upon meeting Lizzy for the first time practically at the carriage door—a different carriage than the ornate one her ladyship had arrived in. Lizzy recognised it from Hertfordshire; it was Mr Darcy's brougham, she was certain.

"Yes, my lady," Lizzy replied, once installed beside Georgiana in the seat facing opposite Lady Catherine. "My family recently had the privilege of hosting him at Longbourn." She prayed Collins had not revealed *every* detail of his recent stay.

"Your father's estate is entailed upon him, as I recall. I see no occasion for entailing estates from the female line. It was not thought necessary in Sir Lewis de Bourgh's family. How many sisters do you have? Collins took a wife elsewhere, although there are a great many of you, I believe."

"There are five of us, ma'am."

"One of you ought to have been clever enough to snatch him up. A pity."

Georgiana visibly cringed and plainly sought to change the subject. "It was certainly a happy surprise to see you in Ramsgate, my lady."

"You ought not to have been surprised. You wrote that I was needed. You should have known I would come."

"Oh-oh, of course, Aunt. It is only that Lady Matlock was so certain that Fitzwilliam—"

"*I* am almost the nearest relation your brother has in the world, *not* my brother's wife," she interrupted. "*I* am entitled to take charge of all his dearest concerns. I came here with the determined resolution of carrying my purpose. Nor would I be dissuaded from it by the earl's sorry excuse for a physician—I have not been used to submitting to *any* person's whims, least of all Mr Younge's. *Such* an unsatisfactory person!"

Lady Catherine kept up a running commentary on multiple topics: the many talents her daughter possessed—or would have possessed had her health permitted—as well as the successes of her manifold interventions in the lives of her neighbours, all intermingled with officious, meddlesome questions regarding Lizzy's upbringing, parents, relations, and marital prospects. Georgiana's tentative attempts to turn the conversation—and to discover any details about her brother's journey—were either ignored or given unsatisfactory replies.

They kept a good pace, but as they pulled into an inn at dusk, Lady Catherine announced that they would stop for the night.

"We will be on our way early, so do not dawdle. I mean to reach our destination speedily."

The inn was a fine one, and Lady Catherine was given all the attention she required. Even better, Lizzy and Georgiana were given a room to themselves, and for the first time that day, they were able to speak unhindered by Lady Catherine's formidable presence.

"I am so sorry!" Georgiana apologised the moment they were alone. "I wished so desperately you could come, but of course, you could not have known beforehand how awful she is. I knew I would have to leave with her—there is never any use in arguing, and besides, she has my brother."

"I was very happy to accept your invitation," Lizzy replied, "however unconventional its delivery."

Georgiana, in her distress, hardly seemed to hear. "I apologise for her intrusive questions. I daresay it was why she allowed me to have you—she is dreadfully interfering and curious, besides liking another excuse to leave Mrs Younge behind."

"It is amazing that she could even care to hear such inconsequential stuff. Her vicar is the man who asked for my hand, received my refusal, and prompted my parents' anger. Thankfully, he must not have revealed to her of his botched proposal."

"No! Truly?" Georgiana cried, surprised.

"Truly. But you must tell me—what of Mrs Younge? Does she mean to follow you, do you think?"

"Oh, I hope not, but she was very sly. She does not dare question my aunt's orders and demands, only saying things like 'Of course Miss Darcy knows how to behave herself' whilst giving me that hard look of hers. I understood her threat—'say nothing or else'."

"Hmm. It would take a bold person indeed to present oneself, uninvited, at your aunt's estate. Of course, I suppose we can expect that she and the doctor will both be sending expresses to Lord and Lady Matlock. But thankfully, it will be Lady Catherine who must deal with them henceforth. She certainly seems fearsome enough to go up against anyone in the realm, even the king."

"Yes," Georgiana agreed. But she appeared troubled, even so. "My aunt is not usually so helpful. Or rather, she imagines she is, but instead is awfully meddlesome. She cares most about the inconsequential doings of her neighbours whilst refusing to let my brother enact changes that are much needed at Rosings. He is usually so very frustrated with her."

But Lizzy could not worry about the modernisation of estate practises. Mr Darcy was free of the Younges, and she was free of Harriet's whims. As she settled into the comfortable inn bed for the night, she could only think that this had been, in all, the nicest birthday she had ever had.

<hr>

'Early', Lizzy learnt, had a different meaning to Lady Catherine than her own definition. It was after the ten o'clock hour before she appeared in their private dining parlour and nearly eleven before they were on the road once more. Daylight was fading long before they finally reached the outskirts of London. Wheeled conveyances of every type clogged the roads, and people of every description drove, pushed, or walked beside them.

The noise is incredible! she thought. She was not quite certain how one accustomed themselves to it all: vendors hawking wares, drivers shouting and cursing, pedestrians calling, dogs barking— the endless din of a million bodies in such close proximity. Finally, however, they turned onto quieter streets—and the quieter the street, the more impressive the homes upon it.

Georgiana, who had mostly ceased trying to make conversation with her difficult aunt, continually peered out the window and finally ventured to ask her plans. "Excuse me, ma'am...but do we stop at Darcy House tonight?"

"Of course. Tonight, tomorrow, and thereafter. I will, naturally, oversee Darcy's recuperation from London."

"Oh, of course. It is only...I thought I heard...did not you say we would go to Rosings?"

Lady Catherine hesitated for a moment. "I have spent the last week in diligent consult with one of the greatest medical minds in the civilised world—my own, personal physician—on behalf of Darcy's recovery. It was his express wish that I bring your brother here. Should I, near the very moment of accomplishing true and curative treatment, be prevented by the earl, who has merely hired your *companion's* relation, an insignificant medic of no importance in the world and wholly unallied to the family? Do I owe any explanations of my conduct to the earl after such neglect, never mind to that toad, Younge?"

"No, ma'am," Georgiana humbly replied. "Thank you, ma'am."

Lady Catherine tilted her head in satisfaction. When she spoke again, she seemed almost to be speaking to herself. "Let them follow my carriage to Rosings. Let them enjoy the red herrings I have in store for them, trails leading to nowhere but further delay."

Astonished, Elizabeth blurted, "But will they not learn of the opening of Darcy House? Someone is bound to speak of it."

Lady Catherine gave her a quelling look. "Foolish girl! Naturally, I have asked Mrs Taylor to keep the household to the barest number of servants and, of those, the most circumspect. I am confident she will act in the family's best interests, keeping our presence confidential. I need not remind you, I am sure, that your own discretion will be required. Letters must not be posted from town. Weekly, I will have one of my people collect any you feel the need to write as well my own. The letters will be posted from, hmm, other places. I trust you understand?"

She spoke in such a forceful, compelling manner, compliance was a foregone conclusion. And if there *was* any mystery regarding her acceptance of Lizzy's inclusion in this little party, it was made clear —she was to be Georgie's sole entertainment, just as Georgie was to be Lizzy's. Evidently, Lady Catherine had no doubts as to her ability to exercise control over them both.

"Yes, my lady," Lizzy agreed.

After all, she had nowhere else to go.

—※—

Mrs Taylor, the housekeeper, was apologetic when she learnt that neither had brought a maid. "I don't know if her ladyship will allow me to put another on, but I will ask."

"Never mind it, Mrs Taylor," Georgiana had replied. "My aunt did not want us to bring any servants, so I doubt she will allow it now. If you have someone to help us dress, we will contrive to make do."

The rooms given Lizzy were grand ones and directly across from Georgiana's in the family wing. Anxious not to be a bother to Mrs Taylor, she unpacked her own trunk before tapping on Georgiana's door; she was immediately admitted.

"Have you discovered whether your brother is in residence?" Lizzy asked as soon as the door shut behind her. She saw that, like herself, Georgiana was unpacking her own belongings—haphazard stacks of undergarments, dresses, and shawls lay in untidy heaps upon the bed. Perfunctorily, Lizzy began organising the piles.

"It was the oddest thing, Lizzy. I asked Mrs Taylor as soon as we were alone, but she behaved very strange, when she has always been most accommodating. It was almost as though she wished to speak but abruptly said my aunt required her and hurried from the room without answering."

"Clearly, your aunt has instructed her to say nothing to anyone, and Lady Catherine *is* a most intimidating creature. Probably her lack of an answer *was* her answer. After all, if he is not here, she would have no qualms about saying so."

"I suppose," Georgiana said dubiously.

"Where could they put him if he is here?"

"His rooms are just down the corridor."

Lizzy nodded. "You should definitely check them. It seems unlikely, though, *if* she is trying to hide his presence. Where else?"

Georgiana was thoughtful. "Perhaps the nursery? There are servants' quarters in the attics, but most of the upper servants have rooms belowstairs. The entire second floor should be vacant." She plunked down in a chair beside the unlit hearth. "It is so unfair! He is *my* brother! Am I to have no access to him? I have practically abducted you from Ramsgate only to be locked up in London!" She sniffed, fumbling for her handkerchief.

Lizzy sighed, moving to the chair opposite. "At least one of those burdens you must not shoulder. I told you my friend is to marry soon, and my visit to her would have drawn to a quick end."

"You also told me that you eagerly await a reunion with your sister. Lizzy, I do not know when any letter you write will even reach her! Your parents will not stay angry forever and will wonder at your whereabouts soon."

"It does not signify. Jane is on her wedding trip, and it may be weeks before she returns or receives any letter of mine. I was in no hurry to present myself in Hertfordshire, I assure you."

"I feel terrible. This is not how I envisioned your visit." Georgiana sighed.

Lizzy paused, considering how much to say before deciding upon the whole truth. She sat down on the large bed, folding and refolding a linen handkerchief. "My father is a gentleman, while my mother was the daughter of his Meryton solicitor. He fell in love with her, and they wed quickly, but it was not long before they discovered a great difference in temperament. My mother was… lively. My father called her a flirt."

Georgie's eyes opened wide, and Lizzy's cheeks pinked with mortification. However, she refused to apologise; salacious the story might be, but Lizzy was its innocent victim.

"My eldest sister, Jane, is golden haired and blue eyed, as is Lydia, the youngest—both resemble my mother. Mary and Catherine are dark haired and dark eyed, like my father. As you can see, I am neither."

"Perhaps some distant relation on either side."

"There was an officer, a Colonel Millar, of ginger-coloured hair and green eyes stationed near Meryton not many months after Jane was born, who fell in love with my mother. He wrote her letters full of bad poetry, and Papa found them just after she told him she was with child again. My parents patched up their marriage, after a fashion, I think. Mary is only a year younger than I am. He repudiated neither me nor Mama, but he has never spoken to me either."

"Never?" Georgiana gasped.

"Not even a request to pass the salt at the dinner table. Mama persists in calling him wrongheaded and unfair. She claims her innocence and that she has always been loyal. Most days, I believe her. But of course, he never would. I think Mama mostly hates us both now, though she was better to me when I was younger."

"I am sorry, Lizzy."

"I did not tell you this to gain your pity but so that you would understand about the book."

"The book?"

Lizzy excused herself for a moment, retrieving the tissue-wrapped volume from her chamber, handing it to Georgiana for perusal. "It is a first-edition copy of the first part of *The Pilgrim's Progress*, signed by its owner, Lady Sarah Ashley, in 1678. Lady Sarah was once a lady-in-waiting to Catherine of Braganza, queen to Charles II, and she is my paternal grandmother, several greats past. Mr Bennet is an avid reader, and I wished to be as well. However, I knew I was not welcome in his book-room, and for years, I would only read those volumes which I thought I could appropriate without his notice. As I grew older, though, my choices grew bolder. I even believed that he probably knew of my borrowings, deciding to say nothing about it—a tacit approval, if you will. One day in my sixteenth year, I slipped in to return *The Pilgrim's Progress* to its shelf when I thought him away, only to have him clap his hand upon my shoulder. I nearly jumped out of my skin, I tell you."

Georgiana shivered, but Lizzy remembered something besides fear. It had been a small triumph, for even if he would chastise her, it would be an acknowledgement of sorts.

"Were you punished?" she whispered.

"No," Lizzy said matter-of-factly. "But that night at dinner, the conversation—as most of my mother's conversations tend to be—centred on potential husbands and settlements, for it is the business of her life to see her other daughters wed. Papa looked right at me and said to her, 'As to your second daughter, *The Pilgrim's Progress* is all the dowry she will get from me.' I am uncertain if she even heard him, for she only looked at him absently and continued talking. But just before I departed for Ramsgate, he handed me the book, Lady Sarah's book. I knew what he meant by it."

"But...if he hates you, why give you a Bennet family heirloom? It might be quite valuable."

Lizzy shrugged. "I suppose it was the easiest way to communicate my utter repudiation, without saying a word to me. And probably he despises *The Pilgrim's Progress*."

"I am sorry, Lizzy. You must...he must—"

"I loathe him," Lizzy interrupted passionately. "I hate everything about him. I hate him, and I would wish he were dead—if it would not leave my mother and sisters homeless."

Georgiana's eyes widened, and Lizzy found a smile, if a rather grim one. "And now you know my greatest fault as well as my deepest secret."

"All the more reason I wish you were treated as a proper guest of Darcy House instead of practically held prisoner here," Georgiana replied.

"You are the dearest girl in the world. I can never go home, Georgie. My great hope for the future rests with Jane and Bingley. I thank you for taking me in at all." She made a better attempt at a sincere smile. "We will be prisoners together."

Georgiana reached over the stacks of folded clothing and took Lizzy's cold hand. "Prisoners together," she repeated.

9

THE ENCOURAGEMENT OF LOVE

Georgiana and Lizzy's first ambition the following day was to discover the location of Mr Darcy. Interviewing the housekeeper might be helpful but could only be accomplished by Georgiana, who was shy and not at all accustomed to exerting herself. Lizzy rehearsed with her the questions she ought to ask—all of which could be answered without directly revealing the secrets Lady Catherine had, evidently, sworn Mrs Taylor to keep.

"Did you have any luck?" Lizzy asked when Georgiana finally returned after her morning interview with the housekeeper.

"A bit," Georgiana replied. "She is very reticent, but I asked her directly for the names of those currently employed at Darcy House and then, of the few names I did not recognise, what they do. She could hardly refuse to answer, but Lizzy...on three of them, she hedged. She said they were Lady Catherine's men. I truly think she wished to say more, but she is afraid of my aunt."

"Her fear is understandable, and those men are a definite clue. What were their names?"

"Mr Sharp, Mr Hudson, and a Mr Stimple. She said that Hudson is employed days, and Stimple works at night. The third, Sharp, only works Sundays."

"Hmm. He *must* be here, Georgie, and these men are his attendants. It sounds as though your aunt has him watched day and night, however."

"It grows worse," Georgiana sighed. "Mrs Taylor said that she does not care at all for Mr Stimple and that it is a good thing he works only at night. I believe she meant it as a warning to me."

After more discussion, they decided to see whether Lady Catherine herself might be a source of more information.

"She must always say whatever is within her head, without restraint," Georgiana said.

They made their way to the breakfast parlour, as Georgiana claimed her aunt seldom took a tray and would expect them to dine with her.

Unfortunately, enduring the lady's unrestrained opinions and prying curiosity was the price to be paid for any discoveries, much to Georgiana's constant chagrin.

"Your hair is an unusual colour, Miss Bennet," Lady Catherine announced, after loading her plate with kippers and rejecting six slices of toast before the footman managed to please her. "I wonder at it. I had a horse once of that shade, but it was too ill-tempered. It had to be put down, and I always thought its colouring a sign. Mr Collins was likely wise to avoid it and, hence, any possibility of having children with the defect."

"Mrs Collins has long been a friend to our family and, I agree, a very wise choice for him." Lizzy bristled but bit her tongue against tempting impertinence.

"Pooh," her ladyship replied. "Collins will be an exemplary husband, and it would have solved your family's problem with the ridiculous entail. How stupid of your father not to have had a son. He ought to have seen to it."

She turned her redoubtable attention upon Georgiana. "And you," she said in awful tones, "I received a letter from the earl—sent last week, though I only just had time to read it this morning—stating that you would shortly be wed to Colonel Fitzwilliam. You are not yet out! Anne made her curtsey in her eighteenth year, and I would not have dreamt of her marrying before one and twenty. To marry before you are presented? Utter nonsense. What were you thinking, to *agree* to a marriage arranged by Lord Matlock?"

"I did not! I–I do not wish to marry my cousin," Georgiana stammered, with unfeigned shock at this announcement. "Or–or anyone."

Lady Catherine's manner abruptly reversed itself. "Of course you do not. You *will* not. I will see to it that no one forces you, including Matlock," she declared.

"Th-thank you, Aunt," Georgiana said humbly. Lizzy nodded at her, and she pressed forward with an enquiry. "I wonder…I wonder if Fitzwilliam is still suffering illness?"

Lady Catherine's nostrils flared. "Naturally, your brother is suffering! But only because I have not yet had charge of his care! His doctor was incompetent. I have replaced that rodent, Younge, with the best medical mind in England. Mr Donavan will shortly commence treatment."

Lizzy felt a surge of hope. She completely agreed with Lady Catherine regarding Mr Darcy's former medical care. If a new doctor was able to produce a restorative treatment—although in her opinion, fresh air, wholesome meals, and sunshine might produce results as no pill or potion could—why, Mr Darcy could prevent Georgiana's wedding to the colonel himself. Freed from Younge's prison and with healthful attention, his place and position would surely be quickly restored.

"Your ladyship is most kind," Lizzy said warmly, forgiving her for the 'horse' remark. "We feel as you do—his doctor was *not* helping."

Lady Catherine graced her with an approving nod. "You need no longer be anxious," she said. "I have the situation well in hand."

Lizzy entered Darcy House's back gardens with a lighter heart, willing to excuse any of the older lady's incivility if only to see Mr Darcy restored to health. She and Georgiana had decided earlier to enjoy the out of doors while the weather was fine, and they quickly found a shady bench on which to relish the garden's summer beauty. Such was her own contentment that it took her several moments to note her companion's unhappiness.

"What is the matter, Georgie?"

"Mr Donavan...he is Anne's doctor."

Lizzy considered this. "So...perhaps *not* the 'best physician in the civilised world' or a 'superior medical mind'?"

The other girl snorted. "Hardly. Anne suffers from digestive complaints. The best Fitzwilliam has ever said of him is that his potions are unlikely to cause any further damage."

This was a blow. Lizzy's feelings of relief vanished.

"My aunt prizes adulation above all else. She would value a compliment to her own ideas above any respected physician's opinion on Fitzwilliam's treatment."

"That explains her preference for Mr Collins. Still...I feel that the sort of care your brother requires has more to do with time and rest than any particular potion. Perhaps it is for the best that she does not allow some so-called proficient to experiment upon him."

They both were silent, staring out at the garden's beauties, trying to hold on to hope.

A clock striking somewhere in the dark startled Lizzy from a light doze. Checking the time, she saw it was an hour past midnight. *Perfect.* Quietly, she left her room and entered her friend's.

"Georgie," Lizzy whispered.

The girl did not move. Lizzy shook her shoulder. Georgiana rolled over, mumbling something. Lizzy tried again, but short of pouring water on her, the effort seemed futile. This would not do. Should she return to bed and forget the exercise?

In the end, she determined their plan could not wait. She had already decided that if she were caught, she would simply claim to have heard noises requiring investigation. After all, there were no footmen stationed in the corridors at night. Still, she halted in every shadow to ensure she was yet unobserved, her heart beating in a frantic rhythm; when a loudly creaking step screeched its alarm, she stopped short, throwing the panel on the dark lantern Georgiana had procured for them. When no one popped out to confront her, she crept on but kept the lantern cloaked and felt her way forward until she reached the empty second floor.

At long last, she reached the door that, according to Georgiana's direction, should be the nursery. It might be locked from the inside, especially if it were in use. Still, it would be a clue of occupancy, would it not? An ugly thought tried to deter her; was she truly prepared to deal with the dislikeable Mr Stimple, who might be Mr Darcy's attendant? What if he could not be reasoned with? What if he were to assume she was some sort of 'woman of the town' and tried to assault her?

For a moment, she shivered in fear. But then, she straightened. Why, she would dash the lantern in his face and run screaming, consequences be devilled. On the other hand, nothing ventured, nothing gained. This was her opportunity to discover whether Mr Darcy was here, and she was determined *to* discover it.

Before opening the door, she paused and pressed her ear against it. She could hear a murmur—were they conversing? Did Mr Stimple read aloud? Plucking up her courage, straightening her spine, she put her most imperious expression on her face and tried the latch, prepared to do her best impression of a formidable matron demanding to see the patient.

But the door opened easily, with no attendant on the other side staring at her in surprise and disapproval. She shut it quietly behind her. Dimming coals burned in the fireplace, doing little more than creating shadows. There was no other light beyond her small lantern. She peered into the gloom.

She discerned the outlines of a bedstead. Must Mr Darcy be within it, since they had bothered with a fire? At the furthest end of the room, a door was ajar, from which emerged the sound of raucous snores—Mr Stimple's? She moved closer, holding the lantern aloft so she could see.

Mr Darcy stared back at her, his aspect as formal and grave as she had ever seen him, and Lizzy, suddenly struck by a wave of awkwardness, stared back. The plan had all seemed much more rational and understandable, even *obvious* an effort, when in discussion with his sister. Supposing Georgiana would be accompanying her, she had not conceived what she would say. Still, her presence in his home, in his *room*, must be explained at the very least.

"Mr Darcy," she whispered, hoping not to disturb Stimple's snores. "I apologise for this intrusion on your privacy and my unforgivable boldness. I know my presence here is highly irregular. I assure you, only your sister's extreme anxiety could bring me to this point, although I share her deep concern, and I cannot blame you for thinking...whatever it is you might be thinking..."

She broke off, rolling her eyes at her ridiculous discomposure, looking at him somewhat helplessly, wondering if he understood a word she said. As though *he* might give *her* some clue about how to proceed. *Foolish girl!*

He had lost more weight since her visit to Younge's, she realised, and yet he was handsome as ever, with one lock of hair falling forward into his eyes; she had the urge to smooth it back. In those eyes, she saw traces of the same impatience she'd held when her mother had launched one of *her* rambling effusions. The comparison stiffened her spine and resolve.

She went straight to him, maintaining that eye contact and, unbidden, remembered again his derision, his mocking taunt.

"You must allow me to tell you how ardently I admire and love you."

Instead of shoving his mockery from her mind, as was her habit, she faced it directly—he was not some stranger, nor even simply someone's patient, but a man, a man with flaws of his own and a sister who worried. She would discover what he knew of his coming treatment and Donavan and see what else he might need, how else she might be of use.

Then she saw what, in the darkness and in her embarrassment, she had previously missed. The fabric cuffs around his wrists had been replaced; he was no longer tethered to his bed with a leather cord.

Instead, he was chained.

Darcy saw at once when someone entered, shutting his mouth upon his speech rehearsals with a clack of his teeth. How long had it been since he had been spirited up the stairs of his own house, into the nursery he had never bothered to fill with his own children? A day? Two? He squinted into the darkness. Mrs Taylor? His aunt? Or...could it be Georgiana? His pulse accelerated, torn between desperately wanting to see his sister and desperately wishing she would *never* see him, not like this.

But no, she was not tall enough to be Georgie, and though he could not see her face, it was certainly not Mrs Taylor. Mrs Taylor had never possessed such a pleasing figure as that, *could* not have, even when she was young enough to have had one.

The woman approached with her lantern high, lighting her face.

Elizabeth. Her eyes were wide and dark in the lantern's shadow—though he knew them to be a striking shade of green. For once without her ugly cap, her hair was drawn up in a mass of shining copper curls, her cheekbones high, her mouth wide, her chin sharp and determined. How had she grown lovelier? How had she come to be here? The answer was obvious; she was not. He had dreamt her again, his own, personal delusion. But he willed the dream to slow its speech, to allow her words to penetrate the mists of darkness in his mind.

It is a dream, another impossible dream. I wasted the last one, trying to bring her into my illness, into my sordid world. I shall not make the same mistake again, but only enjoy the illusion until my sad wakening.

Through many hours of practise, he had finally discovered that if he set his words to a rhythm, almost like poetry or a tune, he could usually get through most of them without betraying himself with filth. He had even memorised a statement for his cousin Fitzwilliam—should he ever bother to visit again—hoping his sanity would be recognised in the normal words, though spoken in an unusual cadence. He almost opened his mouth and began reciting a sonnet to the dream girl, one memorised in his youth, a tribute to his adoration:

'All days are nights to see till I see thee

And nights bright days when dreams do show me thee.'

Abruptly, dream-Elizabeth stopped speaking to stare at his chains.

Once, he had prided himself on his control; indeed, his ability to manage both his own affairs and those for whom he was responsible had been a major source of satisfaction.

Now, he could not even make his dreams behave. A proper dream of a beautiful young woman ought to have placed them in a different setting—Pemberley's gardens, mayhap, where a better version of himself might pluck a rose for his beloved whilst reciting the sonnets she inspired. It would not toss the woman he loved into the scene of his own wrecked despair, to watch him chained like a rabid animal. He despised the brain that would mock him with her vision.

He groaned in frustration; surprisingly, this dream-Elizabeth looked at him as no one ever did any longer, with compassion instead of pity or disgust. Setting down her lantern, her soft, cool hands touched the skin above his shackles. Carefully, soothingly, she rubbed at the precise spot where the metal was chafing the skin of his wrists. It felt so true to life, he had to speak, to ask.

"*Bugger it*. N-no. Please."

She stopped the gentle touch, and he tried to tell her that it wasn't what he'd meant, that she must not disappear again, that he needed her, that he yearned for her to be real.

Unfortunately, he lost any sense or rhythm, the words leaving his mouth vulgar in the extreme—having absolutely nothing to do with yearning or sonnets, a twisted parody of the vision in his brain. He looked away from her, at the wall, completely humiliated. His mouth was a mad thing, uncontrollable, useless. He was equal parts anguish and shame. The dream, real or not, was finished before it had even begun.

<hr />

Lizzy was nearly overset by another wave of compassion when he turned his head away from her. This would not do. She was determined that he should hear her and understand. She took his hand up again in hers. That captured his attention, and his head snapped around to her face.

"I already know you have troubles with your speech, if you recall," she began quietly, slower this time. "I wanted you to know. I am staying here, as a guest of Miss Darcy. We were not sure you were in the house, although we suspected, and I wished to confirm it."

His eyes widened; his mouth worked. "Jupiter! No." He closed his eyes and tried again. "Georg-ie."

"Yes. As I told you before, Georgie and I have become friends, and I am known to your aunt through Mr Collins, if you remember. Lady Catherine. She had you brought here." She paused. "Do you know where you are?"

He nodded, opening his eyes.

"She has decided that her own physician shall treat you. A Mr Donavan. Perhaps he shall be better than Mr Younge?"

He shook his head in a vigorous negative. "*Son of a*—No. *Stubble it.* No. Set me…free. No need doc." He pulled up on the chains, rattling them. The snores from the other room abruptly stopped.

"Mr Darcy, you must be quieter," she whispered.

He stilled, and after a moment, the snores resumed.

"Mr Donavan must quickly see that your reasoning is intact. If I had a key, I would of course…but Georgie, too, will press for your release. These chains are ridiculous, and I predict you will be freed immediately, if he has the sense God gave a goose."

He seemed to deflate a little. "Georg-ie…" he began. "Well?"

"Yes. She is trying to learn courage. It is…difficult to challenge Lady Catherine."

He closed his eyes briefly, as if in agreement, relief, or both. "No… see her."

"She meant to come tonight, but I had difficulty waking her, and since I was not even sure we would be able to visit, I left her to sleep. But tomorrow night—"

"No!"

His tone was too loud. "Hush," she urged, dropping his hand. His breathing had grown louder; plainly, he was in some distress. "Surely you wish to see your sister?"

He shook his head, urgently, in the negative. Lifting his chained arm, he stared at it then back at her.

Mr Darcy was a proud man. Plainly, he could not bear the thought of Georgiana seeing him in chains.

"I think I understand," she said. "You have been almost as a father to her. You do not wish her to see you in weakness, for her to feel fear and dismay on your behalf."

He nodded, agreeing.

She smiled ruefully; he was the very opposite of her own parents. "I think you are being very protective. Your wishes must be considered." *I will not promise,* she thought. *Georgiana's wishes must be considered as well.*

His expression grew steely. "*Yeasty yapcocking codpiece,*" he choked. "Mrs...Mrs...Yuh-Yuh..." But the words he wished refused to come.

"Oh, Mrs Younge, yes," Lizzy put in. "She was left behind in Ramsgate, where hopefully she will remain until you can terminate her employment." She gave him a look meant to convey her disapproval of the woman.

He, evidently, shared her opinion, for his tension seemed to ease, and he rested back against his pillow. His throat worked as he again attempted to speak; after a curse or two, he managed it. "You true here?...near?"

It touched her, the look in his eyes, as if he genuinely *wanted* her to stay close, putting aside all pride to show his need. But then her conscience spoke: *He has been shackled to his bed,* she chided herself. *Any ally, even a Boisterous Bennet, must seem a godsend.* Being unforgivably fanciful would only alarm him, and she sought to lighten the mood.

"I know you must prefer someone more tolerable and tempting," she smiled.

But his brow furrowed. His expression grew immediately thunderous. "No!" he shouted.

The snores abruptly stopped. She glanced over at the room where the attendant rested, then at the nursery door. It was more imperative than ever that she not be caught in his room if she was to be of any use to him at all.

"Mr Darcy, please...I must not be found here—" But she stopped her whisper mid-sentence when she saw the expression on his face.

His eyes were so pleading, yet so full of frustration and despair. He was a man, not an animal. The chains were an insult, and she wished to show him that she knew it, felt the same. What would she do if he were *only* Fitzwilliam Darcy, a young and fine-looking man, and she were *only* Lizzy Bennet, who thought him handsome enough to break her heart?

She took his hand once more. There was no sound from the anteroom, not of snores nor of movement. What could she say to him? But his hearing was not affected, and she bent to speak directly in his ear.

"Do you remember the party at Lucas Lodge? Sir William foisted me upon you for a dance, as the gentlemen around you—for some mystifying reason—seemed compelled to do, and in turn you felt obliged to dance with me."

He squeezed her hand so tightly it hurt, turning his dark eyes upon her. In the dimness, she could not read what he felt, only that some strong emotion possessed him. She tried to smile.

"Someday soon, you will dance again...with your *own* choice of partners."

She had hoped to make him smile, but he did not; instead, he drew her hand towards his face, though the manacles binding his wrists allowed him little range of movement. She watched, spellbound, as he raised himself up off the pillow, using his elbows to support himself, sitting up to the fullest extent his chains allowed, stretching his neck taut until, at last, he reached his destination. Gently, he pressed a kiss to her fingertips, his eyes never once leaving her face.

Abruptly, he released her. For a precious second, she remained where she was, startled and uncertain, his intense, searing gaze burning upon her. Another sound from the anteroom forced itself on her attention, and she slid the dark lantern closed. By the light of the fire, she quickly found her way out of the room, her heart pounding as much from his farewell as from her fear of discovery.

10

AN IMPROPER WAY OF THINKING

Unsurprisingly, Lizzy did not sleep well. Mr Darcy was no longer simply a patient to be tended, the brother of a friend, but a man, *himself*, the man she had both hated and wanted. He was imprisoned in this, his own house. Why had they chained him? It was completely unnecessary; any fool could see it.

"I did it," she said to Georgiana the next morning, once they were alone in her sitting room.

Georgiana's eyes widened. "Why did you not wake me? How did he seem? Was Mr Stimple not there? Did no one see you?"

Lizzy smiled wearily. "It would have taken a pitcher of water to wake you."

The girl's expression fell, and Lizzy reached over to pat her knee. "It was fine, dear, and you obviously needed your rest. He seemed very much...Mr Darcy. He still has troubles with his speech. They...they keep him in restraints, which I find excessive and needless. I hope that Mr Donavan releases those at once. His 'attendant' was not attending at all but rather snoring in the adjoining chamber. I did not see anyone at all except your brother. He asked after you and seemed relieved that you are near."

Tears filled Georgiana's eyes, and she hastily swiped at them.

"He does not want you to see him bound," she added. "I believe he wishes you to think of him as he was before, not as he is now."

Georgiana fumbled for her handkerchief. "I will not lie to you. It is not *only* that—he must blame me for his current state. My wilfulness is its cause."

"I fail to see how that can be so. Nevertheless, we must not think of ourselves. I do believe we should give him time to...accommodate his current situation, but I do *not* believe that we should allow him to hide from you for long. You are accustomed to thinking of him as invulnerable to weakness—I know this because I found myself surprised as well. But though he is not, perhaps, quite as you remember, he *is* very strong, very courageous. In his position, I would be screaming and angry. I cannot believe, however, that anyone competent would keep him in restraints. He is, plainly, the furthest thing from mad."

"You are right, of course," she sniffed. "Oh, I do hope Mr Donavan will set him free."

"If Mr Donavan has a brain in his head, your brother will be joining us at breakfast tomorrow."

⊰❊⊱

Lizzy, Georgiana, and Lady Catherine awaited the arrival of Mr Donavan in the yellow parlour after breakfast. Despite not looking forward to spending any length of time with Lady Catherine, Lizzy was grateful that she had not been evicted from the meeting, not wanting to miss an opportunity to see the physician and hopefully hear an encouraging diagnosis.

Making conversation proved completely unnecessary. Her ladyship held forth on her opinions about everything from the placement of the windows to the upholstery on the chairs, questioning Georgiana but seldom awaiting any answer. Which was a good thing, because Georgiana seldom had one.

Lizzy was interrogated upon each of her unmarried sisters: "None of you draw? All of you out? How very strange." Of course, she thought of several impudent answers to her ladyship's insolent questions, but she swallowed them. This woman would think nothing of ousting her from Darcy House, and Georgiana could hardly prevent her.

Finally, after an interminable hour, the doctor was announced. He appeared not at all how Lizzy expected—she had pictured someone with presence and a noble mien. Mr Donavan was a small, rotund man hefting a valise almost half his own size and panting with the effort.

"Welcome, Mr Donavan," Lady Catherine acknowledged at his bow. "My nephew is much in need of your aid. He suffers from apoplexy, mania, as well as malevolent spirits, disordered speech, and violent melancholia. It is intolerable, as I am sure you understand, and your expert opinion is required."

Lizzy was aghast. While her own visits with Mr Darcy had not been greater than an hour in total, he had demonstrated none of these symptoms, excepting the disordered speech. Had he weakened in the last few hours? Had her ladyship even visited him? How could she believe such if she had?

"I have observed what your ladyship describes many times amongst the Quality," the doctor replied. "Such illnesses are caused by an imbalance in the body's humours. His blood is from two noble houses. When mixed, the two fight for dominion. The stronger the blood, the more the patient suffers. He has had the leeches, I understand?"

"Yes," Lady Catherine answered quickly. "Younge claimed they helped with his violent tendencies."

You mean weakened him into submission! Mr Jones loved prescribing leeches for every complaint, yet Lizzy had never noticed them bring about any significant improvement—and in the case of Jane's most recent fever, believed them to have produced a deleterious effect.

"Despite the improvement in his behaviour, his other symptoms remained," Lady Catherine declared.

"I ought to have been called in to the case sooner," the physician pontificated sorrowfully, shaking his head. "Leeches are only the first step and, frankly, are incapable of discharging enough of the ruinous blood. His treatment was incomplete. The black and yellow bile are now in disharmony, and his phlegm will overpower it all if purgation is not employed."

"Purgation," Lizzy repeated, appalled. *He cannot believe that inducing vomiting will help?*

The physician ignored all except Lady Catherine. "After purgation, we will proceed with vesticulation to complete the process of restoring the patient's equilibrium."

"I understand perfectly." Lady Catherine nodded. "The Fitzwilliam blood is of heroic vigour, but the Darcy potency is not insignificant."

Lizzy had read of *vesiculation,* or blistering, in the war medicinal journals from Mr Goulding's library—although it was considered proven ineffective amongst the opinions she had studied. But perhaps he was not mispronouncing an archaic ulcerating procedure, instead referring to something entirely different—his learning was bound to be greater than her own. "V-vesticulation? What is that, please, sir?" she dared to ask.

The doctor turned to her. "It has also been referred to as blistering amongst laymen, but *vesticulation* is the appropriate term."

"You mean vesiculation?" Lizzy asked incredulously. *The man could not even say the term correctly, but felt he ought to thus afflict Mr Darcy?*

"Yes. Vesticulation. That is what I said."

She fought for patience. "I am an avid walker and have experienced my share of blisters. I fail to see how they could possibly be helpful."

"Permit me to say that there must be a wide difference between the understanding amongst the laity and those which regulate the best physicians. I look upon the trained medic as equal in point of wisdom with the highest rank of the kingdom."

Since the highest-ranking man in England, King George III, was widely considered insane, she could not take comfort in his sentiment.

"Unless at once diverted by the most energetic means, his disharmonious humours are predisposed to attack the brain or spinal cord, quickly disorganising their structure. This is the source of his mania and inability to speak."

Donavan's expression grew truculent, as if daring her to continue arguing. Every part of her wished to; she was not uneducated on the subjects of illnesses and care of the body. She'd always felt a connexion to Grandmother Bennet, whose herbals held pride of place in her father's library—and were amongst the first volumes that she had assumed actual risk in 'borrowing'. She had taken many notes from them in her own journals, and while most of her experience had to do with megrims, nervous complaints, and menstrual difficulties, she could brew a tea to ease fevers, prepare an ointment to relieve burns, hold numerous intelligent discussions with Mrs Bailey, the midwife, and had, on one memorable occasion—and unbeknownst to her parents—delivered one of Longbourn's tenant wives of a babe who had arrived before Mrs Bailey could.

Mr Donavan's explanations sounded like...balderdash.

"Lady Catherine," Lizzy said, hoping to appeal to a voice of reason, "perhaps, before such extreme measures are tried, simpler treatments with proven success, such as—"

"Did I ask your opinion?" the lady interrupted stridently. "Am I consulting *you* for *your* expertise? I am shocked and astonished that you would attempt to interfere with your betters—"

"Excuse me, Aunt. I-I feel I should...see to my correspondence," Georgiana interpolated, standing, swaying slightly, her voice nearly a whisper. She was so pale, she appeared almost ghostly in the bright yellow room—and slightly greenish.

Lady Catherine swivelled to look at her. "Young lady, you look peaked. Perhaps the doctor should attend to you too."

"I am certain Miss Darcy is well. We often rest this time of the day, do we not?" Lizzy invented quickly, going at once to her friend.

Lady Catherine quickly lost interest in them both. Georgiana appeared in great danger of swooning; Lizzy grasped her arm as they took their leave of the doctor and Lady Catherine. Those two remained oblivious, beginning a discussion on ferrous humours and overexcited organs. Neither acknowledged the younger ladies' departure.

At the door to her room, Georgiana paused. "I think I will rest now."

Lizzy nodded dumbly as the girl disappeared inside, shutting the door quietly behind her. For long moments, Lizzy just stood there, wondering what to do. Her impulse was to follow Georgiana into her room, but to say *what*? What possible consolation could she offer?

Absolutely none. This all felt like her own fault—had not she insisted Georgiana write to Lady Catherine, bringing the difficult lady into the situation in the first place? She had no comforting ideas, no words of wisdom, and no reassurance. Besides, it was the man upstairs who was apparently to be tortured into good health. Or most likely, simply tortured.

She went so far as to open the door to her room—so pretty and luxurious—and enter. Her feet sank into the thick rug. The bed, with its fine linens and thick mattresses, called to her. Besides, she was exhausted—not simply from lack of sleep, but from feeling powerless and insignificant. Moving to shut the door behind her, however, a sudden thought speared her soul:

"Miss Elizabeth, it is all in vain. My sentiments cannot be repressed. You must allow me to tell you how ardently I admire and love you."

The memory of his words hurt. It had hurt when he'd spoken them, taunting her, as she'd thought then. What man of honour pronounced such declarations from his saddle, after disdaining her for weeks? But last night's kiss...could he possibly have meant any of it?

Oh, if he had! What would she have replied had she believed in his love? What might be different, now, if instead of laughing off the remark in what might have seemed a callous response, she had questioned him as to why he had said it?

But it did not signify. She could not go back in time and change the past. She could do nothing to offer hope or peace or solutions in the present. The only thing she could do for him in the whole world was to keep his beloved sister from bearing her burdens alone.

With a sigh, she turned on her heel and exited her chamber, closing the door gently behind her.

Georgiana lay facedown upon her bed, shoulders shaking with quiet sobs. Lizzy sat beside her, placing her hand gently upon the girl's back, trying to think of something to say.

Georgiana finally turned to face her, her eyes red and swollen. "I have disappointed him in every possible way," she cried. "His illness is my fault. I cannot explain. I simply *cannot*. You must trust me...I am the cause of his illness. Donavan ought to be blistering *me!*"

"You are correct; I do not understand," Lizzy said after contemplating this for some moments. "But—your brother *does* understand. He already knows whatever it is you are unwilling to tell *me*, does he not? And yet, it is obvious he thinks only of your welfare and happiness."

"I do not deserve his love," Georgiana said at last.

"Fortunately for you, you do not *have* to deserve it. It just *is*. A gift you can accept and even grow and nurture. You know my history. By all rights, my sisters should have hated me. Certainly, had they treated me ill, they would never have been punished."

"I doubt you ever gave them cause."

Lizzy laughed. "I certainly did. We were regarded equally by our nurserymaid, but as I grew older, I realised I was not granted the same parental affection. However, I was endlessly hopeful that if I was good enough and well-behaved enough, this might change. It came to a head upon my seventh birthday. We are all close in age, and I had recently witnessed Jane and Catherine's birthdays. While there was not much in the way of celebrations for any of us, they had each received a doll on the great day. I expected one on mine and waited—not very patiently—for my gift. It did not come. Finally, I went to my mother and demanded it. She told me there was nothing, blamed my father for pinching pennies, and sent me back upstairs."

"That was not right," Georgiana said.

"I was very angry at the unfairness," Lizzy agreed. "So I told my sisters that I had been given a fairy princess of my very own as a gift and even arranged a prank or two proving I had such a benefactress! Oh, were they jealous, and you may believe I exulted in my triumph! The nursery was in an uproar." She shook her head in remembered dismay. "But after a day or two of my gloating, Jane, Mary, and even Kitty, who was only three, came to me with gifts— Mary, a new lace handkerchief, Kitty had drawn a picture, and Jane gave her silver thimble—each humbly asking if they could share my fairy with me. I am certain, had they complained to my mother instead, I would have been punished for telling lies. But they did not. They made peace."

"Or else, they *really* wanted part ownership of that fairy," Georgiana said, with unusual asperity, and Lizzy laughed again.

"Perhaps. But as the years have passed, they have shown kindness towards me, especially Jane, who is all that is good. My point is that my sisters love me, I think, and I love them. Regardless of everything wrong in my life, to possess such love is the greatest of gifts. One ought never to take it for granted." She took a deep breath and made a further confession. "I was supposed to be banished to an unknown uncle in London after refusing Mr Collins. Instead, I went with Harriet to Ramsgate. My sisters *could* have ruined the trip at any time by telling my parents the truth of my whereabouts, but they would not see me hurt. It is what family is supposed to do." Lizzy clasped Georgiana's hand. "Your brother is equally loyal to you. You and Mr Darcy have not *received* that loyalty from your aunts and uncle, however. I understand your feelings, truly—you know I do. But *their* disloyalty is not *your* fault."

Georgiana sighed. "What can I do to be loyal to Brother now, Lizzy?"

Lizzy pursed her lips. "Family has failed him. Perhaps his friends might do better? You might write to…to someone her ladyship would not suspect of aiding you. Mrs Hurst, perhaps? You might congratulate her upon her new sister and include a letter to be forwarded to Mr Bingley, supposedly with a message from your brother? Beg his assistance, and I will include my own note. He is a kind man and will hopefully have an idea."

"What if Lady Catherine reads the letters? I would not put it past her."

"Then you shall have to ask Mrs Taylor to post them without her knowledge and hope she is loyal enough to *you* to do it."

"My aunt will contrive to withhold any response. She doubtless reads everything that arrives in the post."

Lizzy grimaced. "Yes, and we must hope Mrs Hurst will forward the letter in the first place. Perhaps Mrs Taylor has an idea for whom the return post might be directed in order to avoid notice. But it is a plan, is it not? If it does not help, it will not hurt."

They spent the rest of the afternoon writing a long letter of delicately couched enquiry and explanation, praying that it would reach Mr Bingley, and that he would care enough to act.

The doctor did not leave until late in the evening; Lizzy knew this because her window was over the mews, and she watched at it, wrapped in a blanket, until the carriage was called. Then she had to wait an additional hour or so for the house to settle and to ensure all were abed before she made her way again to see Mr Darcy. There was no question in her mind that she must.

The clock showed midnight, and she was beyond tired. Georgiana was asleep in Lizzy's bed; she had tried to wait up with Lizzy and failed.

The route upstairs was familiar this time, and avoiding each creaky floorboard and stair was easier. Lizzy quickly found herself at the nursery, listening for Stimple's sonorous snores. When she was satisfied the attendant slept, she quietly entered, this time closing the door separating Stimple's couch and Mr Darcy before setting her candlestick in the holder beside his bed—she had not bothered with the dark lantern. Stimple's snores were an adequate alarm and loud as ever.

The stink in the room was fetid, smelling of bile.

She gasped, to see the change in him. He appeared utterly white against his sheets, restless, mumbling soundlessly. How was it possible he should appear as though he had lost so much weight in twenty-four hours? His cheekbones positively jutted from his skin, the creases on either side of his full mouth now deep slashes.

"Mr Darcy," she whispered, but he did not seem to hear.

"Mr Darcy!" she whispered more urgently, touching his bound hands.

He started, briefly struggling away as if trying to escape. Then his bleary eyes opened, and she saw when recognition returned.

"*Bug-ger,*" he said, and Lizzy knew he'd meant to say her name. He shut his eyes again.

Daringly, she brushed his hair back from his clammy forehead. He did not respond to the touch, so obviously unwell. What could she do? She did not have her stillroom and possessed very few herbs. Precious little, anyway, that would help him.

She glanced around for the expected pitcher of water, frowning when she realised there was none in the room. Had not there been some the night before, futilely out of his reach, perhaps, but present?

Last night, he had been hale, and while his speech had embarrassed him and he had hated the chains, he had yet been the Mr Darcy she had always known, and had seemed somewhat improved over Ramsgate. Tonight, he seemed…frail.

Heavens above, she thought. *What has Donavan done?* The difference between last night and now was so vast that she truly feared he might be dying.

11

SCARCELY ALLOWED TO HOPE

Lizzy stared at the hated chains. Dared she sneak into Stimple's chamber and attempt to steal a key? She peered more closely and noticed something she had not seen before—the chains were longer than they needed to be and looped around the bedstead to shorten them. Carefully, she lifted them, flinching a bit when they clanked—but Stimple's snores continued unabated.

When she finished, it appeared he had enough play in the chain to stand. He did not seem to notice. She carefully chafed his wrists, her belly clenching when he did not move. But after a few moments, he mumbled something so faintly she put her ear closer to his mouth.

"Please, sir, what do you need?" she asked.

He moved his mouth, but nothing emerged. He seemed slightly more wakeful, however. His eyes stayed closed, but he tried harder to speak.

"*Clot-pole*...wa-ter," he mumbled.

"Water? I shall fetch some," she said.

She raced back down the stairs to her bedroom, so dismayed she hardly cared if she was discovered. *Mr Darcy could be dying while the household slept and his attendant snored!* Carrying the water pitcher, she had to slow a bit returning. She had no cup but would have to manage, somehow.

She was holding her breath upon her return—what if he–he...had worsened while she was away?

He lay upon the bed as still as death, but he had taken advantage of the play in the chains and turned onto his side.

Please, please, please, she thought. "Can you take some water, sir?" she whispered.

At the mention of water, his eyes opened to slits. He managed a nod.

He was too weak to sit up; drinking might choke him if she attempted to pour it into his mouth. She must give the barest amount at a time, which would take longer. Still, something was better than nothing. Pouring a small amount into her palm, she brushed his cheek with the other.

"Please open your mouth, Mr Darcy," she said gently.

It took him several seconds, as if he had to force his mouth to obey him, but he did it. She dribbled the water onto his tongue. Some spilled, but most went into his mouth. After a few seconds, he opened his mouth again.

She repeated the process several times. Finally, he nodded. Enough, she supposed. She set the pitcher down then, and not knowing what else to do, sat in the chair near his bed and simply... watched. He appeared to be dozing.

After what seemed several minutes, he opened his eyes. His lips worked. She could tell he was forcing his unruly mouth and mind to coordinate. "Th-thank...you."

"Perfectly said, sir," she replied, so proud of him for trying so hard, and hurting for the noble, impatient man she had known so briefly. Although reduced to begging for a few drops of sloppily adminis-tered water, he was yet the gentleman.

Slowly, the minutes passed until she was half-dozing, but the sound of the chains' rattle startled her awake when he moved, heaving himself upright. She bit her lip.

"Can I get you anything?" she asked.

He looked over at her, as if he had forgotten her presence in the room.

"Georg-ie," he began but couldn't seem to add any other words.

"Your sister is well," she immediately reassured. "She is very concerned for you, of course. She is sleeping now. I—we were not sure...we met Mr Donavan, and his plan...it sounded very...strenuous," she finished weakly.

He gave her a sardonic look.

She knew the answer to the question before she asked it, but she asked it anyway. "Do you think...his treatment will be of any use?"

He shook his head once, a definite negative.

"I was afraid of that. I understood little of what he was saying about the body's humours." She sighed. "But it sounded like nonsense to me."

"*Weedy*...no...wa-ter...help," he muttered.

"Would you like more?" she asked hopefully.

He stared at her a long moment then nodded once.

Since he was sitting upright, she brought the pitcher to him. "I am sorry I do not have a cup." Trying to hold it at the correct angle not to dribble, she brought it to his lips.

With a trembling hand, he steadied it, took a long drink, then another. He drew back. He nodded. Thanked her again, staying seated. Swayed slightly, which made her fear he might tumble right off the bed.

What would she do if he fell out of it? He was too heavy for her to lift, and the unforgiving chains might hurt him. Placing the pitcher back onto the table, impulsively she climbed up beside him and sat, close enough to shore him up. His toes touched the floor, but her legs dangled, and she tucked her slippered feet onto the bed frame to secure herself and provide more support, placing one fisted hand on the mattress, her other in her lap. She had thought to place one arm around him to further support him—except she had been unprepared for the feel of his body next to hers. It was astonishingly different than she had expected.

How long had it been since anyone had hugged her? Years and years, not since she had been a very young child, and never by her father. Was Papa the same as Darcy, with no softness whatsoever covering lean muscle? Somehow, she thought not. In her concern, she had forgotten he was more than a patient, more to her than a suffering soul. He was her...her Mr Darcy, and even in weakness, his presence was almost overpowering. It had been preposterous to consider placing her arm about him.

Mr Darcy, too, must have been surprised by her action, because he froze into stillness for several moments. Then, slowly, gradually, he relaxed against her, leant into her. He was heavy and warm along her right side. The room grew cold, the fire mere embers. Her gown sleeves were little puffs of fabric, with no protection from the chill, and she stared down at the goose-flesh rising on her arm.

Idly, she wondered what it must be like to be forced to remain in one position, flat upon one's back. *I am a restless sleeper...it would be so uncomfortable,* she thought. How would it be to feel weak, sickly, without even the privilege of rolling over in bed? She ought to have been searching for the key and at least urging Georgiana to try demanding one, for all the good it would likely do. But even supposing they found it, what would be the result? How far from his family could he flee, weak and unable to speak properly?

"Are you hungry?" she asked at long last. Not that she had any food to offer him. But stealing into the kitchen was an option.

"N-no," he said.

And that was all. She sat there with him for what felt like hours but probably was much less, trying to stay awake—fixing upon the odd warmth along her side in order to do so. But it was so late, and her sleep had been so interrupted, it was probably inevitable that she dozed. She did not know it, of course. One moment she was staring at the shrinking candle; the next, she startled awake, wondering what roused her.

Her pillow was hard.

That was when she realised she was curled up, on her side, cuddled against Mr Darcy, her head tucked into his shoulder—in a *bed* with Mr Darcy. He, too, was on his side, facing her, his arm thrown over her bare one, warming her. Watching her. There was so much impropriety in the situation that for a moment, she was paralysed.

"Liz-zy," he whispered. And he smiled, or rather, his mouth quirked at one side, his version of a grin.

Time restarted. The snores were still sounding from the next room, and she breathed a sigh of relief, easing in his arms. It was a mistake. There was something about him, something salty, woodsy, and male, that made her wish to press in closer to him and inhale. Giving in to temptation, she placed her arm tentatively over his broad shoulder.

"Liz-zy," he said again, smile disappearing, as if it were a plea and a prayer all at once.

He pressed her in more tightly to him, and she marvelled at it, at his warmth, his strength, his maleness, his power. *He is more of a man than Papa ever was, even diminished and chained.* His eyes were on her lips, and she wished he would kiss her.

Did you mean it? she wanted to ask. *Did you mean to tell me of your love?* "I should get back. It must be close to dawn," she whispered instead.

He nodded solemnly. She could barely see him in the candle's dim glow.

"I do not wish you to be at the mercy of that awful doctor," she said.

He only shrugged.

She wished she could stay with him even here, order the foolish medic away, tell his aunt to jump from the London Bridge. "Would you care for another drink of water before I leave?"

He looked at her for a long moment. His eyes were shadowed in the dim light of the candle, which must be burning low; he had the longest lashes, she noticed. A temptation to touch them whispered imprudently in her mind, and she gave into it, brushing her fingers against the softness. His eyes closed, and the chain jangled softly as he moved his hand gently into her hair, combing one hand through it.

"Carrot-headed chit," she whispered, smiling.

He groaned then stared so intently she thought he would draw her head towards his, kiss her. And she would return it, oh yes, she would. Her first kiss ought to be *his*, no matter the future.

But she had been foolish, for he only shook his head, slowly removing his arm. The chill was immediate. She lifted herself off the bed and brought him the pitcher while he pulled himself again into a sitting position. He was stronger, she noticed, no longer swaying or trembling.

This time he took it from her, holding the thing with both hands and drinking deeply. At first, she could only stare at the sight of him, neck open, exposing that dark hair at his chest, strong biceps outlined by the thin fabric of his nightshirt. But she bit her lower lip as she realised what he did—drinking fluids so he would have something in his belly to retch tomorrow, if the doctor continued purging him. Preparing himself to face more abuse.

She could think of nothing to support Donavan's story of Darcy and Fitzwilliam bloods battling each other for dominance; it sounded ridiculous to her ears. But the science behind treatment of various symptoms was murky; physicians often disagreed with each other on what was best, all of them showing evidence agreeing with their own claims. Her experience was limited to treating minor complaints, such as a burn, or chronic ones, as her father's swollen joints. She did not hold with bleeding, however, which the doctor favoured, and knew the writings of some physicians who agreed with her. She meant to search Mr Darcy's library for articles, tomes or essays, including any information on purgation, but had already set her opinion firmly against such practises with the evidence before her eyes.

After he finished drinking, she set the pitcher nearby. She would not rewrap the chains again so he could lie upon his side for as long as possible. *Let Stimple be blamed for it, if anyone is,* she thought.

One more time, she took her hand in his, feeling a terrible reluctance to leave him.

"I assume Mr Stimple has a key," she whispered. "Perhaps I should try to steal it from him? I ought to have tried sooner. He seems a very sound sleeper."

But he immediately shook his head vigorously in the negative. "No, no, no." He took hold of her hand more tightly. "No, no, no." His throat worked. "*Friggot,* no good. *Prigging*...no. Promise. No Stimple."

So great was his obvious distress at the idea, she immediately promised. How awful of a person was this Mr Stimple that Mr Darcy genuinely feared her trying to cross him?

The moments passed, and still she stayed, wanting his touch for as long as she could have it, even knowing dawn approached, that the few servants still employed would soon be up and about, and her chances of being caught were growing greater with each passing second. She saw the moment he realised it as well.

"Go *to the devil,*" he said then closed his eyes, obviously frustrated. "Go." He deliberately released her hand, clenching his fist as if to keep from seizing hers again.

The only way she could turn to the door was to remind herself that she must not be thrown out of Darcy House now, when only she and his young sister could be depended upon to look after his interests, however clumsily. She knew she must hurry to her own bed before the maid attending to the fires found her missing.

But she could not resist looking back at him. His head was turned towards her, his expression bleak. Words of pity would not help, and those of yearning even less.

"Good-night, Mr Darcy," she said simply. "I will see you tomorrow night."

His half-smile quirked, the bleakness vanishing. Pretending, for her sake, that all was well. She departed quickly, before she burst into tears.

⎯❖⎯

"How does he fare?" Georgiana asked.

Lizzy yawned, having only had a few hours of slumber before Georgiana woke her to ready herself for the day—for Lady Catherine always wished an audience at her meals.

"Let us just say he shall not be joining us at breakfast. Georgiana, we must find the key to his restraints. You must ask Mrs Taylor to procure it!"

The other girl's eyes filled with tears. "I tried to speak with her this morning about posting the letters, and she...she did not refuse to help outright, but she said it would be better to wait, to avoid trouble and maintain discretion. I can only imagine what she would say if I asked her for the keys."

Not for the first time, Lizzy felt impatient with her timidity. The keys to everything in the place belonged, by rights, more to Georgiana than to Mrs Taylor. She should not ask. She should *demand*. But what could she expect from a child who had been cosseted, waited upon, and never taught to assert herself? Georgiana loved her brother, but her natural tendency was to allow herself to be pulled in whichever direction the most dominant person in her life tugged. Lady Catherine still occupied that position, whether Lizzy liked it or not. It was necessary to challenge the real foe, to find a way to pull her towards a different objective.

But doing so directly was not an option. If Lady Catherine discovered that Lizzy was actively working against her plans for her nephew, she would simply toss her out of Darcy House.

"He is your brother, dear, and you are his heir. If you will insist, she must obey. We will practise the asking together. Just pretend you are Lady Catherine, and care for no one's opinion except your own."

Georgiana giggled at this—a first—and they did actually practise. Although she retreated into herself when their voices grew impatient, after a few tries, she haltingly persisted until Lizzy was somewhat satisfied.

Breakfast was a lesson in endurance, as Lady Catherine marvelled at the doctor's reports of rapid improvement.

"Might Miss Darcy visit her brother if he is so improved?" Lizzy questioned in innocent tones.

But her ladyship denounced the idea immediately. "You do not understand, Miss Bennet, the delicacy of the body's function. I am unsurprised, for the earl is likewise uninformed. I will explain. All of Darcy's humours are being carefully guided into a healing centre, where Mr Donavan's next treatments will converge. Once in place, he will destroy the defective membranes, signalling to his mind the necessity of choosing the stronger Fitzwilliam blood in order to conquer his Darcy weaknesses. Any deviation or intrusion could disrupt the battle and steal the victory."

It was all Lizzy could do not to gape. Even allowing for a romantic explanation without technical terminology, it was ridiculous, and the true facts were undisputed—all Donavan had done thus far was force Mr Darcy to vomit. There was only one conclusion to draw: Mr Donavan was a quack, allowed to experiment upon Mr Darcy, and Lady Catherine was his fool.

Lizzy napped the afternoon away, in the hopes of staying awake long into the night. She wakened to the sight of Georgiana reading a book beside the cold hearth, a candle lit against the chamber's gloom.

"Did the light waken you? I ought to have put up a screen. I am so sorry—I did not think."

Sitting up, Lizzy rubbed her eyes. "No, no. You mustn't apologise. I am very well rested now. What time is it, do you know?"

"I heard the clock strike five not long ago," she replied.

It was as well that she had wakened, for dinner was served early. There was another evening of Lady Catherine's blatherings to endure; after the meal, she would likely demand Georgiana play, but she would jabber throughout every piece without bothering to listen to a note. If Mr Donavan joined them, Lizzy would be hard-pressed to remain silent. Leaving her bed, she went to the window and opened the drapes, allowing in the late-afternoon sunlight.

"I spoke with Mrs Taylor about the key," Georgiana said, interrupting her thoughts.

Lizzy turned to her eagerly. "Oh! What did she say?"

"Firstly, she denied any such possibility—that my brother would be chained in his own house, that is. I could not say it was you who saw it, Lizzy, so I said that Lady Catherine admitted it herself." Georgiana looked away for a long moment, plainly gathering her composure. "Mrs Taylor finally confessed that Lady Catherine had informed her of his madness, that he must be confined lest he harm himself, and on no account was she, or any of the servants, to enter the second-floor rooms. My aunt vowed her physician would cure him, and Mrs Taylor clings to that hope."

"Lies!" Lizzy cried. "Your brother is no more insane than you or I am! Lady Catherine is the one who is mad!"

"I told her so, Lizzy! I had to prevaricate a bit, but I told her a nurse from the hospital assured me that he was well, only troubled in his speech and unable to express himself properly. I told her my aunt made unreasonable assumptions based on nothing except her doctor's opinions. I reminded her that Mr Donavan is Anne's doctor, and his experience lies in complaints of the belly."

"Well done! Would she believe you?"

Georgiana's shoulders slumped. "I do not think so. She said she certainly wished I was correct but hinted that in my affection for Fitzwilliam, I could be deluding myself, and in the meantime, I ought to remain hopeful while we await the results of the treatment. She claims that regardless, she does not possess any keys beyond the nursery door. She provides trays that the attendants fetch and carry and has never seen my brother for herself."

It was all Lizzy could do not to groan in frustration. She ought to have expected it, of course. Lady Catherine's whole purpose seemed much more about besting her brother, the earl, and proving *she* was the expert, rather than healing Mr Darcy—to whom she had yet to pay a visit. Her ladyship would maintain control of every detail possible, including terrifying Mrs Taylor into the highest possible discretion. Unfortunately, the housekeeper would likely know she could not rely upon Georgiana to protect her from the great lady's wrath; if she was convinced that Mr Darcy would never be able to shield her either, her loyalty might be seriously diminished.

"Tonight, I will go with you, Lizzy, even if you must dump an entire pitcher of water on my head to waken me. Promise you will."

Lizzy promised, feeling a return of sympathy for her friend. Her life had changed so drastically, and not for the better. Those who *ought* to protect the Darcys—their own family—had utterly failed them. Lady Catherine believed only what she wished to believe and would no more listen to Lizzy—or the king—than a gnat buzzing near her ear. Georgiana faced something more terrible than being tossed from Longbourn with nary a by-your-leave, and she deserved to support the brother she loved in any way she could, even if it was only an embrace.

It is all I can do for him, after all. At least he would see and know his sister loved him still. Then, perhaps, she could keep her own growing feelings for him in check.

12

IN WRETCHED SUSPENSE

But Mr Donavan did not leave.

When the clock chimed three, Lizzy startled awake from a light doze. She had been huddled in the window seat overlooking the mews for hours, waiting and hoping. Had she slept through his departure? She stood then nearly fell, her cramped limbs numb; she had to cling to a chairback until painful feeling returned to her toes. The room was dark, but a light snore from her bed told her Georgiana slumbered soundly.

What to do? Assume she had slept through the doctor's departure and attempt a visit to the second floor? Another option occurred to her, however. Lady Catherine had ordered a footman to await the doctor and call for the carriage when Mr Donavan was ready to leave. Mrs Taylor had assured her that James would not leave his post for the night until the doctor departed. Would he still be in the entry?

After lighting a candle, she cautiously slipped out the door, moving quietly down the corridor until she reached the staircase. She descended about halfway before she had visibility to the entryway below.

And there was the footman, James, hunched in a delicate chair beside the door, legs stretched out in front of him, arms folded, chin to chest as he slept. It was an answer and a dreaded one.

Mr Darcy's only companionship this night would be Stimple and Donavan.

Georgiana managed to discover, from the housekeeper, that Mr Donavan had not departed until after seven that morning. Lizzy, who had slept fitfully, claimed a megrim to avoid sharing the breakfast meal with Lady Catherine. She truly feared that her ire would liberate her tongue, that she would speak aloud her true thoughts—and be summarily ejected from the household.

The day dragged on. It was with dismay that they greeted Mr Donavan's return, just after tea. He did look rather the worse for wear; dark circles ringed his eyes, and he did not seem quite so cocksure as he had on previous occasions. But he nevertheless spoke to Lady Catherine of 'the battle in progress' as if he were nearly victorious.

At dinner, Lizzy bit her tongue, and Georgiana said less, but Lady Catherine seemed to notice nothing of her audience's silence. Instead, she gleefully related her news from Rosings—the earl's minions had arrived to interrogate her, and her people had dutifully sent them on to Birmingham, her supposed location with the Darcys. Her trail of clues from that point, she declared, would take them all over England and go cold somewhere in Wales. That, at least, was news of interest.

Once the subject of the earl's search for them was exhausted, however, she lapsed into repetitive grievances pertaining to people Lizzy had never heard of, and broadsheet gossip moralising on the fall from grace of those she had. By the time the meal was ended, Lizzy's pretend megrim was real.

Afterwards, they withdrew to the music room, where Georgiana played while her ladyship held forth on the excellent guidance she provided for Rosings, Hunsford, and all points in between, which she explained without any intermission till coffee was served.

When they were finally able to retire, the two girls made their way gloomily to Lizzy's room. Finally, Lizzy suggested that they try to sleep. "When my sisters and I wanted to waken in the night, we would drink as much water as we could before falling asleep. Whoever wakened first, wakened the others."

"Why would you want to waken in the night?" Georgiana asked, curious.

How to explain? Lizzy thought. They bore with lives of restraint and sameness, but she had always urged her sisters to seize what fun they could. When a full moon coincided with a generous snowfall, to sneak out upon pastures made new with blankets of white, to giggle and toss snowballs and dance and make snow statues and snow angels until they were blue with cold and hilarity...all but Mary had looked upon such moments as the pinnacle of life. *Poor Georgiana, to have never had sisters.*

"We liked, occasionally, to play games during the first snowfalls, unchaperoned and unseen by adults with too many dull opinions— to our way of thinking," she admitted, smiling ruefully. "It was not, perhaps, quite the thing, and I admit to being the chief instigator."

"It sounds perfectly wonderful." Georgiana sighed.

They drank their water pitchers dry, refilled them, drank more, and finally, managed to sleep. Even so, Lizzy was so tired that she did not awaken until around three in the morning. But James still dozed in the cold entry.

Neither did Mr Donavan depart after that. At breakfast, before Lady Catherine appeared, Mrs Taylor confirmed that the doctor was yet in the house. What was more, Mr Hudson had failed to turn up that morning. Mr Stimple had departed regardless. Only the doctor remained with Mr Darcy.

"Mr Hudson, he was the best of the lot." Mrs Taylor fretted aloud for the first time in Lizzy's hearing. "Cared about getting Mr Darcy's meals to him timely, he did. It's not like him to decamp like this. I don't like it."

Lizzy did not like it either. Had Hudson wanted no part of what he'd witnessed the day previous? Why had Mr Donavan not asked for Mrs Taylor to provide new assistance from one of the footmen, or even required Stimple to stay longer until a replacement could be found? What was happening in that nursery?

Another interminable day followed, an excruciating combination of tedium and terror. They found excuses to avoid being in company with Lady Catherine until dinner, endured the hour of inanity, and were once again ordered to the music room.

"Do you play, Miss Bennet?"

"A little," Lizzy replied.

"If I had ever learnt, I should have been a great proficient. And so would Anne, had her health allowed her to apply."

Lizzy fought to keep her eyes from rolling while Lady Catherine pontificated.

"This room is sadly out of date. I told Darcy he ought to refurnish it in the Egyptian style."

Mr Darcy suffering above stairs, and she speaks of redecorating! Incredible!

"The entire neighbourhood depends upon me for such advice. It was but Tuesday before last—or was it Wednesday? Yes, Wednesday. I recommended gold draperies to Lady Metcalfe, instead of dark green, and the family is quite delighted with them. Lady Metcalfe finds them a treasure. 'Lady Catherine,' said she, 'you have suggested to me a treasure.'"

Lizzy had long since drawn the only possible conclusion: for all her rank, Lady Catherine had little sense. She could relate the number of courses Lady Metcalfe regularly served for dinner or the titbit that she would take extra helpings of pudding whenever her husband was away but nothing whatsoever of that lady's character or intelligence. Whenever Lizzy delicately enquired as to Mr Donavan's education or successful cases, her questions were brushed aside as meaningless.

"Mr Donavan has ministered to Anne in every condition," she declared. "I trust him with my daughter's life—his triumphs on her behalf are many, his methods proven."

At the piano, Georgiana missed a note, plainly not comforted by his 'successes' with her sickly cousin.

At long last, Lady Catherine said her good nights, her every footstep on the stairs punctuated by the strident thump of her ever-present cane, leaving the girls alone. When Mrs Taylor entered to clear the coffee service, Lizzy nudged her friend.

"Mrs Taylor," Georgiana began hesitantly, "does Mr Donavan attend my brother still this evening?"

"Yes," she said, sounding subdued. "Mr Stimple arrived early for his shift, so it seems clear they did not expect Hudson to return. Mr Stimple took trays up, but...but the tray of broth and such for Mr Darcy...that tray was returned untouched."

Lizzy and Georgiana exchanged a look. The moment the doctor departed, Stimple would go to sleep. It might be their only chance, and seizing it was too important to depend upon imprecise methods of waking.

Georgiana took a deep breath and asked diffidently, "Mrs Taylor...I know not if we have someone...who could—could watch for Donavan to l-leave. I do not mean it should be you," she added hurriedly. "I know we are shorthanded. But if there is someone who—who could inform m-me the moment the doctor departs, even if it means w-waking me."

Lizzy had urged Georgiana to try to be more assertive, especially now that Mrs Taylor was not quite so convinced of the soundness of her ladyship's care. To her relief, the housekeeper complied readily enough.

"James has watched at the front door these last two nights and will do so again tonight, in case the doctor calls for the carriage. He will tell me if I ask him to."

Georgiana lifted her chin "I *will* visit my brother if—when—he departs. And—and there is no need to inform my aunt of it."

"Yes, miss." Mrs Taylor nodded. "It shall be as you say."

It is something, Lizzy thought, heartened by the small victory. Perhaps the housekeeper would take more risks, if necessary, than they had believed. Perhaps Georgiana would as well. *Perhaps, perhaps.*

⬥

Lizzy went to Georgiana's room once she was sure the maid they shared was gone. "Do you mind if I wait with you?" she asked.

They both had changed into simple gowns they could don themselves.

"I was going to fetch you if you did not come," Georgiana assured.

For a long while, they rehearsed their plans and concerns. But as the minutes turned into hours and they grew weary, Lizzy finally suggested they blow out the candles and lie down on the bed to wait. If they could sleep, they probably ought.

"It is likely fruitless waiting up. He did not leave last night at all."

"I believe Mrs Taylor will contrive to let you know when he departs, whenever it is," Lizzy replied. "Lady Catherine left us alone this morning while she attended to her correspondence. Perhaps a morning visit will be possible if he stays tonight. He has to leave *some*time."

But as the mantel clock chimed hour after desperate hour, she wondered if he ever would.

The doctor must not have departed was Lizzy's first dismayed thought when she awakened to the daylight streaming into the room from the open drapes, and she realised the night was passed. She had not even roused to the sound of the maid making up the fire. Slipping out of bed, she pulled the blankets over Georgiana and went to the window. The garden view was cloaked in murky fog, matching her despair.

A light scratch on the door had her nearly running to it.

Mrs Taylor did not look as though she had gotten much sleep herself. "He's gone, miss. The doctor, that is. Just now."

"Did he say when he might return?"

"No, miss, but directly after his departure, Stimple left in a great hurry. It is Mr Sharp's day, but I do not believe he will arrive for an hour yet. Oh, and Donavan was complaining about his lack of sleep...and he muttered something of Lady Catherine's ingratitude in the face of his 'heroic' efforts. I do not know what he meant."

Lizzy briefly closed her eyes, fearing she could guess. "Thank you, Mrs Taylor. I will wake Georgiana, and she will be up to visit her brother directly."

"Should I send Edna up to help her dress?"

"No need. I will help her."

The housekeeper withdrew as Georgiana sat up in bed. "Lizzy?"

"Donavan has departed. Shall we go at once?"

The other girl scrambled out of bed, pulled on her slippers, glanced at her dishevelled appearance in the glass, and shrugged; neither of them was presentable enough for Lady Catherine's critical eye. It mattered not at all.

They hurried up the stairs to the nursery, not speaking. Lizzy stopped, turning to Georgiana.

"Are you certain you wish to enter, dear?" she asked gently. "We do not know what state he is in. I am happy to go first, that you might be prepared."

"I have been a coward long enough, Lizzy," Georgiana said.

Lizzy put a hand upon her shoulder. "We must only think of your brother," she said quietly. "We cannot give way to tears if—if he has worsened."

Georgiana nodded grimly, and they entered.

The room was dark; there was a vile odour—not of bile, as before. Something else. Something bad.

Lizzy strode to the window, pulling aside the curtains so the dull morning light entered. Georgiana gasped, and Lizzy turned.

Donavan's large medical case lay open at the bedside. Upon a nearby table rested various implements, needles, and other unknown apparatus, many of them bloody. Mr Darcy had no blanket. He lay on his side, his feet bound together and tied to the foot of the bed. He wore some sort of contraption...a tight waistcoat with long sleeves extending over his hands and strings attached, binding them behind his back. He was gagged with a leather strap, and there was a swelling bruise over his eye. He appeared to be quite unconscious. Or...was he even alive?

Lizzy hurried to his bedside, placing her fingers beneath his nose. He breathed, but that was the most she could say. She placed a hand upon his forehead; it felt hot and dry.

"Dash it, we must get this off him." She picked at the leather gag, finding it tightly knotted.

A singular noise echoed beyond the door from the direction of the stairwell. *Thump. Thump. Thump.*

Lizzy looked up from her task as Georgiana froze in fear, her eyes wide.

Lady Catherine, she mouthed.

Lizzy did not hesitate, grabbing Georgiana's hand and dragging her to the little room where Stimple had previously napped during his shift. There was no time to close the door behind them—they could only wait just beyond it, hoping she did not enter, hoping she did not seek any attendant. Lizzy glanced around; the settee would not provide adequate cover for even one of them. She pulled Georgiana against the wall to the right of the door and leant against it. Her ladyship would have to walk in and turn to spot them. It was the best she could do.

Lady Catherine's voice suddenly rang out, hideously nearby. "Fitzwilliam Sébastien Montgomery Darcy," the old lady declared in stentorian tones. "How dare you resort to violence, to *madness*! It is *deplorable*! We are *Fitzwilliams*, however polluted your own blood. We do *not* give way."

She waited a beat, as if the gagged, unconscious man on the bed could possibly answer.

"A report equally unacceptable reached me early this morning from Mr Donavan. He says you are declining, despite all his strenuous efforts to rescue you from your weakness. From your infancy, Nephew, you were intended for Anne. It was the favourite wish of your parents as well as my own. I suppose I must be thankful those plans never came to fruition. Honour, decorum, prudence, nay, interest, forbid it. I *never* would have agreed to such a union had I known the shades in your character. Madness. Weakness. And now it is to be presumed, *death*? How could you have failed us so?

"The earl believes I should return you to *him*. Hah! Impossible that the earl should possess you in my place, especially at the cost of the entire family's good name. Why, news of your insanity will be all over London in no time if he goes about marrying you off to some gossipy bride *he* controls, never mind his other threats of *legal* guardianship, all to support his rape of the great Darcy estates! Anne, especially, would be a victim. Her dowry will not help much if madness is thought to exist in the family lines. Is this, then, your gratitude for my attentions to you?

"No. Your death will be a disgrace; your name will never even be *mentioned* by any of us."

There was a long pause. Lizzy stared, aghast, at Georgiana, who had a fist stuffed into her mouth and held a matching look of horror upon her face.

When Lady Catherine spoke again, her voice was different, soft... almost tender. "I do not submit to the earl's whims. I have not been in the habit of brooking disappointment. You were always so good to my Anne, my precious Anne. Obstinate...headstrong boy."

They heard a sniff then another. The woman was...crying?

Then, finally, came the *thump, thump, thump* of her cane as she retreated, making her slow way down the stairs.

13

THE MEASURES OF ARTIFICE

"**G**eorgie...we must stop her!" Lizzy felt all the helplessness of her position, her lack of resources.

"She will let Donavan kill him," Georgiana whispered. "He will die, and she will call it merciful."

Lizzy saw the girl was about to give way to hysteria, an understandable temptation. But it was her own mother's response to ill news, and it never, ever helped. She must distract them both with action, if possible.

She took a deep breath. "Remember, we must think only of your brother. We need Mrs Taylor, and we need her quickly. Mr Sharp must not be allowed in. I feel certain she will know some way that might be accomplished once she understands the situation. Will you—very discreetly—fetch her while I attempt to remove these bindings?"

Georgiana blinked, shuddering. Then, with renewed resolution, she nodded, hurrying out.

Lizzy approached the bed. Had Mr Darcy heard Lady Catherine? His eyes were yet closed; he was as still as death. She began picking at the knotted leather gag. It was impossibly tight. His mouth must be so sore! Her fingernail tore in the futile process, and she told herself her tears were from pain.

"Stupid, stupid," she whispered, swiping at her eyes. Who would beat a sick man? Her own inability to do this simple thing, ease him in this tiny way, shredded her self-possession. A sob escaped, and she bit her lip to stop herself. She checked his breathing again. *He is so quiet!* "It will be well, Mr Darcy. We will fix this, somehow. At least you are no longer chained. Knots can be untied." But those knots were ruthlessly snarled, and she could make little progress.

Where is the housekeeper with Georgie? Does Mrs Taylor refuse to assist her, even now?

Although she was expecting and hoping for assistance, the sound of approaching steps on the stairs several minutes later gave her pause. If it was Mr Donavan, he would throw her out. She did not even care if he tried. Picking up a nearby candlestick, she ran to the other side of the bed, prepared to do battle. She would beat him with all the strength within her if he even tried to approach Mr Darcy, and to the devil with any consequences.

But it was Mrs Taylor, alone, at first astonished at the sight of Lizzy wielding a candlestick—then shocked at the sight of Mr Darcy in such straits.

Lizzy did not give her time to question her presence in the sick-room. Lowering the candlestick, she asked, "Might you procure a knife? I cannot undo these stupid knots."

The woman nodded, plainly too astonished to comment further, withdrawing a tool from her apron pocket and moving beside Mr Darcy. Efficiently she cut the gag, then sliced the bindings at his feet. Finally, she severed the strings fastening his wrists. They flopped to the mattress lifelessly. Lizzy worked with her to withdraw the binding garment from him, pulling it off his arms.

They both gasped at the same time.

Large bloody splotches marked his shirt's back—the garment sticking to his skin where blood had dried.

"Merciful heavens," Mrs Taylor whispered.

"Miss Darcy must not see this. Where is she?" Lizzy whispered back, a lump in her throat preventing her from speaking any louder.

"She came to me and said her brother needed me desperately and that we must on no account allow Mr Sharp entry. I have Frost on the lookout—he will send him on his way. As we walked up the stairs together, Lady Catherine called to her and demanded she play for her—at once. Miss Darcy did not know what else to do except keep her ladyship occupied."

"That is as well," Lizzy said, still staring at the wounds. "I wonder —have you any sandalwood?"

Mrs Taylor looked taken aback. "Why...I do not think so, miss. Whatever for?"

"It can be used in a treatment for ulcerations, I have read. The cloth and any impurities in the flesh must be cleansed and removed."

But the housekeeper was distraught. "I'm sure I don't know, miss! I will call for James, and we will bathe him and dress these wounds with a special ointment prepared from my own stillroom. Something must be done at once!"

Lizzy had been so caught up in thinking of how to ease Mr Darcy's trauma that she had briefly forgotten just how highly irregular Mrs Taylor must find her presence.

"I apologise, Mrs Taylor. I am well-known at home for my remedies."

The woman nodded distractedly, obviously too upset to pay attention to the bleatings of a young houseguest. "If you'll excuse me, I will fetch James now."

Lizzy tried once more, wanting nothing more than to assist in Mr Darcy's recovery. "Lady Catherine will not appreciate any interference. You, James, even Mr Frost might risk her wrath for aiding him."

"James is my nephew and loyal to me as well as Mr Darcy. Frost and I have worked for the family for many years and may be relied upon," she said, in a voice grown suddenly offended.

"Of course. I did not mean to imply otherwise." Lizzy felt she had no choice but to remove herself from the room, but not before she caught sight, as the housekeeper cut off his nightshirt, of what Mr Darcy had endured; it was horrifying, his back mutilated.

After James entered the nursery, she paced to and fro along the corridor, wishing she was allowed to offer something besides pity. It seemed like hours but was probably less than one before Georgiana reappeared, flushed and anxious.

"They are caring for him, dear," Lizzy said. "Mrs Taylor and James."

"Lady Catherine believes us resting now. I did not know what else to do when—" Georgiana began, but Lizzy interrupted.

"You were perfect," Lizzy said. "Not arousing her suspicion was of the utmost importance. Mr Sharp will be sent away. Mr Darcy has a few hours of respite."

"Yes," Georgiana agreed.

"But only a few. We must get your brother away from here," Lizzy said.

"To where, though?"

At that moment, James, looking very solemn and slightly green, exited the sickroom and took his place just beyond the door. Lizzy looked at Georgiana meaningfully then at the door to the nursery.

Georgiana straightened and made for the door. "We will see my brother," she said firmly.

"Ah, miss, 'tis not fit for you to see," James began.

For the first time, Lizzy saw a resemblance to her brother in Georgiana's aristocratic—some would say, stubborn—expression. "I will see Fitzwilliam," she demanded.

When the footman reluctantly opened the door, Georgiana took Lizzy's hand, and they both entered.

He lay on his belly, motionless. The bedsheets had been changed, and he had been washed and redressed; his hair curled damply. He needed a shave, the shadow of his beard only thinly disguising the purpling bruises—the sole colour on his face.

"Oh, Fitzwilliam," Georgiana whispered, going to him, laying a hand upon his cheek. A tear fell, then another. She looked at Lizzy, then at Mrs Taylor, who appeared white-faced and grim.

"Do you have any means of reaching my cousin, Colonel Fitzwilliam? Footmen who have couriered messages to him before on my brother's behalf? I have no idea if he is in London, but we must attempt it."

"I can try, miss."

"The earl could stop her. Unfortunately, he is doubtless at his country seat. Even an express will take a day or two to reach him."

"We do not have days," Lizzy said. "I do not know if Mr Darcy can survive one more night of Donavan's 'treatments'. We must stop them." She turned to Mrs Taylor. "You do not know me, I know, but I believe I *can* help. Please, may I have the use of your stillroom?"

Mrs Taylor's brows rose, but it was Georgiana who protested.

"Lizzy, my aunt will never allow *you* to treat Fitzwilliam instead of her doctor, as much as I wish she would. She will order you from the house if you try!"

But Lizzy had ceased listening; instead, she began examining the many bottles, pots, and decanters in the doctor's medical case. Most were helpfully labelled. The ones that were not, she opened lids and sniffed. After withdrawing several items, she looked up at her audience. "She cannot order anyone to do anything if she is soundly sleeping."

The extent of Mr Darcy's wounds had, evidently, extinguished any possible objections the housekeeper's might have offered to Lizzy's ideas, and she—with a bit of encouragement from Georgiana—had mercifully agreed to Lizzy's 'plan'. It was rather simple—although she was not quite so confident in its success as she pretended. If Lady Catherine were of the same stature as Mrs Bennet, she would know exactly how much of the concoction she must ingest in order to achieve several hours of uninterrupted slumber. However, Mrs Bennet was much smaller, and what was more, she willingly swallowed any of Lizzy's concoctions and asked for more. Lizzy could not force her ladyship to take the potion, nor could she risk giving her too much and causing illness.

"I have noticed your aunt's fondness for sweetmeats. We will serve her these"—she pointed to a tray of small, prettily decorated marchpane cakes—"which have been infused with ingredients to encourage a deep slumber. Sharp did not question Mr Frost's assertion that he is no longer needed, and as it is the Sabbath, Mrs Taylor hopes Donavan will not come—but we cannot take the chance. If he arrives, Mrs Taylor is going to inform him that Lady Catherine requires him to honour the day of rest and perform no work. It is my guess that he will welcome more sleep—he does not appear as one who customarily sacrifices so much for his patients."

Georgiana made an unladylike noise of agreement.

"In the meantime, we will hope that Mrs Taylor's messages reach your cousin while keeping your aunt, um, well rested. And we are certain your express to your uncle will bring results eventually."

It was not an ideal plan on several counts. The Fitzwilliams had not proven to have Mr Darcy's best interests at heart either—but at least they would not *murder* him. She had no notion of whether Colonel Fitzwilliam could be discovered or whether he would be any more helpful than his father had proven, if he was found. Mr Donavan might return early Monday morning and even try to insist upon resuming treatments—with or without Lady Catherine's awareness. She had thought of asking for an express to be sent to the Bingleys in Brighton—they *might* have arrived there by now—but doubted whether it would do any good. Bingley could not stand against an earl, who had already been sent for. How long would it take Lord Matlock to receive the message and travel to London? A week? Did they have time?

✦

The sweetmeats were served at tea. For once, instead of the ceaseless boredom such moments with Lady Catherine usually inspired, Georgiana, Lizzy, and even Mrs Taylor were transfixed by her every word. Well, at least upon her mouth as she swallowed. She was ignoring Lizzy's cakes, however, in favour of biscuits.

Why did they put anything else out? Lizzy wondered. To her surprise, it was Georgiana who intervened.

With a look of desperation upon her face, Georgiana raised one of the small cakes to her mouth, taking a tiny nibble. "Oh, Mrs Taylor," she enthused in an unnaturally shrill voice, "if this is not the most delicious marchpane I have ever tasted. Y-you must send my compliments to Cook."

It accomplished her purpose. Lady Catherine's eye fell upon the little cakes, snatching up a piece with alacrity.

"These are acceptably pleasant," she noted after her fourth helping. "Mrs Taylor, you will provide the receipt for my cook."

The intense strain Lizzy had been feeling eased a bit. Although the lady showed no signs of drowsiness, it *must* take effect eventually.

But after the seventh helping, she began to worry again. Poisoning an earl's sister was not her goal.

"I am feeling very fatigued. I always wish for a nap at this time of day," Lizzy announced, yawning as her ladyship reached for an eighth, hoping to encourage any residual fatigue.

Georgiana chimed in. "Do you? I find an afternoon nap most restorative."

Lady Catherine paused with the sweet on its way to her mouth. "I have always been possessed of energetic spirits. My neighbours often say, 'You always possess such energy of—'" Her self-congratulatory speech was interrupted by a yawn. She gave her head a small shake. "As I was saying, I am a great believer in...in...greatness..." Her words trailed off into a snore, the cake dropping onto her lap.

For two or three minutes, they all simply stared at her, more than half-expecting that she would quickly waken. But her snores continued—loudly—her chins resting upon her bosom. When a thin line of spittle emerged, Lizzy knew it was time.

"We should move her to her chamber," Georgiana suggested.

"Will her maid remark upon her unusual slumbering?" Lizzy wondered.

Mrs Taylor smiled for the first time. "I thought of that and sent her on several errands, supposedly at her ladyship's instruction. She often has me send her out for bits and bobs, and I have noticed the girl is seldom quick to return. When she does, well, there are a few bites left for her, are there not?" She nodded at the plate, where three of the cakes still remained, then hurried to bring James and Frost in to assist her ladyship to her bed.

"How long will she, um, rest, Lizzy?"

Lizzy sighed. "I am unsure. Mama would be out until tomorrow at this time, at least, with half the dosage, but she is much smaller of stature. And of course, she always *wished* for the sleep this potion brings. Not to mention being less, er, energetic of spirits."

But all seemed to go smoothly. As James and Mr Frost hoisted up Lady Catherine, her snores roughened and paused, and Georgiana's expression grew tense; however, soon she was safely ensconced in her chamber. Donavan arrived a few hours later, but accepted 'Lady Catherine's' directive to attend to his worship rather than his patient and departed without even *asking* how Mr Darcy fared.

"What will we do when Stimple returns tomorrow?"

Georgiana and Lizzy were sitting in the sickroom, both keeping watch. James was standing by in case he was needed—though he had had very little sleep the night before.

"I would tell him he has been dismissed," Lizzy replied darkly. "I suppose he applied those bruises."

"I would put him in that contraption he trussed Mr Darcy in," James muttered from just beyond the door. "And poke him like he did Mr Darcy."

They both gave startled laughs, but their smiles soon vanished. Watching the unconscious man, there was very little humour to find.

❖

Lizzy awakened to pitch-black, wondering the time. How long had she slept? Georgiana had insisted upon staying with Mr Darcy, agreeing to waken Lizzy for a shift at midnight, and there was no one to deny her. Was he feverish? Was he in mortal danger? Would Lady Catherine awaken soon? How long could they keep her from interfering?

So many questions with no answers! The clock chimed twelve counts—but there was no sign of her friend. Which meant, probably, that Georgiana had fallen to sleep, and no one waited upon Mr Darcy.

She lit a candle, pulled on an old gown and slippers, and hurried out of her room and up the stairs. James was no longer at his chair but asleep on the floor beside the nursery door; she could hardly blame him, so little rest as the poor man had been given.

Quietly, she opened the door, not wanting to disturb him, and slipped inside the dim room. She did not immediately see her friend, however, and held the candlestick up a little higher to cast the light around the room.

Georgiana lay upon Mr Darcy's bed, sound asleep upon his pillow. There was no sign of her brother. Suddenly, Lizzy was thrust against someone in the darkness, a hand clapping over her mouth, another wrenching the candlestick away.

14

EXCESSIVELY SORRY TO GO

Darcy had wakened to find his sister curled up at the foot of his bed, soundly asleep. He felt like the very devil, and his back and upper arms burned as if on fire. He sat up, sliding to the edge of the bed, looking around more carefully. Still in the nursery. Still at Darcy House. No chains, no doctor, no snores.

The room spun, his gut roiling. His memories were hazy; he remembered deciding that specious quack, Donavan, and his sadistic assistant, Stimple, were killing him and that he must either fight or die here in his own nursery.

His opportunity had arrived while they had lacerated his back; Stimple had freed one arm to turn him, probably thinking that he was too weak to struggle. He was nearly right; exhausted, sick, and suffering, the battle to remain conscious was almost more than he could win. But the hideous pain gave him the impetus to try it anyway.

It had been a doomed fight because one arm remained chained, but he came up swinging and managed a punch to Stimple's ugly phiz. The doctor, in his shock, dropped his torture device—which held a red-hot iron rod—on the mattress, and Darcy snatched it up, waving it at them whenever they neared. It kept them off for as long as they attacked him individually, but of course, they soon began working in concert. Stimple managed a blow to his head whilst Donavan came at him from the other side, and soon Darcy found himself bound again.

However, he managed to draw blood with his teeth when Stimple then tried to force some noxious brew down his throat. What might have happened next, he did not know—likely they would have killed him for the violence, not that he much cared—but at that very moment, a knock sounded at the door.

A note. His life was spared because of a note from Lady Catherine ordering Donavan to deliver a report on his progress that very minute. Donavan ordered Stimple to stand down; the brute, fortunately, stalked from the room and took to his couch.

The doctor disappeared for what seemed an hour or two; during that time, Stimple began snoring, so Darcy dozed, too, but finally Donavan returned, full of fury at Lady Catherine's displeasure, at her nephew's insanity, at the world's idiocy in not recognising his superiority. He ranted—raved, really—as if he were a madman himself. Perhaps he was.

Finally, though, he woke Stimple and ordered Darcy gagged and put into some hideously painful waistcoat bindings, without regard to the mutilated flesh of his back, stating his intention to begin his 'treatment' anew later in the day. Stimple had enjoyed Darcy's pain —but unconsciousness had instead wrought its own peculiar mercy.

Now, uncertain he could refrain from casting up his accounts, he breathed in slowly through his nose, out through his mouth, trying to settle. When he thought he could manage the distance, Darcy dragged himself up, trying to ignore the fire in his skin and the swelling behind his eye, stumbling his way across the room until he reached the chamber pot behind a screen. He did not retch after all, but was able to take care of his other needs. Then, his head clearing a bit, he began to absorb more details.

A good fire burned, one that had been tended not long past. Every binding had been removed, and his nightshirt was a clean one.

Where were his tormentors? Georgiana was here, a good sign. But he was not returned to his own room. He looked over at his precious sister, who had rolled over now, somehow finding his pillow in her sleep. It would, likely, take an explosion to wake her —she had always been a sound sleeper. It made him smile, and then inexplicably, a lump formed in his throat.

He fought against the futile panic of being unable to comprehend why his life had turned into a horrendous gothic novel, why his family employed villains, why his mouth would not work correctly.

He would go looking for answers, he decided, since he was not bound to a bed. He found his banyan hanging on the bed post, shrugged it painfully over his nightshirt, and had just made his way towards the door when it opened a crack. Immediately, he flattened himself against the wall, despite the pain.

If it was Donavan or Stimple, he would kill them or die trying.

A figure entered the room, holding a candlestick. *Perfect. A weapon.* The element of surprise was his only advantage.

The moment he pounced, he knew the form was female—not any female, but *her*. Elizabeth. The girl he dreamt of, the hope he clung to.

And he had nearly attacked her; perhaps he was as mad as Donavan believed.

❦

One moment, Lizzy was furiously resisting the unknown hands detaining her. The next, however, she realised who held her, and she ceased her struggling. She knew he had injuries to his arms and back, and she would not exacerbate them. Nevertheless, for all she knew, he was in the maddened state that might have led to his previous bindings. Would he hurt her?

However, the hand covering her mouth slipped away, the body behind her stepping back. But he retained the candlestick.

"I am sorry," she whispered, turning to face him, her heart pumping at an absurd rate. "I did not mean to startle you. You are up! You are awake! Oh, I am so glad!"

His dark eyes glittered in the candlelight. His jaw clenched, his hair in messy curls; he wore a banyan over his nightshirt, she saw despite keeping her gaze determinedly upon his face. If she had to apply a descriptor, she would call him angry, although the purpling bruise around his left eye might have contributed; she could not tell if he yet meant to thwack her with that candlestick.

"We are taking turns keeping watch, and it is past my turn, but your sister fell asleep, and I hoped to waken her quietly," she added. "Do you need anything? Are you hungry? Can I bring you water?"

"Speak...*slamkin*...slow," he gritted.

"Ohh," she said, realising that in her fright and the surprise of seeing him conscious, she had been babbling. "I am sorry," she said again.

He waved her apology away. Instead, he staggered to the other side of the room, sitting down heavily on a chair, placing the candlestick on a side table. He scrubbed the good side of his face with his hand; she noticed he did not allow his injured back to touch the chairback, resting his elbows on his thighs, breathing heavily.

She felt a bit stupid, truly. If he was fit enough to rise from his sickbed, ought she to leave? The whole world would think so. And yet, he was hardly well and certainly still unsafe in his own home. So instead of exiting hastily, she sat down in the chair opposite him, perching on its edge.

"Mr Darcy," she said, her voice low so as not to waken his sister or James, enunciating carefully but trying not to sound as though she spoke to a child. "Did Georgiana tell you what we have done?"

He shook his head once in the negative.

"We sent for your uncle and cousin to stop your aunt from this torture of your person. We are hoping they can arrive in time to do it."

His head snapped up. *"The devil.* No."

He stood so quickly it surprised her, heading for the door, and she jumped up to intercept him—throwing herself between him and the door to stop him. "Wait!" she whispered desperately. "There are things to consider, things you do not know!"

Betrayal and anger were in the gaze that accused her now. What else could she have done? Where could she take him and his sister to hide from such a powerful family? But neither could she allow him to barrel directly towards instant trouble.

"Listen to me," she said, taking his face within her hands. "I was trying to help."

Help, she thought, *from a man who had already had him imprisoned within his power, a man whose intentions had proven unjust and dishonourable. And what of Georgiana? In calling for her uncle, she had as good as sacrificed herself to an unwanted marriage.*

And it was I who urged Georgiana to write to Lady Catherine in the first place.

Why *should* he listen to her?

Her eyes filled with tears of frustration at her powerlessness, at her inability to fix all that was wrong, words of futile explanations and apologies clogging her throat.

Inexplicably, however, his expression changed, softened. Instead of being shoved aside, she found herself cradled in his arms.

The sensation of it! To be surrounded by him, to feel cherished by him. To breathe in his scent, to inhale him—he became her world in that moment.

Lizzy knew it was wrong. She should not be embracing this man —*any* man—and that he wore only his night clothes compounded the wickedness. Why, then, did it feel right? Why did it feel as if she was doing the best thing she had ever done? Why did the differences between them—hard and soft, muscle and yielding, male and female—meld into a perfect whole? Why did her name, spoken in his broken, gruff murmur, sound the way she had always longed to hear it?

"Liz-zy. Oh, Liz-zy."

She looked up, meeting his eyes. He looked down at her. The rage and frustration in his expression of a few moments ago was replaced with...tenderness? Affection? His head bent towards her. Would he kiss her now? Her eyes drifted shut, anticipating the sensation while fearing it as well. Oh, yes, she was in over her head for certain.

But the expected kiss did not come. Instead, he rested his forehead upon hers. His skin burned.

He is feverish, ill, and I think of kissing. What an excellent nurse I am!

But of course, she did not wish to be his nurse. She wanted something more, an unknown something creating an unnamed longing within.

Stupid, stupid girl.

So instead of words of love to lover, she softly told him the rest of it. "I brewed a—well, it is actually my mama's sleeping draught, but we put it in cakes and served them to your aunt. She has been the next thing to unconscious for several hours now."

He smiled, but she could not return it. "We do not know how long we can keep her asleep or whether she will grow immediately suspicious when she wakens. We sent Donavan away, but we do not think we can make him *stay* away, and the servants are very afraid of your aunt. I am uncertain...how much command we might be able to exercise."

He nodded, solemn again.

"Do you think...it is such a long journey, but...would you be safe if we could find a way to spirit you to Pemberley?"

For a long moment, he held still, seeming to consider. But at last, he shook his head. "No. Look…there first. No *egad*…earl. No Cathrine. Must…go."

"But where? If only Bingley was in town!"

His countenance lightened with what might have been enthusiasm, but he grappled with his tongue, trying to express it. "*Other*. No. Nether-field."

"Netherfield? You likely have not heard that my sister Jane married Mr Bingley," she explained, and his face tautened.

"Bing," he repeated, frowning. "Mar-ried."

"Yes."

His disapproval was plain upon his face, and she bit her tongue against reproaching him for it, reminding herself that while Jane was a worthy bride, Jane's parents and prospects helped Bingley's circumstances not at all. But it did give her the impetus, as one even less fortunate than her sister, to step away from him. He easily let her go.

"Only Miss Bingley and the Hursts reside currently at Netherfield, I believe," she made herself continue, "as Mr Bingley and Jane are on their wedding trip. They went first to Scarborough, you see, to his relations there, and will go to Brighton after. I fear your appearance at Netherfield might only result in the furtherance of Lady Matlock's plans."

He closed his eyes. "No…earl. No…Cath. Must…away." He swayed on his feet, might even have fallen if she had not clutched his arms.

"Sir, you must lie down. You are unwell."

He blinked several times, clenching his jaw. Then, gradually, he straightened. "*Beefwitted barnacle*. No. Bed. *Mine*."

He said the last word with such emphasis that she understood. He took an uncertain step towards the door. Grabbing up the candlestick, she kept hold of his arm, worried that he might fall. Thankfully, James responded to her nudge as they left the nursery, jumping up to assist. The stairs were perilous, Lizzy worrying he would topple forward at any moment; James was of much smaller stature than Mr Darcy, and Lizzy wondered if he could prevent an injury.

When they were mere steps from his chamber door, he sagged. It took the two of them half-dragging him to get him into his bed. When it was done, they looked at each other anxiously. Mr Darcy lay upon the bed on his belly, unmoving.

"After I wake Miss Darcy, I will go to the kitchen and brew a tea to help with his fever." She injected her words with as much confidence as she could muster. "Please see his fire lit and watch him until I can return."

Fortunately, James obediently went at once to the fireplace.

She returned to the nursery, waking a chagrined Georgiana, explaining what she could of his condition. "He is of course very weak and ill and naturally wishes to be away from Darcy House. Once in his own bed, he fell immediately back to sleep—which one might expect."

The younger girl was persuaded to return to her bed, and then with liberal thefts from the doctor's pharmacy case and the use of the Darcy kitchen, Lizzy concocted the tea she had found useful for fevers.

Even with James's help, however, she could not get the half of it down Mr Darcy. It was as she had feared; he was more unconscious than sleeping.

The night was a long one. At first, he was insensible, cursing, his skin hot, and she worried that Mrs Taylor's treatment of his wounds had been ineffective; after a time, however, he seemed to settle. Perhaps the tea had done its work. Alone in the dark and the quiet, with not much to do except gaze upon him, she could not resist reviewing the past.

That look upon his face when he had declared his love—*if* he had meant it—in the fields of Longbourn…had it been a joke? He had not been chuckling or teasing, but then, he was not a chuckling or teasing sort of man. Not a *joking* sort of man. If she had to describe his expression, she would have called it…bewilderment. An impulse? Even now, after having been held within his arms *twice*, she could hardly credit it. If the declaration *had* been meant, he had certainly regretted it quickly enough. He had done nothing to correct her assumption, and she had not mistaken his relief when she had treated it lightly. She must remember that when, in his infirmity, he reached for her.

He did not waken again. When morning arrived at last, Mrs Taylor was dismayed that Lizzy had not roused her sooner. She agreed to administer Lizzy's tea for his fever and sent a maid out to search for the sandalwood Lizzy wished for. Her alarm over Mr Darcy's condition was plain.

Both Lizzy and Georgiana picked at their breakfasts whilst Lizzy considered what might be done about Lady Catherine. Perhaps more of the same ingredients but brewed into a tea that she might be served? A more immediate trouble presented itself, however, when Mrs Taylor hurried into the breakfast parlour.

"Miss Darcy, the doctor is returned. I told him he wasn't to come until Lady Catherine sent for him, but he insisted upon speaking with her. I told him she was sleeping, but he then demanded to see his patient."

Lizzy dropped her fork, and together they followed the housekeeper into the parlour, where the doctor waited.

"This is ridiculous," he announced to Mrs Taylor. "I will go upstairs now—" He broke off as he saw the girls.

Lizzy saw that Georgiana was flummoxed and knew not how to act. "You have interrupted Miss Darcy's breakfast, and Lady

Catherine has not yet risen. You must return when she sends for you. Her orders were clear," she declared.

His eyes narrowed at her. "Orders! *I* received no such orders. I will see my patient now, and you may take yourselves away!"

Lizzy clenched her fists, her temper flaring; fatigue and outrage contrived to break its bounds at last. "She did not care for your ill treatment of her nephew. She said you were unfit, a fool, and if you dared come here again with your nasty, ineffective tortures, she would post broadsheets with your picture all over London, declaring you a public nuisance and a fraud!"

"Why, you little imbecile!" he roared, his face red with fury. "I have never, in all my days, heard such—"

"Mr Donavan," came a cold, imperious voice from the doorway. "You will be silent." Lady Catherine, her hair dishevelled, her dress only partially buttoned, nevertheless emanated an authority that only an arrogance of birthright could manage.

Mr Donavan shut his mouth with a snap.

But then she turned to Lizzy. "As for you, young lady, what are you about?"

Lizzy felt all the hopelessness of her situation. Nevertheless, she *had* to try. "Please, my lady, I beg you to listen. This man has done nothing but torture your nephew and will do nothing to help him. Mr Darcy is not mad at all and would not be ill now except for—"

"That will be quite enough! I am ashamed of you! Prattling about such as you cannot possibly understand, denigrating one whose reputation is so far above your own, as to make yourself ridiculous in the effort."

Within her frustration, Lizzy could see it plainly. To defend her own ineptitude, her ladyship defended her choice of physician. The old lady would never admit to mistakes, his or her own.

"He will *murder* your nephew. Will you give him your permission?"

Her eyes blazed. "Enough. Take yourself to your room while I decide what is to be done with you. Now!"

But Lady Catherine did not see the mangled flesh, the evidence of torture. Perhaps she does not realise the extent of his suffering.

Nothing mattered now, neither pride nor her future, not her low opinion of this woman, nothing except preventing Lady Catherine from authorising the death of Mr Darcy. Lizzy dropped to her knees. "Please, ma'am, I beg you. He has maimed and disfigured Mr Darcy, brutalised him. I believe you must care for and love your nephew. Please, I implore you, send Donavan away, disassociate yourself from such incompetence as he possesses."

But Lady Catherine's eyes only narrowed, suspicion in her gaze. "I am shocked and astonished! Explain how you would know *anything* of my nephew? Sneak! Spy! Are you in the earl's pay? *This* is how you show your gratitude after my many kindnesses towards you? Deceitful, despicable girl!"

Stalking out of the parlour into the entryway, she shoved the footman aside and threw open the massive front door herself, pointing to the street. "I know how to act. Out!"

"Aunt, please, no!" Georgiana cried.

Mrs Taylor gasped, her expression appalled.

Lizzy rose to her feet. "I would retrieve my things."

Lady Catherine brandished her cane as if a weapon. "Begone at once! Lest I call a constable!"

She would do it, Lizzy realised. *She would have me arrested, just because she could.*

With a final apologetic glance at Georgiana, head held high, she walked out the door, only flinching a little when it slammed shut behind her.

15

A CONVERGENCE OF DIFFICULTIES

Dazed, Lizzy found herself on the quiet street, blinking in the sunlight. For a few moments, blind panic wanted its way, but she kept it at bay by the thought that if Lady Catherine watched, she must not be given the satisfaction of seeing her humbled.

With a sigh, she began walking. There were not many people about, and those, mostly servants sent on errands. Dressed as plainly as she was, in her neat linen cap, she probably had the look of an upper servant and had not drawn any notice despite her lack of companion. Thus, she kept moving, attempting to appear as though she had a direction and purpose, and tried to think.

A hackney sped by—how did one make it stop for a passenger, she wondered? And she needed, quite desperately, her guinea, secreted in the lining of her trunk. And *The Pilgrim's Progress*—all she had left of her girlhood. Well, she must have her belongings, that was all. How could she retrieve them?

Perhaps if she returned to Darcy House later, presenting herself at the tradesman's entrance, Mrs Taylor might be persuaded to return her trunk. But where was a safe place to wait until she could? The old lady must suspect she would try to recover her things.

Georgiana would want to help, but how could Lizzy gain admittance to her? And even if she reclaimed her belongings, what then? Again, the wave of panic threatened.

No. I will keep my head. I have strong limbs to walk. The weather is fine. I will not think of Longbourn or my sisters or if-onlys or Mr Darcy or—

Tears threatened, and one escaped. *Mr Darcy!* But she must not consider him, and ruthlessly crushed the thought; she could not fathom, at this moment, how even to save herself.

***

Georgiana stared at the closed door in horror. "Aunt, we must at least—"

But at that moment, Lady Catherine caught sight of herself in the large looking glass over the mantelpiece, startling at her frowsy appearance and wild hair. "Dawson! Dawson!" she barked stridently, turning towards the stairs, paying no mind whatsoever to Georgiana's distress as she hurried away. "Why does everyone require my attendance at *such* an abominable hour? Taylor! I am *not* at home!"

For a moment, the three of them stood frozen in the entry.

Then Donavan's supercilious expression returned. "I shall see my patient now," he announced.

It was all Georgiana could do not to scream. And yet, Lizzy's words echoed in her head—'*Remember, we must only think of your brother.*' What would Lizzy *want* her to do? Delay him, at the very least. It would not take Donavan long to shout the house down if he went to the nursery and discovered the absence of his patient.

"It *is* quite early, Doctor," she managed. "H-have you had your breakfast? I believe the, um, the..." her mind blanked as she tried to think of what foods she had been eating only minutes before.

"The apple tart, did you mean?" Mrs Taylor put in. "With clotted cream, of course."

Georgiana was fairly certain *those* had not been on the sideboard earlier. "Oh, um, yes, that was it. And fig pasties, I think?" Figs were a delectable, rarely found treat, and Cook liked to have them on hand in case a visitor required impressing, so there would probably be some about, somewhere. "With your bacon, of course."

One could see the gluttony blooming in the doctor's eyes. "Why yes, er, I did miss breakfast this morning in my eagerness to attend to the patient."

"Very good, Mr Donavan." Mrs Taylor nodded. "If you will follow me to the breakfast parlour."

The moment they departed, Georgiana raced for the stairs. She wished, *how* she wished, to run after Lizzy—but it was vital that they do something more to protect Fitzwilliam, and quickly. She burst into his chambers, heedless of any kind of propriety, startling James into jumping from his chair.

"Brother, the doctor is here! He insists upon seeing you!"

Fitzwilliam, however, lay motionless and unresponsive. She bit her lip—he looked so very ill. Lizzy had said he was resting, but perhaps it was something worse than sleep. She looked at James, for the first time realising that he was only a few years older than herself. While a sturdy lad, he could hardly pick up her brother and carry him down the stairs.

"We must move him. To, um, somewhere more secure."

"Yes, miss," he replied, then looked at the unconscious man and scratched his head. "Um, where would ye like me to put 'im?"

She took Fitzwilliam's hand in hers. It was hot. "Brother," she said urgently. "Fitzwilliam, please wake up. Please, please wake up!"

Nothing.

"Fitzwilliam! You must arise! Donavan is in the house! He will hurt you again if he finds you!"

Still, no response.

She squeezed his hand. "Brother! Aunt has tossed Lizzy from the house! She put her out in the street, all because she tried to stop Donavan from coming to you! You are in the gravest danger! *Wake up!*"

He opened one eye. "Liz-zy" was all he said.

"Miss," came a gruff male voice from behind her. "Miss Bennet!"

Lizzy turned to see a portly older man, whom she recognised from the journey to London in the Darcy carriage; Mr Frost, the coachman—huffing a little—struggled to catch his breath once he reached her.

"Ye made it further from Darcy House than I thought ye could. I ought to have taken the mare," he said. "If ye'll come on back with me, miss, Taylor will get your things out to the stable, and I'll take ye to The George. The post runs from there to most everywhere in England." He eyed her plain dress and worn half boots. "If ye haven't the fare, it will be provided."

She coloured at his remarks, but this was no time for pride. "I thank you, sir. If the fare to Hertfordshire might be supplied, I will return to my family home." *Or to a little cabin in the woods near my family's home until Jane returns.* Better to face the dangers of the forest than the dangers of London, or even the potential danger of an unknown uncle—one who had never seen fit to be a part of her life in the past and thus could have little interest in her future.

But though she had stifled her pride, she could not go so far as to allow others to be punished for it. When they drew closer to the house, she asked, "Excuse me, sir—but will you be held account-able in any way if Lady Catherine sees you with me? I would not like to cause you trouble. I could come back under cover of dark-ness for my belongings if it will save you any."

Mr Frost looked her right in the eye. "My loyalty be to the Darcys, miss," he said, "and none other, despite what any might think about who be in charge here. Ye needn't fear for me place." He grinned. "And after all, the old lady be on the other side of the house, ain't she? Wait here a moment, and I'll fetch your trunk and the fare from Taylor, with a bit extra besides to see ye through. Then I'll have the carriage hitched and will see ye safely on the post."

He disappeared into the house while she stood where she was, cloaked in the shadows near the tradesman's entrance, feeling conspicuous, guilty for taking his charity, and angry at the fates on every count. Was the doctor even now resuming his torture?

Thankfully, Frost quickly reappeared, hoisting her trunk on a beefy shoulder and directing her towards the stables. But they had no sooner neared them when a panicked voice from within drew their attention.

"Someone, help! Oh, help please!"

Frost hurried in via a side door, Lizzy directly behind him. It took a moment for her vision to adjust to the darkness of the interior, but she made out two stable lads staring, their mouths gaping. Georgiana stood by, sobbing and calling. And then she saw why: James was on the ground, trying to struggle from beneath the weight of a collapsed Mr Darcy.

Georgiana caught sight of her, running to her, clutching at her arms. "Lizzy! Thank goodness! Donavan is at breakfast, so I went to Fitzwilliam. He got himself up and was determined to leave—he wishes Mr Frost to take him...somewhere, anywhere! We helped him get this far, but...I know he should not have left his bed, but—"

"Of course, dear. You did well. Hush, now," Lizzy said, extracting herself to go to Mr Darcy.

James had gotten to his feet, Frost propping up his fallen employer with a broad arm across his back—which must be excruciating for the injured man, not that the coachman would understand. Mr

Darcy's eyes were open, and other than his breath coming in the short pants of the deepest pain, he bore it stoically. She saw the moment he recognised her—his eyes widened with…something. Relief? Pleasure?

He looked at Frost. *"Perdition.* No. Up."

Frost's brows furrowed. "Taylor said ye'd been hurt. Never held with nimgimmers an' their fancy treatments."

"Donavan mutilated his back," Lizzy said, "and he says he means to do more. Lady Catherine will *not* stop him."

"Bloody bled me…first. Cursed…weak."

The coachman carefully helped him stand, withdrawing his arm from about the wounded shoulders; Mr Darcy swayed but remained standing.

"Donavan is inside now, and Stimple might return at any time," Lizzy warned. "We must get him away."

"Stimple's a guzzle-guts. His loyalty's only to the whiskey. Easy enough to be rid of him. James, help the master in, careful-like." He turned to the lads. "Quit your starin', and get the brougham hitched. Chop up now."

His words were mild, but she saw how quickly he was obeyed.

"You must get your things as well," Lizzy said to Georgiana. "Just what necessities you can gather quickly. You must flee with your brother, and at once."

"But what of you?"

"I will ask Mrs Taylor to help me reach the post. Or perhaps take my chances with my uncle. It matters not—what matters is that you *hurry.*"

But Georgiana obviously understood she had nowhere to go. "No, Lizzy. Besides, I know nothing of caring for—for a wounded man. You must come. You must help me! Say you will!"

Lizzy hardly had to think about it. "Of course I shall, if you wish it. Now hurry and get what you need!"

As the younger girl hastily returned to the house, Lizzy watched the carriage be readied with a speed she had never before seen at lackadaisical Longbourn. After her trunk was loaded, she moved to where Mr Frost and James stood at the open door of the carriage. Mr Darcy was now sitting quietly within, observing, still swaying slightly, his eyes drifting shut then widening as he plainly fought for consciousness.

"Where might we take you?" she asked. "Ought we to try for Pemberley after all?"

He shook his head, a firm no. His lips moved as he struggled to speak. "*Blast it*. No. B-bright. Bright. Bing."

Frost looked confused, but Lizzy thought she understood. "Do you mean Brighton? The Breakers, the house Mr Bingley let? But I do not know whether they are there yet."

He shrugged, and she understood. What did it matter? The house was likely open in readiness for the couple. If they said Mr and Mrs Bingley had directed them there, if she were bold enough and self-assured enough, perhaps it would work. Certainly, it might buy them time for Bingley and Jane to arrive. And if it did not...they would find a nearby inn and await the advent of the Bingleys.

"James, Mr Frost, I am certain you, also, must gather your belongings if you mean to take this journey with us to Brighton—or so I hope. Please go quickly to obtain what you will need. If it is possible that you are also able to gather Mr Darcy's necessities, it would be much appreciated."

"The master's things be packed, still, and his trunks here in the loft since Ramsgate," Frost replied. "I didn't trust any at the Lodge, nor that Stimple fellow none, what with the master's travel roll within it besides. Decided they may as well be kept for him when next he needed 'em."

Then amazingly—to her, at least—they swiftly obeyed her directives, disappearing, one into the house and the other to his rooms above the stables. She gingerly sat beside Mr Darcy, lending him the support of her body, just as she had on that night—was it only a few nights past? It seemed years ago. And when he took her hand within his larger one, she experienced a thrill that had nothing to do with fleeing Lady Catherine and her henchman, and everything to do with her own reckless affection.

Here was a man who, horribly wounded, nevertheless refused to wait abed for feckless fate and foolish family to make his choices for him. He would live as *he* chose, or he would die trying. How could she not admire him?

He dropped her hand when James returned, Mr Frost right behind him. But where was Georgiana? Surely she would not be dawdling over her belongings, deciding which dresses she ought to bring? But the mystery was quickly unfolded when Bertie, the footman on duty, appeared in the stables, leading a horse.

Mr Darcy leant out and, taking one look at the beast, swore—and not, she thought, unintentionally. When the boy was close enough, he, Frost, and James exchanged a few words. One of the stable lads took the horse. Bertie ran back to the house, and the two men approached.

"It be the colonel's mount, as ye see," Frost said.

Mr Darcy nodded.

"Miss Darcy told Bertie to tell ye to leave at once. She said she'd stall as long as she could and have her cousin take her to the earl to await your recovery once yer away. Ye must go, and quickly, else let the colonel decide what's to be done."

Lizzy saw the agonised expression on Mr Darcy's face but also his resignation. *Georgiana's cousin*...this must be the earl's son, the one who had returned to his regiment rather than abide by his father's plans to marry. Such actions did not seem as though he were in league with Matlock, but neither had he helped Mr Darcy.

"Can you trust him?" she asked.

He shrugged again, wincing at the effort. He was apparently unwilling to take the risk. "Must...press on."

He had not heard, of course, of the earl's threats to force a wedding; Georgiana now showed a willingness to sacrifice everything to save Mr Darcy. Mercilessly, Lizzy quelled her concern. The girl's best chance for freedom was the restoration of her brother's health. This colonel had evaded matrimony once, and it was to be hoped he could continue to do so.

She looked to James. "Did you tell Mrs Taylor where we are headed?"

He shook his head in the negative.

No one in the house would know their direction, then. She took a deep breath. "Well, gentlemen, let us be on our way, as Mr Darcy has ordered."

She had assumed James would seat himself beside Mr Darcy, and she moved to sit across from him, but he only put up the step and shut the door. She felt the tilt of the vehicle as he climbed to sit beside the coachman.

And then they were away.

⬥

The carriage had cushions of velvet, the most luxurious, spacious vehicle Lizzy had ever travelled within. Nevertheless, Mr Darcy could not be comfortable. He leant forward, probably trying to avoid putting pressure on his wounds. He had not bothered with cravat or waistcoat but had thrown a heavy long coat over shirt and trousers. The pressure of the dense wool upon his wounds must be agonising.

"Shall I help you remove this?" she asked, now heedless of propriety, reaching over to pluck lightly at the fabric.

He nodded once, curtly, and she carefully tugged it off; he made a weak effort to help, but his movements were jerky and uncoordinated. Lizzy gasped. The white linen of his shirt was smeared in bloody blotches, turning the fabric bright red.

And yet all she could do was close the shades so no one might glance within and see. It was still early, but as soon as they departed the quiet neighbourhood, they would be in the thick of London traffic.

As they plodded along, Mr Darcy held his head in his hands, elbows braced upon his knees, teetering unsteadily, clearly miserable and possibly holding onto consciousness or the contents of his belly by sheer will. How to make him comfortable—or as comfortable as possible—in a coach suddenly grown too small? He should have the whole seat…but could he lie down with his back so torn?

The coach hit a hole in the road, jouncing them both—but throwing the off-balance Mr Darcy against the wall of the carriage, and he let out a cry, quickly cut short, as if he stopped himself from screaming.

She *must* try to help. Moving off her seat, she wedged herself as close to the carriage wall as possible. "Lie on your side, Mr Darcy."

He turned to watch her, meeting her eyes. His were fathomless dark pools of agony.

She pushed gently on the front of his left shoulder. "Use me as a cushion," she instructed. "I will do my best to keep your back from touching."

For several moments, he only looked at her, and she realised how much he hated this weakness, this inability to be whole and healthy, being forced to accept her aid. *He might refuse,* she thought. He might choose to suffer instead.

"Must…keep on," he said again, more to himself than to her.

"Yes," she agreed.

He cautiously, awkwardly turned himself, his head on her lap, his gory back facing away from her. She carefully rested her hand upon a spot on his shoulder that showed no sign of blood, hanging on tightly whenever the road roughened in attempts to keep him still.

It was, perhaps, the most scandalous, improper mode of transport she had ever or would ever experience. But she could not care about anything except getting Mr Darcy safely to his destination. Nothing else mattered.

Georgiana walked slowly back to the house, her heart pounding. It had only been luck that she had spotted Colonel Fitzwilliam speaking to the footman from the window, that she had been able to avoid the colonel's notice whilst slipping out to give Bertie her own instructions. She waited at the door until she saw the Darcy carriage pulling out of the mews.

The sound of raised voices told her where the company waited; as she reached the parlour door, she found herself trembling and stopped for a moment to collect herself. *Will my brother reach safety? Has he been irreparably wounded? Will Richard be furious with me? Might Matlock attempt a forced marriage? Will his son agree to it?*

A final question occurred to her. *In my place, what would Lizzy do?*

Well, she would not snivel about what could not be changed, for one thing. Fitzwilliam was gone—to where, she knew not. It was a relief, as she considered it. She could not reveal what she did not know. Her relations had each had the opportunity to help him and, instead, had only treated him abominably, ignored him, or worsened his condition. Whatever happened now, at least he was nominally in control of his own fate.

Secondly, Lizzy might do any number of things she did not particularly wish, uncomplainingly even, but she would not simply roll over and marry someone without protest. Georgiana could decline, dither, and delay—possibly for years—and see what came of it all before accepting defeat. With these bracing thoughts, she straightened her spine and opened the door.

But no one noticed her standing in the open doorway; they were too occupied with their bickering. Richard was levelling questions at an angry Lady Catherine and an indignant-sounding Mr Donavan; he received no sensible answers. Only when the colonel threatened to tear the house apart looking for her and Fitzwilliam did she clear her throat.

Richard looked up at once. "Georgiana! There you are. Since entering the house, I have been accosted by accusations and ridiculous reproach. Where is your brother?"

She lifted her chin against her own nerves. "He is gone, and where, I know not. But he chose to depart of his own volition rather than continue to be tortured by our aunt and her physician."

Her words led to a torrent of protest and denunciation.

"Cease your blathering!"

It was a sign of the colonel's military command that Lady Catherine and Donavan did, indeed, clamp their mouths shut. He opened his mouth to speak, but at that moment, Mrs Taylor entered with an interruption.

"Excuse me, sir, but Mr Bingley is here upon a matter of some urgency, he says."

At her words, Richard's countenance lightened. "Bingley! Darcy has gone to him, I suppose. By Jove—"

But Mr Bingley, evidently, was impatient and poked his head into the parlour. "What ho, Colonel Fitzwilliam! It has been a long while, has it not?" Manoeuvring around the housekeeper, he moved purposefully into the room, trailed by a petite woman with golden curls.

All eyes turned to stare at the couple. Mr Bingley beamed back, but there was something about the tension in his posture that told Georgiana he was not quite so sanguine as he acted. The golden-haired woman could not even pretend nonchalance. Her blue eyes were large and distressed; she clutched a handkerchief, twisting it anxiously.

"I have recently married, as you can see. Mrs Bingley, darling, this is Colonel Fitzwilliam, Darcy's cousin. Best of good fellows. And Darcy's sister, Miss Darcy." He bowed. "A thousand pardons, all. Not wishing to interrupt, not for the world. Just here to collect my new sister, who has been, it seems, a guest at Darcy House since before our wedding. Might someone call Miss Bennet?"

16

A DETERMINED RESOLUTION

Georgiana bit her lip, wondering what to say to Mr and Mrs Bingley. She could not reveal, not before Lady Catherine, that Lizzy had gone in the carriage, unaccompanied, with an ill Fitzwilliam. Neither could she allow Lizzy's relations to believe her to be wandering the streets alone in London. But saying anything at all proved unnecessary—at least in the moment.

"Why, Miss Bennet has gone home—somewhere in Hertfordshire, I believe. Mr Frost, our coachman, put her on the post himself," Mrs Taylor interjected.

"The post!" Mrs Bingley cried with obvious alarm. "Alone?"

"Yes, ma'am." Mrs Taylor added with decided bravery, "Upon her ladyship's orders."

Though Lady Catherine squawked at this revelation, Georgiana knew it to be kinder than the truth. The colonel was furious.

"How could you? Without even sending a maid to accompany her?"

"One could not be spared," Lady Catherine replied with a condescending lift of her chin.

"My father will wish to know why you have subjected our guest to such treatment. Are you lost to every feeling of propriety and delicacy?"

"I do not answer to you *or* your father!" She spun on her heel, giving him her back.

"But, my lady, what about—" the doctor began.

"Shut it," she snapped and flounced from the room.

"Your services are obviously no longer required at Darcy House, Donavan," Colonel Fitzwilliam declared once she was gone. "You may take up your bill with the one who hired you."

The doctor looked as though he dearly wished to argue, but though her cousin's tone had been even, there was warning in it.

"I will collect my things. I do *not* take my leave of you," he sniffed, stalking out.

An awkward silence descended. Colonel Fitzwilliam scrubbed his hands through his hair. "Apologies are weak, Bingley. I only just arrived to find the house in an uproar. Please, let us sit. Perhaps Miss Darcy can apprise us of what has happened here."

Although Mr and Mrs Bingley sat, there was an obvious restlessness to the one and the large blue eyes of the other were tear filled.

"A report of the most alarming nature reached us from Miss Darcy," Mr Bingley said. "Louisa forwarded it along with an earlier letter from Miss Bennet, and we came at once upon receiving them."

Richard's brow furrowed, and he directed a glare at Georgiana. Instead of wilting, as she usually did at every sign of her family's disapproval, she only felt a deep measure of aggravation.

"You departed Ramsgate without leaving me the least idea how to reach you," she said, answering his look.

"I thought you with my parents," he grumbled.

"Yes, well, they thought it best to leave me in Ramsgate with my companion, where I met Miss Bennet quite by chance. Her visit to my neighbour there was concluding, and I persuaded her to come to me instead, as she is the dearest girl in the world. Then Lady Catherine came and took us here, with my brother, who she proceeded to torture with her awful doctor's vicious treatments. I was desperate to reach someone who might help, and Mr Bingley has always been a friend to him. I did direct Mrs Taylor to try to find you, too, although you made yourself so scarce."

Her cousin's glare did not recede. "I received her message after a bit of delay, and it was the *only* action required. No offence intended, Bingley, but this is a family matter."

Mr Bingley spoke with some annoyance. "No offence taken. However, you have, or *had*, a member of *my* family here, in a situation I could not like. Whilst I meant to see Darcy if I could, my first objective was to ensure my sister's wellbeing and bring her away with us."

Georgiana was disappointed in his response, even while understanding it. All his concern was for his new family, plainly wanting no part in protecting her brother from his relations. But Elizabeth had suspected he could not stand against the earl, whether he wished to or not.

At Mr Bingley's words, however, the colonel seemed to deflate, scrubbing his hands through his hair again and sighing. "Yes, yes, you are correct, of course. My father—" He hesitated, as if weighing his words. "It is a delicate time. Not all the earl's plans are, perhaps, in everyone's best interests. Specifically, he desires a match between Georgiana and myself to take place immediately, a match to which Miss Darcy and I are both opposed."

Not that he has asked me one way or the other, she thought. But she was most *definitely* opposed now.

"I rejoined my regiment to put some distance between us, giving Darcy time to recover, but the earl has been hounding me from afar. Thus, I recently accepted an assignment that takes me out of

England for a few months." He met her eyes, then Mr Bingley's. "I sail within the week."

The hours passed slowly, Lizzy's anxiety growing stronger with every mile. At the journey's beginning, and as worried as she was about Mr Darcy's painful wounds, the threat of pursuit by the colonel seemed the greatest danger. It could not be difficult for a high army officer to recruit men to ride after them, especially since it seemed to take forever to navigate through London traffic at their snail's pace, in a carriage which must be well known to Colonel Fitzwilliam.

But once beyond town, travelling as quickly as possible, only stopping as needed for the horses, the journey still seemed far too slow. Mr Darcy worsened as the day dragged, ever more feverish, ever less aware…and finally, out of his head. After a particularly vicious bump nearly threw him off the seat, which required her to clutch against his poor back, he lashed out a glancing blow to Lizzy's jaw that nevertheless hurt dreadfully. When Frost and James discovered what had happened at the next stop, James joined them within, attempting to hang onto and quiet Mr Darcy by turns while she watched his sufferings from the facing seat.

Finally, he did calm, but her dread only increased. He no longer fought at all, no matter how the carriage ride bumped and bruised him, lying still…as still as death.

Mr Frost had no trouble gaining the direction of The Breakers—though it was dark by the time they reached Brighton. It was described to him as a white stone house, not at all large, but surrounded by unexpectedly lush gardens in dense beds and over-looking a private beach from slabs of chalk-white cliff, perhaps three miles beyond the town proper. While the establishment was small, it likely took a regiment of gardeners to maintain—a pearl of great price, despite its size.

The perfect setting for a new bride, Lizzy thought, rehearsing in her mind what she would say. Her explanations and even the tone of voice in which she would say them, must hit the right note—not imitating Lady Catherine, but too authoritative to dismiss.

To her surprise, however, the housekeeper—who introduced herself as Mrs Davis—hurried out nearly the moment the carriage drew up before the house, greeting them warmly. Before Lizzy could interrupt her effusions to explain the situation, the housekeeper added, "We were not sure, from your letter, whether you would come this week or next, Mrs Bingley. We have been anticipating your arrival."

In that moment, Lizzy decided she would not correct the woman. The most important object was to obtain good care for Mr Darcy—and she felt the Bingleys would surely forgive her for the pretence. But neither did her prevarications end with the adoption of a surname.

"Thank you, Mrs Davis," Lizzy said. "Unfortunately, my husband was severely injured in an accident whilst we travelled through London."

She saw the housekeeper's enthusiasm diminish as she peered into the dark interior of the carriage. "Shall I call for a doctor, ma'am?"

Should she? Certainly, not all doctors were the awful Mr Donavan, but one more like him would be the certain finish of Mr Darcy.

Lizzy sighed. "Truth to tell, Mrs Davis, the London doctor's so-called cures have put him into an alarming condition. I fear he cannot withstand any more 'treatments'."

"Londoners. Hmph." The housekeeper snorted. "Our household is not a large one, however, madam. Additional servants should be hired if we're to be caring for an invalid."

"We can discuss our needs in the morning. I am...becoming accustomed to nursing him. Our men know just how to move him to cause the least distress. James, Mr Frost, please bring Mr Bingley in. Mrs Davis will show us the way."

An astute Mr Frost urged a puzzled James forward, and the two carried Mr Darcy into the house, laying him upon a comfortable bed in a large room, well-lit, with a nice fire burning.

Mrs Davis turned towards an adjoining door. "It's a shame, it is, you being new-married and him so ill. Your room is through here, but I suppose you'll be staying with your man."

"I suppose I will," Lizzy replied faintly, just having realised what other assumptions her falsehood implied. "James, I will need your assistance with, um, undressing Mr Bingley."

She caught a smirk on the older woman's face at her hesitation. Well, Lizzy had tasks enough to busy the woman and followed her from the room, while James attended to Mr Darcy. "Mrs Davis, I assume you have honey in the house?"

"Yes, mistress."

"I shall need you to boil a half-pound of honey with two quarts of the purest water you can obtain. Boil it until it is thoroughly scummed, then bring me the reduction. It is a remedy I wish to apply before it grows much later. Also, marrow broth if you have any, barley water if you do not." She glanced worriedly back at the closed door of the bed chamber. "And hot water, salt, scissors, clean muslin, and towelling, if you please."

While these requests elicited an expression of slight annoyance, Mrs Davis did not protest, especially when Lizzy explained that they had eaten on the road—which they had, if only bread and cheese—and would only require such cold collation as was easily available.

Returning to Mr Darcy, she dismissed James with all the borrowed authority of a pretend wife. Her decision had been made. Whilst she had no idea what sort of attack had robbed Mr Darcy of his speech in the first place, and though such an illness was far beyond her ability to mend, he had, she believed, been well on the road to recovery before the interference of a quack. She had treated fevers, burns, and blisters, in *much* lesser degrees, but many times. She told herself that these were the ailments from which Mr Darcy now suffered, and she was likely as qualified as any to treat them.

Gathering her courage, she carefully peeled back the blankets covering him. James had not dressed him in a nightshirt, and it was obvious why. His shirt was stuck to his back with a glue of dried blood. At the visible signs of his suffering, she felt a tightness in her bosom, a lump in her throat. Tears would not help him, but the unfairness of it grieved her.

Mrs Davis returned, finally, with the requested items, grimacing at the prone figure on the bed, recoiling at the sight of his injuries. It was obvious she wanted nothing to do with either of them. "Is there anything else needed, ma'am?"

Yes! I need help, the help of true physicians, people of wisdom and experience! I need Mrs Hill with her powders and Cook with her soups! I need Kitty to sit with me, Jane to share the burden of worry! I need to be anywhere else in the world! He needs too much from too few.

But she would find no succour here, not from the rented servants of a rented house, and the comforts of Longbourn were long gone. There was only young James and old Mr Frost...and herself. Thus, she reluctantly spoke the words of dismissal the servant wished to hear.

"Nothing more, Mrs Davis."

Then they were alone. Steeling herself, she cut away broad swaths of the shirt until only the cloth plastered to his back and arms remained. Carefully, she wet the wounds with warm water, patting gently, picking at the blood-saturated cloth. Once or twice, he let out a groan when a piece of cloth was particularly stubborn—and Lizzy both cringed at this evidence of pain and was callously thankful for the sign that he lived. Mixing a bit of salt in with the last of the water, she gently cleansed his bared skin. When finished with the process, she straightened, stretching against the cramp of maintaining one position too long.

His back lay naked before her, the violation of his flesh in stark contrast to the strength and beauty of those portions of his form uninjured. Moving away, she opened the windows to the sea breezes, breathing deeply, trying to settle the nauseating feelings at so closely witnessing such brutality. After a few fortifying breaths, she returned to Mr Darcy.

The cooled honey mixture she applied to strips of muslin and gently laid across each wound; a few were minor enough that she decided the open air would do better for them. At least this procedure caused no pain, but neither did he stir again; his skin was hot.

By the time she finished, and had tried and mostly failed at giving him some nourishment, she was so exhausted she could hardly see straight. Briefly, she contemplated trying to sleep in the chair by his bedside, but the enticements of mattresses and pillow were too alluring. Moving to the opposite side of the bed, she placed a pillow at its foot—as far from her patient as possible but close enough to hear him if he cried out. She fell fast asleep almost instantly.

"Ma'am? I'm sorry to wake ye, but…"

Lizzy opened her eyes, momentarily disoriented, looking around at the strange room and strange maid, before remembering where she was…and with whom. Morning light shone through the opened window. She sat up abruptly.

"Mrs Davis asked me if you'd be wishin' fer a tray? And fer yer husband?"

"Oh, yes…for me, that is. And let us try more of the marrow broth," Lizzy replied, heaving herself out of bed and padding around to the other side. Mr Darcy appeared not to have moved, and she touched his heated skin to ensure he still breathed, conscious of the girl's curious eyes. The open wounds upon his back appeared red and angry still.

"I usually do fer the ladies who stay here if they doesn't bring their own maids," the girl continued. "I'd be happy to do for you." Her brow furrowed, and her voice lowered. "I've got me a tincture that could help with yer hair colour. Make it not so...marked."

Lizzy closed her eyes briefly against the maid's impertinence. "No thank you to the colouring, but yes, I will require assistance otherwise. Your name?"

"Susan, ma'am. He looks about ready for old Mr Grim, don't he?"

A flash of anger coursed through Lizzy at the unfeeling remark. "You may bring the tray, now, Susan, with more broth, and you may help me dress later. That will be all."

Something in her tone must have warned the girl she had crossed a line. "Yes, ma'am. Beg pardon, ma'am."

Once the maid departed, Lizzy turned back to Mr Darcy. The girl's observations, however unwelcome, were not incorrect—he was unmoving and pale against the white sheets. Carefully, she removed one of the dressings to peek at a gash treated with honey. It appeared slightly less red and raw. Or was she only imagining a result she yearned for?

Foolishly, she had failed to ask for more hot water and rags. Also, he must be cooled down, and a better means of giving him her fever tea determined. She would rather not hire any new servants to help if it could be avoided—for all she knew, Mr Darcy was well known in the area. Would Mr Frost be willing to help her with some of the more arduous tasks of nursing? For she must henceforth ask James to watch him at night—she had been useless to her patient once she'd fallen asleep and had no idea of the time now.

A fine wife you are, Elizabeth Bingley!

But she was all he had. And she could do only one thing, as Mr Darcy had gritted out at the beginning of their journey: *Press on.*

ONE GOOD SONNET

As the week passed, she grew accustomed to being thought of as the sick man's wife and managing the small establishment; even James and Mr Frost seemed to almost believe it, deferring to her as if she were—and both serving Mr Darcy with unflinching devotion.

"If I was to go through the world, I could not meet with a better man," Frost said to her once, after she thanked him yet again for his help. "But I have always observed that they who are good-natured when children are good-natured when they grow up. He was always the most even-tempered, kindest lad in the world. All who've known him as long as I would count it a privilege to help him in his troubles now." His voice lowered. "'Tis for the best that we lie low with him, missus, and have no truck with earls."

The household, she had learnt to run from her mother, of course. Other lessons, however, came only by hard experience. She grew to understand that there were no rules of gender and propriety on the battlefield of illness. Perhaps a small part of her had believed, at the onset of this journey, that she might heroically be Mr Darcy's saviour, envisioning his thanks and deep gratitude for her accomplishments of rescue and restoration. All such pride was swallowed up in the beauty and ugliness of real care. His body's demands dictated action. When weakened, it still must be fed. If it vomited the broth she'd managed to get down it, it must be bathed then fed again. When overheated, it must be cooled. When insensible or distressed, it must be calmed, coddled, or commanded. He was not a man, although his body was so different from her own, nor an object of romance—but he *was* a person, whose daunting needs must somehow be met.

Mr Frost had suggested a method of nourishment similar to one used in the stables for ill horses, involving towelling twisted and soaked in water or broth and placed upon his tongue. Instinctively, he usually sucked upon it, though at his worst, he spat it out and fought against its intrusion into his mouth.

She spoke to him constantly, and he sometimes obeyed her wishes, often enough that she was hopeful he'd somehow heard.

"Come now, my love, you must lie still and not disturb your dressings. You know your sister requires you to be well and healthy." Although not quite conscious, he, at times, allowed himself to be soothed. It gave her hope during the times he would not, when he blindly struck out as she changed his bandages and she was forced to have James hold him. She would not bind him, no matter that, occasionally, he hurt her when she did not move away swiftly enough. Never again would he be bound, if she had aught to say about it.

Thus, one day bled into another, with Lizzy scarcely aware of the passage of time. Sometimes she thought he worsened—insensible, feverish, crying out. Just when she decided she must find a real physician, he would quiet and cool. James, of course, watched him nightly while she slept. But she could never sleep for long; once her initial exhaustion was satisfied, she found herself again at his side.

Naturally, she wondered where Jane and Bingley were and why they had not come and if the earl sought his nephew and whether Georgiana was well. All these worries lived at the back of her mind. But for the most part, seeing that Mr Darcy lived through one more day was all the consolation she required and all the anxiety she could endure.

Darcy regained awareness to the sound of mild cursing. It was not the voices from his nightmarish past, praise heaven, nor any of his relations. His vision gradually came into focus. A comely girl with ginger curls peeking from a linen cap stood by his bedside—some thick viscous substance streaming down the front of her apron.

"Devil take it, Mr Da—I mean, Mr Bingley—I am attempting to help you!" she muttered.

In his disoriented state, he could not offer up his own name, much less hers. *Bingley? I am Bingley?* But the pretty girl before him, he knew. Even before his beleaguered brain identified her, instinctively, he associated her with safety. Affection. Peace. *Not a gaoler.*

In the moment, however, his thirst overrode all other considerations; he shut his eyes, trying to fix on the correct words. "*What the flaxwench.* No!" He closed his eyes, tried again. "Wa-wa-ter."

"Sir?"

He opened his eyes.

"Oh, it is—why, you are awake! You cannot know how glad I am to see you thus!"

Her voice grew into a rapidly flowing mishmash of syllables; he could not follow her words. He reached out, snagged her sleeve. The syllables stopped abruptly.

"*Frig*-no, wa-ter," he said.

"No water," she repeated, carefully echoing his own tangled speech.

"No!" he shouted, more loudly in volume than he had meant, his inherent frustration with his muddled tongue escaping his control.

And she threw up her hands as if defending against a blow.

What? Why would she...she could not think he would ever—ever—hurt her, or any female. Could she?

But how had she come to be covered in...in whatever it was? Had he...no, surely not. He was *not* the animal his captors believed.

Slowly, she lowered her hands, looking at him warily.

He tried harder to make his blasted mouth work. "Wa-ter," he managed.

"Oh! You wish a drink. Of course." She went to a nearby pitcher, poured a cup.

He knew he must move, get himself up, and made a futile attempt to roll over. Noticing, she hurried back to his side. "No, no, you must be careful. Your back, sir...it is very painful."

But the very act of moving released fiery, smarting waves, freeing his memories within the torrent of pain. Donavan and his torture instruments. Escape. Georgiana, James, Frost, and Elizabeth breaking him free. *Lizzy. Lizzy.* She was still here; she had not left him.

They must have gotten him away, although he could not recall the journey. But she was talking again.

"Frost devised...means" she was saying, her voice fading in and out of comprehension, "which...easier...awake." She took a piece of cloth from a large stack of them on the bedside table, dipping into the cup. "Open." She tapped his chin.

Reluctantly, frowning, he opened his mouth.

She inserted the wet cloth into it, waiting. Then it was her turn to frown. "When...ill...unconscious, somehow knew...suck, drawing...moisture out...it."

Had he? Was he reduced to stable yard meals now? It was cool and wet upon his parched tongue, but dash it, he was a man, not a horse.

However weak, he was nevertheless determined to sit up. She clucked and sputtered over him but helped too—had she not, he would have toppled right out of bed and onto his face. When at last he managed it, he had to remain very, very still while the room tilted and whirled about him. Finally, however, he steadied, extending his hand for the cup. It took her a moment to realise what he wanted, but she gave it into his trembling hands at last.

He swallowed, the fresh, pure liquid trickling down his throat in a moment so beautiful he nearly cried.

His back was sore, unquestionably. But compared to the screaming agony of pain he'd endured in London, it was...bearable. As he sat quietly, elbows braced upon his knees, a salt-scented breeze entered through an open window. Were they in Brighton, at the house Bingley had leased? How long had he been insensible? Where was Bingley?

"Liz-zy." Oddly enough, it seemed he could manage her name every time he tried. "*What the devil*...no...what hap-pened?"

To his surprise, she knelt at his feet, looking up at him so she could see his face. Her eyes were wide, a fathomless green, thick-lashed. Beautiful eyes, intelligent eyes, darkened circles beneath, testifying to her fatigue. Her flaming hair was hidden beneath ugly linen instead of flowing over her shoulders as he had once dreamt of seeing it. A fading bruise faintly yellowed upon her jaw. He reached to touch it; she flinched back, just a little.

And he knew. *He* had done this to her. *No, no, no!* Not acceptable, not had she been the lowest creature in England. But to her...? He ought to be shot. Carefully, he traced its outline up the smooth skin of her jaw while she simply looked up at him, a little puzzled, a little...bemused.

"I...*harpy*—No! Hurt." He closed his eyes. "Sor...sorry." As apologies went, it was woefully inadequate.

"Must forget all," she said dismissively. "Cousin...Fitzwilliam arrived...Darcy House...escaped to Brighton...ten days ago, remember?"

He gave a short nod of agreement; the action caused discomfort, and he must have winced, for she talked of his wounds.

"I have tried...keep lesions clean...treating...honey. Seems helped. Old...remedy...burns. Drawn away...poisons from...wounds. Or something." Her cheeks pinkened with a pretty blush, a few freckles adding character and kindness on otherwise pale golden skin.

Suddenly, he realised that he sat here shirtless, clothed only in breeches. This young maiden had plainly been caring for him, caring for him intimately. But she was talking again, and it was all he could do to follow her words.

Lady Catherine had ejected her from Darcy House for attempting to stop Mr Donavan, and Lizzy had to pause in her narrative until he could restrain vocabulary that, for once, expressed his feelings perfectly. In fact, it was necessary, over the next hour, for her to stop her explanations a number of times, and not simply because she spoke too quickly.

Lord Matlock, it seemed, planned to marry Georgiana off to Fitzwilliam!

He remembered more clearly now the distress of leaving Georgiana behind, but he had believed, in the moment, that the colonel would *always* protect his sister. Now, too much of his faith and trust in his family had been shattered; could he trust him still? It did explain, however, why Fitzwilliam had so quickly abandoned Darcy in Ramsgate—believing, perhaps, that avoiding his father was the best thing he *could* do to protect her.

Meanwhile, had Lady Matlock proceeded with her plans to marry him off to Caroline Bingley? Would her ladyship begin gossip and rumour about the match, enough to make the marriage expected? His aunt was ruthless enough to do it. He had most recently stayed with the Bingleys, had several times danced with her, had never definitively rejected her. His thoughts raced.

Then Elizabeth began to explain the misunderstanding she had taken advantage of to permit their stay here. Together. *Mr and Mrs*

Bingley. The real newly wedded couple had never appeared for some unknown reason.

She finally ceased her explanations, looking up at him expectantly. As if he somehow held the answers, could take charge of the tangle. Jupiter, he could barely even string a simple sentence correctly, much less fathom how to fix all that was wrong. She appeared very weary; even so, she was so pretty, he nearly ached with it. And she was posing as his wife.

"Liz-zy," he said. "Devil take it."

Her smile started in her eyes long before it reached her mouth. Life made more sense when he looked into them; there was laughter there, and hope, not to mention strength and caring.

He had so many difficulties—problem upon problem stacked in limitless piles around him. Against all that, there were her beautiful eyes, her priceless smile. He had been at death's threshold, he knew. He had felt it, the longing to give way, to let go, to leave the pain and ugliness behind. But always, always, at his moments of greatest weakness had been her voice calling him back. She had cared for him with little assistance, directing his journey earthbound, although he must have hurt her more than once in his maddened, feverish state.

He would love Elizabeth, he knew, until the day of his death— which, thanks to her, was likely years in the future. It was an ironic stab to his heart—realising he would never be able to reveal to her that plain and simple truth.

❦

Lizzy was beginning to feel great hopefulness. Since Mr Darcy's— no, *Bingley's*—fever-free awakening of one short week past, he was recovering in many ways. His speech was unreliable, and his handwriting worse still, but he grew stronger daily. The hollows in his cheeks were beginning to fill as he put on weight, and a daily stroll down to the beach had provided him healthy colour. Now that Mr

Darcy was out of danger, James had taken over the dressing of his bandages and acting as valet. But Mr Darcy dined with her at meal-times—which she looked forward to more than was perfectly reasonable, telling herself it was a natural consequence of her weeks of care and attention. She ruthlessly quelled her attraction in every way she could, but it was not easy. In certain ways, he relied upon her, especially in assistance with his correspondence. His estate, financial, and business concerns were vast, she discovered, and although he apparently trusted the men in charge of those affairs, he wanted them to be assured of his soundness of mind as quickly as possible.

"Liz-zy?" he would ask, holding out pen and parchment.

They would sit together in The Breakers' small book room, and she would proceed to ask questions and interpret his answers—in the beginning, especially, a tedious process.

"To whom shall I address this letter?"

"*Strumpet...*no...Stewart."

"A Mr Stewart?"

He shook his head, negative.

"Steward? Your steward?"

A nod.

"*Pribbling puttock.* No. *Puny priggles.* No! Derby. Pen."

"Derby...Oh. Pen a letter to Derbyshire?"

"Yes. No."

Finally, she had 'Pemberley' in 'Derbyshire' and understood he wished her to explain his circumstances to the steward there as well as provide instruction on a number of estate issues. The process of communication was wearisome and frustrating to him, certainly, but she noted that he never lost his temper with her inability to understand. All his vexation was self-directed.

"Are you worried?" she asked him once, after finishing the dictation to another of his men of business—he seemed to have numerous such men employed. "Do you fear that your finances will suffer due to your absence from town and Pemberley?"

It was a bold question, born of the subjects just dictated, and she only realised it to be none of her concern after the voicing of it. But he did not appear to notice.

He shook his head in the negative. "*Fiend seize it*. No. Many." He gestured expansively. "Good men."

"You have several different men managing your interests. Is that not dangerous? You are at the centre of all your business concerns, yet if you are unable to lead, who else will be able to sort out the intricacy of it? Might the pieces fail to unite, risking the collapse of all?"

He shrugged then smiled. "Fall…slower."

The letters exhausted him, and she knew he chafed at his slow pace. He was apparently accustomed to doing the work of many men—certainly her father had not even a particle of his varied affairs. Tradespeople, solicitors, importers, exporters, and manufacturers formed a complex web of associations and investments. The earl could not touch most of it—would not have the slightest idea *how* to do it. Matlock would likely fix his attention on Pemberley and let the rest go to the devil, if it were up to him. And Pemberley, Mr Darcy explained, while the jewel of his holdings, was responsible for only a third of his profits—naming sums that she wondered at. Ten thousand a year was the least of it.

A lifetime spent with an indolent father who squandered—she did not think it too harsh a word—his fortune and failed to plan for the eventuality of his death for *any* of his family, never mind his least-favourite daughter, gave her a special appreciation for the complexities of the management of his affairs. As if she *needed* another reason to admire him.

The few non-Darcy servants took their orders from Lizzy and left him carefully alone. She could only imagine how he might be treated if he were to grunt nonsense and curse at them. Still, one had only to see how much improvement Mr Darcy had made in a single week to know that there was ample reason for optimism.

One niggling worry, however, only grew: Where were the Bingleys?

After dinner each evening, they did not separate but removed to a favourite parlour. Darcy did not talk, staring into the flames, exhausted from his day's activities. He liked that Elizabeth felt no need to fill the space with words but simply let him be. He wondered what she thought of him, whether she considered him merely a pathetic invalid under her care. He had loved her before, as a daughter of Longbourn; now, a confluence of gratitude and appreciation heightened his early admiration. She was nearly perfect in his eyes, and sonnets memorised as a youth bloomed again within his mind.

He must have watched her too intently, for she looked up from her embroidery to meet his gaze.

"Is anything the matter, sir? Is there a draught?"

Shaking his head, he forced himself to speak. "Thinking...book." It was not exactly what he meant to say but close enough.

She cocked her head. "Is your reading improving? Shall I fetch one for you?"

Actually, he had tried to read, again, earlier that day, but the words swam on the page, as they did when he attempted writing. He opened his mouth to say—or attempt to say—that he was simply tired but instead uttered, "'Lo, thus, by day my limbs, by night my mind, for thee, for myself, no quiet find.'"

Her eyes widened, dawning excitement on her brow. "Shakespeare? Perfectly said! I cannot believe my ears! Can you remember the rest? Can you try?"

Just as surprised as she, he tried again for more. *"Fiddlesticks,"* he blurted then closed his eyes in frustration.

"No, I am sure you can do it," Lizzy cried, leaning forward in her seat. "Say it with me: 'Weary with toil, I haste me to my bed, the dear repose for limbs with travel tired...'"

"'But then begins a journey in my head to work my mind, when body's work's expired,'" he quoted.

Lizzy clapped, bouncing a little on her seat. "Very good! Do you know this? 'I love to hear her speak, yet well I know, that music hath a far more pleasing sound. I grant I—'"

"'Never saw a goddess go, my mistress when she walks, treads on the ground,'" he finished.

"I always loved that one," Lizzy said, plainly elated by his newly discovered talent. "This is marvellous! You see, your words are all there, within your mind! It will just take time to set them free."

He gave her a look. *"Pogy*...no...poetry-spouting...madman."

She laughed, the sound of it shivering down his spine. "It could be very useful! A well-placed sonnet or two at just the right time, and the ladies will leap from admiration to love within a moment. 'My love is like a red, red rose...'" she began slyly.

He refused to take the bait but could not help smiling at her impertinence. "You...know Shakes-per...from memory? Governess...*bloody* strict?"

"Oh, we never had a governess."

"No?" He was much taken aback by this. *"Chick-a-biddy*...neglected," he managed.

"The Bennet henhouse." She laughed but then grew thoughtful. "I suppose...there was plenty of 'feed' scattered about, for my sisters, at least—had they wished to learn, they never lacked the means. They were always encouraged to read and had all the masters that were necessary. Or if they chose to be idle, they certainly might."

"Not you? Enc...encour..."

"Was I encouraged? Not exactly."

He frowned, and a situation he had foolishly failed to even consider overtook his thoughts. "Ben...Bennet par-ents...s-search for you? Why not home, Liz-zy?"

She sighed, and for several minutes, she stayed silent, biting her lip and obviously fretting. Finally, as if reaching a conclusion, she asked him to wait. She was gone for a bit, returning with an old leatherbound copy of *The Pilgrim's Progress*. She showed him its inscription then told him an incredible story of its history and how she had obtained it.

"My father...my father was unconvinced of—of the legitimacy of my birth."

He could only gape. There had never been a word of gossip uttered amongst her Meryton neighbours suggesting this, and certainly Caroline Bingley *would* have uttered it, had there been.

"He did not like me to—to share in the privileges of my sisters; however, he could not do much without alerting the neighbours to my mother's supposed shame. My mother was usually good to me. For the most part, I did not go without. But he did not encourage my learning, or much of anything in me, I suppose." She shrugged and grinned, as if this revelation of the unfairness of her entire life meant little. "In trying to make my own place, however, I only sought more diligently for every advantage. It has not been easy, but since when are the best goals easily achieved? We none of us have wealth enough to make a good match, and I have even less. I truly never thought to marry, and even my sisters must rely upon character and providence. Jane was fortunate indeed."

"No...*son of a*...no...settlement? Noth-ing?"

Her smile disappeared. "There is a little from my mother, but I have been informed it will not come to me—just this book, as I told you. I am no longer welcome at Longbourn and am hoping to make my home with Jane in the future. Mr Bingley foreswore

Jane's portion to leave a bit more for Mary, Kitty, and Lydia. He is the best of men."

Darcy shook his head. How many times had he told Bingley that it was just as easy to fall in love with an heiress as a cookmaid? And now *he* had fallen in love with a girl who had less than nothing. The fates must be laughing uproariously.

Despite his confident words to Lizzy earlier, his own estate *was* in a precarious position, with so many of his business interests neglected for weeks, not to mention his family believing him insane and doing all they could to destroy him. To take an impoverished bride of uncertain birth would be more proof to them of his weakness. It was imprudent, at best—and dangerous at worst—to give way to this love burning in his heart. Even if she could recite Shakespeare and had, quite probably, saved his life. Not even then.

18

FOR THE HAPPINESS OF BOTH

T he mysterious nonappearance of Mr and Mrs Bingley had become their major topic of discussion. Lizzy wished to write to Mrs Hurst at Netherfield, and at once, but Mr Darcy was understandably reluctant.

"Caro...read," he contended.

"Surely not," Lizzy disagreed, fearing how anxious Jane would be; if Mr Bingley had received the letter from Georgiana and herself via Mrs Hurst, it would place her whereabouts with the Darcys. At the very least, Jane would wonder why no letter had arrived after the one from Ramsgate, begging for sanctuary. But none of it explained why the Bingleys had failed to arrive in Brighton, and Lizzy was equally anxious, hoping and praying that Jane was well.

Still, she understood Mr Darcy's concerns; Caroline Bingley *might* be in the pocket of Lady Matlock. If she was, and Louisa Hurst shared the information, she *might* inform the earl. Even if Lizzy did not mention Mr Darcy's presence, he insisted it to be unsafe. Although Mr Frost claimed he could vouch for the silence of the stable boys, and James for Bertie's, Colonel Fitzwilliam could be a ferocious interrogator. He *might* have discovered Lizzy's departure with the Darcy carriage, and for all either of them knew, the earl was combing hill and dale for his missing nephew. Mr Darcy wished to gain as much strength as possible before that discovery. They finally compromised;

he gave one of his trusted men of business instructions to reveal to them that he had provided her with a safe, if hidden, place to reside until his full recovery. They might be appalled, but they both agreed that the Bingleys would keep the secret.

But the letter no sooner was sent than a letter arrived, and although providing some news, it also increased her puzzlement. Mrs Davis brought it from the nearest receiving office, looked at it curiously, and handed it over to Lizzy. 'The Breakers' and 'Brighton' were both legible on the front, but the rest was an indecipherable scribble. She took it to Mr Darcy at once in the book-room. He glanced at it and laughed.

"Can you read the name? Do you know to whom this is directed?"

"Never...*rutting* read...at my best. *Clay-brained* Bing. Seal is his. Know...anywhere."

"Mr Bingley? This is from him? You are certain?"

He nodded, and she studied it carefully.

"Do you know, I think he meant this to go to Mrs Davis—he does not use her name, but I believe he writes 'To Caretaker or House-keeper.' Oh, I am dearly tempted to read it."

He glanced at her then held out his hand for it. She handed it over, but he only broke the seal, unfolded it, and handed it back.

"You," he said. "Care-take."

She hesitated, but there was no question that she was running the establishment, so to speak. Seating herself near a window for the best light, she scrutinised the document. It was not lengthy, but it was so full of blots and scored words, it took her some time to make it out.

"Mr and Mrs Bingley have been unavoidably delayed by business, he says, and will be unable to occupy the house. He instructs her to close it and not to expect him at all! What could have happened?"

"*Nutting*...n-nothing else?"

She shook her head. "Nothing. Do you think he will have sent a similar letter to the house agent? Will the house be leased to someone else?"

Mr Darcy shrugged. "Bound for...term. Michaelmas earliest."

"Michaelmas? That is but a few weeks away!"

He looked surprised, a little. And a bit sad. Time had no meaning, she supposed, when one was ill or recovering. The desk before him was covered in blotched, ruined attempts at writing; in contrast, she recalled the strong, even penmanship she had witnessed in his letters from Netherfield Park.

"Shall I take a letter for you?" she suggested, only hoping to distract him, and was pleased by his quick agreement.

In his trunk had been a stack of letters, which he now handed across to her—obviously wanting her to search for the desired correspondents from amongst them.

"*Rutting*...no...writing...my men of biz."

She read the names aloud as she thumbed through them: "George Saxelby, Edward Gardiner—" she halted, peering at the letter more closely. "I have an uncle by this name, evidently—I have never met him. But your man has a different address—mine resides in Cheapside." She shrugged and continued reading. "William Grayhurst, Henry Nelson."

"Gard," he said, "Sax."

She nodded, setting aside the requested correspondents and putting pen to parchment.

"George Saxelby, next to the Dove & Olive Branch, in the Cloisters, near West Smithfield, London," she recited, reading the direction aloud in case he had anything to add to or change about it. "My father has always been contemptuous of those who, like my uncle —apparently—'sully their hands' with commerce, accepting payment for their labours. I admit I do not quite understand his hostility."

He looked over at her with that little half smile she loved, the one revealing his dimple. It was one of the things she liked most about him, that he seemed pleased by her questions rather than annoyed, never chiding her for her curiosity in topics none of her concern. Also, even though his muddled speech embarrassed him, he never hesitated to offer answers and did so once again now, explaining how youths were leaving farms in favour of factories, how England's manufacturing capabilities were transforming the very fabric of society.

"Future...England...*fawning   footlicker*...no...not   agri-culture. Must...change with country," he concluded.

She considered this. "If all you say is correct, it hardly matters that my father's property is entailed away from us—for it could not support us all indefinitely regardless."

He shrugged. "My...groats...in *motley* manufacturing. Trade... inventions...promoting *bloody* efficiencies. For...grandchildren. Would that *frigging* farms...survive. Hope. Plan if...not."

She sighed. "My future seems limited by the options I can see. I like how you are trying to imagine a different one, with different rules, and are planning all these means of coping." Then she smiled. "However, if you are tutoring Bingley, and he and Jane agree to take me in, I suppose I need not waste time in worry. My future will be secure enough."

He looked at her a little oddly then—if she had to describe his expression, she might have called it *wistful*—but undoubtedly, she was being fanciful. He began dictating again, and the moment passed.

Lizzy wakened to the sound of what she first thought was a fog bell, a common sound, especially when she left her window open at night. Sleepily, she listened for it again but heard nothing except the pitch of the waves hitting shore. It nearly lured her back to sleep until another noise disturbed the quiet night.

It sounded like a growl, or moan, coming from Mr Darcy's room— loud enough for her to hear through the door kept shut between their chambers. Shut but not locked.

Should she go to him? Had his fever returned? Pushing the covers back, she rose and went to the connecting door. She stood there, listening, motionless, for several moments, the floor cold beneath her bare toes. Then she heard it again—pain, terror, or some combination of both. She opened it.

Despite the parted drapes and pale moonlight, it was nearly dark within, the fire all but a few embers. But of course, she knew her way, going at once to the man in the bed, reaching to check his forehead for fever. He twisted away from her touch, but his skin was cool.

"Mr Darcy," she called softly, knowing a false name would never reach into his dreams.

His only response was another groan that twisted her heart, his mouth working with screams he could not voice within the prison of his terror.

"Mr Darcy," she called a bit more loudly, touching his shoulder, shaking it gently. "Mr Darcy!"

His eyes fluttered open, his neck twisting back and forth, plainly disoriented.

"Mr Darcy?" She made her voice calm, as she had when he'd been feverish. "Are you well?"

She felt his gaze fix upon her.

"You were having a bad dream."

He nodded. His mouth worked. "Sor."

"Sorry? You have nothing to be sorry for. It would be unusual to have no lingering effects from such traumas as you have so recently experienced. I hope your rest will be more peaceful now. Goodnight." She took a step away.

"Way...wait." He sat up, the white of his nightshirt in gleaming contrast to the room's dimness. It was open at his chest, revealing an expanse of skin, the sight a flare of warning and a reminder.

"I should go."

"*Slattern...sleep now?*"

Would she? It was doubtful. She only shrugged, but he caught the motion. He stood, grabbing his banyan from the bedpost and pulling it on before going to the fireplace and lighting a candle. Along with a neat stack of small logs, she now noticed a few pieces of driftwood in a leather basket nearby. Unexpectedly, he built up a neat little fire from within the dying embers, as if he commonly tended his own fireplace, and when the flames were steady, put in a single piece of driftwood. It added a violet flame to the yellow and red, entrancing her. He stood, dusting off his hands, and pulled the settee a few inches closer to the fire's warmth, making a motion for her to sit.

Hesitantly, she did, folding up her knees and wrapping her arms around them, resting her chin upon them, and staring at that single purple flame. The settee was not large, and when he sat beside her, the heat from his body created another source of warmth at her side. The breezes from the open window chilled in stark contrast. They sat like that for some minutes, not talking. But then he reached out and touched her toes, where they peeped out from beneath her nightgown.

"Cold." He reached out with one arm, pulling her securely into his side.

She looked up at him, brow raised. "I notice you do not offer to fetch me a blanket."

He smiled that little half smile.

She knew it was wrong. She knew that it was dangerous. She was not stupid. Or perhaps she was, because she snuggled into the shelter of his body, feeling safe and warm and peaceful for the first time since her mother had declared she must leave her girlhood home.

***

I am a stupid, stupid man, he thought, and not merely because of his ridiculous vocabulary. Had he persuaded her that his first proposal was a serious one, he would be married to her now, not battling base urges and thrilling desire. The feel of her shivering beside him had been too intense to ignore, the need to hold her a near compulsion. And now, with her body half-sprawled across his lap, his embrace became an exquisite torture. Her hair, her unbound hair, smelled of lavender and spice, and he wanted to kiss her so badly he ached with it.

No, he reminded himself. It was a blessing to *her* that he had failed to secure the match when he'd had the voice and power to do so. Had he been successful, she might be tied for life to a man perpetually battling his family over his sanity.

His dark thoughts were interrupted by her soft breath upon his skin, her head upon his chest now. Did she feel what he did? The temptation to touch grew past his ability to control, and he put his other arm around her, pulling her closer. She looked up at him, those big green eyes wide with...what? Fear? Wonderment? If he could ask her without a string of nonsense emerging, he would have. But she spoke instead, and it was as if she understood his every unspoken thought.

"I wish I had not laughed," she said. "I did not believe you had any feelings for me except contempt. That you might have been serious truly never crossed my mind. I did not see you for who you are, only for who you showed the world. I am sorry, sorrier than words can say."

"Wish," he replied. What had his mother used to say? *If wishes were butter cakes, beggars might bite.* "Wish," he repeated, the only word he could manage at the moment.

He wished, too, that he had courted her properly, wished that he had shown the world his feelings instead of assaulting her with them unexpectedly, giving her no warning, seeking first neither favour nor friendship. He wished he had asked her father's permission, wished he had offered for her with all the world's pomp and ceremony, in a way no titled family member could ever refute or deny.

"We cannot do this," she said, looking up at him from where she fit so perfectly within his arms. "It is only pretend."

He nodded, tracing the supple skin of her cheek, the softness of her brow, the sweet plump of her flawless lips with a hand suddenly grown unsteady. He wanted her, wanted to kiss her, to feel the taste of her in his mouth, to ruin himself for any other. He wanted to see her clear, direct gaze grow dazed and fogged with passion, with need, with *him*. Her eyes, those lovely eyes, told him that the feelings of the person who once refused him were now very different; those eyes, her lovely eyes, begged him to repeat his proposal, to make the pretence real.

"Wish," he whispered once more, all the anguish of his broken heart in that solitary word.

She nodded, her grief a living wound between them, and rested her head again upon his chest; he held her there until he knew she slept.

⊰⊱

The next morning, Lizzy was wakened by the shout of gulls from her open window. She was alone, of course; Mr Darcy must have brought her—*carried* her—to her lonely bed when she slept. The room was chilly, but she left the warmth of her covers to watch the sun rise upon the horizon. She wished she had not fallen asleep, that she could recall him lifting her, holding her to his chest, tucking the blankets around her. Had he left her with a single kiss, although she could not remember it?

Too much! Too much pain, too much hurt! I must leave here, and soon! I have fallen in love, while he has only regrets.

I will do it, she thought. *I will go to town, discover how and when the post runs to Hertfordshire.* She wondered if Mr Darcy would agree with her decision. Not that there was any reason why he should not, other than requiring her help with his letters and with the servants' understanding. Nevertheless, his speech was improving daily, James was growing better at interpretation, and a trusted man of business—she had written to them all now, but only Saxelby and one other were given his exact location—would certainly be arriving at any time. Very soon he would not need her for anything at all. It was utterly ridiculous to imagine him begging her to stay.

But it was too early for such errands. Instead of packing her trunk, she dressed in dull garb and linen cap, slipping out into the cold morning and down to the beach. And as it often did, the sight and sound of the ocean brought her a measure of peace. One could hardly gaze upon its mighty, vast splendour and be overly concerned by one's own small troubles. She walked much further from the house than she usually did, trying to push away her sorrow with the exercise, and in her preoccupation, she nearly stumbled upon a small cache of men's clothing and boots. The beach was a private one, separated from the town by rocky cliffs, and she'd never met another soul. Squinting at the waves, she saw the figure of a man stroking against the surf, swimming out towards the horizon, the sun glistening off his shoulders and strong limbs. At first, she was frightened for the unknown swimmer.

To take such risks with the vagaries of nature, the chill of the waves, and all the hidden dangers! She nearly called out in protest, though he was much too far away to hear.

But no. He turned his strokes back towards the shore, and as he neared, the man's identity became obvious. It was wrong to watch him in his unclothed state; she knew she ought to turn away, *must* turn away, and leave immediately. And yet she remained where she was, entranced, as powerful muscles glinted, his broad, scarred back, shoulders, and biceps working towards his goal, every inch of his body chiselled and fit, lean and athletic, aggressively combatting the ocean itself.

Only…let me have this moment: surrounded by a magnificent sea, while a lone man pits himself against the strength of ocean waves, emerging victorious against all his battles. He never quits, never falters, never surrenders, no matter his struggles.

And she knew she would not pack, would not hurry home to Netherfield, would not protect herself from a love she would carry for the rest of her life. *If these last few days are to be all I ever have, I will seize them while I can.*

She tarried for only a moment longer, before making her way back to a pretend life so much better than the real one awaiting her.

How Humiliating a Discovery

They were together in the book-room after tea one afternoon, sitting innocently, even sedately, side by side on the settee but several polite inches apart, as she read aloud from an epistolary novel.

When the heroine indulged in her fifth swoon in as many chapters, she looked up at him. "How did it begin?" she asked. "Your illness, I mean. Mr Goulding was lifting a heavy chest on his own, without benefit of a footman's assistance—even though one was within calling distance—when he collapsed. Was it sudden? Or a fever?"

Instead of answering, he leant forward, forearms on his knees, his head drooping.

"I am sorry!" she cried. "I should not have asked. I have an unhealthy interest in the details of illness, my friend Charlotte has often informed me."

But sighing, he sat up again; when his arm moved around her shoulders, it seemed only that he had need of a closer connexion before he spoke, rather than an impropriety. When his hand delved into the mass of hair beneath her cap, it was an absent gesture rather than an intimate one.

"It *was*...sudden, in a s-sense," he said. "Collapse, I mean. But... had not felt well...*pish*...no...precisely, for month or two p-previous, although symptoms...vague. And then...*devil it*...no...directly preceding c-collapse...I...lost temper. Utterly, completely. Lost...all semblance of control."

"I can hardly fathom it," she said, giving in to the luxury of his warmth, his strength, his nearness. "You seem the epitome of restraint."

He looked upon her, cradled in his arms, his dark eyes intense, their faces mere inches apart.

"You...have no idea," he said lowly.

Dangerous, a voice within whispered. *You pretend a connexion that does not exist.* Still, while he seemed as unable to resist the joy of touch and closeness as she, he had never taken advantage, not even one stolen kiss. He *did* have feelings for her, she knew, strong ones. And who was to say that later, once he was healthy and had regained his life...well, she did not allow her thoughts to stray too far, but hope was alive within her heart. It seemed prudent, nevertheless, to provide some distraction.

"Shall I continue reading?" she whispered.

He nodded curtly but did not let her go.

The novel was an amusing one, with a self-deluded heroine making terrible choices based upon excessive sensibility and utter foolishness. Tension easing, they both laughed at her antics until he added, chuckling, "Miss Ly-dee."

Lizzy felt her smile disappearing. "My sister, you mean? Lydia?"

That he did not recognise her affront was obvious by his continued smiles, his head shaking. "Wild."

She knew that Lydia had given no good impression of herself. None of her family had, it was true, especially at any party where punch was served, with both Kitty and Lydia likely overindulging, and neither parent restraining either. It was why she had thought him joking when he declared himself—he was so plainly and fully disapproving of her every connexion. She shuddered to think of how foolish those two girls would be with a regiment in nearby Meryton; she could only hope that her father was extending himself a bit more, with such an obvious onslaught of masculinity afoot.

She sat up, putting some space between them, looked him in the eye, and tried to explain. "Mama had difficulty carrying Lydia, and she was born early. It is amazing that she lived." She did not explain her father's nonchalance on the subject of her survival after learning he had another daughter. "It was plain Mama should have no more children, and she clung to her last infant. Lydia learnt early that the best way to persuade my mother to do her bidding was to be very, very noisy about it. She is not stupid—she simply does what works for her. It is not an effective tactic for the rest of us, however," she added wryly.

Mr Darcy only frowned. "Spoilt."

"Yes, she is much indulged. However, you do not understand what she could have done with the power she wields. My father pays little attention, and my mother caves to her every demand. She *is* spoilt—spoilt, selfish, and careless. And yet...she can be kind, when she notices." It was true. Lydia had stood for Lizzy more often than Jane ever had. It was only that she so seldom noticed anything beyond her own needs and desires.

He rolled his eyes. "No dis-discip...wild."

"She is also brave, fun, and clever."

He shrugged, as if there were nothing redeeming in those traits. Even though she well understood her sister's flaws, something in his dismissiveness irked her, and she could not simply let it go.

"If I were put into a hospital and she wished to see me, she would not merely wring her hands and accept refusals. She would not take no for an answer. If she wanted to see me, she would see me, and no one would be able to prevent her."

It was not, perhaps, fair to pit Lydia's strengths against Georgiana's weaknesses. After all, if she found herself in Mr Darcy's position, would Lydia sacrifice for Lizzy the way that Georgiana had sacrificed for her brother? One could never tell with her youngest sister, for she was nothing if not capricious. Nevertheless, he did not *know* Lydia. Lydia at her best was fearless, bright, and curious. She was also still very young; it was surely too soon to label her uncivilised.

"Georg-anna," he said, in frigid though broken accents, and she knew he resented the comparison. "Miss Darcy of Pember. Behave. Higher…" He made an encompassing gesture to cover the words he could not summon.

"Miss Darcy of Pemberley? She is held to a higher standard, I take it, than the Bennets of Longbourn?"

"Yes," he said, a note of defiance in his voice.

"You must be relieved, indeed, that I did not take seriously your offer. Think what a foolish family you might have tied yourself to so inextricably! Think who would, even now, be your relations!"

Ever after, she did not know why she had goaded him. Too much pride and not enough sense, most likely. Even though her family had hardly given Mr Darcy cause to respect them, it hurt that he did not think them as good and as worthy as his own. Even though she had accepted it, it hurt to know he'd had second thoughts regarding that proposal. Most pathetically, within that hurt, perhaps she had even imagined that if confronted, he would confess that his antipathy towards *them* was nothing compared to his deeper feelings for *her*.

"No!" he said, his throat working as he tried to speak.

She bit her tongue against the need to interrupt, to apologise, to pick up the book again and read as if nothing had been said. "Is that why?" she asked boldly instead. "Is that why you will not repeat your proposal?"

"Must…m-marry," he blurted haltingly. "Likely…Matlock's ch-choice…Caro. With…support…I might *gudgeon*…no…regain… estates…Georg-anna…control. Am not…madman! Need…earl."

She felt the colour drain from her face. It was one thing, she suddenly discovered, to accept that he was no longer as ready for marriage as he once had been. It was quite another to be found lacking in comparison to the arrogant, self-centred Caroline Bingley. It was a terrible awakening to learn that he had already made plans, plans in which neither she nor her foolish love had *ever* had any part. Only then could she feel how much imprudent hopefulness had taken root within their shared affection. She scrambled to her feet.

"I perfectly comprehend your feelings, sir, and have now only to be ashamed of what my own have been. I shall make arrangements to return to Hertfordshire, and at once." With a hasty curtsey, she hurried from the room.

<hr />

"Lizzy!" Darcy shouted, but he heard her, the next moment, open the front door and quit the house.

He was filled with an indescribable sense of loss, the tumult of his mind painfully great. Until this moment, the plan to marry Caroline had been an imaginary sacrifice, one to be contemplated at some future date—and as far in the future as he could possibly push it. He had not fully appreciated how in planning for that future, he must destroy every bit of happiness, now and ever after.

It was not fair to Lizzy, of course. She had his love, but he had foolishly pretended that she understood its hopelessness. And to watch her learn her replacement must be *Caroline Bingley*, of all people, the woman who had mocked and degraded her at every opportunity, who of course had been the one pointing out her family's every foible and folly. It had seemed dishonest not to say it, but now it seemed even more dishonourable that he had.

Her astonishment was obvious; she had looked at him with such mortification and incredulity.

Because of course, he had been luxuriating in the enjoyment of holding her in his arms only moments before. The confession had cheapened his affection, turning it to something illicit, tawdry even.

All the if-onlys of his life choked him now.

<hr />

Because her distress was too obvious, Lizzy did not call for Mr Frost to accompany her into town immediately to find the post, to pack, to leave. Instead, she escaped to the oceanside, its beating surf calming the wild pounding of her heart, the blustering sea winds drying her salt-laced tears.

As always, nature outdid her in emotion, whipping her hair from its moorings so even the cap could not contain it, its strands stinging her face.

She must, of course, face him again. Regrets, however, could always wait awhile before they must be dealt with, the choppy surface of the sea seeming an apt reflection of her own spirit.

My feelings are not his fault. She had told him they must not pretend, but she had eagerly indulged regardless. For a few brief days of affection, she had traded peace of mind and common sense. Sighing, she drew her knees to her chest and wrapped her arms about them; regrets were determined to have their way immediately. Why could she not be a practical, sensible girl? *'Life isn't one of your plays, Lizzy,'* her mother's voice drilled into her head. *'You'll find it out soon enough, and don't say I did not warn you.'*

But Lizzy had insisted upon fairy tales and princes and happily-ever-afters. She had easily accepted his affection despite *knowing* she was no longer his choice. *Pretending.*

The icy wind lashed at her thin dress, slicing like knives, desolate chill shrouding her.

The sudden screech of gulls finally startled her into looking up. There was Mr Darcy, striding purposefully down the sandhills towards her. His overlong hair blew back, tangling; even though James had shaved him this morning, his chin was shadowed with a day's growth of beard. The black of his coat gusted in the wind, like some gothic prince's cape. There was no sign of weakness in the strength of his stride. In appearance, all told, he looked much more the part of a pirate than a country gentleman. She shivered, and not entirely because of the cold.

He knelt beside her, gently drawing his coat around her shoulders before looking away. The heat of it suffused her in a sudden rush. For long moments, neither said anything while the wind reproached and scolded. Then, they both spoke at once.

"I...*frigging*...apologise."

"I am sorry."

Lizzy was struck by a sudden sliver of humour. "I prefer your words this time. I frigging apologise too."

She wrapped the coat more tightly around her, burying her face within her arms. After a few minutes, she felt the warmth of his body beside her as he settled himself in the sand, not attempting to touch.

"No...apology," he managed, or something very close to it.

"I do not apologise for my feelings, only for expecting more of you than you are capable of giving," she said at last. "And after all, who, of the two of us, will suffer most? My heart will heal, in time, whereas you intend to tie yourself to an arrogant, selfish woman at the whim of your uncle." Then she sighed. "Also, a woman who is pretty, fashionable, rich, and the sister of your good friend. A good match, by any standard. I do not like her, but then, she does not like me. It is to be supposed that you might have a much better experience than any predictions of mine."

He shook his head. "No."

She looked at him. "I hope you are wrong. I wish you happy."

"Frigging happy," he said wryly.

She snorted, turning her head to peer at him.

He faced the sea, his arms also around his knees.

"Perhaps you do not have only two alternatives. You can offer for someone else entirely, someone who meets all of your needs."

He shrugged. "I do...not...no...*bloody*...choice."

She thought of that for a moment before nodding. "There are always choices...it is just that sometimes there are no good ones. I had the opportunity to secure my family's future when my cousin, Mr Collins, proposed marriage to me. I rejected it. I thought I did right at the time, and perhaps I did. But there might always be a part of me that wonders if I should have stepped forward with a more courageous acceptance instead."

He reached out, as if to touch her, but withdrew his hand before he did. "No," he protested, the distaste upon his face obvious. "Differ."

"Not really. You act to save your estate's future as well as your sister's. The only shame in all of it is that neither your relations nor my parents care enough about either of us to save ours." She gave him a crooked smile. "You scorn Lydia, but she *did* help me at my lowest. She is no heroine, but she does care. Georgiana cares deeply for you. We will take such love as we possess and look at the past only as it gives us pleasure. I will always cherish your friendship, but you can see, I hope, that I must leave at once."

"No!"

She frowned.

"I...*blazes*...behave. Trust. Please. A...*nugging*...week or two. More...health. Please."

His earnest appeal for just a bit more time was too close to Lizzy's own inclinations. After all, he could not perfectly communicate on his own yet, James did not write, and reading was still a tedious process. It would, perhaps, be a week or so before any of his men of business arrived. It was the Christian thing to do. How much more pain could a few extra days bring?

Mr Darcy was not the first man to discount her because she had no fortune. It was a hurt she had faced down years ago; the Caroline Bingleys of this world were always offered first choice. Large fortune cloaked every vice of malevolence, insipidity, or foolishness with a pleasing desirability. Perhaps Jane's near miraculous marriage had given her an unwarranted hopefulness, but the future *might* yet present another man for whom she could feel such affection and respect, who would be happy with an impoverished gentlewoman.

I am a frigging fool, Lizzy thought. *A blasted, frigging fool.*

The very next afternoon, she received a letter from Jane.

Mr Saxelby, one of Darcy's trusted men of business, had written to Bingley with the assurances of Miss Elizabeth Bennet's wellbeing and an offer to forward any return correspondence. Thus, when a large envelope arrived from him, she was not overly surprised at its contents.

"From Mr Bingley!" she said breathlessly when she came upon it, after thumbing through each of the letters it contained.

Mr Darcy looked up sharply. "Bing."

"Yes...should I begin with it?" She clutched the letter to her bosom.

She could see the reluctance upon his face, and in a way, she understood. The drama of their story together was in its final act and would end unhappily for both. Bingley and his sister, Caroline, represented a future Mr Darcy must accept.

But...home. Jane. Longbourn. Netherfield. News of any of it was a longing in her breast and a comfort for her own future.

He nodded. His brow furrowed as she broke the seal. A folded note with her name written across its surface fell out, a letter from her sister. But she set it aside in favour of the first. It was stained with blots, scores, and crosses, but its message was clear enough.

> *Darcy,*
>
> *Where the devil are you? What have you done with my sister? In the meantime, your sister resides with my wife and me, and both Mrs Bingley and Miss Darcy worry day and night, for your safety and for Elizabeth's. I have endured a visit from an earl, an experience I am not anxious to repeat anytime soon. I could tell him nothing, but of course, I hope Saxelby knows more than I do about how to reach you. Avoided mentioning him to your uncle this time, but if he continues to push, I must give him something. I do hope you are recovering, but dash it, we must hear from you.*
>
> *Bingley*

It was as unlike Bingley's tone as she could have imagined. "He is upset," she said with some understatement, and bit her lip. "And why would he have Georgiana?" Suddenly, she joined Mr Darcy in reluctance to read her own missive from Jane. But the thing must be done.

Jane's script was neat and flowing, unlike her husband's. She gave a great deal of added detail, without the cursing. But the gist of her message was the same. Because Mr Darcy had to sacrifice privacy to hear his letter, she felt it only fair to read hers aloud as well.

> *Dearest Lizzy,*
>
> *I cannot imagine where you have gone and why you would not write to me. We have been home to Netherfield for nearly five weeks, every day expecting word, and every day disappointed.*

"Why does she assume I know where she is?" Lizzy interrupted herself. "Last I knew, she was in Scarborough, and she was supposed to come here!" She ignored the niggling voice reminding her that she had known Jane would not be arriving for nearly three weeks now.

> *We received yours and Miss Darcy's letters, forwarded by Louisa, whilst still in Scarborough. How alarmed we were to hear of Mr Darcy's illness! And how astonished we were to learn you had departed Ramsgate and the care of Harriet Thorpe, a place of which our parents approved, at least. Instead, you have been in a house of illness!*

"Well, if that is not the outside of enough," Lizzy protested. "'You have departed the care of Harriet' she complains, as if Harriet cared a tuppence for me, and *my parents* assume I meekly put myself into the hands of an uncle who has never bothered to meet any of us! *My parents* assume I was dropped at an address in Cheapside, with my only introduction a letter demanding that uncle find me something to do. *My parents* could care less where I am now!"

For the first time in two days, Mr Darcy touched her, cautiously laying a hand upon her shoulder, his dark eyes full of compassion. He said nothing, but she knew he wished to be a support, a true friend. She pushed her anger back into the small home in her soul she allowed it, managing a rueful smile as she continued reading.

> *Bingley assures me that Lady Catherine was more than enough chaperonage for you and Miss Darcy, and thus I do not doubt it. And yet, I could hardly rest, knowing Miss Darcy's fears for her brother's health and the delicate nature of his illness.*

"At least she did not outright accuse you of madness," Lizzy interjected, grinning up at him impishly.

His soft smile nearly undid her, and she hurriedly returned to Jane's letter.

> *We arrived at Darcy House mere minutes after Colonel Fitzwilliam and but a few hours after your departure with Mr Darcy—although we did not, of course, know you accompanied him at the time.*

"Oh, did you hear that? Georgiana, Mrs Taylor, even Bertie and the stable boys fooled them all, if they believed us to have had a three-hour start on them. You owe Mr Frost and James apologies—they *told* you they would inform no one."

He nodded in agreement.

Of course, we discovered at once you were not there, and, Lizzy, I do not quite understand how the confusion arose, but Lady Catherine and the housekeeper believed you to have returned to Hertfordshire! On the post! Miss Darcy did not like to correct her aunt, but she knew all along that you had not. I would tell this to no one but you, but I cannot feel any fondness for Lady Catherine, though she is sister to an earl. I believe her to have been understandably distressed by Mr Darcy's departure, but she was not polite. However, I digress.

Colonel Fitzwilliam was terribly concerned for Mr Darcy and also for Miss Darcy. It seems that the earl wished to promote a match between them— between Miss Darcy and the colonel, I mean. Both oppose the idea most strenuously, although I am not quite certain why, as it would serve quite well. However, having married Bingley for love, I am the last person to object to the notion in others. Nevertheless, Colonel Fitzwilliam had an additional motive for speedily wishing a resolution to Mr Darcy's troubles, for in an effort to thwart his father's matrimonial designs, he accepted a military assignment taking him out of England. He expects to be away for several months, at least.

"Fitz," Darcy muttered, shaking his head. "*Bloody* sneak."

Without ever checking upon his cousin. Such neglect had to have hurt him, if they were close. But she tried to paint his actions in the best possible light. "Clever, I suppose. And we shall be charitable and assume that he only promotes your sister's welfare. I still believe we fled just in time, however. I cannot trust Lady Catherine's reason."

"*Mammering* madwoman," he muttered.

Lizzy turned back to the letter.

The colonel wished to return Miss Darcy to her companion in Ramsgate, but Lizzy, she was adamant that she would not and that if he tried to take her to that 'horrid woman' she would run away! I was appalled at her outburst, but what else could we say except that we would take her back with us to Netherfield? (As Mr Bingley believed the cottage leased in Brighton unsuitable—we never were able to go.) Fortunately, Miss Darcy has been most agreeable—although she failed to tell us that we would not find you awaiting us in Hertfordshire until we were nearly home.

Lord Matlock came to us last week in a most dreadful humour. I suppose I can understand it, for he is doubtless worried about whatever assignment the colonel has undertaken as well as Mr Darcy's health. We could tell him nothing, further upsetting him. He wished to take Miss Darcy away with him, but she once again objected most strenuously until he conceded. I swear she has not been much in company with Lydia, but the resemblance was marked.

Lizzy met Darcy's gaze again with raised brow; he looked sheepish.

Sadly, Lydia and Kitty do little except traipse after the officers, while Mary has taken to praying aloud for their souls every time there is a pause in conversation. We used to bicker, but now we can hardly bear to be in each other's company. Your good humour and sweet spirit are sorely missed.

I suppose you feared coming to us without warning, but, Lizzy, I ought to have assured you before my wedding that you would always be welcome. I have often reread the letter you sent from Ramsgate, and I grieve that you ever felt the need to write it. I was so terribly anxious just before my marriage and regarding the reception of my new sisters. I was not myself. It is my fault, I think, that you hide away from us now. Please come home, Lizzy.

Yours ever,

Jane Bingley

20

WHEN CUPID IS NOT BLIND

Lizzy thought of little else besides Jane's letter over the next four days, rereading it several times. She'd had to sit, so great was her surprise at this open invitation—almost a plea—to come to her.

But though she had longed for the safety and security of a home with the Bingleys, now that it was assured, she was conscious of another emotion, mixed in with real gratitude and relief. It took her some days to identify so foreign a feeling, and she instinctively shied from it. But finally, she knew: it was a sense of dread, almost, as the forced donning of an ill-fitting garment.

One night after dinner, she and Darcy sat quietly in their favourite parlour, side by side upon the settee. He did not touch her—he was very careful to 'behave' as he had put it. But he watched her, alert to her troubled mood.

"Liz-zy…you well?" he asked.

And because she knew he cared, truly, for her feelings, she told him what had been bothering her. "In the beginning of her letter, Jane says she cannot imagine why I do not come home and, at its end, confesses to fearing she is the cause for my absence." Sighing, she turned to face him.

"She is not wholly correct, but she is not wrong either." Lizzy had never voiced aloud her feelings on this subject, had never had a friend close enough, willing enough to share her burdens, to say it. Even with Charlotte, protecting her sisters had been too important —protecting herself too. "I worked so hard, all my life, to keep peace in our family. I used every wit I possessed to coax and cajole and entertain and amuse. I cared for each one of them in every illness or physical complaint. When I needed them the most, my sisters did not desert me, but neither did any of them make a stand. Lydia thought of a way to delay my punishment for a time, and Jane, under duress, promised to make a future effort, but... essentially, I was left to fend for myself."

He shook his head in mute commiseration, his gaze sympathetic.

"Perhaps I ought to have done what Mama ordered and gone to her brother in Cheapside. But who is he? He certainly never bothered to take any notice of us. Mama is difficult enough, and I cannot imagine any brother of hers to be an improvement."

Darcy nodded in understanding.

"I resented your opinion of Lydia, but your accusations were not baseless. With a full regiment of men in redcoats to attract her, and Kitty following in her footsteps, neither sister likely gave me a thought. Instead, they make a laughingstock of themselves and our family name whilst my parents do naught to restrain either. We are just as foolish as you worried." She tried to smile, took a deep breath. "Thankfully, you may congratulate yourself at having successfully avoided such an inauspicious connexion." And she buried her face in her hands.

Seconds later, she felt his tentative touch; perhaps, even, she had allowed him to see too much of her pain simply for the affection of it. She had no more pride and so little time left with him. A bit of comfort, a bit of understanding—was it asking too much?

"Jane said...missed good humour, spirits," he said. "You, Lizzy. Kept all..." He tried to summon the word 'together' with his tangled tongue and was only partially successful.

Still, she understood him. She usually did now.

"But what good was it?" she questioned. "In the end, my efforts were in vain. Even now...I worry that it may be the only reason Jane wants me back—to rein in my younger sisters. But they are no longer children. I cannot persuade or distract them into good behaviour any longer, not if they are determined to do as they will."

"Georg—"

"Georgiana. Yes."

"Wanted...more. More atten-tion, more friend. I wanted...her stay little, stay girl. Not think about wed-dings and bed-dings. Repulse. No want. So. I did not. Gave...her to Lady Mat-lock. Approved all asked. Paid lit-tle attention. She...she gave her to..."

"Her companion, Mrs Younge!" Lizzy finished for him. "Georgiana told me the most horrible things about her. I did not think you would have hired such a person for her. She would not allow your sister to see you, and she had her maid dismissed by telling lies. By fostering dissent and disharmony amongst the household, the best servants left. Finally, she managed to completely isolate her. Georgiana grew so desperate that at one point...well, let us say she was beyond despair." She met his gaze. "That was when I met her, actually. Upon the cliffs of Ramsgate."

He did not misunderstand, she saw, closing his eyes briefly. Sweetly, he took her hand and kissed it in gratitude and affection; she clutched it, so pitifully grateful for the connexion.

"There was...a man," he managed.

"A man?" Lizzy asked, surprised.

"Told you...once. Lost temper...before c-collapse. It...was him." In fits and starts, he got out the details—the son of Pemberley's steward, George Wickham, a beloved godson of his father's, who had been given so much and yet who only took, only wounded, only ruined.

"An elopement?" Lizzy asked, appalled. "Surely Georgiana would never hurt or offend you in such a way. She loves you!"

"Love," he murmured. "I showed none. I regarded her...feelings... burden. Retreated. Left alone. Vul-vulnerable. When dis-covered... with Wick...I lost temper. Lost mind. Woke...hosp-ital. More Younges." He looked straight into her eyes. "Your sister Bing... knows. Like I know. Should have stayed close. Loved *blasted* better. Not lose you. Liz-zy...you...better than us all. Not run from chal-lenges, from hard. Embrace. Conquer."

Confusion filled her; his form grew misty within her unshed tears.

"Only you." The words came out easily, as if he had rehearsed them. "Only you, my Lizzy."

And suddenly, without even being aware of how it happened, she was in his arms, and for the first time, finally, she gave expression to the feelings in her heart. Her need was voracious, lightning in her blood and a fever in her soul, and she tried to withdraw, to find her restraint.

But he seemed to want no such reserve, his longing as greedy and ravenous as her own. His fingers went to the linen cap, unpinning, loosening until, at last, her hair was free, and he buried his hands within the masses.

"Liz-zy...my Liz-zy," he said over and over, drawing her close until they were intertwined in each other's arms. "Be...be mine, Liz-zy. Pl-please. Need you. Need you...so much." And then his mouth, hot and strong, was on hers, and she was lost, lost to the same yearnings, to the kisses, both sweet and overwhelming. What did it matter? It was all she had ever wanted. Just him—not his name, not his wealth and properties, not the trappings of prosperity. Only his love. Only that.

Almost viciously, he tore himself away, breathing hard, his cravat ruined, his hair mussed, his desire obvious. He stared at her, his eyes wild. Moments later, she was alone in the empty parlour.

He did not return. For the first time since his recovery from the fever, she dined alone that night.

Since she could not sleep, Lizzy packed her trunk. Obviously, she could not stay any longer. Even a frightening ride alone on the post seemed a better option than lingering at The Breakers, falling more in love daily with a man she could never have—who would never have *her*. Her will to resist him was gone. She was too vulnerable, immune to sense or reason; she might even have been guilty of luring him into kisses he had rather not given—she no longer knew herself. Rather than continuing to compound her mistakes, she must make haste to Hertfordshire as quickly as was possible, not looking back.

Her plan for the next morning was to tell Mr Darcy of her decision and ask for his aid in procuring transportation back to Netherfield. However, when he finally appeared after breakfast, he seemed full of a suppressed energy and will, his hair wet, damply curling at the ends.

She tried not to remember him powerfully swimming alone through ocean waves.

"Need...letter," he said, unsmiling, intent.

How I despise the thought of leaving him alone! Even though she knew it was the right thing, nay, the *only* thing to do, it was difficult to find the words to tell him so. Still, she could help him with this one task before asking him to help her find a means of immediate departure.

"I will help with that," she assented. "Then we must talk."

"Will...write...earl," he said instead of agreeing.

"The earl?" she questioned. "Confrontation at this point seems... unwise. What if you anger him?"

"Will...write earl," he repeated with more force.

"Very well," she agreed. Who was she to decide to whom he should or should not write? After today, he would be making all his decisions without her participation. It was as it ought to be. Still, he had already worried aloud that time might be short before the earl acted, taking further steps to ruin the Darcys and cement his own power thereby. The threat of a declared insanity might remain for years. Would such a letter help or hurt?

"Mat-lock," he began dictating with none of the usual niceties.

Dear Lord Matlock, she wrote.

"Will do...as you pro-pose. M-marriage."

Lizzy dropped the pen, but he did not seem to notice. *Marriage!* How could he be so callous? Only yesterday, he had pledged 'only you, my Lizzy'! While that was not precisely a declaration, his demanding she write this letter was especially cruel in the wake of his recent passion.

But then...she had practically begged for that passion, had she not? Letting him know of the reasons he should be grateful to her, inspiring his pity with her own losses. Ultimately, he was the one who stood strong against *her* passion, not the reverse.

What they had shared was a brief, impossible moment in time, and she had already resolved to leave—today, if possible. A pretend wife she might have been, but she must not pretend to herself. Better to face it as straightforwardly as he was. Telling her directly was the kindest thing he could do.

So she took up the pen again, struggling to keep up as he dwelt with some warmth on the subject of his bride's inferiority. While it gave her no pleasure to imagine him tied forever to one who suited him so ill, at least her heart could not be wounded by his senti-ments—or lack thereof—towards his bride.

"Not best...choice. Not...not...suitable. Family...undeserving... Darcy name," seemed to be the gist of his remarks. Repeatedly.

Well, this would not be how I would speak of my betrothed, Lizzy thought. However, it was true enough—Caroline's birth was much lower than Lizzy's own, for instance. She had not dwelt upon how such things mattered to him, but it had to be a consideration, or he might have married Caroline and her magnificent portion years before. Did he insult the Bingley lineage to emphasise his own, building up his worth in Matlock's eyes by slandering the earl's chosen bride? She tried to gentle it as much as she could.

"But...accomplished," he offered. *Of course, he must add that.* What were Caroline's claims from that silly drawing room conversation of so long ago? "A thorough knowledge of music, singing, drawing, dancing, and the modern languages," amongst others. *I suppose I should list them all,* she thought. Too, Caroline had the running of Netherfield. Mr Darcy might not think of it, but he was also, plainly, stating the good reasons he had for accepting the earl's choice, regardless that it was not his own.

"Good to sister," he said.

I would rather have said Caroline's sister is good to her, Lizzy thought. Nevertheless, Mrs Hurst and Caroline did seem to rely heavily upon each other, even if Mrs Hurst seemed the more submissive of the two. She wrote his sentiments quickly despite the agony each one caused.

"Family...for most part...ill-behaved," he relayed. "Will...require... some intercession. But not all...bad."

Her family is the best part about her! Well, at least her brother; Mr Bingley was the very best of men. *Of course, Louisa Hurst is a dreadful gossip, while Mr Hurst is a winebibber and a clunch.* Perhaps Mr Darcy intended to demand that his distinguished family provide some incentive for Hurst to drink less and contribute more to dinner party conversations, while encouraging his wife to contribute less? It *might* be beneficial. At least, beneficial to their future dinner partners.

"Witty, charming," he added, and she quickly wrote down those adjectives, resisting the temptation to add 'arrogant' and 'self-centred'. Was she to hear all of Caroline's strengths now, every one of his reasons for accepting the earl's bride? It did not matter; Caroline had the earl's seal of approval.

"I am...un-unconcerned...her ability to...navigate society of...her betters."

Truthfully, Caroline, with her seminary education, was well-suited to navigating the world of earls and countesses. However, Lizzy could not truly consider his relations a family of 'betters'. Lady Catherine had nearly killed him with her senseless trust in a quack, while Lord and Lady Matlock were more interested in maintaining control of the Darcy wealth than their good health. No, there were not any heroes in his family tree, despite their bluer blood.

"Again...again, I reassure...consider Georg-anna welfare...believe me. Bride...good influence...if regret-table. Bride's...family...insufficiency of income and conduct...difficult to accept. I...am not mad. Your idea...will not do. I...will have my choice...or none."

Insufficiency of income? Caroline Bingley had no lack of income.

Who then? No...he would not—*could not*—be referring to...herself? Lizzy very carefully set down the pen and reread all she had written. He, however, did not appear to notice whether or not she wrote a word, remaining lost in contemplation of further demeaning adjectives to describe his future bride.

"I know...I sacrifice...in this...m-marriage. Do not...think me mad. It...perhaps...m-mortify to you, to see tying...myself to such. I... own...its disgrace, I promise. But...misery...of losing her... greater...than hu-humiliation...of keeping."

And he looked up at her with his dark eyes...smiling at last, proud of himself. He had listed out her—and her family's—many failings with hardly a missed or vulgar word.

Darcy looked at the woman he loved, expecting to see a smile of dawning comprehension as she realised that *she* was to be his intended bride. Instead, her face was white, pale. Was her surprise too great? Or had she not yet comprehended the honour bestowed?

He went to her then, hands outstretched. "Liz-zy."

Softly, she drew her fingers across his; but when he tried to clasp them, she backed away from his grasp.

"It is impossible," she said.

"I *bloody* thought so...at first...as well!" he exclaimed. "But for... every det-detriment, there is...a positive! Yes...m-match...*inap*-inappropriate. But...when family...meet you...come to...know you...th-they will see...s-sacrifice...worthwhile."

To his dismay, a tear tracked down her cheek. He opened his mouth to speak, but she put her finger to his lips to stop him.

"Your very belief that it *is* a sacrifice is the reason I cannot. You care for me, I know. But an unequal connexion such as this cannot survive our unequal feelings. My family would continue to embarrass you, I promise."

"'Love looks not with the eyes,'" he quoted, "but with the mind; and therefore is wing'd Cupid painted blind.'"

"You, however, see only too clearly. There is nothing of blindness in this letter and only satire in your poetry," she said—caustically, it seemed to him.

His brow furrowed. "Yes...but...no live Longbourn. Most... Pember...Derbyshire."

"Ah. A place where you might hide your inappropriate bride. How convenient."

Anger flared. "Liz-zy...I...*dash it*...cannot...h-help..." As usual, as he grew upset, he grew less able to elucidate his feelings.

"You cannot help who I am," she replied. "Let us not quibble on particulars. Miss Bingley, whose birth is lower than mine, you do not consider a degradation, for she has the approval of your family at a time when you desperately need it. It all comes down to that— whatever attractions I possess, I have not the fortune or family to earn *your* approval, never mind your relations'."

His hands went to his hips, offended. "I...choose...*blasted*...you!"

"Since you choose me against your will, and since you so plainly worry this choice will prove to your family an absence of reason and character, I can assume you will have little difficulty over-coming any regrets at my refusal. I meant to ask you earlier today to hire me a carriage to return me to Hertfordshire. Perhaps one of the maids could be convinced to accompany me. I am already packed, and it is past time I leave."

Darcy gaped at the woman he had just proposed to...again. And this...*this* was all the reply she could give him? *Surely* she could see why his choices must be examined and dissected through the lens of his family's approval! He must couch his defiance in a manner that showed he knew exactly what he was doing; he was not deluding himself, not claiming his bride to be someone whom she was plainly not. Rather, he was *declaring* himself!

And she had *already* packed! Had already decided to *leave*, to *leave him*. She had apologised for misunderstanding his first declaration, but there was no doubt she had comprehended this one. He would not humiliate himself further, trying to beg for *her* approval—the one person on this earth he thought believed in him already. Turning on his heel without another word, he quit the room.

21

GONE WITH SUCH CELERITY

Lizzy found herself trembling. Had she really refused the opportunity to marry Fitzwilliam Darcy, the dearest wish of her heart, the man she yearned for more than anything in the world?

Yes, it seemed she had.

Fool! her heart declared. *There would be plenty of time to convince him of my merit once I was Mrs Darcy!*

However, the greater share of her mind knew she had done right. She loved him. She truly did. But since the day she was born, she had been judged not 'good enough' to be treated as her sisters. One could grow accustomed to it, but it was a wound that never healed. Loving him as she did, she could imagine how it would be —apologising for the rest of her life for not being wealthy enough or wellborn enough to please the difficult family whose opinions he so valued. And what if they *did* use her inferiority against him? What if her father openly disowned her out of spite, just to embarrass them? What if the earl used their union as proof of insanity?

All terrible possibilities.

Although she would not exactly call his recent declaration a true proposal, she had easily seen that he'd had no doubt of a favourable response, his countenance expressing real security; he had been quite certain of her affections, as well he might be. Her refusal had shocked and humiliated him. Would he hate her now?

Better that he hate you now, than after you are inextricably wed. He has judged and found you unworthy, just as your father did. Imagine watching his resentment grow with every passing year!

A tear fell then another, but forcibly, she quelled them; Mr Darcy must not see her heart breaking. It took her some time to gain control, however, so by the time she was ready to ask for assistance in hiring a carriage, she discovered that Mr Frost had driven Mr Darcy out, taking James as well. She could ask Mrs Davis to see to it—but it would be thought exceedingly odd.

"Mrs Bingley." Mrs Davis interrupted her morose thoughts, tapping at the door as she entered. "There is a gentleman here to see Mr Bingley." She handed over his card.

'Mr Edward Gardiner' it read. Just her luck that one of Mr Darcy's most trusted men of business should arrive while he was nowhere to be found. And of course, Mr Darcy had written him an explanation of the ruse of his own identity but had never mentioned hers —only Saxelby knew of her connexion. What a pickle!

Still, Mr Gardiner had been one of only two of his entire acquaintance with whom Mr Darcy had trusted his exact whereabouts; not even Mr Bingley or Georgiana possessed such information. It meant that he expected the men to stand against earls, should they be so confronted. It meant absolute fidelity. Could she hope that his loyalty would extend to her? It seemed she had little choice but to find out.

"Show him in, Mrs Davis," she replied.

Mr Gardiner was a handsome, sandy-haired man with laugh lines at his eyes, and much younger than she had pictured. His personal prosperity was obvious, as was his good nature. "Mrs Bingley," he said once the housekeeper departed to bring the tea Lizzy requested, his brows raised. "I had no idea of a Mrs Bingley," he said politely, "but perhaps congratulations are in order? I have been telling our mutual friend for some time that he ought to take my own example of matrimony. As a groom with a decade of marital bliss and four children under his belt, I feel well qualified to offer the advice."

Were it not for his name, she might not have noticed it—but of course, he *did* share the same name as her absent uncle. It was too preposterous a thought, and too large a coincidence to be believable, but there was a certain something in his appearance that seemed vaguely…familiar. *His eyes are the same colour and shape as Mama's,* she noted, though his were warmed by those crinkled edges.

"I wonder," she said tentatively, "if you might bear some connexion to the Bennets of Longbourn. It is a small estate in Hertfordshire, near—"

"I know exactly where Longbourn is situated," he said, interrupting her with a strange intensity.

"I have a relation by your name," Lizzy continued, more cautiously still. "But of course, it is a common one. And the direction I was given for him is in Cheapside. Corner of Dean's Court and George Street at Folter Lane."

"This is remarkable," he said, his brow furrowing, "I have not lived there for some three years, at least. Can you be…? You cannot possibly be one of Frances's girls, can you?"

"Yes, sir," Lizzy replied, uncertain of how to proceed, wishing with all her heart that Mr Darcy was at her side to provide explanations. How would this man take the news that she, probably his niece, was posing as a wife to one of his important clients? Did she dare even reveal it?

He was already shaking his head in astonishment. "But this is incredible. Absolutely incredible. Only one of Frances's girls had hair of such distinctive colour. You would not be little Lizzy, would you?"

This reminder of her hated hair had the effect of summoning her pride. "Little no longer, sir, as you can see. Would you care to take a seat? Mr, er, Bingley is not at home, but we expect him anytime now."

He still shook his head with some astonishment and remained standing. "What a surprise you are! And such a great beauty! 'Tis no wonder Mr Bingley has tied the knot without warning. You must tell me, though, all about your mother and sisters and how they do."

His reference to her beauty she assumed to be a flattery; she required none and ignored it. But his enquiry regarding her family seemed even more false, since he had never bothered to know them. "They were well, last I knew. Could it be that you take an interest?"

He showed, briefly, some affront, but then he let out a sigh. "You would have been too young to remember me, I suppose, although I had hopes. You were only six years and such a darling thing, for all your mama worshipped Janey's golden curls. Lydia was not even walking! But I did wish you might remember. I was a great favourite of yours once, you see."

"A favourite?" Lizzy asked with some astonishment. "But...that cannot be. I remember other details from my earliest years. Why can I not remember you?"

He sighed again, and a sorrow unusual to his obvious good humour showed in his face. He finally sat heavily in the velvet armchair, remaining silent as Mrs Davis entered with a tea tray. Lizzy dismissed the housekeeper and used the excuse of pouring to gain control of her own disquiet.

"I lived nearby and was a constant visitor, although your father was none too fond of me. I ignored him, for the most part, and he ignored me, for the most part," Mr Gardiner explained quietly. "It was fine until you were old enough to talk. Such a sharp little sparrow you were, cleverer than any of your sisters, and practically doing somersaults to get your papa's attention."

She coloured a little at this.

"It wasn't fair, how he treated you. And I tell you this because you are a woman grown now and deserve to know—Frances was devoted to Bennet once. I can believe he lost her affection afterwards, but he still had it when you were planted. She oughtn't to have kept any foolish letters from foolish admirers, but she did enjoy being flattered—she was silly, almost childlike about such things. Anyone could see there was only Bennet for her, but he was a jealous old gudgeon from the day he met her, and probably still is."

She could not recall this man; yet knowing that he was aware of the family secrets, but clearly believed her to be legitimate, had wonderful effect—a wound within healed just a little. She nodded.

"The nursery was overfull, and you and Jane, with your sweet, sunny smiles, were allowed out—I do not think anyone minded either of you. Janey would play quietly but not you—you spent your hours trying to please your parents. You'd bring Bennet a this or a that or whatever he'd wished for aloud, whilst he shunned you. He did it one time too many in my presence, breaking your little heart, until I lost my temper and explained to him just how ridiculous, how disgusting, how *ungentlemanly* his behaviour. He ordered me to begone and never return, told Frances my name was never to be mentioned again. I was sorry for it later, but in the moment, I was too angry." He shook his head sadly.

"You...wished to return?" The remnants of the lonely young girl she had once been clung to this notion—inexplicably wanting this man, yet a stranger, to care.

"After I moved to London and had cooled down a bit, I tried writing my apologies again and again. I renewed my efforts after my marriage then again after the birth of my eldest. When Frances never answered, I knew it was no use—either he did not give her the letters, or else she stood with him on the situation. Either way, it wasn't worth the price of the postage to keep bothering her. But I have many regrets, and you are the biggest of them. I would have loved to...to have been allowed to be your uncle, perhaps even brought you to us after my marriage, if only I could have held my tongue."

"But this is fantastic," she murmured. "Nothing is as I believed."

Something about him *exuded* safety and familiarity. Another wound in her heart even eased a bit; Mama's decision to send her to her Uncle Gardiner was not quite the act of cruelty she had believed. Negligent, of course, as she had plainly neither verified his direction nor written to him regarding the situation—but Mama had always been thoughtless and silly. Mr Bennet, of course, was neither. He simply had not cared *what* became of her.

Impulsively, she asked, "Will you excuse me for a moment? I need to fetch something."

He nodded solemnly.

She hurried upstairs and dug about in her trunk until she found the letter her mother had given her before she left. It had her uncle's name and the direction in Cheapside on the front of it; she had never broken its seal, only assumed it contained an introduction and an order to find her a place. Returning to the parlour, she shut the door behind her as she approached the man who, incredibly, was her near relation, the guardian her parents had chosen. Taking a deep breath, she held out the letter.

"It is a long story, but I refused a marriage proposal against the will of my parents. In punishment, they have, well, disowned me. They sent me to you—or rather, to your old address—with this letter of explanation," she got out in a breath.

"They did what?" he exclaimed in shocked astonishment.

"Plainly, I did not go to Cheapside. Instead, I went to friends in Ramsgate then, quite by accident, stumbled into the situation of the Darcys. Mr Darcy spent a month at an estate near Longbourn, so I knew him, and as I have some skill with nursing, with him being quite ill and his family—"

"Yes," he interpolated, and she recalled Mr Darcy's dictation and how he had explained most of his recent past to this trusted advisor. There was a pregnant pause. "He did not mention taking a wife, however."

"I am not his wife," she admitted baldly. "The housekeeper here assumed I was, and I did not correct her. When we arrived, he was so very ill. I did not know whether he would live or die. All I cared about was his recovery, and I had nowhere else to go, regardless. I expected my sister and her husband—Jane recently married Mr Darcy's good friend Mr Bingley, you see—to arrive at any moment and provide whatever explanations were necessary. It turns out, however, that they recently took Miss Darcy into their care and returned to Netherfield Park instead of journeying on to Brighton as expected."

"Posing as his wife." Although his tone was even, she could not help but listen for disapproval.

"Yes, we have been staying here under the alias of Mr and Mrs Bingley, although only as a ruse." She blushed, remembering the kisses, the longing. But she lifted her chin. Whatever mistakes she had made, she could not apologise for that which she did not regret.

"I understand why, originally, you undertook to care for him," Mr Gardiner began carefully. "However, I do hope you can see why he ought to have sent for me, or someone else he trusted, much sooner. You cannot remain here another minute with him, alone like this. Surely you know it."

Some resentment stirred within her at his easy assumption of authority over her; but he quickly seemed to think better of his approach and sighed instead of continuing. "Perhaps I should read the letter," he said, reaching for it.

Lizzy handed it over, her heart beating hard, her emotions nearly escaping her control, although she was uncertain why. In essence, he was a stranger to her still; his opinion of her could not truly matter, no matter how unkindly her mother had chosen to describe her, no matter how imprudent he believed her decision to act as 'Mrs Bingley'. Nevertheless, as he opened it, she could not help moving so that she could see what had been written.

It was in her mother's messy scrawl and embarrassingly brief, with blots nearly obliterating a word or two—though still legible, for all that.

Edward—

You wanted her. Now, you may have her.

Frances

The events of the next hour blurred in her mind. She hoped against hope that Mr Darcy might return before her departure, but it was not to be.

'Tis for the best, foolish girl.

She tried to write him a letter of farewell, but Mr Gardiner—she could not, as yet, think of him as 'uncle'—watched her as he waited, and she could not express a hundredth part of what was in her heart. Gardiner was obviously desirous of protecting her; if he knew that Mr Darcy had actually spoken of marriage, she could not tell *what* he might insist upon. In the end, she wrote only a short note explaining the barest facts of her uncle's appearance and his offer to accompany her to Netherfield. She ordered her trunk brought down while an astonished—and suspicious—Mrs Davis looked on. "My...husband will be staying on for a bit," Lizzy said. "In a fortunate coincidence, my uncle has travelled here for another obligation and is able to return me to our home estate in Hertfordshire, where I have many commitments."

"Do ye wish me t'give Mr Bingley a message?" she asked, obviously probing.

"We discussed this possibility earlier. He will not be concerned," Lizzy prevaricated. "Leaving now with my uncle will prevent him from a tedious journey he is not yet up to undertaking. He will come home when he can."

"Your uncle. Very well, madam," the housekeeper said, scepticism writ plain upon her face. "No message, then."

Lizzy nearly turned away without saying anything else, but found she could not. One message, one last exchange. All of her words, all her feelings demanding expression, clogged her throat: *I will miss you. I will think of you every day. I could have loved you. Be happy, be safe. I wish…I wish.*

But no. There was nothing in any of them appropriate for a pretend wife to tell a hired housekeeper of a leased house to the man from whom she fled.

"Tell him…tell him to take good care. To be well."

The woman appeared even more curious. "Peculiar, you leaving so sudden like this," she dared.

"Promise you will not forget," Lizzy admonished forcefully.

Mrs Davis nodded, and Lizzy made herself walk away, her footsteps echoing. Down to the entry, out the front door. Into the carriage. And thus, more quickly than she could have ever imagined, her adventures in Brighton, in nursing, and in falling in love were all finished.

Do not weep.

It was a mantra she repeated often for the first several miles as she stared silently out the window. Mr Gardiner spoke a few pleas-antries and comments upon the scenery, which she believed she answered casually, as though foolish dreams did not lie shattered at her feet. But perhaps not, for he lapsed into silence within a mile and left her alone. Over and over, her memory echoed Mr Darcy's expression at her refusal. There was anger, yes—but also a hurt, a deep confusion. Had she done wrong? Had her pride betrayed her into a ruinous answer?

But no. He had not really asked a question, had he? He had only attempted to defend a decision that his family would find repulsive and he believed a possible proof of insanity. She could not blame him for it, but it hardly showed overwhelming love. They would believe him grown dependent upon her and that she had taken advantage. They would use it against him. And as he grew ever stronger and more capable of fighting his own battles, he might believe it too.

"What will you do?"

The question startled her, so accustomed to silence she had become. She abruptly met Mr Gardiner's eyes, finding them filled with a grave sort of kindness.

"Wh-what?"

"Have you reflected upon what you will do when you return to your sister's home?"

The question seemed almost nonsensical. "The usual things, I suppose," she answered, brow furrowing.

"I cannot imagine you netting purses, covering screens, or painting tables—the usual occupations of young ladies. Unless you enjoy those pursuits."

She shrugged, utterly helpless to identify much of interest. "I do enjoy reading. And I have much to improve upon in my playing."

He appeared thoughtful. "My business connexion with Mr Darcy came about—in a way and in part—due to my banishment from Longbourn," he said. "I was only five or six years older than you are now, and my father planned to ease into retirement whilst I took over his practice. Vindictively, your father wrote to mine, exclaiming his displeasure over my behaviour to him, threatening to withdraw his patronage. Meryton is a small pond, as you know, and Bennet was—*is*—a rather large fish within it."

"Surely not," Lizzy whispered.

But of course, it was utterly in character. It would not have been simply the loss of a client, although that would be damaging enough to old Mr Gardiner. It would be the public humiliation of it. It might have ruined her grandfather, who had died when she was nine or ten years old. She *could* just remember him, although he had rarely visited or had a word for her if he did.

"Sadly true," he nodded. "But Thomas Bennet offered a suggestion by way of penitence. My father should offer the firm to his clerk, Philips, instead of me, if he would marry our eldest sister. Ida seldom in her life made a remark touched by sense, common or otherwise, and hadn't the looks of her younger sister to compensate. It solved Father's problem of how to care for her, whilst it was an excellent match for both of them. Bennet's good will could thus be restored."

Lizzy briefly closed her eyes. She had often wondered at the union of her uncle Philips, a solemn, pedantic man, to her silly, flighty aunt. "And my father ensured that he would never be called upon to take in my aunt once her father died."

"That too," he agreed. "Of course, I parted ways with my father's firm, as Bennet knew I would. But I then used every connexion I had made in my previous seven years of apprenticeship to gain an introduction to George Saxelby, a well-connected solicitor. I managed to impress him. His most important client was old Mr Darcy."

Lizzy was listening carefully now; she feared she always would at any mention of a Darcy.

"When his father died five years ago, Mr Darcy was distraught—it was completely unexpected, and he was not prepared. There was some trouble, afterwards, with one of his legacies, and in assisting him with it, we grew to be...friends, after a manner of speaking. I understood him, you see. I, too, had once lost my world. I encouraged him to follow my example: keep on, press on. Not shovelling smoke, so to speak, but purposeful actions, one foot in front of the other. One day at a time."

Keep on, she thought. *Press on.* The phrases Mr Darcy had repeated over and over. Looking into his sympathetic eyes, she saw that she had not hidden her sorrow from Mr Gardiner, not at all. He was trying to help. He *did* care.

"He trusts you," she said at last. "I knew that because he only shared his exact whereabouts with one other—Mr Saxelby. And I think he has relied upon you as well." She took a deep breath. "I hope I may rely upon your advice, too, if you would be so kind as to give it."

"Nothing would make me happier," he said, and she felt her throat constrict at the kindness in his expression.

"The thing is…" She swallowed around the lump. "The thing is, you know already what my life was like at Longbourn. One of the ways I survived with my happiness intact was to…to cease hoping for things to be any different. I did not dream of the future like other girls do. I thought I would not marry, as my mother decreed it could never happen. Receiving a marriage proposal was such a surprise, and the expectation from my parents that I marry him even more astonishing. The offer was from my cousin, Mr Collins, the heir to Longbourn. I would have become mistress of Long-bourn, eventually—which I thought my father would not tolerate."

Mr Gardiner frowned. "I would guess Bennet's cousin to be quite elderly. He and Bennet were estranged, as I recall."

"You must be thinking of the father. I never met him, but his son offered an olive branch, so to speak." She told him of her ridicu-lous cousin, his ludicrous behaviour culminating in his absurd proposal of marriage. From there, and with a few promptings, she revealed the whole tale of her journey to Ramsgate, how she had discovered Mr Darcy, meeting Georgiana—even, the desperation of the poor girl at that first meeting, and the earl's desire to force a marriage to her other guardian upon her.

"Heavens above," he murmured.

She told him most of the rest, omitting any of Mr Darcy's declarations, lest her uncle want to insist upon their fulfilment, and any of their shared affection. "Mr Darcy is improving daily. He no longer requires a nurse but rather a secretary and his loyal retainers. Who knows what the earl will do?"

"As to that, I do not believe he is, any longer, in as much danger as he fears. The earl's heir has been embroiled in scandals requiring Darcy monies in order to extract him. He turned both of those affairs over to Saxelby and myself; I refused to pay out such sums in question without explicit, witnessed, documentation regarding the viscount's culpability. I will inform Mr Darcy of the existence of these documents as soon as possible. We will then remind the earl, ever so tactfully, what information Darcy's solicitors possess, should we be displeased."

Lizzy bit her lip. "Is it wise to anger an earl?"

Mr Gardiner smiled, and for the first time, she noticed something besides kindness—a strength of purpose. "No, no, no, my dear, it will all be quite civilised, I promise. I would know how to speak with the regent himself, should such a thing ever become necessary. We will simply come to a right understanding together."

Lizzy absorbed this. "Had Mr Darcy been incapacitated in truth, what would your role have been?"

"I would always see to Mr Darcy's interests to the best extent I could. It would have been much more difficult, however, had he not managed to communicate with Saxelby and myself privately. We were able to move certain assets into defensible positions, knowing, as we did, that Mr Darcy *would* someday resume his duties. We would always have challenged the earl's diagnosis, but had he been permanently debilitated, had we not understood his true condition, had he still been within the earl's control, and had the earl been able to force that marriage on Miss Darcy, our position would have been less certain."

For all his amiability, Mr Gardiner's gaze was penetrating. "If your actions have saved his life—which from your descriptions of every circumstance in which you took part, I do not doubt—you are owed a great deal, Miss Bennet. My employer is a generous man. You should consider what your future happiness requires."

It requires him! a part of her soul wished to cry. But she would not allow that to be true, and she would rather walk on hot coals than accept one penny for her time, her care of him. Besides, if there was a single skill at which she was more proficient than caring for the sick, it was the ability to find happiness no matter her situation. So instead, she gave him her most assured smile.

"For the present, I believe I will simply press on, as you once so wisely counselled Mr Darcy. Perhaps you should call me Lizzy, sir. All of my family do."

22

SOOTHED, IF NOT CONSOLED

W hen Darcy returned to The Breakers that evening, Lizzy was gone. He had known she meant to leave— had known that she *must*, since she would not accept him as her husband. But he had believed there would be one more evening...perhaps, even, one more chance to put into words the tangled feelings of his heart. However, Mrs Davis had, with an eager curiosity, given him Gardiner's card and said with whom she'd departed.

"*Said* you already knew her plans," the housekeeper added. "*Said* she wished you well. Made a fuss about me remembering to tell you that. As if I'd forget," she sniffed, her opinion of fleeing wives clear.

Darcy only nodded his dismissal, relieved when the housekeeper was gone. He found speech difficult, still, with people less known to him. When he spoke with James or Frost, he could make himself understood; but when he *tried* to think of the correct words, they tangled madly. Only with Lizzy had he achieved anything close to real lucidity. And she was gone—what had Gardiner thought of finding her here? Obviously, he had thought she ought to leave without delay.

Spotting the letter to Matlock—his marriage proposal, the last thing she had written, full of his unrequited adoration—lying on the writing table, he crumpled it and tossed it into the grate. Restlessly, he roamed the house, soon finding himself entering the room she had so recently occupied. It had been so sweet, imagining her there, just beyond his connecting door, knowing if he called, she would come; knowing if she called, he would run to her. Yet, it had also been dangerous—their unspoken passion for each other, too great. She had felt it too. He *knew* that.

He had been angry at her refusal. And hurt. But he would not dwell upon it. What he would do, he had decided, after today's long drive through the countryside to nowhere in particular, was keep on with his plans take his life back, without acquiring any bride at all.

Still, he wandered through her room, hoping against hope that she'd left some sort of note for him. There was nothing. But upon entering his own chambers, on his pillow, a sheet of parchment lay folded and sealed. He touched it, half-afraid it might disappear, a figment of his desires.

Carefully he opened it, then had to light more candles to better see it. Reading was still difficult for him, and it would likely be more easily deciphered in the morning, when he was fresh.

There was no possible chance of waiting.

It *was* difficult—and took what seemed an hour—but a word at a time, he made it out.

> *Dear Sir,*
>
> *Your man of business, Mr Edward Gardiner, arrived today with the papers you requested and an earnest desire to see you much improved. Imagine my surprise—and his—to discover him to be the brother of my mother. A great rift between my parents and himself precluded my ever knowing him. Of course, you must recognise how trusted a companion he will make for my journey back to Netherfield. He will write, he instructs me to inform you, to let you know when I am delivered safely and to determine what next you wish him to do.*
>
> *I will only add, God bless you.*

E.B.

He lay awake for a long while that night. *Incredible! The feared and unknown uncle had been Gardiner! A most trusted man of business, one of unshaken and unshakeable character and integrity, proven a hundred times over—he is her uncle!*

Gardiner must have been appalled that Darcy would keep a young lady of her family, goodness, and virtue to *nurse* him.

Still, Elizabeth had taken no risks with *his* reputation, he noticed, even in that final note—sealing it and avoiding the Darcy name and her own. If the housekeeper had been so audacious as to break the seal and read it, nothing contradicted what she had been told, protecting him to the last, and her adieu had been charity itself.

Finally, the hours passing in wakeful sorrow, knowing he was being ridiculous, he went to her room, retrieved one of her pillows, and brought it back to his own bed. With the scent of her in his lungs, he finally fell into a troubled sleep.

The next morning, he spoke with James. "Leave…Pember. Pack."

The footman broke into a smile. "'Tis about time, sir," James replied with a candour he once would never have dared. "Yer people be there. 'Twill all be better from Pemberley."

"Hope," Darcy replied.

The earl might discover him there, but in the night, he had made his decisions. The devil with the earl; the ache of Lizzy's loss was a missing limb, the urge to follow her to Netherfield and beat upon Bingley's door a relentless temptation. But no; her decision had been made. And if he was not going to bow and scrape to the earl, it was time to take his life back. His speech was not perfect, his reading abysmal, his writing illegible…but he was whole; he was improving. He would instruct the housekeeper to forward any letters on to Pemberley in Derbyshire, then close up the house. *Or perhaps have James tell her,* he thought ruefully and went to speak to Frost.

Just before his departure, Darcy walked through The Breakers a final time, gathering memories. It was foolishly sentimental besides being painful. But the first time he'd attempted swimming in the ocean, he hadn't been able to remain in but a minute or two —the combination of freezing cold and the sting of saltwater in his sores nearly felling him. Yet, he had grown to be glad he had faced it, persisting, strengthening his resistance to the cold and the pain until he could manage an hour at a time.

He would gather these memories now: Lizzy embroidering some delicate piece, reading to him by candlelight, writing at the desk, encouraging his every effort. Even those memories he hated, ones of pain and weakness, she had been here, caring for him, helping him, teasing him for some misspoken vulgarity until he laughed too. Finally, he pulled that last letter, his aborted proposal, from the cold, empty grate, smoothing it and folding it carefully.

The recollections were painful and stinging at present, but he would collect them, regardless, to hold in the most private regions of his heart.

Lizzy approached Netherfield's grand front entrance with head held high and teeth gritted; she was not quite certain what to expect, but was taking Jane at her word that she would still be welcome.

"'Tis not too late, Lizzy. We can climb back in that carriage and return to London. Margaret and the children hated to see you leave so quickly."

"It is a temptation." Lizzy smiled gratefully at her uncle. "But I need to smooth things over with Jane and reassure Georgiana, who must be worried—despite the report she received from Mr Saxelby."

The day before, they had driven straight through to Mr Gardiner's lovely and spacious home on Egerton Crescent in London. He must have sent his wife an express from one of the inns where they changed horses, because she was eagerly awaiting them with an excellent meal and charming hospitality. Their four children—ranging in age from eight to three years—were each a delight. That very morning, Lizzy's aunt had begged her to return to them soon.

Her uncle grinned. "And naturally, you wish to show your father that you *will* take your place in the neighbourhood, with or without his blessing. I understand it."

"Better than myself, I think," she murmured, for she had not considered, in the morass of emotions vying for expression, that defiance was one of them.

But before her uncle could lift the knocker, the door flew open. "Sister!" Jane cried, throwing her arms about Lizzy. "Oh, you are home! I am so glad! Tell me you have come to stay!"

In that hug, Lizzy found a welcome she had not quite expected and a love she had once longed for. She relished it with a deep sense of gratitude, and only a small part of her remained a bit detached, unable to feel it as strongly as she once would have. "I will, if Mr Bingley agrees I might, but now you must meet someone. Jane, do you remember him? You would have been quite young upon his last visit, but here is Mr Edward Gardiner of Highview House in London, Mama's brother and our kind and good uncle."

Jane's brows rose in astonishment, and she looked from Lizzy to Mr Gardiner. "Uncle? Oh...oh. You know, I think I do! At least... how familiar you seem! Oh, Lizzy! How many questions I have for you!"

Thankfully, she asked none of them, as Mr Bingley joined his wife at the entry. In *his* welcome, she saw a man as besotted as ever with his bride, shaking Mr Gardiner's hand and immediately agreeing with Jane that *of course* Lizzy must stay with them at

Netherfield. In Mr Gardiner, he could obviously see a relation of whom he need never be ashamed—not only was her uncle outwardly prosperous, but he was in every word and manner of expression thoroughly gentlemanlike.

"Enter, enter," Mr Bingley cried, shepherding them towards the largest front parlour. "You are so welcome! Mr Gardiner, it is very good to meet you—I believe Darcy has mentioned you before. And now to discover we are family! And how is our mutual friend?"

"Apparently, much improved," Mr Gardiner replied. "I am very happy to meet you, too, Mr Bingley, and to meet you again after so many years, Mrs Bingley. You must plan a lengthy visit to Highview House and come to know your aunt and cousins."

"They are wonderful, Jane, all of them," Lizzy asserted as they entered the fine parlour.

"Or you must bring them all here for a country holiday, and as soon as may be," Mr Bingley invited. He paused as another figure appeared in the doorway. "Ah, Miss Darcy, come in, come in, for we have visitors to become acquainted with. Or do you already know Mr Gardiner?" He carefully shut the door behind Georgiana, Lizzy saw.

But Georgiana, quite heedless of genteel behaviour, ran to Lizzy and threw herself into Lizzy's arms with a more joyous greeting than even Jane's. At this, Lizzy's heart wrenched with feeling— their shared experiences of terror and love having created their own sisterhood, of a sort.

"Lizzy, Lizzy," was all she said.

Lizzy hugged her tightly for a moment before releasing her and addressing the others; Bingley's sisters remained nowhere in sight. Here, in this room, was everyone who knew the secret of her sojourn with Mr Darcy. It was vital to her peace of mind that she try to make them understand why. "We should all talk whilst we have a moment of privacy."

All eyes turned to her—her uncle encouraging, Jane slightly bewildered, Georgiana tearful, Mr Bingley suddenly sombre.

"Please, sit, all of you," he offered.

"Jane, I am sorry for not writing," Lizzy began once all were seated. "It could not be helped. You are aware that Mr Darcy was ill and that the earl of Matlock held designs upon his future. I tell you now, he was not simply ill, but as close to death as ever I have seen a man who yet survived. After the tortures—for they were nothing less—that Lady Catherine's doctor inflicted, a fever nearly took him to his grave. For a time, I wondered if he could possibly recover. The servants speculated openly that he would not." She took Georgiana's hand in hers and gripped it tightly.

"Thankfully, and because he is the strongest, most determined man any of us will ever meet, he has recovered much of what he lost at Donavan's hands and is now progressing daily. But his strength *alone* did not see him through." She took a deep breath. "I did. I saw to his care hour after hour, sometimes with teas and with poultices and with herbs and—when I felt him slipping from me despite whatever I know of nursing—with my pleadings for him to stay. *I* did not heal him. But neither is it an exaggeration to believe that—had I not been so devoted to his care—he might not have survived. There was, simply, no one else to do it."

Jane's mouth was an 'o' of astonishment.

Bingley's brows were raised. "I suppose it was not quite the thing —" he began, but Georgiana spoke over him.

"None of you saw him," she said, low-voiced. "I did. I witnessed first-hand the burned, torn, and bleeding flesh upon his back and shoulders as I helped him from his bed to escape the next onslaught of Donavan's torment. He was hanging onto consciousness by a thread that last day. And I truly believed it might *be* the last time I ever saw him alive."

"But Fitzwilliam *had* arrived," Bingley said. "Had you waited a few hours, the colonel—"

"Would do *what*, precisely?" Georgiana interrupted, and Lizzy was proud to see she neither faltered nor trembled. "Deliver my brother back to the earl, who had already put him at the mercy of those whom I know *for a fact* are villains? And even if not the earl, Richard planned to be on a ship in less than a week. How much attention and devotion *could* he give my brother? More hired servants who could not care less whether he lived or died? Another specious doctor? Lizzy is a heroine, and if you cannot see it, why—"

But it was Mr Gardiner's turn to interrupt. "I am certain *none* of us wish for any blame to fall upon Miss Bennet," he said calmly. "In fact, I believe we in this room would all be best served if we make it known that she spent her weeks away from Hertfordshire in my home, with my wife and children, as her parents previously intended. She did, in fact, visit us, and we are eager for a repetition. I am equally certain that we each understand the danger of speaking to *any* others of this *very* private family matter." He met the gazes of every person; in his eyes, Lizzy saw confidence and authority.

"Of course, of course," Mr Bingley was quick to agree. "We none of us have mentioned a word of her whereabouts to this point. The important thing is that she is home now, and the past is all to be forgot. Dearest, shall you ask Mrs Nicholls to bring tea?"

Jane—smiling with relief at her husband and plainly wishing to discover *nothing* else regarding Lizzy's absence—stood. "Of course. Lizzy, I will tell her to ready your room at once. I shall put you in the blue room, with its view of the garden, which you shall love. Uncle Gardiner, one shall be prepared for you as well. We would love to have you."

"I had thought to be returned to Highview by dusk, but I find myself anxious to at least stay the night and to renew my family's acquaintance," he agreed.

There were a few moments of awkward silence after Jane's departure to see to rooms, then Mr Gardiner asked Mr Bingley regarding

Netherfield's farms, quickly sparking a conversation, and so she turned to Georgiana.

"You have been well?" Lizzy asked quietly.

"As well as I could be, what with my worry. He is truly improved?"

"Every day better. I know he will come to you as soon as he can, for he misses you dreadfully."

Georgiana took a shuddering breath and would have replied, but at that moment, the door opened, and Miss Bingley entered.

Lizzy had forgotten, in her memories of malicious speeches and cutting asides, just how pretty was Caroline Bingley. In her elegant rose silk, lace sleeves, and rich brown ringlets, she was the exact opposite of Lizzy's dusty, drab dress and matron's muslin cap. *Had he ever stolen a kiss from her?* she wondered with sudden jealousy. But she crushed the thought in an instant. It was heretofore none of her concern.

"Eliza, how...surprising to see you." Caroline glanced at Lizzy's grimy hems with disapproval. "Or were you just leaving?"

But Mr Bingley gave her a firm look. "Caroline, it is good you have come down, for Elizabeth has just arrived with her uncle. Jane has invited her to make her home with us, and she has graciously agreed. Mr Gardiner, my sister, Miss Bingley."

Caroline looked as though she had swallowed something unpleasant.

"Miss Bennet—oh, pardon, Elizabeth and I were *just* getting acquainted," Georgiana said sweetly, plainly pretending they had never before met. "I believe we will become the greatest of friends."

"Thank you, Georgiana. I look forward to it."

Caroline gave a pinched smile. "I am sure. Perhaps I had better see how Mrs Nicholls does getting tea. If you will excuse me." With the barest curtsey, she swept out.

The men resumed their conversation, and Lizzy watched Georgiana's smile fade. "She has been hinting that she would like to address me less formally, but Lizzy, I cannot stand her simpering, unctuous manner. Rather, I try to avoid her if at all possible and ignore her fawning," she whispered. "And for her to be so unwelcoming towards you, of all people…"

Lizzy put a hand on her elbow and murmured, "It appears Mr Bingley will keep her in line, for the sake of peace in his home. You need not fight my battles. But I thank you for it."

When the younger girl contrived to move them further away from the men, on the pretext of showing Lizzy a view, she was further impressed. Georgiana, it seemed, had come a long way from the timid, cringing creature she had been—was it only two months past?

"When Matlock visited, did he have a private word with Miss Bingley?" Lizzy asked quietly.

"Not that I could see," Georgiana said. "I do not believe so. She behaved no differently before his visit than after. And if he *had* spoken to her, or if she received a letter from my aunt suggesting a match, she would not have been able to resist hinting of it to me. Besides which, she has shown no more than the shallowest interest in my brother's health, and that mere curiosity. If she thought to be his bride, she would be hounding me regarding his symptoms and illness."

"Good news, then," Lizzy whispered. "We have a bit more time. And every day that passes, Mr Darcy grows stronger. Soon this will all be an unpleasant memory. Things are looking up."

23

SOMETHING NEW TO BE OBSERVED

Pemberley. *Home.* For a day after arriving, Darcy basked in the comforting feeling of being surrounded by familiarity. But the differences within himself soon became obvious as well. Not simply that he had difficulty reading and writing but that his senses were...disordered, especially in the evenings, when fatigued. He would forget servants were in the room only to be startled when a small movement reminded him. He could not remember it happening with Lizzy—he had always been aware of her, no matter how quiet.

Too often, he missed what others were saying and had to ask for repetition. Darcy had always enjoyed business with, as his father had sometimes worried, an 'unnatural interest' in trade. He had mountains of correspondence, only some of which his solicitors had dealt with previously. It required his own attention, and yet his brainbox scrambled letters and words into Gordian knots that he must painstakingly unravel, taking hours to do what he had once done in minutes. It was vital that he hire a secretary, but it was one thing to ask Mrs Reynolds or Dobbs, his steward, to repeat themselves and quite another to trust a stranger. Any negative publicity could be fatal to his reputation. With every day that he was able to manage his *own* affairs, his sister and his future stayed within his control. So, he took an absurd number of hours producing a legible note explaining his whereabouts and had it sent to Highview via express. Perhaps Gardiner would agree to act in that stead for a time.

He missed Georgiana. He longed for Elizabeth. He envied Bingley, who had the privilege of watching over them. Vexation and despair flooded him. *I ought to be the one to safeguard and protect them both.* Painfully, he acknowledged the truth: Lizzy was right to have refused his suit. If he could not even take on a secretary, he was hardly ready to take on his uncle. It had been hubris to ask her as well as a sign of how much he had taken for granted—she had done so much to make his life run smoothly, whilst he pretended he could have everything simply because he wanted it.

❖

Once upon a time, Darcy thought the day wasted if he did not work on seven schemes at once, if no letters were written or business transactions negotiated, if his stewards were not given multiple assignments, if projects were left unplanned.

He could no longer even *think* of seven things at once, much less work on so many. Although he felt his strength build daily, and there was definite improvement in every aspect resulting from his relentless efforts, the frustration was a constant weight of worry. Each day, he practised his letters, forcing his fingers to copy the pages before him while they coiled and curled in his brain. The *helplessness* of it, to look around him at Pemberley's library, the work of generations, and know how difficult it would be to decipher any of it. But because it took ages to make sense of reports from Dobbs, he rode the land with the man instead. Because he could not depend upon his tongue, he spoke little and listened much. Because he could not easily write out orders, he thought carefully before he gave them, using as few words as possible to communicate clearly.

And to his surprise, he discovered things he had never known.

Dobbs began sharing more of his own ideas for improvements, many of which were astute and prudent. Had the man always possessed such ingenuity? And the land. How long since he had connected with the acreage itself, the farms, the fields, and the forests? When had it become merely recorded lists of assets and ledger entries instead of the soul of his prosperity? When had he ceased participating in harvests and barn raisings, coming to better know his tenants and letting them know him?

Not all his discoveries were pleasant. Several of his tenant homes were lacking, with large families expected to share tiny spaces. How could he have failed to notice that more was required than roofing repairs? How could he expect the children of his current tenants to remain here when they were housed so inadequately? What was to become of those who the land could not support if he could not increase its yields? What was to become of the farms if the majority of his tenants could earn more in factories elsewhere?

Many of the answers to his questions were uncomfortable. His father had taught excellent principals of thrift, industry, and diligence but allowed, encouraged, even *taught* him to follow them in an overbearing, selfish manner. He was accustomed to thinking of his father as all that was good, even benevolent, because he had generously rewarded behaviour of which he approved. It did not mean, however, that he had been particularly generous.

He had prized thrift—so money was saved in housing and wages amongst his people. True, the farms were, during some years, unprofitable, but in putting aside and storing against those seasons, he had neglected liberality during times of plenty.

There was no school on the estate for the children, so many of them must be as he: powerless to unravel the knowledge surrounding them, at the mercy of those who would take advantage. 'Too much education will create discontent, son,' his father's voice whispered. "The most important knowledge they receive comes in listening to their parents, in teaching them a love for the land."

But if they could not afford to marry, would love for his land help them sleep better at night?

Wherever he looked, he saw too much needing improvement. Nothing was as it seemed. Never had he needed the fine education his father had provided him as now, whilst sweating over the recording of a simple thought. Never had he wished he had seen more to the schooling and nurture of his tenants and servants than now, when the skills and knowledge he had unthinkingly hoarded were trapped uselessly inside his mind. The little he had done in the past was plainly not enough to ensure prosperity in the future.

And yet, helpless as he felt, incompetent to deal with so much as he was…as the days passed, he never ceased wondering about Elizabeth, how she fared, and if she ever spared a thought for him.

Lizzy stared at her dress choices, an unfamiliar feeling of despair filling her. She had attended assemblies in Meryton since she was fifteen, and while the plainness of her clothing had always been a challenge, she'd had four sisters. None of them had minded if she borrowed a ribbon, a necklace, or made over a dress they had tired of to improve her appearance. Not even Mary, although she was prone to offer annoying praise upon her own benevolence.

But something about their divergent lives before the wedding had damaged the degree of intimacy required to casually rummage through Jane's jewellery and lace. Lizzy's best dress was of good fabric in a dark colour somewhere between brown and black, with absolutely nothing in the way of trims. She'd worn it to most of the parties and dances in Ramsgate without thinking much about it. Why should she care now?

With a sigh, she acknowledged to herself that it was all pride. Her uncle had been correct; she had wanted to show her father that she had not only survived but had thrived during her absence. That she could come and go as she pleased without reference to his feelings on the matter.

Which you can, Lizzy, she reminded her reflection. *Forget not, you are fortunate that your father ignores your presence at Netherfield.*

A tap on the door interrupted her self-lecture.

"Come in," she called, and Georgiana entered. Lizzy grinned. "Have you changed your mind and decided to attend the assembly? Or did Lydia and Kitty scare you off it?"

"Oh! Oh no. They have been most kind," Georgiana replied, a little flustered by the question.

Lizzy knew her brash younger sisters made Georgiana uncomfortable.

"I was wondering whether you might like to wear my lace collar? I think it would look lovely with your dress."

Her cheeks were pink as she held out the thing, and Lizzy knew that kind, sensitive Georgiana had been the only one to worry about Lizzy's appearance. Her own sister had never given it a thought—she was so accustomed to seeing Lizzy dressed sombrely and for Lizzy to be the one who did all the asking...she had never *had* to give it a thought. Jane would willingly agree to whatever was requested of her, but it was not quite the same as being empathetic. And of course, pleasing Mr Bingley was her life's work now.

"Thank you, Georgie." Lizzy smiled at the younger girl. "You know, there will be other young ladies in attendance who are not yet out. A large group, in fact, will be watching the dancing in chairs put up near the floor for that purpose. I would stay beside you and introduce you around. Several of the families are quite nice and, ahem, a bit calmer than my younger sisters."

"You are very kind. But...I truly am not ready for such entertainments. I...well..." She bit her lip, bowing her head, and dropped hard into the nearest chair. "Please understand. I am *happy* I am not yet out, and I have that excuse not to participate. I...I have made mistakes, in the past. I hope you do not take offence if I share no details, for I still have not learnt to view them with equanimity."

Lizzy felt her heart turn over at her friend's sorrow. What had Mr Darcy told her about the man who had taken such extreme advantage of Georgiana's youth and loneliness? A man who had grown up on the estate, who was well known to her from childhood, and who was their father's godson as well, someone whom Georgie had no reason to suspect of nefarious motive. What was his name? Wilson? Wexham? *No matter.*

Lizzy went to her, knelt at her feet. "Of course I am not offended. I never could be, not by you. I pray you will look forward rather than back. All will be well."

"Oh, Lizzy...I wish I had not..." Georgiana whispered, her voice small. "I...until I know for sure that my brother is well and healed, I cannot possibly go to parties and pretend I have not a care in the world. Oh, how I wish I had not...made those mistakes."

"Mr Darcy told me, once, that he was not feeling...himself just before his illness struck. He would hate for you to feel responsible. I understand not wishing to go tonight. To be honest, I am not enthusiastic about the evening myself. But as your brother often said, we must 'press on'— and I am trying to do as he might wish. Oh, I hope you understand! You are as dear to me as any of my sisters. Perhaps more so," she said.

Georgiana finally looked up. "I...I will try to deserve your friendship."

Lizzy reached up to embrace her friend. "All is well, then, for there is *nothing* you can do to lose it."

Georgiana managed a smile. "Here, then, let me fasten the collar for you."

They went to the looking glass together, and Lizzy smiled at her reflection. "An enormous improvement. I thank you."

A look flashed in Georgie's eyes. "If you were to remove that cap... and perhaps, burn it, it would improve *everything* enormously. Your hair is lovely, Lizzy. I do not know why you hide it."

"Why, because my—" Lizzy began but then halted. *Because my father hated seeing it, hated seeing* me. *Because* I *hated it, whenever I saw myself through his eyes.* A sudden memory assailed her: Mr Darcy, his hands in her hair, the intent look in his eyes as he mussed it, the groan he'd sighed, what his eyes had revealed about what he wished to do, to her and with her, at that very moment. It was silly, even, that she had ever kept her hair hidden from him.

"Do you suppose Sally might have time to do it up before the carriage leaves?" she asked instead.

"I will find her at once!" Georgiana cried eagerly, hurrying to the door. "I am sure she will!"

Lizzy turned back to her mirror and began unpinning the linen covering. "Press on, Lizzy," she whispered to her reflection. "Even if you never see *him* again, you can see yourself as *he* saw you."

Beautiful.

⸻

"Lizzy, there you are," Jane called once Lizzy finally appeared downstairs. "Oh! You look quite nice. Does not she look lovely, Mr Bingley?"

"Indeed, you do, my sister. I shall have to beat the fellows off with a stick! And I am the most fortunate man alive, surrounded as I am by such beauty." He laughed good naturedly, crooking out his arms to offer them both escort.

"You shall be surprised, I think, at our numbers, Lizzy. The regiment has improved attendance exceedingly."

"I am happy to hear it. Will Miss Bingley and Mrs Hurst be joining us?"

"Oh, they have already departed for the assembly hall in Hurst's carriage."

The three of them chatted merrily during the drive, and Lizzy tried to join in their enthusiasm for the event. But although they had warned her, Lizzy was unprepared for the sheer number of men gathered for the assembly. She was accustomed to a scarcity of partners and knowing every person in attendance; now, there must be three men to every female! It was probably just as well that Georgiana had chosen to remain home, for it would likely have been a more intimidating gathering than she had envisioned.

But there were benefits to such a crowd. For one thing, her uncovered hair caused little notice, as it might have once upon a time. For another, she was swept into the dancing immediately, after Mary King introduced her to an officer, a Mr Chamberlayne. There were, of course, many other familiar faces as well, and her welcome from them was equally gratifying. She looked about for Lydia and Kitty, both of whom had been very excited by the probable return of a young captain, a Mr Denny—who, according to Lydia, was not handsome but considered quite eligible. And although she tried not to, she continuously watched for the arrival of Mr and Mrs Bennet.

But her sisters were late arriving, and when they did, they did not come with her parents but with the Lucases—evidently her mother's edicts against *that* family had gone the way of all her others— her sisters' laughter somehow louder than any others, despite the noisy rooms. She went to greet them, and they readily included her in introductions to the officers they conversed with. One was the hoped-for Mr Denny, and another, a Lieutenant Wickham of Derbyshire. He seemed to take an immediate liking to her.

"My friend Denny tempted me to join the Hertfordshire militia with his report of the very great attentions and excellent acquaintance here. Society, I own, is necessary to me. I have been a disappointed man, and my spirits will not bear solitude. I can plainly see he did not lie." He gifted her with a most charming smile, conveying both respect and admiration.

Oh, to feel something, anything! She *ought* to have, for his appearance was greatly in his favour; he had all the best part of beauty—a fine countenance, a good figure, and very pleasing address. If only he were taller, broader of shoulder; if only he had a curl inclined to fall upon his forehead and eyes of the darkest chocolate. How long would she search for another's face and form amongst strangers?

Lydia quickly—and in the most forward manner—demanded Captain Denny lead her into the country dance whilst Kitty procured another partner with very little less presumption. But the rest of the party remained standing and talking together, very agreeably, when to Lizzy's surprise, they were joined by Mrs Hurst and Miss Caroline Bingley—who generally ignored anyone of the surname Bennet. She could do no less than introduce them, but was further surprised by the questions Miss Bingley asked the lieutenant.

"We hosted another gentleman from Derbyshire earlier this summer, for the grouse," she said. "Mr Fitzwilliam Darcy of Pemberley. Do you know him?"

"Yes," replied Wickham. "His estate there is a noble one. A clear ten thousand per annum. You could not have met with a person more capable of giving you certain information on that head than myself—for I have been connected with his family in a particular manner from my infancy."

Lizzy could hardly fail to be deeply interested in the subject, and longed to hear anything he would tell her of the Darcys. However, it seemed rude somehow not to mention that Miss Darcy was currently a houseguest, and she opened her mouth to say so. But Mrs Hurst spoke first.

"He has been ill, as I understand, and is recovering slowly."

Lizzy took immediate offence. How dare she probe for more information, for *gossip*, from this stranger? It was ill bred in the extreme. But her offence only grew at Wickham's reply.

"I am most sorry to hear it, although his behaviour to myself has been scandalous. But verily, I believe I could forgive him anything and everything, rather than his disappointing the hopes and disgracing the memory of his father, who was one of the best men who ever breathed."

"Disgraced," Lizzy repeated coldly, her temper beginning to boil. Who was this man? How dared he make such accusations?

"It is difficult to hear, I know, as difficult as it is to say. Old Mr Darcy was my godfather, you see, and I cannot do justice to his kindness. He brought me up for the church and bequeathed me the next presentation of the best living in his gift. But when the living fell, it was given elsewhere."

Godfather! Godfather? No, it could not be! Not Wilson. Not Wexham. Wickham. Wickham! She glanced at Miss Bingley and Mrs Hurst, expecting to see identical expressions of outrage.

They wore identical expressions...but of avid interest.

"Really?" Miss Bingley breathed. "Do tell!"

"How could that be?" Lizzy questioned. "How could a will be disregarded? And if so, why did you not seek legal redress?"

"There was just such an informality in the terms of the bequest as to give me no hope from the law." He sighed sadly. "A man of honour could not have doubted the intention, but Mr Darcy *chose* to doubt it—or to treat it as a merely conditional recommendation. I cannot accuse myself of having done anything to deserve to lose it. I have a warm, unguarded temper, and I may perhaps have sometimes spoken my opinion of him, and *to* him, too freely. I can recall nothing worse. But the fact is, we are very different sort of men, and he hates me." He adopted a pose of piety. "Of course, he deserves public disgrace, but it shall not be by *me*. Till I can forget his father, I can never defy or expose *him*."

"And yet—" Lizzy began, intending to point out this contradiction, for he had most certainly both 'defied' and 'exposed'; but Miss Bingley spoke *over* her, tossing Lizzy a snide glance.

"I suppose you know Miss Darcy as well?"

"Oh, of course. I wish I could call her amiable. It gives me pain to speak ill of a Darcy, but she is too much like her brother—very, very proud."

Miss Bingley smiled.

"You must be feeling a good deal of pain now, then," Lizzy said acerbically, "for you have spoken very ill indeed."

His eyes narrowed in anger before his charming mask instantly cloaked it. "I do not blame you for disbelieving me, not at all. The world is blinded by the Darcy fortune and consequence, or frightened by their high and imposing manners, and sees them only as they choose to be seen. I have a different bias. Such has been my treatment at Darcy's hand, it is impossible for me to be an impartial judge, and thus I have no right to give *my* opinion." He beamed at Miss Bingley. "But enough of awful subjects! It is the prospect of constant and good society which has brought me to you. Is there any possibility your next set has not been spoken for?"

He led a tittering Miss Bingley onto the floor; Mrs Hurst turned away the moment Wickham's attention was gone from her, without even a by-your-leave.

THE INFLUENCE OF FRIENDSHIP
AND AFFECTION

Mrs Bennet, after ignoring Netherfield for two weeks following Lizzy's arrival—a slight for which Mr Bingley seemed rather grateful—resumed visiting shortly after the assembly. While Lizzy had been anxious about facing her mother again, Mrs Bennet talked away as though there had been no proposal, no rift, no expulsion. Granted, most of her conversation was directed at Jane, with suggestions on how to spend Mr Bingley's money, but it was not in any way pointed. Lizzy noticed that Georgiana, although having little to say, seemed unoffended by the blatant crassness, and thankfully, Mrs Hurst and Miss Bingley did not join them.

At the end of a very long hour, Mrs Bennet exclaimed, "Oh, Lizzy, you have not made my tonic for me in some time. Also, Lydia's monthlies are troubling her fiercely. I hope you do not mean to neglect us for long."

Lizzy bristled. *How dare she expect that I continue on as before, as if I was not thrown out on my ear!* "Yes, well, I have been gone, have I not? Jane's stillroom has not any of my herbs. Perhaps Mr Jones can provide something, or Mrs Hill."

"Oh, nobody is on my side. Nobody takes part with me! Nobody feels for my poor nerves. I have no pleasure in begging my undutiful—"

But Jane, seeing the conversation descending into no good place, found some mettle. "Mama, perhaps you could have Mrs Hill pack up Lizzy's, um, herbs and such and send them to Netherfield?"

This, Mrs Bennet agreed might be done and finally took her leave, but Lizzy found herself unable to dismiss her own anger. When Mrs Nicholls brought in the post, Lizzy used the distraction to slip out into the park, where she might regain her composure.

She understood Mama. She did. Mama was neither sensible nor even-tempered and was so far from compassion as to make herself unfeeling. And yet, she was almost childlike as well: easily distracted, easily entertained, quick to anger, quick to laughter. There was no use in expecting sympathy or rapprochement—Lizzy had wanted too much from her. Had her father possessed the patience of a gnat, he might have been able to influence and guide Mrs Bennet; however, when she was not instantly and easily managed, he only dwelt upon his resentment and jealousy. Mama had come to Netherfield, but had no skill for restoring what must be restored; she was as a child in many ways and probably always would be. But she *had* come, saying nothing of the past.

The silence and peace of nature was just what Lizzy needed; she had hoped to be calmer before meeting anyone, but Georgiana appeared on the path, and Lizzy certainly owed her better company after an hour of Mrs Bennet's.

"I apologise for my mother's...er, enthusiasm on certain subjects," she said upon joining Georgiana.

"Oh, she—that is, you listened to my aunt on so many worse occasions. Please, think nothing of it."

For the first time, Lizzy noticed that her friend was as pale as a ghost. "Has something upset you, dear?"

Georgiana sighed. "Yes. I have received a letter. A terrible...that is..." She stopped and started several times but finally got out the whole story. "I suppose I must start at the beginning. My father had a steward, who was also his good friend for many years. He had a son, my father's godson. As a child, he was kind to me. My father died, then his did—I did not see him for years. But this summer, in Ramsgate, I met him again."

She has learnt of Wickham's presence in the area, Lizzy thought. *Frankly, I am surprised the news was kept from her this long. But it is good that she speaks of it, exorcising these feelings of shame and guilt.* "Yes, with the awful Mrs Younge," Lizzy said encouragingly.

"Yes. She and this boy—a man, now—were well known to each other. She reintroduced him to me."

"How very unprincipled of her," Lizzy replied. "You were under her care, not even out, and alone without family. Lady Matlock could not have hired a person less suitable had she tried."

"I fell in love with him," Georgiana blurted. "I thought he loved me too. He wished...he said he wished to marry. To elope. I began to—to change my mind about the elopement, but I did not quite know how to withdraw. And of course, I was quite desperately in love, I believed."

Lizzy reached over, taking Georgiana's hand in silent reassurance.

"One day, he visited me. As always when he came, Mrs Younge made herself scarce. He was—was bestowing his affections upon me in our own parlour when Brother unexpectedly arrived. The scene will live forever in my mind. Fitzwilliam was enraged, very red in the face, then suddenly, he collapsed. I went to him, screaming at Wickham to get help. But he...he laughed."

Lizzy squeezed Georgiana's hand, fury at Wickham's callousness filling her.

"I could not believe the evidence of my eyes and ears at first. He left me there. To go for help, I hoped, but no one came, and I realised he...had not. *Would* not. The truth could not have been more obvious; he never had loved me, not really—his chief object was unquestionably my thirty thousand."

"How awful," Lizzy murmured.

"Mrs Younge, when she finally returned…she pretended, at first, to be as she always was, kindly and helpful. She called for her brother-in-law. Then the earl."

Lizzy sighed.

"Yes. As the situation grew steadily worse, Mrs Younge changed. She began reminding me of the cause of my brother's illness—which I had stupidly told her myself—wondering aloud whether or not she ought to tell the earl the whole story."

"Threatening, you mean?" Lizzy asked, barely hanging on to her temper, even though she had guessed this part. "Extorting you?"

"Yes," Georgiana agreed. "Demanding small things, at first. Then speculating about what might happen if she intervened with my brother's care unless she had my jewellery as well. I thought my pin money never came, but I would not be surprised if she found a way to steal it. By the time we left Ramsgate, she had taken everything I had of value."

Lizzy grimaced. "She was purely evil."

Georgiana nodded.

"I only wish I could have her thrown into Newgate!" Lizzy cried. "But Uncle Gardiner promised to see you receive your pin money here and also to ensure that you are never required to see nor speak to Younge again. She is in the past, and it is done and over."

"No. My past will haunt me wherever I shall go."

She withdrew a letter from her pocket and handed it to Lizzy, who unfolded it and read:

Dearest Miss Darcy,

Notice the respectful salutation. You are quite accustomed to it, are you not? To being thought the perfect young lady, looking down upon those lesser mortals surrounding you? We two know better, perhaps. Do you look down upon me now? Or do you remember me holding you within my arms, the feel of my lips upon yours, as once we shared so much more than mere friendship?

Do you remember the letter you wrote to me? I have read it so often I know it by heart. Sadly, the memories do not keep me warm when the nights are cold. Imagine my surprise to learn that you are so near! Come to me, my dearest love. It is all I can do to refrain from expressing my recent disappointment. But my lips are forever sealed, if I only learn you love me still. I will be in the village square tomorrow to happily shop for ribbons with you.

G. W.

"The cad!" Lizzy cried. "The lowborn, misbegotten scoundrel! He did not deserve even one of your kisses and does not merit another of your thoughts. How bad is the letter he refers to? Do you remember your words?"

"Only too clearly. I wrote him a poem, Lizzy, a stupid one about my love and his and...and babies with eyes of his colour." She turned bright red with mortification.

"Dearest, I know it is embarrassing, but it hardly sounds dreadful. It is the love of a young innocent and scarcely a stain upon your honour."

Georgiana only bit her lip. "But...what shall I do?"

"Do? Why nothing at all. Imagine he says the worst he could say. You deny it with true disgust. Deny, deny, deny, even if he shows your poem around. He makes himself appear as a liar at worst, a despoiler of young females at best. What good would it do him? And suppose some few idiots listen to him. What do you care? These people have no power over you or influence in town, and we can take cover with my uncle if need be."

"I would not mind that."

"Exactly." A darker thought occurred to Lizzy, however, and she felt obliged to voice it. "There is a possibility, I suppose, he is laying a...a foundation for a prospective demand."

"You think he may be after ruining my future rather than simply my present," Georgiana whispered.

Lizzy made herself shrug. "Very well. Let us say he waits a few years, until a betrothal or an engagement is announced. You ignore it. I might recommend confessing the childish error to a soon-to-be husband, perhaps. It would be embarrassing, yes. But you will hold your head high. It *is* in the past."

Curiously, at this notion, Georgiana brightened. "It is the best possible outcome, Lizzy! Because I plan *never* to marry—I am *finished* with sentimental attachments. They bring nothing except pain. I intend *never* to be so used for my fortune again!"

Lizzy turned to face her, forcing Georgiana to meet her gaze. "Do not you see? This rogue writes to a girl who is gone forever. Perhaps, had you received this letter a couple of months ago, you might have felt you must grovel before him or do whatever he demands or try to earn or pay for his good will. But the girl who lured Lady Catherine into eating sweets laced with sleeping draught, the girl who stood up to her guardian—a medalled colonel in His Majesty's army—the girl who refused to submit to an earl's demands that she accompany him, the girl who never allows the overbearing Miss Caroline Bingley to bully or intimidate her, the girl who told me to burn my caps...why, *she* would never care a tuppence for *anything* this worm says!"

Georgiana opened her mouth then closed it again, appearing thoughtful.

They walked together in silence for some time; Lizzy was thankful to notice the girl's colour was restored, her expression more peaceful.

"I met him, you know," Lizzy said at last. "Your brother told me about Wickham importuning you, and you must only imagine my surprise when, at the assembly two weeks ago, I heard a man declaring himself your father's godson, spreading lies and rumours about Mr Darcy. I knew at once it was he. I had even thought him pretty, in a way, until he opened his mouth. I predict his soiled character will soon be laid bare for all to see."

"You knew? All this time, then? But of course, I do not blame Fitzwilliam for telling you, even though a foolish part of me hoped he might forget."

"He does not blame you, Georgie. He never did. I hope someday you, too, will forgive your younger self for her mistakes. And I hope that if those mistakes are ever used to try to humiliate you publicly, you will think, 'The girl who made them is not who I am any longer, the poor dear.'"

"'The poor dear'…as if I were an infant at the time instead of one who ought to have known better!" Georgiana protested.

"Well…you really were. Cannot you remember? I do not think I have ever met a girl so timid and biddable in all my life."

The admission startled a laugh from her friend. "I suppose I was," she agreed.

"And I suppose those stupid linen caps I wore did nothing except announce to the world my own lack of confidence. But I shall encourage you with the same advice I once gave your brother: we shall remember the past only as it gives us pleasure to do so. Pact?"

And after a moment, "Pact," Georgiana replied.

It had been three weeks since he'd seen *her*; it felt like months.

Gardiner would be here at any moment, the thought filling Darcy with a mixture of dread and eager anticipation. Dread, for he was guilty of absconding with the man's niece and…*and what?* he thought defensively. *Falling in love with her? Asking her to marry me?* But then his shoulders slumped. If he had not been precisely dishonourable in his intentions, the fact remained that she had cared for him, intimately, for weeks. However heroic *he* believed her, if the world were to learn of it, she would be castigated, perhaps ruined. Still, even knowing he deserved Gardiner's censure, he could not help but hope to also hear news of her. Or would Gardiner pretend none of it had ever happened? After all, Lizzy might have told him the extent of Darcy's humiliation, of her rejection. Or told him nothing, inviting his fury.

But to his relief, Gardiner shook his proffered hand and seemed in all ways as usual. He took Darcy's speech issues in stride—but of course, his speech had improved a great deal. If he could not always hit upon the word he wished for, he seldom blurted completely inappropriate ones.

His reading had greatly improved, too, even if his writing still resembled Bingley's, and they worked for hours on his correspondence, making tremendous progress in the stacks of mail. The news Gardiner brought from town was almost uniformly good. His business interests had suffered but not as badly as he had feared; Gardiner had met with bankers, pre-empting any action from Matlock to interfere with his finances. He had prepared a letter to the earl, which was the perfect balance of warning and clemency, and only required Darcy's signature.

"I first learnt of your illness from Saxelby," Gardiner explained. "The earl wrote him, claiming you permanently incapacitated and demanding a full report of your assets to be used for your care. Of course, we were alarmed and took every step we could to trace you. Saxelby discovered your whereabouts in Ramsgate but arrived after your departure with Lady Catherine. He then followed as far as Rosings Park but shortly thereafter felt he was being led a merry chase and returned to London. Meanwhile, I uncovered some rather nefarious legal issues involving Mr Atticus Younge. We responded to the earl with our proof that his physician's reputation was hardly one that could stand legally against a Darcy and demanded your own physicians be included before any such diagnosis be noised about. I like to think the action delayed the earl in his immediate plans, and he lost you before he could simply hire a more reputable physician."

Darcy smiled for the first time. "Good...man. Younge is...snake."

"Oh, quite so. In truth, I believe Matlock has now retreated from all his former plans. He lost control of you, of the colonel, and of Miss Darcy. His visit to Bingley was a lame attempt to reassert himself, and what did he find? Not only were your friends standing with you, but he could not even intimidate the formerly docile Miss Darcy into falling in with him. Your sister's defiance was an enormous shock, I would say. Truthfully, he has nothing to gain, except the loss of his own family's reputation, if he betrays the Darcys with accusations of insanity."

"Georgie...come home. Pember-ley."

Gardiner's expression grew pensive. "Yes, there is no reason she should not. Except one, perhaps. I believe she is my niece's only real friend in the world. I think you owe Lizzy that, at least."

25

AN UNDERSTANDING OF THE FIRST CLASS

Darcy stared over at Gardiner. "Liz-zy," was all he could force his mouth to say. There it was, the name he had been longing to utter all day, the saying of it swallowing every other word in his hard-won vocabulary. "Liz-zy." He scrubbed his face with both hands, trying to get past it, to say more, but what?

I am her friend! he wanted to shout. *I would be so much more. She will not have me.*

"Until Brighton, I had not seen her in well over a decade, not since she was a sharp-chinned little pixie. But the instant she mentioned Longbourn, the years melted away." Gardiner sat back in his chair, looking up at the ceiling as if lost in memories.

"The day I last saw her, those many years ago, she had escaped from the nursery—again—and joined us in the parlour. Bennet wished aloud for his book, and she raced to bring it to him—the right one, too, amidst so many other titles. There she was, holding it out to him whilst he ignored her, second after second, her little arms beginning to tremble because it was such a heavy tome, my temper burning hotter with every passing moment. Finally, she dared say, 'Papa, here is your book for you, please' as sweetly as a tiny child could. Does he even glance at her? No. Instead, he calls meanly, 'Frances, take your brat back to the nursery and out of my sight before I throw her out of my home'."

"Devil take it!" Darcy roared. "Hanged, drawn, quartered." But his wrath choked off his words, and he pounded his desk in frustration and rage.

"Hold, man, hold." Going to the pitcher, Gardiner poured him a cup of water.

"'Come not between the dragon and his wrath'," Darcy muttered but took the cup anyway, drank it when he rather wished to throw it at something; not since trying to leave Younge's imprisonment had he been this furious. It took him some moments to gain control.

"Liz-zy...not deserve. No one deserve, least all her."

"I agree. I told you once that my falling out with my family indirectly brought me to you. That was the crux of the breach, and afterward, Bennet did what he could to ruin me. Not in his power, of course."

"Ruined...you and Liz-zy. Enough."

"But the fates decreed otherwise, did they not? They intervened in a rather miraculous way. She saved your life, I think."

Darcy nodded.

"You have compromised her. When I understood the situation, with her so alone, so friendless, I nearly lost all my powers of diplomacy; it was all I could do not to await you there and demand you do the right thing by her. In all honesty, my inclination is to demand you do it *now*. It is only my respect for Lizzy that prevents me. Her payment for all she has done on your behalf ought not to be the loss of all her powers of choice. I would not wish her tied to one who does not want her, for she is the very best of women, and deserves someone who realises it."

How could I explain? She does not want me, would not have me! And who could blame her?

After a moment, he realised he had only one recourse—to show Gardiner that he had already proposed and had already been rejected.

He stood. "Wait," he ordered, unable to prevent his peremptory tone. He was prepared to humiliate himself, but he did not have to like it. He went to his study, to his desk. Working the key, he unlocked a particular drawer and withdrew a book, recently purchased at a shop in Lambton, cheaply bound and not at all worthy of the grandeur of a place in Pemberley's library; it was a copy of *The Pilgrim's Progress*. It had reminded him of Lizzy, of her pathetic inheritance, and he had found he could not leave it behind.

Inserted within its covers was the last letter he had dictated to her, addressed to Lord Matlock but meant to ensure *she* knew his intentions. He hated to read it, to invite the pain of it again over wounds barely scabbed over, but if he were going to allow Gardiner to view it, he ought to at least be able to face, himself, those sentiments that had once so disgusted her. He could not imagine speaking aloud any of it.

The sight of her handwriting was still familiar, though back then, the words slid off the page whenever he attempted to read them. He could see her even now, covered head bent over a writing desk, stray curls escaping at her nape, her face lovely in profile.

> *My dear Lord Matlock,*
>
> *I am to be married.*

"Bold," he said aloud, "as...had not yet asked." Shaking his head at his overeager beginning, he continued.

> *She should not have been my first choice, or any choice at all—I perhaps should never have looked at her. Her family is more closely related to trade than to aristocracy. I assure you I understand the ramifications of this. I have thought it through carefully, and while I cannot be happy at the idea of*

bringing such a family into our circle, other principles guide me. I know your
special interest is the same as mine—wondering if such a bride will have a
deleterious effect upon Georgiana's prospects. I am convinced, however, that
my sister can rise above the embarrassment—I would never have chosen one
who would bring shame upon us, despite her deficiencies of blood.

He felt his face flush as he read the paragraph. Although he had meant to reassure Matlock that he understood her inferiority of birth and the consequence he was wounding, those conditions were dwelt upon with a warmth which was very unlikely to recommend his suit. Had these been his exact remarks? It seemed impossible; she *must* have edited them. But would she have made them *harsher* than his own? Hesitantly, he continued.

You will, perhaps, wonder if my choice means I am not in my right mind.
Whilst I cannot fault your concern, I ask you to withhold judgment. A rose
may blossom amongst weeds—I only remove her from such before they choke
her. Miss Bingley is accomplished in music, singing, drawing, dancing, and
all the modern languages. As well, she shows an affection towards and
reliance upon her sister that speaks well of family felicity. She has had the
running of her brother's house for some time, a not-insignificant accom-
plishment.

Miss Bingley! She had believed him to be speaking of *Miss Bingley!* Since he was certain he had not dwelt upon Caroline Bingley's accomplishments, those additions to the letter *must* have been Lizzy's—who, he remembered, seldom hesitated to embellish his words when she thought them lacking. He felt an instant of overwhelming relief. If he could blame his ineptitude on a misunderstanding, he was more than willing to let it stand. His memory *was* sometimes spotty of those earlier days—although he had been on the road to recovery by that time, he had still been, in retrospect, not at all himself.

But no. One of the last things she had said to him had echoed in his mind ever since:

"Since you choose me against your will, and since you so plainly worry this choice will prove to your family an absence of reason and character, I can assume you will have little difficulty overcoming any regrets at my refusal."

He had picked at her words in his memory often, like a scab he could not quite leave to heal. His words in this letter were not completely unfamiliar—he *had* worried that his choice indicated an absence of reason. The feelings of being so overwhelmingly attracted to a young woman of such obscure origin *had* disturbed him, had disturbed him since those feelings had begun in early June. In the time since their parting, he had almost *waited* for his feelings for her to subside, along with the rest of his madness.

However, they never had—and now he knew, they never would. Every time he reviewed the past, he could only remember her kindness and compassion, her fearlessness, her care for his sister then himself...and of course, her beauty, the passionate kisses, holding her in his arms, even talking for hours. His memory of *those* things refused to fade; he expected to grow old warming his heart with them.

No. By the finish of whatever was contained in this letter, she had understood his intentions. He nearly groaned aloud, despairing of what he would next read.

> *Her family has its imperfections, which may require some intercession. I am not quite certain how it will be accomplished, although I feel sure that exposure to their betters can only be beneficial.*

> *But my bride, of all of them, is witty and charming. I am unconcerned regarding her ability to navigate the society of her betters.*

Blast it, could he have thrown in the word 'betters' more often? As if Elizabeth, dearest, loveliest Elizabeth, had *any* betters! Were her 'betters' Lady Catherine and Lord and Lady Matlock, all determined to see him put away or dead, even? Was his own sister, who had fallen victim to the seductions of a rogue, a 'better'? Yes, Lizzy was witty and charming—but she was so much more.

Again and again, I reassure you: I have considered Georgiana's welfare. My bride is a good influence, although from a regrettable family. I know I sacrifice in this marriage. Her family's insufficiency of income and conduct are difficult to accept. Do not think me mad.

There was nothing more. Evidently, this was the point at which she had finally realised he was not speaking of marriage to Miss Bingley. He dared not try to recall what other words he might have blathered, making certain she comprehended just how far beneath him she and her family stood.

There was *nothing* in it of what he ought to have said. How could he have omitted her bravery in seeing him through his escape from the quack who had nearly killed him? Where were the words explaining that she had willingly risked *everything*, her very reputation, in order to nurse him back to health? In fact, in those feverish days of illness, it was the promise of her, the scent of her, the sweetness of her voice, the softness of her hands giving him courage, incentive to return to the land of the living. For days, she had barely slept. Even when he'd unknowingly hurt her, her only aim had been to do all she could for his recovery.

If she had never come, he would have died in the nursery of his own townhouse. His fragile sister, most likely, would have preceded him in death. The vaunted Darcy line—of which he was so proud and protective—would even now be extinct.

This, *this* was what he had offered her in return for her selfless care. Degradation. Humiliation.

He had made her cry.

Crumpling the paper in his fist, he loosed a string of expletives such as he had not uttered since that day months past, finding himself tied to a bed, a prisoner of his mind and of his family.

Wherever Lizzy went, talk centred around the upcoming ball to be hosted at Netherfield Park. Lizzy felt she would be heartily glad when the thing was over and done with, but of course, she did not blame her neighbours for their enthusiasm. Lydia and Kitty never ceased arguing about who would dance with whom, but when they began bickering over Wickham's affections, she could not remain silent.

"He is very poor. Would not you find it annoying if your husband could not spend upon you a tenth of what your father does? But of course, I shall not warn you against him, lest it only encourage you to pursue him more blatantly."

"He would be nicely set up if only Mr Darcy had not cheated him of his inheritance," Lydia sniffed.

"That horrible Mr Darcy," Mrs Bennet agreed.

"You have only Wickham's word on that," Lizzy argued. "Miss Darcy told me that the truth was quite the opposite and he was paid out many thousands—which he has obviously wasted—after *refusing* the living. I believe her."

"You would," Lydia argued. "*He* says she is the dullest creature on earth and believes everything her brother utters without question."

"Please, Lydia," Jane pleaded, trying half-heartedly to intervene. "Miss Darcy is our houseguest and deserving of our esteem. I would be mortified if she heard you say any of this."

Lydia only rolled her eyes. "Most days she is too busy practising her music to even notice that we have arrived! How boring it would be to do nothing except pound the keys, day after day, like Mary."

"There is no comparison between Mary's playing and Miss Darcy's," Lizzy interjected dryly.

"Her brother was *so* disagreeable, Lizzy! How can you take his part?" Kitty cried.

"Oh, of course, why believe in a man of well-known, upright, respectable character, whose dearest friend is your brother, Mr Bingley? Any girl with a grain of sense in her upper storey would fall in love with the impoverished soldier instead, for it is a good deal more romantic."

"Pooh, Lizzy, you are becoming as dull as Miss Darcy. I am not in love with Mr Wickham. But he is, beyond all comparison, the most agreeable man I ever saw, and Papa is partial to him too."

Thankfully, Mrs Nicholls brought in the tea at that moment, or Lizzy might have expressed her thoughts upon her father's ineptitude. Why did Mr Bennet do absolutely nothing to prevent Lydia and Kitty from behaving so poorly? She understood Jane's fears for them, for they went into Meryton every day that it did not rain and traipsed after the officers, flirting outrageously, making fools of themselves over the men everywhere they went.

Mr Bennet had apparently given up any idea of preventing Mrs Bennet and Lizzy's sisters from visiting Netherfield, for now they came three or four days a week; only Mary had followed his original edict to stay away but only because the time, she had relayed, could not be spared from her studies. And while Lizzy appreciated the contact with her sisters, it had been a good deal easier not to worry about them when they were beyond her reach. At least her anxieties about Lydia and Kitty kept her from dwelling upon her own losses; she thought she defended Mr Darcy very well and coolly now, with no one possibly the wiser that she had been in love with him, once.

Jane presided over the tea tray, looking very pale. She had been far quieter than usual recently, was arising much later in the day, and retiring early. Although she had shared nothing with Lizzy as yet, her complaint was obvious—but of course, Mama, being Mama, noticed nothing. Probably, Jane was worried that she would, else she would likely be napping right now.

But as Lizzy listened to her mother laugh uproariously at Lydia's story of some prank she and Wickham had played upon another officer—instead of helping her younger sister understand that she was making herself ridiculous in the eyes of anyone respectable—a new thought occurred to her.

Mama, never one for contemplation, lived with a husband who mocked and belittled her and whom she probably hated. Instead of becoming morose, she sought diversion. She might love her other daughters more than Lizzy, but she did not *mother* them—she wanted their company, wanted them to provide her with amusement, as if she were of an age with them.

We, all *my sisters, are starved for true parental affection,* she realised. *But what can I do?*

When he could delay no longer, Darcy slowly made his way to the library where Gardiner waited, closing the door behind him, leaning heavily against it. He still held *The Pilgrim's Progress* clutched in his hand. Gardiner stood, looking alarmed.

"Is something the matter, sir? You appear—"

"I...made mistakes!" he blurted. "Said wrong. Bad as brute, Mr Bennet. Drove her...away. Lizzy...deserves better man. But I do... love her. Most sincerely." The words came easier as he expressed the feelings of his heart, clarified them to her uncle and to himself. "Asked her to marry—no. *Assumed* she would marry because I bothered to say I...willing. Two times." He held up two fingers. "Once before ill, once after. Cannot...blame illness. 'Tis me. Mutton-headed sapscull. Do not deserve," he repeated. "Never...has a man wished...wished could go back...unsay...stupid, devil-damned words from his foolish mouth." He stared at his feet.

"'Tis unlikely to be the last time you wish that," Gardiner said dryly. "As marriage will surely teach you."

Darcy's head snapped up. Inexplicably, Gardiner was grinning.

"You do not…understand."

"No, I surely do not and am grateful it is so. I have made too many of my own mistakes, you see, to sit in judgment of yours."

"How can I convince her…apology? Will change. Must change, prove. How?" He stared at *The Pilgrim's Progress* still in his hand, its bindings a far cry from the gilt and leather of Lizzy's edition, hers signed by…some relation of Charles II? No, that was not quite it. He tried to recall Lizzy's words about the inscription, but instead, the monotonous, stringent voice of his old tutor rang in his ear: "Catherine of Braganza, Queen of England, Scotland, and Ireland, 1662 to 1685."

But a queen had not signed Lizzy's book. Why this memory?

And suddenly, it came to him. He knew exactly. Knew what he had long ago forgotten and the probable, impossible thing he needed, somehow, to discover now. "Gardiner," he said with an urgency unlike any he had ever felt before, "what would do if…I required something most desperately, but…not mine?"

"I suppose it depends upon whose it is."

Darcy considered. "Rightfully…His majesty…the king?"

Gardiner raised a brow, cocked his head. "Well," he replied amiably, and not as if his employer had lost his newly healed mind, "our beloved regent possesses well-known and oft-lamented empty coffers. Perhaps we ought to discover just how valuable a prize it is, oughtn't we?"

At the conclusion of another visit from her mother and sisters, Jane escaped to her nap whilst Lizzy made her way into the music room. The younger girl's attention was solely fixed upon her playing; Lizzy thought a cannon could go off in the next room, and Georgiana would not notice.

Mrs Nicholls entered, carrying a letter. "Will you give it to her, miss, when she's finished?" the housekeeper murmured.

Lizzy nodded as she accepted it, recognising the handwriting as her uncle's. Then she saw that it had been posted from Lambton, a town which Georgiana had told her was near to Mr Darcy's estate...Pemberley.

She smoothed her hand across the folded parchment, knowing *his* words must be within. In that instant, she realised another truth: however dispassionately she spoke of him, now or in the future, whatever happiness she managed, however tranquil her outward spirits...she would yearn for him all the days of her life.

The music stopped abruptly. "Oh, how long have you been sitting there? You ought to have said something! I am so—"

Georgiana paused her apologies as Lizzy held out the letter, summoning a smile for her friend. "It is my uncle's writing, but I think this is something you have been waiting for."

Georgiana took it eagerly, opening it immediately. Lizzy felt her fingernails biting into her palms as she waited. *Do not be foolish,* she told herself. *He will not ask after you.* Except...she longed for some small indication that he did not hate her. Perhaps a 'Please pass along my greetings to Miss Bennet and her family' as an adieu? An acknowledgement that they held an...acquaintance, however trifling?

Georgiana, with shining eyes, handed it over as soon as she had read it through.

> *My Dear Georgiana,*
>
> *If it seems unusual to be hearing from me in another hand, you may, even so, be grateful to Mr Gardiner for his better penmanship; although mine is improving, it still resembles Bingley's too closely to attempt anything of length. (I will address a separate letter to him, and I will be sure to omit that remark—neither need you mention it, for I am full of gratitude for his kindness in caring for you when I could not, and owe him and Mrs Bingley too much as it is.)*

On that score, you may be assured I am seeing good progress daily—not so quickly, perhaps, as I wish, for you must appreciate my impatience to reunite with you and put the past behind me in every particular. Still, I am tolerably well, and to be clear—the condition of the person you last saw and the strength and vigour of the one who writes you today are so widely different from what they were then, that every unpleasant circumstance attending it ought to be forgotten. My speech gives me some trouble, but mostly at night after a busy day, and Gardiner assures me it is acceptable enough.

I have written our uncle, giving him to understand that his intervention in our affairs is no longer required. I feel confident that his lordship will find my arguments sufficiently compelling. As for Lady Catherine, it will be some time before I find myself able to consider renewing our connexion. For Anne's sake, I suppose something must be done eventually, but you need not worry we will ever again spend our Easters at Rosings. Darcy House is cleared of any servants not under Mrs Taylor's direct report; Saxelby will see what can be done to ensure Donavan is not allowed to inflict himself upon other victims.

As to another matter that might trouble you, let me reassure you that I hold you blameless for any issue regarding my health and only regret that we were much deceived as to the character of Mrs Younge. Her employment has, of course, been terminated and without references. All else is to be forgot. I mean to sell the Lodge, as I cannot imagine either of us wishing to return to Ramsgate. Speaking of which—I understand Younge let go your maid, Evans. Efforts are being undertaken to find her, and she shall be offered her position again, if she wishes it.

I leave for London today and am unsure the length of my business there but expect to bring you home to Pemberley by Christmastide. Please know how deeply you are missed and how very much I look forward to our reunion. You may write to me at Darcy House for anything at all.

Your Affectionate Brother,

F.D.

It was a universally good report and all of what Georgie had wished to hear.

JULIE COOPER

The complete absence of the slightest mention of Lizzy, his desire to 'put the past behind him in every particular'...well, it told her the rest of what she needed to know.

THE APPREHENSION OF
DISGRACE

Jane had sent Lizzy to Meryton to select a dress for the ball. It was very kind of her—their figures were quite unalike, so of course, she could not simply wear one of Jane's new gowns, and the dress would be lovely when completed. But neither had Jane felt well enough to accompany her, and it was impossible not to feel she should be as conservative as possible with her choices and spend as little of Mr Bingley's money as she could. It was equally impossible not to envy her sisters, who would each be decked out in the most expensive, loveliest fabrics and trims; Jane's had been sewn in London by a town dressmaker of great repute, and Jane appeared angelic in it.

Nevertheless, Lizzy knew she had little of which to complain. Even though her dress was not lavish, it was the prettiest she had ever owned. Besides, she cared nothing about whom she would dance with and certainly had no interest in the officers; it was merely a pleasant opportunity for entertainment and recreation.

Mr Bennet, evidently unable to think of a good enough excuse to miss the neighbourhood's event of the year—held in his eldest daughter's honour—would be in attendance. Lizzy had about as much desire to see him as he doubtless did her; they maintained a tacit agreement of avoidance, which was not a lot different from what she had experienced her whole life with him. But Aunt and

Uncle Gardiner intended to come, and she did look forward, very much, to enjoying their company.

Truth to tell, she wished to speak to them about the possibility of spending Christmas in London at Egerton Crescent, leaving Netherfield just before Georgiana would. The thought of facing Mr Darcy again as a disinterested acquaintance was beyond imagination.

Three days before the ball found her alone in her sitting room, putting finishing touches of delicate embroidery on her new gown's bodice, when Kitty burst in. Lizzy glanced at her sister and set aside her fabric.

"Oh, Kitty, you are arrived early this morning! Have you come to fetch me? Is Mama downstairs with Lydia?" Lizzy asked. "I shall put this away and go down, if you will give me a moment."

Instead of a reply, Lizzy heard the tell-tale sound of a sniffle.

Inwardly, she sighed, for she had hoped to finish her stitching this morning, but she patted the cushion beside her, contriving not to allow Kitty to see her impatience. "You are troubled, Sister. Come, sit, and let us talk it out. I daresay we can cast a better light upon things if we try."

Kitty answered nothing but did plunk down rather gracelessly beside her. For some moments, there was silence between them, and Lizzy wondered whether she dared take out her sewing again until such time as her sister decided to reveal her sorrows.

"Did you walk over?" she asked, simply to have something to say.

"No," Kitty blurted at last. "I took a horse. It is not as though they would allow me the carriage, would they? I suppose if Lydia wanted it, *she* could have it." Then she began to sob in earnest.

Lizzy patted her sister's back while she waited for the tears to subside. She could sympathise with Kitty in many ways; Lydia had always been made much of, even in comparison to Jane. "I know," she soothed. "But you did not ride all the way here to inform me that Lydia took the carriage. Tell me what is the matter, dear."

Kitty tried to speak, but it took her some time to get any words out through her sobs. "She...she...she..."

"She? Lydia, do you mean?"

"Ye-yes. Sh-she w-will have...have...a n-new...dress!"

It was all Lizzy could do not to roll her eyes. She had seen the pretty pink gossamer net and white satin that was to be Kitty's gown for the ball, likely nicer than anything Lizzy would *ever* own. *Stop,* she chided herself. *Kitty is still but a girl, and fortunately her troubles are the troubles of a girl, although they seem as tragic to her as the real ones of a woman grown.*

"Lydia...will receive yet another new dress? Besides the Venetian crape that Miss Beckford is sewing?" she guessed.

"Miss Beckford!" she cried. "'Tis all her fault! She showed Mary King the whole of it, and what does Mary do but go to Spafford's and buy fabric of the exact same! Of course, she has not asked Miss Beckford to make it, but Mrs Latouche—who hates us, you know, since Mama would not pay her in full for that ghastly crimson Merino, even though she admitted its flaws. Lydia is certain Mary King has described the pattern to Mrs Latouche in every particular!"

"That makes little sense," said Lizzy. "Why would she wish to imitate Lydia?"

"Oh, she thinks she is so superior with her ten thousand," Kitty raged. "She will add stones or fur trims, anything to flaunt her wealth. Wickham has asked her for the opening set and will doubtless be impressed. He shall think Lydia the one who copies! It is not to be borne!"

It was good news, in Lizzy's estimation. As selfish as it might be, what a relief it would be to let Miss King's relations take a turn worrying about the scoundrel. Georgiana had prevented Lizzy from saying anything to Jane regarding refusing him an invitation; Georgie had not answered Wickham's letter nor acknowledged him in any way, but neither did she fancy antagonising him with an

JULIE COOPER

open denunciation. "I will not attend the ball, and I am leaving in a few weeks. Why provoke him now?" had been the girl's argument. If Lizzy had believed her younger sisters or her parents would listen to the opinions of Miss Darcy, she would have pressed Georgie harder, but it was likely a useless exercise. Besides, there was talk of removing the regiment to Brighton soon enough—*oh, happy day!*

"It sounds as though you are very sympathetic to the reasons for the, um, additional purchase," she began gently.

"I do not care about her stupid dress!" Kitty cried. "All I asked for was ostrich plumes and a few ribbons! While she shopped for a whole new ensemble, I only wanted a few trims! But no, only Lydia was to be given *everything*. Everything! She gets everything! It is not fair!"

What am I to say to such a trifling matter? Lizzy thought. *Have you ever studied your face in the looking glass for hours, my sister, searching futilely for some feature of Father's, some means of convincing him that you belong? Talk to me of fairness!*

But it mattered not; if Kitty had more of a place than Lizzy did, she yet had no parent who would try to understand or care. "It often seems so, to be sure," she agreed.

"I should not be so angry, I know," Kitty admitted. "But Lydia gets everything! A new dress, satin slippers, Chantilly lace, jewelled pins, even Wickham himself! Why begrudge me a ribbon or two?"

Warning flared inside Lizzy, but she kept her tone casual, gentle. "It sounds as though she will not 'get' Wickham, if he has asked Miss King for the opening set. 'Tis practically a declaration, to my way of thinking."

"Oh, no, you are wrong, Lizzy! Well, I admit, Lydia thought so, too, at first, and I daresay Mary King thinks it, but *she* is wrong too! He *loves* Lydia!"

"Loves her," Lizzy repeated dubiously.

274

"But he does! He *admits* it, but of course it is dreadful to be so poor, and how can he live? But he is very torn up about it."

"I daresay."

"I hear your disbelief, but he does. He *does*! He will prove it. You will see."

"That alarms me," Lizzy replied. "Kitty, dearest, you can see, can you not, the imprudence of falling in with a man who cannot provide for a wife or children, who cannot give the slightest security—"

"Because of Mr Darcy!"

Lizzy swallowed her indignation and resentment; it was more important to try to reach her sister. "Very well. Let us suppose there is some truth in his complaint. How does it help Wickham if there is? I asked him to his face if he had any legal recourse. He admitted he does not. The law will not help him regain what he has lost, however he lost it. At the end of the day, he is still poor. And now, he pursues Miss King, hoping to marry her and her ten thousand. You can see this, can you not? He hopes for *another* woman's fortune. Is this your wish, for yourself *or* for Lydia? To be the woman he supposedly loves whilst he pursues comfort and ease with another?"

Kitty bit her lip. "He is very handsome. I am certain he would not be so false."

Lizzy's patience slipped. "He is a monster with pretty manners, Kitty. Please, you cannot believe that beauty is any sort of distinguishing sign of good character and intelligence. You might as well call Miss Bingley a wit."

Kitty appeared shocked but then managed a little smile.

Lizzy tried the last weapon in her arsenal. "And now, we have an uncle, an uncle we were unacquainted with until recently. Do you suppose he knows of no respectable young gentlemen?"

In that moment, she surrendered her pride. Uncle had said she was owed something for her care of Mr Darcy. She would ask him to have Mr Darcy help her younger sisters with the addition of something to their portion, to help them achieve a different life than the desperation—for it was nothing less—leading Lydia to consider a false love like Wickham's. Uncle would know some way to get around her stubborn father. She was sure of it.

"Papa says Uncle Gardiner is so far beneath us as to be a worm, an elbow-rubbing cit," Kitty replied, albeit a bit uncertainly.

Lizzy closed her eyes, praying for forbearance. "Dear sister, he is our mother's brother. As our mother is, so is he, and so are we."

"My father is a gentleman!"

"A gentleman who has not saved a penny for your future or Lydia's. Is his neglect a point to his honour? How can we boast of such a father?"

"Well, he is not yours to boast," Kitty snapped.

It was a slap, a direct hit, unlike any she had ever sustained. Some unspoken sort of loyalty, loyalty to their mother, loyalty to Lizzy, had hitherto forbidden any such verbal accusations. She coloured and was silent.

"I am sorry!" Kitty blurted. "I did not mean it. I should not have said it. But Lydia *will* get Mr Wickham's love, she *will*! Her scheme...or rather...well, she cannot be so pretty for nothing. That is all! You should not be so cruel to him!"

The temptation to quit the room and leave her younger sisters to their fates was nearly overwhelming. Yet, Lizzy could not easily accept that Wickham was to be allowed unfettered access to ruin them, while every single person in their family circle looked the other way. She *must* try for a different outcome.

"Kitty...what scheme does Lydia mean to employ to 'get' Mr Wickham's love?"

Her sister retreated into silence.

"If you know of any plans Lydia has made with Wickham, you must tell me. You have insulted me in the most hurtful manner by scorning my birth. Can you imagine how it will feel for *you* to be on the receiving end of those sorts of accusations? If it becomes known that Lydia is indiscriminate with him, if she ruins herself, do you suppose *you* will not be tarred with the same brush? For he will *not* marry her, not for a penny less than Miss King's ten thousand. Do you believe Papa has enough money put by to pay him to do it?"

"He...might," she replied hesitantly.

"No. Do not delude yourself on that point. You know he has not. You *know* it."

"No one will discover it," she hedged.

"And if Lydia becomes with child?"

There was a long silence while Kitty looked at her feet, at the ceiling, anywhere but at Lizzy. "I know nothing. It is unkind of you to suspect her of such things!" But her voice was pitched unnaturally high; she was no great liar.

Lizzy cupped Kitty's face, forcing her sister to meet her gaze. "Do you suppose your father will forgive you, *ever*, for concealing the truth, should she be ruined? Do you suppose you will not be blamed?"

There was a longer silence, but at last, Kitty's shoulders slumped. "She will hate me forever if I tell," she whimpered.

She sighed and dropped her hands; shadowing Lydia was Kitty's life's work. "I know it is painful to consider." Lizzy allowed the sympathy she felt for Kitty's predicament to infuse her words. "Sometimes, if you truly love a person with your whole heart, what is best for them and what is best for you are not the same. You must make a choice. Whom do you love the most—yourself, and keeping the comfort of affection, or a most beloved sister?"

Tears again dripped down Kitty's face; finally, she said in a very small voice, "They plan to sneak away during the ball. It will be a crush, and no one will miss them. They will go to that old woods-man's cottage, the one where once you thought to hide. It is less than a mile, an easy walk under a full moon."

One of Mr Darcy's more vivid curses came to mind; Lizzy had to force herself to speak evenly. "Well. That would certainly ruin her new hems."

Kitty giggled, but her laughter quickly turned again to tears. "I knew it was wrong. But somehow, when Lydia confides in me, I envy her! How can I blame her for wanting his love? I wish he loved me instead. I *do*! I wish he loved *me*!"

It was maddening to hear, and Lizzy's first instinct was to describe just how low was the rat upon whom she bestowed her affection, to snap at Kitty for being vain and foolish and imprudent. But Kitty's—and Lydia's, for that matter—blatant desperation to be loved by someone handsome and desirable, however reckless, was also pathetic. And had she not felt the same anguish? For a better man, of course, and she'd had enough sense of self-preservation to finally remove herself from the situation. Even so, the wrenching feelings of loss beset her still, aligning perfectly with her sister's weeping.

And because she had longed for a mother's affection and concern, yearned for a father's care and counsel, because she had been so alone with her own grief in a way no young girl ought ever to be, she withheld her words of frustration and criticism. Instead, she gathered her sister into her arms, smoothing her hair, taking her tears into her own bosom. "There, now," she murmured, holding Kitty close as if she were a young child, murmuring the words she used to comfort herself against despair. "All will be well. You cannot see it yet, but all will be well."

After Kitty departed at last, Lizzy pondered her options. How to stop him? Confronting Lydia only meant that she—and Wickham —would henceforth better conceal any intrigues.

Obviously, Lydia would only submit to her father's authority; equally obvious, informing Mr Bennet of the trouble was fraught with difficulty. Her mother would be an unlikely mouthpiece, making a hash of the telling—and there was no guarantee she would believe in Lydia's guilt in the first place, her instinct to spoil and protect her youngest.

There was only one man whom Mr Bennet would likely receive with respect—his son by marriage. As little as Lizzy wished to burden him, doing so was her only recourse. With a sigh, she went looking for her sister and Mr Bingley and the succour she now so urgently needed.

27

A Picture of Conjugal Felicity

S he found Jane still in bed, although sitting up, looking rather pale.

"Lizzy, do come in and sit beside me. I am so sorry I have not come down for breakfast...I have not felt quite in spirits of late." Her face took on a pinched look. "Of course, Caroline says I emulate my mother."

Naturally, Jane would not wish to share the truth with such a sharp-tongued shrew; she must believe it too soon to share with anyone. Lizzy took her sister's hand in her own. "It is good that you already know she has not a brain in her head, else she would not say such stupid things," Lizzy replied. She hesitated, wondering if she should try to speak to Mr Bingley privately instead. "I have learnt something...something unpleasant. Perhaps this could wait a bit, however."

But Jane straightened, setting aside her tray. "Oh, Lizzy, please tell me if there is anything that I can do to be of assistance. I want to help."

Lizzy took a deep breath and told her what Kitty had revealed. She had not been sure what Jane's response would be—perhaps anger, perhaps sorrow and disappointment. She had not expected hysteria.

"It cannot be true. Mr Wickham would not behave so unworthily! You are mistaken! Oh, you *must* be mistaken!"

"I am afraid *you* have been much deceived by amiable appearance and graceful conduct, dear sister. I *told* you that he was untruthful in his criticism of Mr Darcy, but you chose to defend them both."

Jane turned utterly white at this. "I have!" she cried loudly. "I did. I have made a muddle of everything once again. *Again.* I cannot do anything right! Anything at all!"

Jane's maid, Harper, poked her head into the room, alarm on her face.

"No," Jane cried again. "Do go away!"

Lizzy nodded reassurance to the maid, who quickly made herself scarce, and for the second time that morning, Lizzy saw a sister fall to pieces. Jane's normally placid nature made the scene all the more distressing.

"No, no, no, no," Jane sobbed, rolling away from Lizzy to weep into her pillow. "It is all t-true, everything Caroline has said, everything she *will* say. I cannot s-stop it or escape it. How could I have known? You look at me, believing me to be the happiest of women. I have everything, d-do I not? But I never would have married him if I had kno-own!"

Alarmed, Lizzy did her best to comfort, patting her sister's back while Jane's shoulders shook. "You...you do not love Mr Bingley, Jane?"

"No! That is the p-problem!" She wept, going off into another round of sobs. "I d-do, I do. Oh, I d-do!" It took some time for her to be coherent enough for Lizzy to make any sense of it.

"It b-began in Scarborough, with his widowed aunts who married cousins. They look so much alike, and their names are Mrs Dora Smythe-Jones and Mrs Cora Jones-Smythe, and I c-could not get them straight. I am so stupid! He-he laughed every time I m-misspoke and made a joke of it to everyone."

"Dearest, he only thought it funny. He did not mean to be unkind. He does not think you stupid."

"B-but they did. It was so obvious. The harder I tried to b-be pleasing, the stupider my mistakes and the louder his laughter. I might have o-overcome my embarrassment, but of course, they wrote to Caroline and Louisa. At least his aunts were never vindictive or mean, but his s-sisters—they hate me, Lizzy. Every time I make any mistake, he makes a joke, and they p-poke at me."

"I have not noticed this, Jane. I believe you are being too thin-skinned." *And your husband needs to shut it,* she thought.

"They are m-more restrained when you are present, for you are just as likely to turn any tease back upon them without a thought. But Lizzy, I c-cannot. They pick and pick at me, in the subtlest ways, and I t-try so hard to make them like m-me, but they do not and n-never will. He...he w-*will* say something to them of Lydia, of what she is d-doing, of Kitty knowing. And I...I will hear of my sluttish relations all the rest of my life."

"Surely he would understand the need for gravity, for silence upon this particular matter," Lizzy tried.

"Oh, he would...except to his sisters. They are so loyal to him that he cannot imagine they are not loyal to me as well."

"Yet, if we are able to prevent any of Lydia's misdeeds, surely it will all be forgotten. Putting a stop to it early is the most important thing."

There was a long silence before Jane spoke so quietly her voice was almost a whisper. "It is like the store-closet at Longbourn."

"The...store-closet?" Lizzy asked, wondering if Jane was growing hysterical again.

"Yes. Do you remember? At first it was just a little drip, nothing to cause any mischief. Then more and more until it was a steady stream, and we had to move everything out of it, leaving it to splash itself as it liked. It is like that, Lizzy. Drip, drip, 'I wonder at the chintz, Jane—do you never grow weary of last year's styles?'

Drip, drip, drip, drip, 'Joints of mutton again! What a menu!' Splash, splash, splatter, spray, 'Dearest, never change, for Charles fell in love with your country manners!' Over and over again, at everything I do, until I fear rearranging a pillow or shifting a vase. Even if Mr Bingley s-somehow never mentioned another word about Lydia, *I* would know that *he* knows of our mortification, how weak and corruptible my relations. I can barely hold my head up as it is. I should never have brought him d-down as I did. He might have married a wealthy heiress. Instead, he only has me, and I...I am not enough." Her sobs began again in earnest.

It was all Lizzy could do to calm her sister's agitation with reassurances, to put her back to bed, promising that she would gain her uncle's assistance instead, and that Mr Bingley should know nothing of the matter. She sat beside her sister until Jane was finally sleeping then sought out a very curious Harper.

"Is the mistress well, miss? I never seen her go off like that before!"

"She is, or soon will be if she is not disturbed in her rest. Please, see that no one does," she instructed. "I will send up a special tea later that will help set her to rights. And Harper—there is no need to tell *anyone* of Mrs Bingley's distress."

"Oh, I wouldn't!" she assured, wide-eyed. "I'll take good care of her. You needn't worry."

But worry, apparently, is my new and constant friend, Lizzy thought.

Lizzy escaped to the park, not wanting to see anyone else—especially her mother or Lydia, although it was to be hoped they were too consumed with last-minute ballgown creation to visit. Her mind was in a tumult...but surprisingly enough, her first reflections were self-congratulatory.

This is what you avoided, Lizzy, she told herself. *Sneers, put-downs, and cold shoulders.* Choices had to be made, difficult choices. Jane had listened to her heart, taken the unequal connexion offered and look what it brought her!

But here, her thoughts came to a sudden halt.

Jane was wife to a man she loved, a man who could well support her and the child she was carrying. Irrespective of Jane's current perceptions, Lizzy had often seen his tender regard for Jane; he did love her, he *did*.

The real problem was not even his shrewish sisters. It was Jane's meek acceptance of their spite, as if it were her due. Lizzy had never noticed Mr Bingley teasing Jane excessively, but if Jane found his remarks hurtful, she must *tell* him. If the sisters were rude, she must put them in their places! This was *her* home!

Jane's unwillingness to do so, Lizzy laid at the feet of Mr and Mrs Bennet. All her life, Jane had been taught that her only value was her beauty. It was not true. Bingley's regard was not at issue, and Jane brought enough to the marriage—she brought *herself*, an intelligent, loving wife who would manage his home and mother his children with grace and kindness. Her parents always withheld affection when displeased. However, simply because she could not please his *sisters* was no reason to fall into despair; she still had every opportunity for happiness.

And what did it say about Lizzy's own decisions, her own difficult choices?

I am just as good, just as worthy as Jane. Did Mr Darcy really believe I was not? Or was I so ready to accept his ill opinion that, like Jane now, I cringed away from any mention of mine or my family's shortcomings? Have I unthinkingly accepted my father's opinion of my value? Was there truly only one possible outcome to his declaration?

But it was too late to unsay what had been said, too late to undo the past. All she could do now was help Jane rise above her current despair; meanwhile, Lydia's urgent situation must still be dealt with.

Lizzy had assured Jane she would reach out to their uncle—yet, what could he do? Keep an eye on Wickham during the ball, certainly, as she would be closely watching Lydia. Still, the scoundrel would certainly try again. Could he contact Mr Darcy, see Wickham run from town? Possibly, given enough time. But time was a luxury they did not have, and he had no authority over Lydia, regardless.

An unsigned letter, perhaps? But if Lizzy addressed a letter to her father anonymously, she would have no way of knowing whether he had read it. Mr Bennet was a most negligent and dilatory correspondent, who often put off reading his letters for days at a time— probably for fear of someone asking something of him or expecting the honour of a reply. Besides, who would believe the words of a nameless stranger, especially words one did not *wish* to believe?

To expect Kitty to confess Lydia's proposed scheme to her parents was ludicrous—she never would. Mary, of course, would be happy to tattle. But of them all, Mary was the most like their mother. Oh, her faults were different ones, but they revealed an essential silliness—such as the deep pride she took in being virtuous whilst having no truck with charity. Like her mother, she was apt to present the problem in such a way as to guarantee Mr Bennet would not listen, even while casting the household into an uproar.

"Devil take it!" she swore, borrowing one of Mr Darcy's curses.

"Lizzy?" came a voice just behind her, and she sighed.

"I beg your pardon, Georgie," Lizzy said. "Please pretend you did not hear that."

"Oh, think nothing of it," her friend reassured once she caught up to Lizzy on the path. "I was hoping to find you here when you did not come down for breakfast. Is all well?"

Lizzy could not think how to answer; so much was wrong that it seemed like none would do.

But Georgiana answered it herself. "Forgive me, I ought not to have asked such a silly question. You need not share with me whatever is distressing you. Just know that I do have an acquaintance now with trouble's tricks and tests. You will please tell me whether I can be of any use to you?"

Lizzy smiled, remembering that long-ago day on the windy cliffs of Ramsgate when she had asked much the same thing of Georgiana. Even if one's friends could not assist in any meaningful way, it was a very good thing to have a friend at all and not to remain alone with one's problems. Because of Wickham's involvement, she had thought she should not confide in *this* friend, but at Georgiana's invitation, she found herself blurting out the whole of Lydia's reckless scheme.

"Oh, Lizzy, I am so sorry," she said, after hearing the story. "There is no question but that Wickham selected Lydia as his victim at least in part due to my connexion to your family."

"Possibly so," Lizzy replied. "However, his motives for villainous conduct do not change who is at fault for his actions."

"I suppose," Georgiana mused, but she did not sound convinced. "What will you do?"

"That is the difficulty. I cannot think of anyone who my father will listen to, excepting Mr Bingley, yet Jane is adamant that he should not be told."

"That is unfortunate. He would be my first choice too. But even so...whatever Mr Bennet believes of your parentage, he must know of your good sense. You are absolutely certain he would not listen to you?"

Would he? she thought. He might pretend not to, but it did not mean, once she was away, that he would do nothing.

"And, Lizzy...if you think it would help him understand, please... tell him how Wickham took advantage of a young, foolish girl, importuned her to elope, and left her to deal with the consequences. You may use my name, with my permission. Mr Bennet must understand that the danger is real."

"A part of me wishes to see my father brought low," Lizzy admitted. "Humiliated before the town he believes himself so superior to, mortified before his neighbours and friends. His disgrace would be so *satisfying*." She could hardly believe she'd said the words aloud. There was a long silence.

"I suppose you must decide if you hate him more than you love Lydia," she said.

"You must think me awful to even consider the notion."

"Lizzy," Georgiana reproved, "I never would. Should you prefer I address him? I know whereof I speak."

Dear, sweet Georgie. "No, my friend. I thank you for listening to me, but it is time I cease postponing my errand and be done with it. Even though my sister will not thank me for saving her, whether it even does."

"Let me thank you for her then," Georgiana said. "On behalf of the woman she might have the opportunity to become, simply because you care."

And that was all that mattered, was it not?

"For her," Lizzy agreed.

28

THE COURAGE TO TRY

Lizzy walked the three miles to Longbourn. Over and over, she practised and discarded approaches to the man she had *avoided* approaching most of her life. "He will not welcome me, however carefully I say it," she reminded herself. "A pretence of ignoring me will be the best I can hope for. My only plan must be to speak quickly, before he can walk away."

She entered Longbourn through the back entry, slipping into the kitchen. There, Cook and Mrs Hill were sitting at the table, having tea, and she was directly greeted with all the warmth of home-coming that she could have wished.

"I have come to speak to my father," she explained, much to their obvious surprise. But the loyal pair were only helpful.

"I just brought him his tea to his book-room," said Mrs Hill. "You can find him there. If you are of a mind to be private, use the back stair, and no one else will see you. Your mother and sisters are all in the front parlour."

"And when you take your leave, stop here again," Cook added. "I'll have spice cake, fresh from the oven, wrapped and ready to go with you."

How dear were these two! Lizzy thought. *How much better they made my childhood because they cared!*

But once she left the warmth of their good company, some of her resolution faded. The dim, quiet staircase seemed to stretch a mile upwards. *Courage, Lizzy*, she whispered, facing the climb to his book-room, daring to face her father. *Time to press on.*

❈❈❈

Darcy faced the façade of his London home with some hesitation. In all respects, it looked just as it ever had—an impressive, elegant edifice on this impressive, elegant Mayfair square.

"How can it look just the same as always, when everything's changed?" James asked in an uncanny echo of his own thoughts.

Whilst his people had located his former valet, Pennywithers, that man had discovered that he enjoyed retirement; Darcy had seen to his pension and raised James to the position. He was not, perhaps, as sartorially proficient, but was learning rapidly. He had also begun teaching James to read and write, discovering in the process that as he taught, his own abilities improved and strengthened. What was more, he *liked* the sensible young man, who said what he thought instead of simply 'yes, sir' and 'no, sir'.

"Truth," Darcy muttered and made himself press forward. *Press on.*

The difference within was marked. Taylor had, plainly, rehired most of the servants, and it was a bustling household in comparison to his previous stay. The housekeeper was there to greet him, appearing anxious.

"We are so happy to have you returned, sir," she said, and he smiled and nodded. No matter how disappointed he was that she had followed Lady Catherine's dictates so exactly, he understood better what it felt like to have so little control over one's own life and position. The earls and Lady Catherines—and the Darcys of this world, too, for that matter—had the ability to assert an unfair dominion over those around them, and it was up to him to try for changes. And should he forget, he had James to subtly hint how it

289

was for her and for so many others. He was as good as a second conscience.

"I...thank you for listening...to Miss Bennet and Miss Darcy, when...called for you...in my extremity," he said, finding a rhythm in the words to get them all out. If others found his new cadence odd, he could not care. "The nursery," he added. "Please have... stripped bare. Furn-ishings...give away, wallpapers...remove. Every bit."

"Yes, sir. It will be done at once," she agreed immediately.

If he ever did marry, his wife could have the pleasure of redoing it. And if he did not, it would be Georgiana's problem, or her heirs. He could not even imagine allowing his own children in there.

Of course, if Lizzy would not have him, he could not foresee marriage at all. It would seem so wrong to marry another when he only wanted her, and he could not conceive of his feelings changing. *Oh, to have another chance!*

How could he show her that he had taken her reproofs to heart, if he and his solicitors were unsuccessful?

At least his study was unchanged, a safe haven, and he breathed a sigh of relief to be here again, whole and healed. A stack of correspondence forwarded by Saxelby in anticipation of his arrival lay neatly piled upon the desk. He was in London not only for this latest project but to acquire a secretary—Saxelby wished for him to interview his favoured three candidates, then make the final decision. Darcy felt a brief longing for the days when he had easily managed it all himself, but quickly set those feelings aside. He was fortunate in every respect, and he knew it.

He picked up the top letter from the stack, read the direction, then broke the seal to read the neatly inscribed invitation:

*Mr and Mrs Charles Bingley beg
the honour of the company of Mr
Fitzwilliam Darcy for a ball to be
held at Netherfield Park,
Hertfordshire.
Tuesday, November 26, 1811
The favour of a reply is requested.*

He set the invitation down with a suddenly trembling hand, his heart beating hard within his chest.

Lizzy did not bother to knock. She was not coming to her father in politeness or subservience. She had a message for this man, and she was determined to say it. Nevertheless, everything within her quaked at the idea of confrontation, of his fury and indignation. She had been sneaking into this book-room for years, always covertly and, except for the one time, had never been caught. To boldly enter and demand his attention was such presumption, she could hardly imagine herself doing it.

The door swung wide; her father glanced up, a cup of tea in his hand, a newspaper before him, annoyance on his brow—then open resentment when he saw the source of the interruption.

But something happened within Lizzy as she stood facing the man whose good opinion she had always longed for and never had the least chance of earning. Somehow, while she was away confronting new situations, challenges, adversity, even death itself...either her world had enlarged, or Mr Thomas Bennet had shrunk. He was physically smaller than she had ever remembered, a puny man with a puny heart. Her courage rose to meet his narrowed gaze.

"I have received information that Lydia has agreed to an assignation with Lieutenant Wickham the night of the ball. She means to steal away with him to the old woodsman's cottage. It matters not to me whether you believe me. I only feel compelled to remind you that *your* importance, *your* respectability in the world must be affected if she continues wild and unrestrained. I and my sister Jane and her family will be touched but little—Mr Bingley can certainly give up the lease and have nothing more to do with any of you, if the association brings disgrace upon Jane. I must speak plainly. If you will not take the trouble of checking Lydia's unguarded flirtations and of teaching her that her present pursuits are not to be the business of her life, she will soon be beyond the reach of amendment. In this danger, Kitty is also comprehended. If you refuse to provide her any other source of guidance, she will follow wherever Lydia leads. Can you suppose it possible that they will not be censured and despised wherever they are known, and you shamed alongside them for your negligence, if you will do nothing?"

Lizzy looked him in the eye as she spoke; in his surprise at her impudence, he had heard every word. There was no need to bring up Miss Darcy's experience to try to convince him of the truthfulness of the charges she had laid against Lydia. He was free to accept her warning else pay the price; in fact, she had already said more than she had meant, but she was not sorry, even as he began sputtering.

She had already turned to leave when he bellowed, "Frances, take your brat out of my home before I have her tossed out!"

In that moment, she was thrown back into the past, six years old again, trembling before her papa; there was shouting, cursing, her beloved uncle furious, whilst she knew *she* had somehow caused the commotion. When Uncle had stormed out of the parlour, she had run after him, chasing his long-legged stride as he'd hurried to his horse, catching up to him only as he had been about to mount. She remembered her uncle's tight embrace as she had wept into his woollen coat, his soothing words as he'd murmured that she mustn't cry, that it was not her fault her papa was a fool, that she was the best girl in the world, that he loved her with all his heart and always would.

She remembered the piercing agony of watching him ride away, knowing, even then, that she would never see him again. How had she forgotten him, put him out of her mind so completely? But after all, she knew; remembering had been too painful. He was twice the man her father ever would be.

Feeding the flame of her hatred, reminding herself of the wrongs Thomas Bennet had inflicted, suddenly seemed so very useless. What? Had she thought that if, somehow, she failed to constantly hold his proverbial feet to the flames, he would be free of *any* consequence?

It is not true; he has lost my respect and devotion. That alone would have been a gift worth having. All her hatred had accomplished was the kindling of a relentless burn of anger and pain in her own heart. It might not be the work of an hour or a day to forgive him, but she would do it; any other course would require endless reigniting of sorrow or resentment or hatred, and she refused to give him or it so big a part of her soul.

She thought of telling that to the blustering man behind her, but she walked from the room instead. The shrivel-hearted Thomas Bennet would never listen, and it was no longer her duty to try.

For the rest of the day, Lizzy felt nothing but relief, even cheerfulness. She had informed her father, giving him every opportunity to fulfil his obligations as parent and restrain his youngest child. Her uncle would arrive Monday in the afternoon, and she would make him aware of the situation, beg his assistance in both keeping a watchful eye on and making efforts towards ridding Meryton of the pox on humankind that was George Wickham. Her dress for the ball was finished, and it fit her well. Jane had come down during the afternoon, declaring herself feeling much improved.

Miss Bingley and Mrs Hurst did not join them for tea, choosing to nap instead, and so she, Jane, and Georgiana had the most pleasant meal imaginable, with much laughter and light-heartedness. Jane seemed to forget about Lydia's situation utterly. When Mr Bingley arrived a bit later, having taken his new hunter for a gallop, he was in high spirits and plainly delighted to see his wife in such looks; Lizzy had the satisfaction of witnessing his obvious and tender regard.

Sunday morning, it rained torrentially, but the inclement weather did not keep away as many worshippers as it might have, had the neighbourhood not had a strong mutual interest in conversing about the upcoming ball; old Mr Whittaker's sermon suffered from a serious lack of pious attention. Lizzy found herself able to join in the general excitement and anticipation of the ball with tolerable optimism. The Bennets, it was noted, remained dry, their padded front pew empty.

Monday morning, Jane, Georgiana, and Lizzy were up early, seeing to last-minute details; Jane especially was very anxious that all should be perfect, and Lizzy meant to see that she did not overexert herself.

Hence, when Mrs Nicholls informed them that their mother and sisters had arrived, Jane betrayed an unusual impatience. "Could they not put off calling for a few days? They must know how much there is to do and how little they mean to help do it."

"I shall go to them, Jane, and make your excuses. You must not worry about them."

"No, no, I did not mean it," Jane said, immediately repentant. "Of course, I shall join you."

"I shall continue arranging these flowers for the small dining room," Georgiana offered. "We are almost finished here anyway. And then I shall check to see if the awning has been successfully raised and threaten any clouds that dare appear in our sky."

With these reassurances that an officer was still in command of the troops, Lizzy was able to shepherd Jane to the drawing room, reflecting that it was as well that she encourage her to sit for a few minutes. One look at the three faces of Mrs Bennet, Kitty, and Lydia, however, almost convinced Lizzy to spirit her sister away again. Mrs Bennet was blowing her nose into her handkerchief; Kitty's eyes were rimmed red, while Lydia appeared furious.

"Lizzy, how could you have?" Mrs Bennet lamented. "You have no regard for my poor nerves!"

"And this is all the thanks I get for giving you my place with Harriet!" Lydia cried. "And now she is married to a colonel! It could have been me!"

Kitty continued to sniffle, twisting her handkerchief into knots.

"I do not understand," Jane said, bewildered.

"What you must *understand* is that you are housing a traitor under your roof! Lizzy has ruined my whole life! *She* called on Papa with *tales* about poor Wickham, so Papa went to Colonel Forster to complain about him, and there was a ridiculous hullabaloo, and Mr Chamberlayne called in his markers. Everyone else followed, and suddenly, they all were heaping shame upon him, and now he has run off, and no one knows where he has gone!" Lydia delivered this speech in accents of great feeling, but Lizzy saw she had not managed a single tear.

"I went to our father and told him of Lydia's planned tryst with Wickham," Lizzy informed her eldest sister.

"But...but *you*, Lizzy? Was that wise?"

"Who else, Jane? Who else?" Lizzy cried, exasperated. Still, this was all good news; so why did she feel as though the guillotine was about to drop?

"She shall hear how wise it was now," Lydia muttered.

But no one seemed inclined to tell her what dreadful consequences approached. Mrs Bennet groaned.

Kitty finally met Lizzy's gaze with her own watery one. "Papa says...Papa says...you are not to attend any event which he must also attend. If you do, he will reveal...will t-tell Mr Bingley, Miss Bingley, and Mrs Hurst...your true f-father's name."

Jane gasped. Mrs Bennet moaned.

"He says we must choose, Lizzy! Choose whether to cease acknowledging you as our sister, else *he* shall cease indulging us with pretty gowns and shoe roses and ribbons! He says we shall discover how spoilt we were once we are wearing the same dresses year after year! Unless you return to our uncle, he will take out his anger at you upon *us*!"

Lizzy's shoulders slumped. She looked into the eyes of each sister —Kitty, tearful; Lydia, angry; Jane, dazed. *When Uncle arrives, I will ask him to take me away, she thought. I will not beg for their support. I do not deserve this.*

But she glanced over at her mother, who was nearly cringing in her chair, as if she could make herself smaller. She was not a sensible woman, and to say that their connexion had not always been a smooth one was a vast understatement; however, *she* did not deserve this, either, and had been bearing up under his anger and jealousy since the day of Lizzy's birth. Lizzy went to her, kneeling at her feet.

"Mama," she said gently, as if she were talking to a young child. "Mama." Finally, the older woman met her gaze.

"Tell them, Mama. Tell my sisters the truth now, if you please. The truth about me."

"What does it matter?" she complained bitterly. "When has the truth *ever* mattered?"

"It matters to us. To me, to Jane, to Lydia, and to Kitty. If they are going to make a decision about whether or not to acknowledge me, they ought to know. If they turn their backs upon you and me now, they should know whether they do so unfairly or if they possess some sort of moral imperative to justify a more comfortable position." She gave her mother a soft smile. "Your brother has always believed in you, always defended you. And so will I. You have my word, regardless of what you say here and now. Always."

Mrs Bennet shut her eyes tightly at that. Two tears leaked out, even so. But finally, she took a deep breath, gave a great shudder, and stood, opening her eyes to look tiredly at her daughters.

"I don't care what that old gudgeon tells the Bingleys, and I don't care whether any of you believe me or not. But Lizzy is every bit as much a Bennet as you are. Do what you will." With that, she marched out the door.

For several moments, they all remained where they were, staring at each other.

"Well," Lydia said drily, "either Lizzy is legitimate, or none of us are."

And Lizzy began to laugh—the absurdity, the silliness of it was too comical to contain—and laugh and laugh and laugh. Lydia's giggles, always close to the surface, joined in—then, of course, Kitty's followed. Finally, Jane let out the most impolite, unfeminine of snorts, which only set the others off into peals, laughing until they wept.

Gradually, the snickers faded into smiles, and Lizzy looked around at her sisters, sprawled gracelessly across Jane's fine drawing room as they had so many times in Longbourn's parlours, and she wondered if she would ever see them thus again.

Jane was the first to straighten, and she sighed. "Lizzy," she began, and Lizzy's smile faded. "I shall go to my husband now and tell him what my father threatens. I-I hope he shall support you, as I do. Perhaps, if we are very fortunate, he will not find us all as ridiculous as it appears we are."

Lizzy's smile returned. "If he does, remind him of your delicate condition and the need for a husband's excessive patience while his wife is increas—" Too late, she realised she had spoken aloud—in front of her younger sisters no less—that which Jane had not yet even shared with her.

But Jane only looked puzzled. "Delicate...what?"

Lydia was not so slow to understand. "Janey! Are you with child?"

Kitty whooped. "Oh! Jane! How wonderful! Am I to be an auntie?"

But Jane only slid bonelessly down onto the cushions of the settee, in a dead faint.

"She swoons so prettily," Kitty grumbled, looking askance at her fallen sister. "I am sure I could not do half so nice a job of it, did I practise for a year."

Lizzy rolled her eyes. "Call for Mrs Nicholls, Kitty. Lydia, fetch Mr Bingley from his study. And then you may both make yourselves scarce. Upon my word, neither of you had better say anything of Jane's condition to *anyone*, else you will suffer your monthlies henceforth without any help from me *or* my stillroom."

At that moment, Georgiana hurried into the drawing room, her face alight with happiness. "Lizzy! You will never guess! I have just received an express. It is the best news in the world. My brother is coming to the ball! Oh! What has happened to Mrs Bingley?"

29

EVERY PROSPECT OF HER OWN

Once Mr Bingley arrived in the drawing room, having been informed in a not overly helpful fashion by Lydia, pure panic ensued—even though, by this point, Jane was recovering from her swoon—and Mr Jones was immediately summoned. Lizzy was obliged to tell Mr Bingley her suspicions as to the true cause of the faint, lest he allow the apothecary to treat her with leeches again. The information only increased his anxieties on his wife's behalf, and his determination that everything within his power should be done for her.

Hence, Jane was put to bed with a hovering Mr Bingley in constant attendance. The midwife was called, and Jane ordered to stay there until tomorrow evening's entertainment. Lizzy worried for her sister, but where once she would have been welcomed to sit beside her, Mr Bingley now eagerly seized that duty. It was best for Jane, but Lizzy felt a certain new loneliness.

The express from her uncle arrived about the time she had begun peering out of windows towards the drive, expecting to see his carriage, and her disappointment was great, for she had wished for his advice upon what her own decision ought to be. Should she go at all tomorrow night?

She did not *want* her mother humiliated before the Bingley ladies, even though, for their own sakes, she was sure they would say nothing to anyone else. She did not *wish* for her sisters to be forced to bear the brunt of Mr Bennet's capricious temper. At the same time, to find that he blamed *her* that he had been forced to confront a situation almost entirely of his own making was ridiculous. His desire to deprive her of every comfort of familial affection was evil, and to yield to his demands, insupportable. It was as if her private vow to forgive him had only doubled his offences against her.

Jane had said she would stand with Lizzy, but had she spoken with Mr Bingley about it? And if she had, would he encourage the quietest possible outcome, especially in light of Jane's current fragility? Certainly, it would be easier for him if Lizzy absented herself from the festivities.

As if this all were not enough to contemplate, Mr Darcy would be *here* within a day.

Lizzy read the note from her uncle for, oh, the hundredth time, at least, since its arrival.

> *Dearest Lizzy,*
>
> *I apologise for such a last-hour delay, but we will not be to Netherfield Park today as I had hoped and will instead arrive tomorrow, likely just ahead of the musicians. Hopefully, Mrs Bingley will already have received Mr Darcy's acceptance of her kind invitation, with his apologies for the tardiness of his arrival; it is business of his which delays me. We look forward with all our hearts to seeing you tomorrow evening.*
>
> *Yours very affectionately,*
>
> *Edward Gardiner*

It was a temptation to hide herself in her rooms, if only to avoid seeing Mr Darcy again, avoid viewing his indifference towards herself, avoid facing all that she *might* have enjoyed in happiness, had she only had more courage. That last day in Brighton, she ought to have insisted upon one last conversation, upon waiting for Mr Darcy's return; she ought to have ensured he understood every reason for her refusal—or at least that none of those reasons were due to a lack of deeper feeling. And yet—if Mr Gardiner had *known* that there had been a proposal, however unwise a one, he might have tried to insist upon its fulfilment, whether or not it was the most sensible decision for the happiness of both. On the one hand, she wished she had done differently; on the other, she was convinced of the essential correctness of her original decision. Despite her fatigue, her sleep that night was a troubled one.

But there was no chance for staying abed the next morning as Jane was required to do. For some reason, the servants preferred to take every question related to the ball to Lizzy instead of Miss Bingley, so she found herself thrown into the position of final arbiter of all decisions related to it, with hardly a moment to call her own. The day passed in a flurry of tradesman deliveries, errand boys, and busy servants. She met with Mrs Nicholls at least three times over several small adjustments, inspected floral and candle and polish in the ballroom, and reviewed every detail of the dinner and supper menus with Mrs Schmidt, the Bingleys' cook.

The sun was disappearing before she realised the time, and she knew she ought to request water for a bath soon—*if* she were going to go downstairs again. Should she?

A light tap on the door interrupted her infernal musings. "Come in," she called.

Mrs Nicholls opened the door. "Excuse me, Miss Bennet. The mistress is asking for you."

So. Here it was. Jane's—or rather, Jane and Mr Bingley's opinion. She made her way to Jane's chambers, wondering if she would be sad or relieved if she must miss the entertainments. *Probably both.* She sighed, for never had a girl been of so many minds.

Jane appeared lovely and pale in her white lace undressing gown, her golden hair perfection. Kitty was right—she really did look unfairly perfect for a woman ailing. "Lizzy," she called, stretching forth both hands; Lizzy took them.

"I am quite fit and well able to be up and about." She sighed. "I only promised to stay abed today so that Charles would not worry about my attendance at the ball tonight. I am so looking forward to it! Thank you, my dear sister. Thank you for everything."

"No thanks are necessary, Janey. I am happy to do whatever I can to help. And Miss Darcy has worked tirelessly as well."

Jane smiled, but there was something else in it that Lizzy could not read. "I shall thank her, too, but it is not only about the ball of which I spoke. Lizzy...I had no idea of being with child. I could not really believe it, not until Mrs Bailey confirmed it. You shall call me stupid, I do not wonder—"

"Never! You are not stupid and never have been. Neither have you ever been *enceinte*. I should have said something! It is a subject of particular interest to me and always has been, for as long as I can remember, but I forget that not everyone shares my fascination—I have always enjoyed listening to Mama and her friends speak of such things, and your symptoms are very like how she has described her own experiences."

Jane squeezed Lizzy's hands. "You are very kind. But you shall agree with me when I tell you how *I* diagnosed my complaint. I thought I was dying. I am so tired and often dizzy. I was very afraid and very...not myself. When you told me of Lydia's folly, all I could think of was how relieved Mr Bingley would be to be rid of me and of his sisters dancing upon my grave and rejoicing. And yet, neither could I say anything aloud of my fears, lest I discover I was correct. It was very foolish of me."

"Oh, Janey. My poor sister."

"And so again, I left you to cope with what I would not. I told Mr Bingley everything, and he said neither of us is to worry about anything that Mr Bennet says to him or any member of his family —he will put our father in his place if he dares repeat aloud such ridiculous accusations so irrationally. He is sending Caroline back to London with the Hursts directly after the ball—he is quite indignant that they should have made me feel so unwelcome. He truly had no idea of my feelings and has assured me that I must always come to him with them—that he trusts me implicitly not to be dramatic or ridiculous, as I feared any accusation would make me appear." Her cheeks pinkened. "And I have promised him that I shall trust in his affections and not leap to the worst possible conclusions if I am teased."

"I am so glad. His happiness to have you as his bride has been very obvious to everyone."

"Can you forgive me, Lizzy? Yet again?"

"There is nothing to forgive. You are my sister. I am so grateful for my home with you."

Jane sighed. "You are a much better person than I will ever be."

No, thought Lizzy. *I have had so much less to take for granted than you. But I am not sorry that I have learnt to cope with greater difficulty either.* "Life has a way of teaching us that which we need to learn, does it not? Now, you must rest, as you promised your husband."

But Jane did not let go of her hands. "Will it be hard for you, Lizzy? Seeing Mr Darcy again?" And Lizzy saw that her sister had understood much more than she had ever said about her time away with him.

"Yes," she answered simply. There did not seem to be much else she could add.

"I am sorry, then, that we invited him. I thought that perhaps...but I should have consulted you. Mr Bingley is searching for an estate for us, something much further away from Longbourn. He was considering land close to Pemberley, Mr Darcy's estate. But we will look elsewhere, Lizzy. I promise you, we will find a place where we can all start afresh and be happy."

Lizzy closed her eyes and, for the first time in months, felt—*truly* felt—Jane's acceptance and sympathy and love. "Thank you," she whispered, finding it an effort to project her voice around the lump in her throat. "And, Janey, whilst we remain at Netherfield, I will not provoke my father. I am more than happy to forego the dinner altogether and come down only for the ball."

"No!" Jane cried with such vehemence that Lizzy was startled.

She tried to make Jane see reason. "You planned a dinner for our family and closest neighbours at eight o'clock. It means that for two hours, our father will be forced to endure my presence under his very nose. This is your first entertainment as Mrs Bingley, Janey. I want it to go perfectly, and it seems foolish to annoy him with so much at stake. At ten o'clock, another seventy or eighty people will arrive to dilute his temper and my presence."

"Lizzy, no! That is not acceptable! We shall not hide you nor make silly excuses for your absence. You are an honoured part of *my* family!"

Even though Jane's protest warmed her heart, Lizzy felt to disagree. "I must try to show our father that I have no intention of presenting public defiance. If he is at all sensible, he will come off his high ropes and realise that the prudent course is to return to our strategy of ignoring each other."

"No, my dear sister. It seems to me that we have all spent our lives trying to placate him. I, for one, am done with it. I find him barely tolerable, but I *love* you. You have made me see how insufficient were all my pretensions of upholding a sister worthy of *being* upheld. I have vowed to do better, and Mr Bingley agrees."

"Oh, Janey," Lizzy said, words failing her.

With her husband to champion her, Jane had finally found her spine.

Lizzy sat with her sister for another half an hour before she decided they would both be late for dinner unless they began their ablutions. But she had no sooner departed the bedchamber when she nearly walked into Mr Bingley pacing Jane's sitting room.

"Oh! Mr Bingley, I beg your pardon."

"I have been waiting for you," he said, a seriousness unusual to him in his air. "I will keep you but a moment. I only wish to apologise that you were required to speak to your father on the matter of our youngest sister, whilst I remained unaware. I hope you will call upon me as your brother in *any* circumstance you find yourself in and for any reason. If I may ever be of service, you may always depend upon my discretion and loyalty to Jane and to yourself."

Touched again, she thanked him warmly.

His expression lightened. "If it eases your mind to know it, I have an aunt in Scarborough, my mother's elder sister, who—who runs a tight ship, so to speak. She is a high stickler, and yet, she *does* have a sense of humour. I shall strongly suggest to Mr Bennet that Miss Lydia be sent to her for a time. I believe I can impress upon him the necessity, and since it can all be accomplished at very little trouble to himself, I do not foresee any difficulty."

It sounded almost too good to be true—surely the aunt would run out of patience before Lydia ran out of misbehaviours. "Would your aunt agree to such a task?"

"I would not have mentioned it if I had the slightest doubt."

A great weight upon Lizzy's soul lifted at his words. "Are we speaking of the aunt named Cora, or is it Dora?" she asked with a twinkle in her eye.

"Oh, neither of those two fussy old hens," Bingley replied, grinning. "It shall be Mrs Nora Pringle. Her patience is endless, I can testify, for she had most of the job of raising me. I have often believed that Caroline and Louisa would be better company now, had they stayed more often with Aunt Pringle. But Cora and Dora were wealthier, you see, and Father allowed my sisters the choice."

At just before eight o'clock, Lizzy gave one last look in her mirror. She suffered a moment's temptation to change her dress into the dull gown she had worn so often, designed not only for its drab-ness but to blend into obscurity. The new dress, although simple in design, showed her figure more than any she had ever worn—or at least, showed that she *had* one. Sally had styled her hair into luxu-riant curls, and somehow, the blue of her dress set off the red of her hair so that she looked a rather…gleaming picture. *But not an ugly or vulgar one,* she reminded herself. Whilst she did not wish to provoke Mr Bennet, neither was she the dull creature he had expelled from Longbourn. She had, in fact, taken great care with her appearance, for although her prospects with Mr Darcy were hopeless, pride demanded she look her best. With a quick prayer for courage, she left the safety of her chamber.

"Lizzy, you look beautiful!" Georgiana said, poking her head out of her door.

"Thank you, dear. I hope your wait is not too much longer."

The younger girl was keeping vigil at her window, waiting and watching for her brother's arrival. At least the delay to the Gardiners also meant a delay in greeting Mr Darcy.

"Oh, me as well!" the other girl cried. "Back to my post! I am determined to be the first to welcome him."

Smiling at Georgiana's eagerness, Lizzy made her way to the grand dining parlour, where the six-and-twenty select guests would be dining before the ball. As she could not talk Jane into excusing her from the dinner, she had taken some liberties with the seating, placing herself in relative obscurity at the very end of the table between Mr Harrington and the vicar. Since she had also arranged the seating so that she was as far from Mr Darcy as was possible, perhaps there would be time to accustom herself to his presence before anything so difficult as polite conversation became necessary.

She had waited to go downstairs until the last conceivable moment and now listened from just beyond the pantry-side entrance of the dining room until she heard murmurs and laughter and the slide of chairs, the sounds of guests finding their places. Carefully, she nudged the door open, meaning to quietly seat herself. But she had only taken a step into the room when she saw that Mrs Long was in the chair she had designated for herself. She glanced around in some confusion.

"Ah, there you are, Elizabeth," Mr Bingley hailed. "I was about to send Mrs Nicholls to find you! We have just been explaining to our guests why the unusual seating arrangements. As I was saying, we missed Miss Bennet's twentieth birthday whilst she visited her uncle in London, and thus her sisters wished to include its celebration in tonight's festivities. Come, my dear."

There was nothing for it but to go to the head of the table, where stood all her sisters, even Mary—although she appeared slightly uncomfortable. But Jane held out her arms for a brief embrace and kissed her cheek; Kitty, Lydia, and Mary did the same. Jane then guided her to a seat at her left, with Kitty just beyond, and Lydia and Mary on her right; a small pile of gifts lay beside her plate. Then, of all people, Mrs Bennet began clapping, quickly joined by the other guests.

"Many happy returns of the day, Lizzy!" Mr Bingley called.

The dinner service began at once, with servants carrying platters, and attention quickly turned to the lavish meal. However, all unspoken, the message was obvious: her sisters had taken a stand, and every one of them stood with Lizzy. From her seat, she could not see Mr Bennet's face. But she could only imagine.

"Janey, I thank you! But should we be so...obvious?" Lizzy whispered.

"Should we be afraid of doing too much on your behalf? We are your sisters," Jane murmured. "We had planned to make a little celebration of your birthday tonight these two weeks past. But it is time *he* understands how little his threats mean. We chose. We choose you." She lifted her chin.

"Even Mary?" Lizzy asked, gratified but a bit uncertain. "And Lydia has forgiven me?"

"With a drop of encouragement, yes," Jane said, smiling serenely. "Open your gifts."

From Jane, she received an exquisitely jewelled hair pin. There was a lovely fan from Kitty, a fine silken shawl from Lydia, and a pretty garnet cross from Mary. Lizzy was not fooled. The Bingleys had, plainly, financed the shopping expedition—and had probably reassured her sisters that their clothing, ribbons, and shoe roses were safe from retribution. Nevertheless, it did not negate their courage in taking such a stand. She thanked them all as best she could, receiving congratulations from those seated nearby. Bingley was directly across from Jane, but to his left were three empty settings —plainly for the Gardiners and Darcy—with the Lucases at his right. Her parents were mostly—and happily—beyond sight on Kitty's other side, and she could only wonder at what her father's response would be.

Well, I will hear about it later, I am certain. We all will.

"I am sorry for the disruption to your numbers and places," Lizzy apologised, feeling somehow responsible—for of course, it *was* an odd seating arrangement.

Jane waved this away. "I do not give a fig for that. Most of our guests have known you all your life. They can indulge us."

The meal was a lengthy one, planned with four courses and perhaps a dozen dishes in each.

"You, and Mrs Schmidt, too, have outdone yourselves," Lizzy said after the second remove of roast. "As I went over the menu today with her, I saw that you both had done Mama proud."

"Just wait until you see what she has done with the dessert," she murmured.

It did not take long to discover it. In marched Bingley's entire livery—in full regalia—the butler hoisting a generously sized torte gleaming with colourful, flaming candles, twenty in all, the tallest one stuck in the middle. The other footmen carried more traditional sweetmeats, cakes, and pies around to the rest of the long table, but the butler set the flaming treat before Elizabeth with a flourish. Everyone—or so it seemed—clapped and cheered, and Lizzy laughed in astonished surprise.

"Mrs Schmidt described it as something they do in Germany for the children, when I wished aloud for something dazzling for you, Lizzy," Jane explained, smiling hugely. "One candle for each year to celebrate too many birthdays gone unappreciated."

"How old *are* you, Lizzy? I believe you will set my ceiling ablaze!" Mr Bingley chuckled, along with the rest of the table.

"Help me put them out, then!" She laughed, standing to blow on the uppermost ones, and laughed still more as he puffed at it in a facetiously frantic manner from his seat—too far away to be useful —to the great amusement of the other diners.

The high-pitched screech of a dining chair across the marble floor interrupted the laughter.

"How dare you!" bellowed Mr Bennet to the sudden astonishment of the entire table.

Lizzy turned sharply towards him and, at last, saw his furious response to her sisters' support, to her mother's small defiance, to this celebration, all clearly written in the rage upon his face. His was purple with it, and a small part of her mind wondered if *he* was having an apoplexy.

"You!" he fumed. "You! If you are so anxious to expose yourself, well then, allow me!"

Mrs Hurst glared. Miss Bingley tittered nervously.

And Lizzy realised with a sudden foreshadowing that she was about to witness his best efforts at ruining them all.

30

A FAITHFUL PORTRAIT

Lizzy stood motionless, her thoughts frantic. Mr Bingley appeared equally astonished, the rest of her family frozen in place whilst all others looked on in avid curiosity. What could she do? Nothing better came to her mind than to begin a scream that might drown his ugly words, and she opened her mouth to try it.

"Enough!" roared a voice from the dining parlour door, a voice absent these two long months, a voice she had longed for every day since she'd heard it last. But something was different in it now, and it was not simply his anger.

But there was plenty of that—anger, and command, too, his coat of black superfine emphasising the breadth of his shoulders, stone-coloured kerseymere breeches and silk stockings of the same colour showing off long, muscular limbs. He strode into the dining parlour as if he owned it, coming face-to-face with her father from across the table.

"Sit!" he ordered as if Thomas Bennet was a mongrel cur.

Mr Bennet blinked rapidly, as if suddenly waking to find himself in an ill dream. But it was Mr Bingley who arose at that moment.

"Darcy, my friend!" He beamed, and Lizzy was fairly certain that only she—and probably Jane—could tell that it was not his normal bonhomie. "You have arrived! And Uncle Gardiner with you!"

For the first time, Lizzy saw that her aunt and uncle were several steps behind Darcy. She hurried around the table to greet them, then a flurry of introductions followed. There were faces who looked curiously at Mr Bennet, waiting for him to greet his brother-in-law or respond to Mr Darcy. He only slunk down into his chair.

Mr Bingley laughed. "I say, is it time to water down the wine for this side of the table? 'Tis early for tipsy displays!"

Sir William loudly protested this course of action, and normal chatter quickly resumed. Lizzy was not mistaken, she was sure, at the continued curiosity on a few faces, but most only seemed a bit puzzled and not much concerned.

"Greetings, Mr Bingley, Mrs Bingley," Uncle Gardiner said in a carrying voice that drew the attention of everyone except Mr Bennet—who only stared intently at his plate. "I see many faces I recognise and some which are new to me. My apologies for our tardiness."

"Uncle Gardiner, Aunt Gardiner, we are only happy you have arrived at last," Bingley assured.

He bowed. "Please, do not allow me to interrupt your meal. It is only that I have brought a birthday gift for Elizabeth, and I hope you will indulge me in its presentation." With the exception of Mr Bennet, not a single eye looked away.

Lizzy, surprised, turned to her aunt, who only smiled and took her hand, squeezing it encouragingly.

Her uncle gave a nod to someone behind him, and a liveried footman entered carrying a rectangular package, not too large but rather unwieldy, swathed in coverings. Carefully, it was unwrapped whilst Lizzy stood behind it—she could see it was a framed picture, but had no idea of what. Murmurs circled the room; Jane covered her mouth, and Mrs Bennet frowned. Her uncle turned to her, smiling kindly, and her aunt relinquished Lizzy's hand to his. He led her around to view it for herself.

And that was who it was—herself, right down to the bright-green eyes—except that she was dressed in the style of one-hundred fifty years past. Lizzy looked at him with puzzled incomprehension.

"Here we have a portrait of Lady Sarah Ashley, a woman of the bedchamber to Catherine of Braganza, Queen of England and wife of King Charles II," her uncle explained. "She was painted by Sir Peter Lely—a well-known portraitist and court favourite at the time—just before her marriage to the Earl of Montclair. She bore the earl three children, one of whom, Genevieve, subsequently married a gentleman, Percival Thomas Bennet, who sired six children himself, the eldest of whom was Percival Earnest Bennet, born in 1689. Frances, is Percy's portrait yet hanging in Longbourn's back parlour? What a sour face he had!"

Amongst the general laughter, Lizzy noticed her mother smiling faintly. Mr Bennet now had eyes only for the picture before them.

"Percy's eldest son was Thomas William Bennet, father to Franklin Percival Bennet. And of course, Franklin Percival is father to Frances's own Thomas Franklin Bennet of Longbourn estate."

Uncle Gardiner seemed to study the framed face for a few moments before he continued. "This portrait, until recently, hung in St James. It was rescued from the fire of '09, after which it was moved to Carleton House. Elizabeth, meet Lady Sarah, the grandmother of your father's great-great-grandfather. She is yours now, as seems only fitting—you were made in her image."

There was a pause, a moment of silence. Then Lydia, of all people, began clapping noisily. "What fun!" she exclaimed, laughing, with Kitty's immediate support. The rest of the room followed, and finally all eyes turned appreciatively to Thomas Bennet as he stood. He looked at the portrait, then at Lizzy. Without a word, he turned away and stalked out.

It might have hurt, once. Instead, Lizzy felt a nearly irrepressible urge to laugh.

"I see my brother is *overcome* with emotion," Uncle Gardiner said mildly, unperturbed. "We shall give him time to recover. Now, Mr Bingley, do we not have a ball to attend?"

Darcy knew he ought to follow Gardiner and his wife, who were being led out by Sir William and Lady Lucas. Certainly, it had been plain that Caroline wished him to—he'd been required to blatantly ignore her hints that her first set was not yet spoken for. She finally gave up, following the rest of the guests exiting en masse for the ballroom.

He, however, could not help but stay to watch Elizabeth a moment longer, the sight of her a feast for starving eyes. She had been lovely in her ugly dresses and linen caps, but now, wearing some delicate blue gown that showed her figure to great advantage, her glorious hair revealed, she appeared nearly overwhelmingly beautiful. She was surrounded by her sisters, all of whom openly marvelled at her resemblance to the portrait. But as the last of the other guests abandoned the dining room, she slipped away from them to approach her mother, who had remained seated, clearly dazed.

"Mama," she said with a light hand upon her shoulder. "Are you well?"

Mrs Bennet's voice was as quiet as he had ever heard it. "All this time...all this time..." she muttered. "It was so very unjust." She fumbled for a handkerchief, found one, and dabbed at her eyes. She finally looked up at Elizabeth. "So many times, I searched your face for something, *anything* of your father in you. I could not see either of us, as if you were a changeling come to curse me. I-I blamed you for what wasn't there. I blamed you."

"I know, Mama. I searched too."

"I'm not clever like you. Always two steps behind. And I blamed you for it. I used to tell Edward that I only needed to be as clever as it took to fetch a fine husband." She shook her head, as if in disbelief at her own words. "I blamed you," she repeated.

"I know, Mama," Elizabeth said again. "But if I ever blamed you, I stopped some time ago. As you said, it was all unjust. Let us put the past behind us."

Mrs Bennet caught her daughter's hand and kissed it.

The action caught the attention of Elizabeth's sisters, who drew nearer. Miss Mary and Miss Kitty appeared bewildered, whilst Mrs Bingley looked sympathetic and even sorrowful.

"Mama, I hear the musicians warming their instruments," Miss Lydia said stridently, only sounding impatient. "I am going to the ballroom. It will be such fun!"

Mrs Bennet's head snapped up, peering at her youngest daughter as if she had only just noticed her. "I shall be watching you, Lydia Bennet. You *will* keep your distance from the punch bowl, and stay in my sight *in* the ballroom, or I shall directly lead you home by your ear. Do you hear me?"

Miss Lydia rolled her eyes but agreed easily enough. "Yes, yes, but let us go *now*!"

With a sigh, Mrs Bennet stood, and as she did, she met Elizabeth's eye. "We are of a height, you and I," she said. "I never noticed that before."

"Yes, Mama," Elizabeth replied, her voice still kind. "Yes, we are."

It is true enough, Darcy thought, although he found it inconsequential. Mrs Bingley was shorter, and her other sisters were a little taller.

With a nod of something like satisfaction, she turned towards the door, the three youngest trailing after her.

Suddenly, he realised he had been standing there, oafishly staring at a private family scene, and he turned to leave too. But Bingley, having been briefly waylaid by another guest, chose that moment to return; Mrs Bingley joined him, looking a bit...tremulous. Darcy saw it then, the quick and ready concern his friend had for his wife, their unspoken communication, the way he steadied her, the strength she took from his support. *A good match,* he thought. He remembered Caroline approaching him in late June, begging him to intervene in Bingley's budding romance, to quash it.

For the first time, he was grateful that he had not felt *himself* during his earlier visit to Netherfield. Leaving Bingley to work out his own life had been one good result of his illness. He already knew he would have made a muck of his love for Elizabeth, no matter his health, as wrong-headed as he'd been. And he would not trade the opportunity to spend his future with her for an easier path to it.

"Ho-ho!" Bingley cried, taking the few steps towards him, shaking his hand with a tight grip. "It is good to see you looking so well, my friend. Of course, you remember the former Miss Bennet and new Mrs Bingley, Darcy?"

"Mrs...Bingley," he said, bowing. "Pleased...to meet you again. Congratulations on your marriage."

"Thank you, Mr Darcy. We are happy to see you so recovered," Mrs Bingley replied sweetly. "Will you not accompany us to greet our other guests?"

Without being rude, he could only nod in agreement.

"Mr Darcy!" Elizabeth's voice interrupted, and he turned to her abruptly.

He had been mistaken, he saw, now that he was so close to her, in thinking the portrait an exact replica of Elizabeth. How could one reproduce such eyes as hers? The artist had copied the startling colour, it was true, but the sparkle, the vivacity, were impossible to capture.

"Have you seen your sister yet?" she asked.

"I...yes. Too long a greeting. Apologies...for late arrival."

"You arrived just in time, I think."

They stared at each other for what seemed a minute but was probably only seconds, his heart too full to speak. *Will you dance with me? Will you marry me? How soon can I say the words?*

"Shall we, Lizzy?" Mr Bingley interrupted, offering her his arm. "I have promised my guests the briefest receiving line in the history of receiving lines so we can get right to the dancing. You haven't forgotten that you pledged your first set to me?"

A keen disappointment cut through Darcy, but ingrained good manners provided him words. "Mrs Bingley, is...your first set promised to another...as well?"

She accepted his invitation, and he turned towards the ballroom, only able to watch the departing back of the woman he loved.

This is Jane's doing, Lizzy thought. It had never been the plan that she open the ball with Mr Bingley; Jane had given up the honour in what she doubtless believed was a rescue.

She followed Mr Darcy with her eyes, envied everyone to whom he spoke, had scarcely patience enough to answer Bingley's remarks, then was enraged against herself for being so silly.

A man who has twice been refused! she reflected. *How could I ever be foolish enough to expect a renewal of his love? Is there a male alive who would commend such weakness as a* third *proposal to the same woman?*

She forced herself to attend to the steps of the dance instead, a country dance, which thankfully left little time for conversation beyond the polite. She was even happy, as Mr Gardiner led her mother down the line, happy to see Mrs Bennet's smile returned, happy to see the reconciliation of brother and sister. Still, she could not help but watch Mr Darcy lead Jane with the perfect grace of a man born to wealth and ballrooms and grand society. It seemed, even, impossible to remember that she had seen and cared for every part of him, that she knew his body as well as she knew her own. That he had kissed her, fully and passionately. That he had *wanted* her, as she had wanted him.

Although she reproached herself for noticing, he sought Mrs Gardiner for the next set. *Better than Miss Bingley,* she thought. Still, she must prepare herself for that eventuality, for she had also seen how that lady contrived to be as near to him as was possible. Miss Bingley was in her best looks, expensively and exquisitely dressed; he must see how perfectly *appropriate* she would be as his bride.

Her uncle claimed her for the set, but she was determined to have a private moment to express her gratitude. She took him a little aside before saying, "I must thank you for your unexampled kindness to me and to my poor mother. I do not know how to express my appreciation—how you even discovered such a portrait—"

"Lizzy," he chided gently, "you are not much in town, but surely you know who resides at Carleton House? It was Mr Darcy who knew of the portrait's existence—all I did was discover where the thing was hanging. Saxelby put a flea in the ear of people who know the regent, who were able to make Darcy's interest in the object known to him. It was Darcy who had to go to such parties and merrymakings as His Royal Highness required of him—for these matters are delicate, you see. Nothing so ham-fisted as a straightforward sale or trade. Knowing the regent, I was somewhat surprised Darcy managed it so quickly, yet it took weeks of routs and revelries as it was. *I* feared it might take months."

Lizzy felt herself go pale with astonishment at this enormous effort from a man who disliked an endless onslaught of society.

Her uncle saw her surprise. "Let us take a turn about the room, my dear."

He walked with her, holding her arm, greeting others whilst she could barely hear what was said over the ringing in her ears.

"It went against my grain to take credit for its acquisition before everyone," he said at last. "But of course, there was no other way to make the portrait known, and so quickly. It seemed we were barely in time as it was. I think my brother Bennet is cracked."

Lizzy sighed. "He had just witnessed a spectacular loss of control of his whole family." She explained what her sisters, and even her mother, had done for her and what, to him, must have seemed an open defiance before the entire neighbourhood.

"I cannot accept excuses for him," her uncle said. "He is a bully and a fool."

"I am not waiting for any apologies from him," Lizzy assured. "But he is no worse than many others of his sex. There is no indignity so abhorrent to their feelings as a natural child and the woman who bore it!"

"That is too often true," he agreed sadly, "even when the judgement of blood is mistaken, as it was in your case."

But she did not wish to speak more of Thomas Bennet. "Uncle," she began hesitantly. "Do you know how Mr Darcy knew of the picture in the first place?"

"Oh, yes. He explained that he came upon it when he was a lad of sixteen years. His old tutor, you see, a gentleman of some learning, connexions, and influence, took him to view the gallery at St James, where he saw the portrait of Lady Sarah—although he did not then learn its subject's name. It made an impression upon him at the time. He had forgotten it completely, however, until he first saw you. There was something so familiar about you, something making him look and look again, he explained, to try to place you. It nagged at him, at least at first. But his attention, once captured, could not be liberated. Or so he said."

"But why did he acquire it? Gratitude, for—for what I did for him during his illness?"

He smiled. "Ah. I do not pretend to speak for Mr Darcy, but as indebted to you as he doubtless feels for *that*, it seems to me that gratitude is the least of his feelings where you are concerned."

Lizzy turned her head to find Mr Darcy amongst the dancers and saw, at that very moment, he was looking at her from across the room; she looked quickly away.

"He will not appreciate my divulging any of this, although I did tell him I would not keep secrets from you," her uncle added.

"Why tell me anything then?" she asked with some asperity and not a little frustration. "He is hardly hurrying to my side. He has barely said ten words to me."

Mr Gardiner smiled, his kindly eyes twinkling. "A man who felt less might say much more" was his only reply.

31

WHAT IT IS TO LOVE

It was a terrible thing, Darcy found, when one's mind and one's heart seemed, suddenly, to speak entirely different languages and refuse to speak at all to each other. He had watched her walking and talking with Gardiner. There was no question but that her uncle was informing her of who had truly purchased that portrait—then he saw her glance over at him and quickly look away. What did it mean?

His heart urged him to race to her; even if she would not have him, he would *know*.

His mind counselled him to patience, that it was too soon, that a slow and steady courtship would be the proper approach.

Proper or tepid? He was not a man to dither for long, however; he must at least learn if there was any hope. Once the set ended, he searched for her. The ballroom was crowded, and for several minutes, he was unsuccessful. But just as if he had dreamt her, she suddenly appeared at his side, looking up at him with eyes that revealed so much—a bit of bewilderment, a little fear...but a good deal of hopefulness, too—or at least, that is what his heart told him. His mind was scrambling, fearing he only saw what he wished.

"Mr Darcy" was all she said in greeting, but it was enough to make his heart race.

And of course, now that he was brought to *point non plus*, his tongue, predictably, tangled.

You are the woman of my dreams, he wanted to tell her. *I will spend my life in your service. Only hear me out. I am sorry. I am yours, forever. Say anything, except no.*

"Liz-zy," he managed. He opened his mouth. Closed it again. The first time, he had proposed like an afterthought, without warning, without courtship. The second, he had allowed his fears to mangle and strangle his feelings.

Quit gaping at her like a fish! Say something, idiot! he thought. And with sudden conviction, he realised there was only one thing he *could* say.

Lizzy was feeling a bit tongue-tied. Colonel Forster in his medals and regimentals could not compete with Fitzwilliam Darcy for display of power and authority. That Darcy was the most hand-some man she had ever known did not help matters. How could she dance with him, pay attention to the steps, to the rhythm, to the other dancers? When he spoke her name, in that dear, still-fractured way, her heart melted, and she could only watch his struggle to speak with a throat as constricted as his own. But he quickly regained control, not murmuring his words but pronouncing them clearly and distinctively enough that those closest *must* overhear.

> "'Passions are liken'd best to floods and
> streams:
> The shallow murmur, but the deep are dumb;
> So, when affection yields discourse, it seems

> The bottom is but shallow whence they come.
> They that are rich in words, in words discover
> That they are poor in that which makes a
>   lover'."

And with those silly verses, she found her own tongue. "Sir Walter Raleigh? Surely the situation is not so desperate that it requires a descent into poetry?" she asked, smiling tremulously.

"Poetry...is love's food," he said, taking her hand in his strong, warm one, his crooked half smile nearly destroying every bit of composure she had gathered.

"Of a fine, stout, healthy love, it might be. Everything nourishes what is strong already. But if it be only a slight, thin sort of inclination, I am convinced that one good sonnet will starve it entirely away," she quipped, trying to be light-hearted while her voice cracked on the words, ruining the effect.

"Let...me nourish," he begged with a pure sincerity that pierced her heart. "Let me feed."

At that very moment, a small commotion not far from the dancers caught her eye, and her heart sank.

Lizzy had only seen her once, but she would never forget the woman—Lady Matlock, resplendent in a gown of green crape and Turkish turban, bedecked in jewellery of gold and amber, on the arm of an equally imposing and elegant gentleman who *must* be the earl. They were here, now, in the ballroom at Netherfield. *Lord Matlock*—who, plainly, was not giving up, as her uncle had predicted he would. The last thing he must witness was a *dance* between herself and Mr Darcy, never mind anything more personal.

Then, with a timing only the angry fates could have supplied, Mr Darcy dropped to one knee.

"Say...you will marry me. I asked...before but in the wrong way. I said I could...do better. No one is. No one could be. *You* deserve... better. I knew it then. I know it now. Take me...anyway. I will try harder...to deserve you, although I never can."

He got the words out, finally—only a small part of what was in his heart, but truth, nevertheless. He looked into her eyes and saw it.

She was going to refuse him. Again.

What was more, they had drawn a crowd.

"Liz-zy," he said, shaking his head, knowing he was pathetic, and yet, still too desperate to let her go without trying again. *I must get the words right this once, if I have to use every poet in memory!* "Would... Burns change your mind?

"'Oh wert thou in the cauld blast,

On yonder lea, on yonder lea;

My plaidie to the angry airt,

I'd shelter thee, I'd shelter thee.'"

But it was another voice who answered him, harsh, incredulous, and infuriated. The last voice on earth he wished to hear.

"Fitzwilliam Darcy! What do you think you are doing?"

Oh, great gads. It only wanted this.

"What is this poetry-spouting nonsense before the entire country-side?" the earl hissed. "You are making a fool of yourself! Or...is it a sign of something *worse?*" The threat in his accusation was unmistakable.

"He did not mean it!" Elizabeth cried, dropping his hand, desperation in her every syllable, her bright-green eyes awash with tears. "He-he..."

And with those words, he *knew*. He understood at last. She had seen his relations and was trying to protect him, even if doing so made her the laughingstock of the countryside. He caught one hand again and smiled up at her. She bit her lip, one of her tears spilling over her lashes. He caught it on the tip of his index finger.

Without even turning to look at his uncle, he made him an answer. "My lord. Please...do not defame me...before my chosen bride. You might at least wait...until she has agreed to wed me. For any *useful* assistance...provided during my illness, I thank you. But your advice...as I have already warned...no longer required."

But Lord Matlock refused to capitulate. "We *might* have spoken privately, but you have forced my hand! I have barely arrived in time to prevent this disaster! Did you think I would not hear? I have many friends at court! The entire *ton* is awash with speculation regarding your incredible *infatuation* with a country miss. Ten thousand pounds, Fitzwilliam! Ten *thousand*, for a portrait of a nobody that *nobody* wanted!"

He saw Elizabeth's eyes widen. *Drat the loudmouthed fool!*

"I know who her father is," Matlock added coldly. "*And* her mother. It does not speak well for your case."

It was, once, his worst fear—for his family to make a mockery of his reputation, to accuse him publicly, to attempt to take away all of what was most important. But no longer. *True* fear was discovering he had entirely muddled the most important part of his life—his love for Elizabeth. If she loved him, his family's machinations became unimportant. He would confront this, now, once and for all.

Sighing, he kissed her hand, squeezed it. "Wait for me...shall you?" he murmured. "I will be...right back."

For a moment, he thought her anxiety over him might carry the day, but quickly, she caught hold of herself, smiling through her tears. "For as long as you wish," she said with only a slight quaver. "I am quite at my leisure."

He gave her a wink, stood, and turned to face his uncle, stepping close to the older man. He was half a head taller and far more fit—

324

he let his uncle see that, see that he was no longer helpless, no longer his victim, and completely in control. His uncle possessed hauteur, but no one could outshine arrogance like a Darcy; he saw when the uncertainty, a real hesitation crossed Matlock's features.

"Do you really...think *regent* believes...whatever I paid him...for such unique...possession was too much? Or does he now...call me the...sharpest fellow in England...his own good friend?"

Matlock frowned. Plainly, he had not stopped to consider just how much favour Darcy had recently purchased from the future king.

Hands upon his hips, Darcy took in the gathered crowd; even the musicians had ceased paying any attention to their instruments. The eyes of the entire assembly were fixed upon this scene, many mouths open in shock, curiosity, astonishment, and avid interest at the display.

"How many here," he called, in a voice loud enough to be heard at the back of the ballroom, "believe...receiving Miss Elizabeth Bennet's...hand in marriage...be an honour to *any* gentleman...no matter how...grand?"

"Hear! Hear!" An uproar sounded, immediate and deafening; while he did not imagine Louisa or Caroline were joining in, he saw and heard all of Lizzy's sisters, her mother, her aunts and uncles, Bingley, the Lucases, the Gouldings, the vicar, as well as many, many others clapping and cheering. This was her home, where people knew her best.

Lord Matlock backed up two or three quick steps; only now did it seem to have occurred to him that in selecting a site for confrontation, he had chosen poorly.

Darcy peered at Elizabeth over his shoulder. "You see...my darling. You heard...Matlock's opinion of *me*. I really...*cannot*...do better."

She snorted in laughter and stepped forward to face him again, giving his relations her back. "I adore you," she mouthed.

He took both her hands in his, then, in his deep, carrying voice, shouted,

"'Or were I in the wildest waste,

Sae black and bare, sae black and bare,

The desert were a Paradise,

If thou wert there, if thou wert there.'"

At this point, several of the more well-read voices joined in. Some, it was true, simply shouted along with him for the fun of it. But to his surprise, he saw Bingley take his wife's hands, and Sir William seize Lady Lucas's; a few others, men and women, looked into each other's eyes as they recited along with him:

"'Or were I monarch o' the globe,

Wi' thee to reign, wi' thee to reign;

The brightest jewel in my crown

Wad be my queen, wad be my queen.'"

He looked into her eyes. "Dearest, loveliest Elizabeth...would you be my queen? You are already...my heart."

"Reciting Burns gives you unfair advantage." She sighed, shaking her head, speaking through laughter and tears and the noise of shouts and applause. "I suppose I *must* marry you, since my heart has been yours for so long now, there is no hope of its rescue."

"Was that an 'aye'?" Lydia cried.

Darcy kissed both her hands, holding them fervently to his lips.

"It was! She has said yes! Good gracious! Only think! Dear me! Two daughters married and married so well! I shall surely go distracted!" Mrs Bennet shrieked as deafening cheers nearly shook the chandeliers.

"These people are *all* mad!" Lady Matlock exclaimed.

"About that," Darcy heard Gardiner say to his uncle—speaking so lowly he could not think anyone else could make it out. "Perhaps, sir, there are one or two points about a recent letter you ought to have received of Mr Darcy that you would care to discuss? I fear you believed it a deceit or a bluff, and I would dearly love to disabuse you of that notion."

Lord Matlock looked down his beaky nose at Gardiner; Gardiner stared back, and there it was—the ferocity so well hidden by Gardiner's benevolent features. Darcy grinned. Lord and Lady Matlock sniffed and made noises of outrage and denial—and finally —declaring they would not stay to be insulted another moment, departed speedily, calling for their carriage.

"Did you invite them?" he asked Bingley.

"Why ever would I do that? Are you mad?" Bingley rejoined. Then he broke into a grin. "No pun intended."

Darcy groaned, but laughingly.

Elizabeth looked up at him with a seriousness returned to her expression. "You should not have paid half so much—or even a hundredth."

"More fool...our regent. I would have paid...twice the sum."

"Oh!" she said, her eyes wide.

But with the removal of the Matlocks, the congratulatory crowd invaded with kisses and handshakes and back-clapping and many expressions of joy.

Then—as if there hadn't been enough fodder for the gossips for the next year, at least—when the next dance was *finally* called, Bingley cried to the musicians, "Will you play a waltz instead?"

A few brows were raised. A few of the guests gasped in dismay, but several couples eagerly took the floor.

Darcy bowed to the most beautiful woman in the room, in the world; she curtseyed, eyeing him winsomely.

"I have never waltzed," she said. "You will be my first. If you—or your toes—are disappointed, you have only yourself and Mr Bingley to blame."

"I will be...your first, your last, and all the waltzes...in between," he assured. "As you will be...mine."

Then his Elizabeth was in his arms, as the music and his heart soared.

EPILOGUE

December 4, 1812

Thomas Franklin Bennet ignored the sounds of laughter and gaiety coming from the front parlour; how his most exasperating daughter had become the bosom companion of his wife, he had little idea, but it was Mary's high-pitched giggle, for certain. She, Frances, and Lady Lucas and her daughter were certainly making a lot of noise and fuss over a simple letter. He liked to hear Frances's laughter; it was one of the first things he had noticed about her, her delight in so many simple things. *Whilst I, as the Bard declares, am prone to 'summon up remembrance of things past, sigh the lack of many a thing I sought, and with old woes new wail my dear time's waste'.*

Old woes caused by Frances's betrayal were all to be forgot because, it turned out, it never happened. And yet, a wound nurtured for twenty years did not disappear because of a surprising lack of existence. At least, so she had informed him.

But ignoring his women and their wounds was his habit, and easily done. The door to his book-room was thick, and shut tightly. Not so easy to bear was his curiosity, the urgent, burning need to *know*. What news was there from Derbyshire? Would Frances leave the letter lying somewhere convenient that he might surreptitiously

329

read it? Or would he be forced to search the house for it when no one was about—a difficulty because, whenever a letter arrived from the renowned Mrs Darcy, Longbourn seemed to fill with company for the next three days, and barely did the crop of visitors die down before another letter arrived. He paid for the postage, of course— the only thing he *could* do for her now. It was a temptation to simply open such missives when they came. But *if* he read the letters first, everyone would *know*...know his secret pride, his hidden shame. It was better to feign nonchalance, that it did not affect him in any manner, that his life was the same as it had always been. *Which it is,* he reassured himself. In essence, nothing had changed.

He caught the image of his own face in the looking glass perched atop the mantel. What a stupid place for a mirror! Why would one ever be required to inspect one's appearance in one's own book-room, where one was seldom disturbed? He hefted the thing, turning its glass face to the wall.

Satisfied, Mr Thomas Franklin Bennet, the last Bennet of Long-bourn, returned to his newspaper, still pretending not to wonder, although there was no one to see if he did.

"Georgie," Lizzy called loudly—even though it was the middle of the night—not bothering to whisper, heartily shaking her shoulder. A whisper would never waken her sister-in-law, who always could sleep like the dead. "Wake up! Time is wasting!"

Georgiana opened one eye. "Something...matter?" she muttered then rolled over as if to go back to sleep.

Lizzy jerked back the covers. "No! Make haste! Rise and shine!"

This time her sister sat up, rubbing her eyes and peering around confusedly. "Wh-what?"

"Get up! Put on something warm. It is snowing! Kitty is already dressing."

It only took the girl another moment to understand. "Oh!" She scrambled from her bed. "I shall meet you downstairs in a very few minutes!"

It was hardly possible to sneak out because Pemberley was a very secure home with night footmen in the corridors and at the exits, but neither did Lizzy worry about the necessity of secrecy. She was mistress here; this was her home. If she decided that day was night and night was day, the servants would move the heavens about until it was so. Still, a clandestine departure was part of the fun, so she had dismissed the footmen to take their suppers, and she threw open the heavy door herself for her sisters, who were already giggling.

"Oh!" Georgiana cried at the sight.

A full moon shone down upon a perfect, undisturbed layer of frosting-white snow spread across the vast surface of the front lawns. Light flakes drifted gently down upon the absolute stillness of the scene. Kitty whooped and practically dove down the steps. Georgiana followed at a more sedate pace, but the two of them were soon thereafter immersed in a project to build the 'most colossal snow sculpture ever seen' and began rolling snow—*boulders* was the only suitable description—across the lawn; how they would ever build anything with them was, evidently, a problem for some future consideration.

"We shall sculpt a snow-gentleman," Kitty cried. "Lizzy, we need one of Mr Darcy's hats!"

"I will gather some supplies for his costume and return shortly," Lizzy assured—although they were laughing so hard, it was doubtful they heard.

It was so good to hear their laughter. The recent news of Wickham's death in a barroom brawl had, briefly, recalled the past to Georgiana's mind, but it appeared she had finally and forever put it behind her. Lizzy heaved open the front door and slipped in—only to be hauled into the powerful arms of her husband.

"Oh!" she yelped, startled—but any potential further outcry was halted by a hungry kiss.

"Your lips…cold," he murmured, barely lifting his mouth from hers.

"Surely not any longer." She grinned.

His curls were falling down messily over his forehead, his banyan exposing a bare, muscular chest, his day's growth of beard fiercely shadowing his chin—in all, he appeared like a pirate disturbed from his slumber, and just as she preferred to see him.

"I wakened…you were gone."

"I warned you it might happen when you said we might get the first snow tonight. A first snow on a full moon…it can mean only one thing." She glanced down his form. "You did not mean to join us, barefoot and only in your banyan and breeches? Talk of cold!"

"I meant only…catch a glimpse of you, ensure all dressed…warmly enough. But you made…mistake…allowing me to entrap you. Now I may not…let you go."

"Our sisters might worry if I do not reappear shortly with the trappings for their project. They mean to build a snow-sculpture of massive proportions and dress him as a gentleman."

He glanced over at the door; even through its heavy barrier, the faint sounds of giggles yet penetrated. "They seem…very anxious, indeed," he said drily. But then his smile gentled, and he tucked a ruby curl behind her ear. "Thank you for…doing this…for Georgie. To hear her laughter…to know her happiness…it is everything."

"Her influence upon Kitty is wonderful to see. Georgiana has blossomed beautifully—I am so fortunate to call her sister, to know that Kitty now uses her as an example of how a lady ought to be."

"My darling," he said, shaking his head. "Do you...not see? Both Georgie, Kitty...have taken *you* as...model for behaviour. Thus...*they* become...ideal and idyllic."

"They are becoming the best versions of *themselves*, which is all anyone could ask," she countered. But then she grinned again. "However, if you notice a bit too much impertinence, I fear I must take the blame."

He smiled again, the half smile she loved, starting in his eyes and visible even in the low light of the entryway. But there was something else in it tonight, some other reason for his sleeplessness besides missing her nearness.

"You are feeling troubled." She looped her arms around his neck.

"Why...should I be?" he asked, his tone nonchalant, pulling her in more closely still.

She raised a brow. "Perhaps because you have invited Colonel Fitzwilliam to come to Pemberley, when you have not yet decided whether you can forgive him?"

"What...to forgive? He did...best he knew to do...protecting my sister. Most important thing...he *could* do."

She shook her head at him, glad he was finally releasing a few of these feelings, the ones he had borne most stoically.

"Of course it was not. It was never simply a conflict between his powerful father and his beloved cousins. Whilst he is apparently able to fight brilliantly on the battlefield, when it came to the wounds of his dearest friend in the world—you—he ran like a coward. He knows it, and you do as well. It is why he has not been invited before this, nor presented himself at Pemberley, although he has been home for a six-month."

Her husband briefly closed his eyes. "Perhaps."

She took his face within her hands, his dear, dear face. "I am so proud of you."

"Did...not much. Sent letter."

"You made the first, the hardest overture. You will bring him here and give him the chance to begin again, to hope he has learnt something from his errors. I hope you also share with him what truly happened to you and how his flight nearly killed you. He ought to know the full truth of it."

He shook his head. "His flight...saved my life. Brought you instead. Would rather...have you, did it mean ten Donavans."

She shuddered just a little, thankful to remember that Donavan had been prevented, upon penalty of arrest and other dire, perhaps less *legal* threats, from ever treating a patient again. "Well then, perhaps *I* will tell the colonel. But I mean to forgive him too. He is the nearest thing you have to a brother, and we shall make allowances, as he comes from a pig-headed father."

"Well," he said, "you managed...a pig...with your soul intact. Perhaps...instruct Richard."

"I can give advice on forgiving the pigs amongst us, but I keep my boundaries firm. My mother explained to me that when I attracted Mr Collins's interest, she saw in it *my* salvation as well as her own. When I refused, her frustration with me peaked. My father did not care either way. Had I accepted Collins, *he* would have refused the suit, I am certain. He only used the excuse of my mother's rage to rid himself of me. I have forgiven him for it. But he is not welcome here, for no longer am I required to cope with his abuse—it was nothing less. If the colonel wishes to keep his father *in* his life, I have no real experience. But our situations are entirely different. I suppose the earl *loves* his son, for one thing."

"Was it...love to force Georgie...on him? I call...greed. I not...so good as you. Angry still."

"As long as it is not an anger you think about—or suffer for—take all the time you need. I found it easier to let all that go. Let God sort it out with my father and the earl, as I do not have the patience for either of them."

"My nature...a resentful one."

She shook her head in disagreement. "Not at all. I lived for years with a man of *truly* resentful nature; yours is of the most loving sort, but you were betrayed. I am proud of you for attempting to see whether things can be put right with your cousin. Family is important. Or it ought to be."

"Keep on...seeing my best self...when you...look at me. Now... how much longer must I...await your return to bed?"

He, plainly, was finished speaking of the colonel's upcoming visit. Lizzy was not too worried about it, however. A man of as much goodness, sense, and compassion as her husband would navigate this new challenge as he did all his others—with honour and grace.

"I would not like for you to lose sleep from any activity of mine," she hedged. "We are to build the largest snow-gentleman in the world, you might recall."

"On contrary—losing sleep from your...activities...my very favourite loss." He bent down to kiss her, aiming for a sensitive spot on her neck rather than her lips. "I will...wait up," he murmured.

❈

An hour later, after bidding her still-giggling sisters a cheerful goodnight, Lizzy crept back to her chambers. Her maid would be unhappy when she discovered the sodden skirts and coat, but how else were snow angels to be made? It had been a great deal of fun, not the least of which was seeing the developing friendship between the two younger girls. Georgiana may have gone through fifteen years of her life without any sister, but in the last year, she had adapted well to the increase.

Kitty had come to live with them three months ago, when in desolate spirits—for it had become clear that Lydia had no intention of *ever* returning from Scarborough. Lizzy could not blame her youngest sister; under the tutelage of Mrs Pringle, a woman of rare tolerance, indomitable nature, and endless energy, Lydia was evidently becoming the belle of Scarborough society. Mrs Pringle, plainly, was the mother Lydia *needed*, one who cared enough to discipline her and, likewise, to show her love and approval for every small improvement. Lydia's letters showed a refinement that went beyond committing steps of etiquette to memory—she, too, was becoming the young lady she always was meant to be.

Unexpectedly, Kitty was readily able to accept the invitation to make her home with them—Lizzy had supposed her father would put up more of a protest. But then, his ability to challenge much of anything had been compromised.

After the ball at Netherfield, she and Darcy had decided to marry immediately. Rather than worry that Mr Bennet might voice an objection when the banns were called, she had gone to her aunt and uncle in London—for she knew her father hated town and would never rouse himself to pursuit. To her surprise, her mother had followed shortly after, insisting upon fitting her out with wedding clothes and sending the bills home to Mr Bennet. The wedding was held within a month, her uncle standing up with her, her mother giving every expression of joy. When she had asked Mama whether she worried about going home to face Mr Bennet after these shows of defiance, Mama had only shrugged. "Who cares what he thinks?" seemed to be her attitude.

Lizzy had not returned to Hertfordshire until Jane's confinement had begun, doing everything she could to ease her sister's discomfort and nerves. To everyone's surprise, the babe had been in a great hurry to arrive, and on a sunny day in late June, before Mrs Bailey could even be summoned, Lizzy had safely delivered her sister of an adorable, healthy baby girl—Flora Elizabeth. Lizzy smiled to think of her dear little niece—and how wonderful it was to remember that they now lived within thirty miles, for Mr Bingley had recently purchased Ashland Hall. She rejoiced whenever she thought of it. Miss Bingley and the Hursts did not care much for Derbyshire weather, remaining in town—yet another reason to enjoy the snow.

It took some time to remove her damp clothing, for Lizzy would never dream of rousing Tilson to request assistance at such an hour. She did not even glance at her own bed but went directly to her husband's—she loved his room, with its eclectic art, walls of bookshelves, two fireplaces, and overstuffed leather sofas. The bed was vast and luxurious, and he encouraged her to consider the room her own. He had told her, of course, that she might redo her chambers any way she wished, but what was the point, she had replied, when their mutual preference was to share his perfect space?

Quietly she slipped through the connecting door, enjoying the warmth of the good fires after the chill of her own room. He looked to be dozing, but she knew him to be a very light sleeper; carefully, she crawled in under the covers, hoping not to disturb him. But before she knew it, she was flat upon her back, her hands pressed against the mattress, staring up into piratical masculine eyes glittering in the shadows.

"I did not mean to startle you," she teased.

"I was…thinking," he said, "about our…wedding night."

"Oh, *those* thoughts," she said, smiling up at him.

"I had never wanted…anyone or anything…in my life so much…as wanted you that night. It was…exquisite torture to be…gentlemanly, to protect you…from my own imaginings."

"I believe you have since overcome most of your chivalrous instinct." She grinned, nipping his chin, feeling his response all the way to her toes.

He did not smile back. "I thought…it would fade," he admitted. "Not my love…never that—but the…intensity of my passion. I believed…it would grow comfortable…familiar."

"Like your favourite banyan?" she said, still smiling. "Or a cosy chair?"

His expression remained serious. "How can I...want you just as much...tonight as a year ago? More, even. How do these feelings... grow ever stronger?"

"I am not sure of the science of it," she replied, "but whatever the alchemy between us, I have only one wish...that you press on."

He smiled at her then. Their commitment to keeping on, pressing on, no matter their difficulties, was as much a part of them as the wedding vows they had shared.

"Oh, my dear," he said. "Nothing...gives me greater pleasure." In the dark and the quiet, his mouth found hers.

Darcy was a man well contented. He had just loved, and affirmed his love for, the most beautiful woman in England—his wife, his world. For their first anniversary, a mere fortnight away, he had planned an estate-wide celebration, with the Gardiners and all their children braving the weather and roads to attend; of course, their new neighbours, the Bingleys and little Flora, would be here as well. He would shower Elizabeth with jewels, too, but that sort of thing meant little to her; whilst she liked pretty things as well as the next woman, what touched her heart was more intimate—connexion, loving kindness, and family. After much deliberation, he had invited his cousin Richard to be here for the festivities. Still, whatever Elizabeth believed of his own character, he was not so forgiving as she, and he was not *quite* ready. But would he ever be? For her, he would try, not only so she could adore having more relations to fuss over but to be the man she considered him to be. It was as she said—family *ought* to be important.

But he had not counted on the invitation releasing something within his soul, something dark and disturbing...the frightening memories he had all but shoved aside in favour of the wonderful life he lived now and the anxiety that somehow, some way, his happiness, his future might disappear in a blink. It had once, after all.

The coldness of the thoughts drove him from the warmth of their bed to build up the nearest fire to a better blaze. After doing so, instead of lying down once more, he went to one of the tall windows facing the moonlit, snow-covered lawn. Its pristine appearance was marred by dozens of boot prints, snow angels, and what looked to be some kind of a snow fort with several apple-shaped snowballs stacked beside it—a surprise for him in the morning, no doubt. It made him smile.

A pair of arms wrapped around his waist, and he glanced over his shoulder.

"Did not mean...to disturb your rest, darling," he said.

She only pressed him even closer, a warmth along his back, saying nothing. He had always loved that about her—she had no need to fill their silent spaces with talk, her quiet support upholding him nonetheless. He clasped her arms where they embraced him and just stood, looking out, enjoying her nearness.

"Where is...world's largest snowman?" he asked at last.

She peered out from behind him to look over the lawn, pointing. "Over there, beside the fountain. Do not you see it?"

He squinted. "I see three big lumps, one beside the other."

"That is it. His name is Sir Goliath, and he is lying on his side, propped up on one arm and leisurely enjoying a carrot whilst looking up at the fountain. You must view him from the other direction to take him all in, of course. We planned to bring you out in the morning to see and appreciate our artistry."

"And perhaps be bombarded by snowballs?" He chuckled, and she giggled without a trace of guilt.

He pulled her around to his front, resting his chin on her soft curls as he wrapped his arms around her. "Have I...told you today...how much I love you...Mrs Darcy?"

"I never tire of hearing it. Will you tell me what is the matter, my love?"

He felt the warmth and strength of her in his arms, smelt the fresh floral scent of whatever she used in her pretty hair, and he wanted her all over again. He sighed.

"What if...it happens again?"

She did not ask what he meant. He knew, even; the idea of another apoplexy must be a fear she lived with, had accepted would be a part of her life when she agreed to be his bride. He had ensured her settlement was more than ample, had done everything he could to better safeguard her future as well as Georgiana's. It would never be enough.

"Would...be harder now," he tried to explain. "Lost...all once...but I had nothing then...in comparison. To...lose all...after having... everything." He clenched his teeth against the very thought.

"What do you see now? Right this minute," she asked quietly.

He felt some surprise at her question but answered anyway. "The front...expanse of Pemberley. A good deal...of snow. A...silly snow-gentleman."

"That is because you are trying to look too far out," she said. "What do you see before you?"

He brought his eyes back to the glass itself, mere inches away. The firelight showed their reflections in it, ghostly images mirrored within the panes—two people, merged and entwined, becoming one.

"I...see us," he replied.

She tilted her head up to brush her lips against his jaw. "Let us hold no rehearsals for some possible, imagined future tragedy. We will look at what we have here and now, right in front of us, and rejoice instead."

She was right, of course. And ever so fortunately, right *here*, and he was the man who held her. "I could...look at you...at us...forever," he told her.

Elizabeth turned within his arms, her soft, sweet hands tantalising upon his bare chest. "Then look. Touch. Love me again now. And press on with me, always."

And so, he did.

The End

THANK YOU FROM THE
AUTHOR AND PUBLISHER

Receive a free ebook when you sign up for the publisher's newsletter! *For the Enjoyment of Reading* contains short stories by Jan Ashton, Julie Cooper, Amy D'Orazio, Linda Gonschior, Lucy Marin, and Mary Smythe. Its yours, free, for signing up for the Quills & Quartos Newsletter

Get it at www.QuillsandQuartos.com

ACKNOWLEDGMENTS

Many thanks to Lisa Sieck for reading too many drafts, to Jan Ashton for her editorial prowess, to Sarah Cooper for finding excuses to keep me on the island, to Allyson Kuykendall for her encouragement, and to Ashley Wyckoff for being a gorgeous, gutsy redhead I could use to model this Elizabeth.

ABOUT THE AUTHOR

Julie Cooper, a California native, lives with her Mr Darcy (without the arrogance or the Pemberley) of nearly forty years, two dogs (one intelligent, one goofball), and Kevin the Cat (smarter than all of them.) They have four children and four grandchildren, all of whom are brilliant and adorable, and she has the pictures to prove it. She works as an executive at a gift basket company and her tombstone will read, 'Have your Christmas gifts delivered at least four days before the 25th.' Her hobbies include reading, giving other people good advice, and wondering why no one follows it.

BB bookbub.com/authors/julie-cooper

ALSO BY JULIE COOPER

NOVELS
Nameless

Tempt Me

The Perfect Gentleman

NOVELLAS
A Yuletide Dream

Part of the 'Tis the Season Collection

Lost and Found

Seek Me: Georgiana's Story

A companion novella to Tempt Me

www.ingramcontent.com/pod-product-compliance
Lightning Source LLC
Chambersburg PA
CBHW011430240626
47153CB00011B/2924